1, 1, 2022

To Andy & Jan,

Our days in Jupiter Narrows will always be fondly remembered. Your kindness & friendship helped make the experience so apt of the phrase 'Another Day in Paradise'.

It was in Jupiter Narrows that I spent a good deal of my time writing the first draft of this novel. You were so kind to review it & provide me feedback that helped me move it forward. Finally, finished, I hope you enjoy it.

Warmest wishes from Florida,

OPERATION
HAWK'S NEST

JOHN FITZGERALD

ISBN 978-1-09836-1-433 eBook 978-1-09836-1-440

In memory of Pamela Jean Walsh

ACKNOWLEDGEMENTS

Four women stand out in making this book a reality.

The first is Mary LaDuca, who found me lost in grief after my wife's death and never gave up on me. She not only encouraged me to write, she read every word, every draft and stayed with me through eight years of on again, off again commitments to the story. I tell people she saved my life. That's another story for another time, a love story.

The second is Marjie Lambert, who I met on my birthday after my wife's death. She is a distinguished journalist and editor from the Miami Herald who took the time to read my early drafts and was the first to give me constructive criticism. As the early drafts evolved, she jolted me into a true journey of discovering what it takes to write a novel. In the process, I finally found my voice. Our paths crossed for a reason. I will forever be indebted to her.

The last two women are sentimental favorites. They have been my biggest fans. They are my mother and my sister who share the same name, Joy, and I sometimes think share the same heart. While this story is a tribute to my Dad, (someone I really did not know well, as he died when I was so young) it truly honors my Mom, who kept his spirit alive. She was 35 years old when he died with six young children to raise. She taught me early on that novels are a great escape from reality. It was not until I too lost a spouse did I realize what she meant. My mother's story is one of the richest ones in my stories yet to write, but I certainly wasn't ready to tackle that as my first. My sister, Joy, is just a year and a half older than me. She paved a promising path for me in schools and life as I grew up. She is beautiful, intelligent, and a caring soul. When people found out that I was her brother, I coasted in her shining path. My mother loves this book (yet she cautions that she is my mother) and my sister has read and proofread every version. She and Mary will perhaps be the most thrilled that this book is finally published.

I also would like to thank my brothers, Joe and Peter, and my other sisters, Anne and my late sister Patty. They too enlisted to read the early drafts and encouraged me to keep on writing. Peter started writing his first novel too and we shared afternoons at the lake discussing the joys of writing.

When I first began writing this novel, three neighbors watched over me in my incubator and cheered me on. Jerry Frank, a retired New York City Detective, is probably one of the most avid readers of books I ever met. You can find him in the library on any given day. He gave me constructive enthusiasm as he gently prodded me to make some changes. I think he will recognize them. Andy Payne, from the U.K., dropped off books to aid in my research and offered me a brutally honest take on my first draft. As much as it hurt, it helped me get back on my feet to try again. From Canada, Greg Stewart took the time to go through the first draft, as well. He called it creative. Canadians should always be on your list of early adopters. They are the kindest people on the planet and will always find something in your book to make you feel good.

I also want to thank Thomas Andersson, a former business colleague and good friend from Sweden. He took the time to read an early draft and encouraged me to finish it, publish it and think about a movie.

Finally, I want to thank my children, John and Hadley. They are the gifts that my wife Pamela Jean gave to me. They watched as my world, and theirs, collapsed. They let me go when they probably needed me the most. My father died too young for me to know how to be a proper Dad. I only hope they know how much I love them and how proud I am of their accomplishments. No matter how far I would run in search of what I was running from after their mother's death, they never faltered in their support of me, and of my dreams. I am the luckiest father of all time.

PROLOGUE

Somewhere in the Arabian Desert
February 26, 1993

A giant sun sets slowly in a sea of sand. Desert storms blow over a junkyard of war machines, past and present. Sands shift over broken boots and unexploded bombs. Men in white flowing robes, with rifles and horses, lay prostrate chanting a Muslim's call to prayer. The song lingers and drifts lazily and long over a heat shimmering landscape of a vast Arabian desert. The chant is eerily exotic seducing the red ball of fire in the sky to finally subside, dropping below the lifeless horizon ushering in a new age of darkness. The chant gives way to a sadistic chorus of satanic impulses. Darkness falls and casts a shadow of terror on the West.

These men who pray do not seek peace. They are radical Islamic fundamentalists - Jihadists that hijack their religion. They trade in terror. The end justifies the means. Can you hear their song?

A bomb detonates nearly 7,000 miles away blasting the foundation of the World Trade Center in New York, killing six and wounding over a thousand in the Twin Towers. It reverberates here in the desert. On this day, terrorism dared entry inside America as the 20th Century came closer to an end.

Will it be an isolated incident or a harbinger of horrors to come? Can you hear their song?

On the days that follow, the rumble of terror becomes increasingly foreboding. For those that watch from around the world, the reality of such a distant disturbing image is so horrific that words fail to capture the absolute fear, as only a picture can. For the terrorist, their fantasy of inflicting fear is central to their purpose. Words are inevitably found, however, to blunt their terror as we find a way to connect words to instant images of unimaginable terror. No matter how horrifying. No matter how tragic. No matter how unbelievable. No matter how far it stretches our imagination. Or belies our beliefs.

The desert sands shift in thirst for rain. Yet such rare desert rain is like tears. It streams from the faint cheeks of daytime moons in a cloudless sky, but evaporates before ever touching the ground. Tonight, the sands no longer drift; they shift, they swirl, and sound an alarm. Do they warn us of a coming flood of human tears -- an omen for an all too certain, uncertain future?

WINTER 1993

CHAPTER 1: THE OMEN

Where Europe meets Asia
February 26, 1993

He sits pensively at his desk staring out at the sea in solitary satisfaction. Sweat is visible on his scrubs. He folds his hands together and presses fingertips to his lips, as if in prayer. It is dusk in Istanbul yet the sea sparkled, as if it was the brightest part of the day. The sun begins to fade far out on the sea, hesitant to withdraw on the horizon. Yet, even as darkness slowly invades his den, it does not overshadow the end to his extraordinary day. Not until the telephone rang.

Dr. Deniz Osman is relaxing comfortably in his private sanctuary. His study is perched high above the Sea of Marmara, on top of a hill, situated near the west end of the most secluded island of all the Princes' Islands, known throughout Istanbul as the Soyakadasi. He had just completed a complex facial reconstruction on Patient 12195, which began in the morning. It was now 8:23 in the evening. He is unwinding, soaking in the sliver of sunset left with a glass of his new favorite red wine from California, a Stag's Leap Cabernet Sauvignon. A silver plate of assorted cheeses, fruits and figs accompanied the wine.

This isolated regimen had become a ritual of sorts since he took on business from a new client from Afghanistan. A Saudi. Very demanding but willing to pay a premium for perfection. Dr. Osman is no ordinary plastic surgeon. He does not strive for perfection. He believes his powers extend beyond this distinction. He sees himself as a surgeon with divine power to perform miracles. Today, he proved that by transforming a human being into the exact likeness of his Saudi benefactor.

A perfect double.

This is his first double created for his newest client. It was the fourth and final operation on this patient over the last year and it lasted a grueling half-day using the latest microsurgery technology available in the world. This patient will need several weeks to recover. When the patient fully heals, he will be transferred to his owner in Afghanistan.

A perfect double.

For Dr. Osman, his reputation at the Soyakadasi for performing modern miracles in plastic surgery was slowly spreading across elite circles of the billionaire class throughout Europe and Asia, and most recently, expanded to a few highly noteworthy clients from the United States. A glamorous woman TV broadcast anchor in New York was now his most famous client, yet no one will ever know about this arrangement, due to an exclusive, highly secretive, physician-patient privilege. The security and remoteness of the Soyakadasi further guaranteed the strictest of confidentiality required for Dr. Osman's prestigious clientele. The TV news anchor from New York had just recuperated from her recent cosmetic surgery in a luxury cottage on this very island just days ago.

However, none of his famous patients know of his extraordinary surgical accomplishments in transforming one human being into the exact replica of another. This aspect of his pioneering plastic surgery skills remains a carefully guarded secret among his most notorious clients in the darkest corners around the globe. Dr. Deniz Osman is their surgeon of choice, without equal. For this distinction and discretion, he isn't as much choosing fortune over fame, he is simply choosing to play God.

In his den, Dr. Osman quietly celebrates the total reconstruction perfection of patient number 12195 as the flawless replica of another human being. He reflects on his surgical feats having now performed this miracle two times. His first was for Saddam Hussein and today for his most aloof and dispassionate client, a Saudi, from Afghanistan. As he savored his second glass of wine, his silent jubilation was interrupted by a telephone call. It rang from a secure phone on the side of his desk. A phone installed solely for one client. He swiveled back to his desk and picked it up reluctantly, displeased to have his moment interrupted.

His eyes winced forcibly within minutes of a conversation where he had not uttered a single word. His free hand now embraced his head and he began ever so slowly massaging his temple. His mood transformed from jubilation to trepidation. When he did finally speak, it was to say a single word, yes, in Arabic:

"Na'am."

Upon hanging up, Dr. Osman appears ashen. The call was from his Saudi client from Afghanistan. He suddenly struggles with choices he's made in his life that prompted this call. He may not have understood why his benefactor was willing to pay such a premium for perfection of his own likeness, yet he is not naive. He understood the risks and rewards of taking on this particular client. This call, from this client, at this moment, however, truly frightened him. He wondered how he could possibly cancel the standing order for two more doubles by his client who has now transformed into an international terrorist.

As his mind raced through scenarios that could alter choices before him, he picked up the remote from his desk and turned on the television. The images were just as the caller said. His client had just bombed the foundation of the World Trade Center in New York City. He looked at his calendar on his desk. It was February 26, 1993. In an instant, he realized he was in far too deep to cancel.

His television set projected scenes of a horrific crime unfolding in New York City, yet no ordinary crime. Instead, a whole new form of global terrorism has finally reached the distant shores of America. It is a brand of terrorism that he knows nothing about and has nothing to do with. Yet, it hits him that somehow he will be connected to this violent act.

Without thinking, he turns up the volume from the remote. The TV anchor reporting on the attack on the World Trade Center is the same journalist that Dr. Osman had operated on just weeks ago. She bore no telltale signs of major cosmetic surgery. He knew that would be so. She was breathtakingly beautiful, he thought, a momentary respite from the tragic news she is reporting. Yet the video images of terror rocked him back to this grim reality.

When traumatic video footage is synced with words to match terror's intensity, it not only calibrates human comprehension, it releases a spontaneous flood of fear. Yet when these words creep into the mind of an accomplice to terror, a different kind of combustible fear is unleashed. For an accomplice to terror feels a completely different emotional response to such a violent atrocity. The fear is simply of getting caught. It is magnified when paranoia sets in.

No one yet knows who is responsible for the terrorist attack on the United States of America, except for Dr. Deniz Osman. He turns off the TV. He sits for a minute profoundly stunned. Then he pushes his chair back, stands up, and walks straight over to his liquor cabinet. Within moments, he pours a shot full of whiskey, trying to calm his nerves. Something he seldom ever does. He tosses it back. With bottle still in hand, he pours another.

The sun had not quite set. Yet his den had suddenly turned pitch black.

CHAPTER 2: NO ORDINARY DAY

The Adirondacks
September 11, 2001

"Noooo!" he cries out in the darkness. He bolts up in bed from a deep sleep in a clammy cold sweat. It is 2:16 am.

Two moons dominate over the majestic mountains of the Adirondacks. One moon shines brightly over the Atateka cabin nestled in towering pines just 100 yards up a hill, from the boathouse dock. The other, just as magnificent, but merely an illusion -- a lifelike reflection of the moon on the glassy, calm lake: a perfect double.

Staring out at this phenomenon was a lone sentry inside the cabin's Great Room overlooking the lake. Here stood a large, black, fearless dog, a Golden Doodle, motionless, on guard. Full alert. A man awaking in terror interrupts the silence prevailing at this ungodly hour. The man is jolted awake by his own nightmare. It is a recurring nightmare that he awakes to every morning, more terrifying since his wife died.

Yet it is one he will never tell anyone. One he cannot tell anyone.

The Golden Doodle hears the cry. She turns and walks powerfully and purposefully toward the familiar sound. She cocks her head quickly to take one last look at the dual moons at opposite ends of the earth and sky. When she reaches her master, she leads him out of bed to the window.

He sees it too.

Scott Walsh gently taps the head of his trusted big black Golden Doodle. "Everything is going to be all right, Ollie Girl."

CHAPTER 3: WHEN THE MORNING COMES

Madison, New Jersey
September 11, 2001

Jennifer Clarkin knew Reed had tossed and turned all night. It was unlike him. She knew something was bothering him.

He had been working around the clock on an important analysis for the Fed for nearly two months and had finished his report just days ago. He never mentioned what it was about. In his line of work, he wasn't allowed to share confidential information even with his wife. She wasn't concerned about his work and respected his need for privacy, yet this morning she was worried. She sipped a cup of freshly ground coffee while staring out of the back screened-in porch of their home in Madison, a New Jersey commuting suburb of New York City.

Her husband entered the adjacent kitchen. He slipped something in his briefcase and closed it before grabbing his own cup of coffee that Jennifer had waiting for him. He walked out towards Jennifer on the porch, cup in hand, checking the time on his watch. He knew he had only a few minutes before leaving to catch the 6:32 morning train to Manhattan.

As soon as he appeared on the deck, Jennifer turned to him, "No wind, not a cloud in the sky. Isn't it beautiful?" She said it softly, romantically. "It is." Reed replied dryly, not capturing the moment. "You're up early, I'll make breakfast." Jennifer said with just a hint of enthusiasm. Reed was a late riser, by habit, so being up this early only underscored his sleepless night. He pointed to his watch. "No time. I'm in a rush - early meeting." She sensed his anxiety. She confronted him directly. "Is something wrong?" she said calmly yet pleadingly seeking an answer. He could sense her concern but chose to ignore it. "Not really. Just an office issue," He put down his coffee and picked up his briefcase. "I'm late. We'll talk tonight." Then, in an instant, he was gone.

No goodbyes. Jennifer slumped into a rocking chair on the porch. They always kissed goodbye every morning. Not this morning. What was so terribly wrong?

CHAPTER 4: PAST IS PRELUDE

Upstate New York – Friends Lake
September 11, 2001

Scott Walsh fell back asleep after his nightmare only to wake up again, well before sunrise. The ringing in his ears, an incessant tinnitus since he lost his wife three years ago, was always loudest when he got out of bed. Today it seemed as powerful and menacing as the day it started -- at the very moment his wife died in his arms.

Scott is an early riser by nature despite his erratic and restless sleep. Ollie Girl, his black bear of a dog, usually wakes Scott daily by whacking her head against his body at the side of the bed at 6:00 am routinely. Not today.

Scott was already up, showered and dressed before 5:00 am. Ollie Girl never stirred from her own bed at the side of Scott's. Yet her eyes defied sleep, as they followed his every step. When she saw him leave the room, she jumped to attention and followed him. If she suspected something was wrong, she didn't alter the rest of her morning routine. When Scott let her out for her morning run to the lake, she didn't hesitate.

By the time his coffee was ready, Ollie Girl was back at the porch door, almost anxiously sensing Scott was up to something. He let her in before taking his coffee to his study. He wanted to select a book to take on his fishing trip this morning. Not a fishing trip really. He was here to pay homage to his late wife. He was returning to the Hudson River site where he released her ashes just three years ago. In his den, he picked up a picture of his late wife, Amy. She was standing, yet a study in motion, holding an overflowing basket of daisies and strawberries, in a silky, short colorful summer dress and floppy hat. Deeply tanned, her long, beautiful curly dark brown hair brushed across her face exposing her giant brown eyes and radiant smile. The backdrop was the lake. Amy always had the flair for the spectacular, but in this spontaneous shot of her, you could feel how powerfully she embraced and loved life. It made Scott smile every time he looked at it. It made him realize how lucky he was that a woman this beautiful and so full of life had once loved him.

Since her death, he started each morning holding this precious image, silently speaking to her, and putting it down only when his hands would eventually begin to tremble. Today was no different. Except this morning, when he put the picture down, he glanced over to a picture of his father, a reminder of another painful loss, when he was just ten years old.

Perhaps there is no heavier a burden for a boy than losing his father at such a young yet formidable age. Except when that same boy struggles to become a man, and a father himself, only to lose the woman he loves most, the mother of his own children. When it is death that prematurely steals everything from you, it never neglects to take a piece of you in each encounter. When they are stolen from you at an early age, grief part paralyzes you; part mobilizes you. It will either destroy you, or trip you forward into the unknown. No matter what happens next, your life now will always be from an observation deck, as you will move forward alone, trusting no one. No one heals from a broken heart. Ever. Yet it does secrete power to make a difference in this world, if only detected.

Scott Walsh woke up early this morning carrying this intense grief. He still had not come to grips with the loss of his wife. How could he? He had yet to recover from his father's loss over forty years ago. He still carries his father's death like an albatross of stifled emotions, the curse of the Irish.

His wife was the only one aware of it and understood how it shaped Scott. His children, a son, James, and daughter, Sara, knew it defined him too.

For his wife, Amy, the image of Scott's late father in uniform, on a piano in his boyhood home, made a significant impression on her when she first met Scott. She was always somewhat in awe of Scott's mother too, especially how she had kept his father's spirit alive so many years after his death. It made her realize how vulnerable Scott was, despite his own heroic military background. It was another reason she had loved him, because she knew that he needed her and that she could help him.

Scott had this strong persona yet was susceptible to his deeply repressed emotions of grief. He was physically strong yet gentle to the touch. He was a rugged individualist yet a watchdog for the weak. He carried a memory of his father, but it was overwhelmingly of his final days on earth. An image of his dad being taken out of his house on a stretcher, wrapped in an oxygen tank, when he was ten years old sticks with him like an indelible tattoo to his troubled soul. Somehow he knew it would be the last time he would ever see his father alive.

What he didn't know then was how that awful scene would surface every night from then on. He confided this recurring nightmare only to Amy, his therapist wife, referring to it as the coldest winter. He was awakened by the sounds of a distant wailing of a lone ambulance. He would look out his second floor window of his suburban home and see snow falling on what was already a high accumulation of snow that had fallen throughout the night.

He could see it clearly because of the light post attached to a telephone pole just outside his window on the street. It was so dark yet a single strong beam of light in this darkness projected a clear path to his doorway amidst high winds, a heavy snowfall and bitter cold. In the dream, the lone wail of an ambulance's siren grew louder as if it was coming home. His home.

Even from a distance, he knew it was coming for his father. The strobe lights of the ambulance reflected off the snow banks of freshly plowed snow and the front Christmas-decorated facades of neighboring homes, as it slowly made its way up the steep hill on his street. It was getting nearer. It stopped in front of his house.

The nightmare found its way of recirculating this grim reality of a frightful night he would never be able to forget. Perhaps, his psychoanalyst wife would later tell him, that he kept it alive because he didn't ever want to forget that moment. It didn't really disturb him anymore. What troubled him most, he would tell his wife, was that he never had a chance to say goodbye to his dad.

Men in white coats took his father out on a white stretcher through the white falling snow to a white ambulance. Only the amber lights betrayed the whiteness of this dark, white night. As they departed, the siren returned, only this time becoming feint the further it left the scene. When the siren stopped, he knew then that his father would never return. He never did come home.

The hole that tore open his heart upon hearing of his father's death a day later, and the flood of tears that followed, would have never ceased except for his mother tenderly holding him and letting him know he had to stop crying, because he now was the man of the house. At ten years old, those five simple words resonated. The man of the house. This was the day ten-year old Scott Walsh became a man. He didn't know what that was really. Yet, he would soon find out that it meant he had to skip growing up. Reality had to become his best friend.

Only his wife knew the conflicts that Scott would bear in trying so hard to be a man, when his rebellious and childlike side would erupt on rare occasions, followed by bouts of depression. She understood she married a great man, but one vulnerable and tormented. She loved his sensitive side and understood his grief and was able to channel the very best in him.

When she died so young of breast cancer, the hole in Scott's heart that Amy tried so hard to help Scott reconcile only widened and her death tore open another larger, more gaping hole in his heart.

How was Scott going to climb back emotionally from such tragic loss? He felt like he never would. So he started to spend more time at this lake house -- his safe haven.

Friends Lake was Scott's refuge. The spot reserved on earth that served to protect him as a boy through his father's death and the safe place where he most recently scattered his wife's ashes on the Hudson, on the back side of Friends Lake. These premature deaths became permanent holes in his heart. These deaths defined him, for better or worse. Going forward for Scott was only possible if it was propelled by his past, like rare double rainbows that follow sensational storms. Yet, going forward for a former soldier was necessary to protect his children, the gifts Amy gave him to survive.

Today, Scott's nightmares would pale in comparison to the realities of the attacks this morning on America. It is September 11, 2001. For the shadow of death is about to knock at his door again. That awful news would be delayed because right now he was unaware of any of the horrifying events unfolding in New York City this morning. Ironically, he is at his safe haven in the Adirondacks. He never traveled home last night nor took his seat this morning at his company's management meeting in the South Tower of the World Trade Center.

CHAPTER 5: WITHOUT WARNING

New York City – Ground Zero
September 11, 2001

Reed Clarkin arrived by train in downtown Manhattan well before the rush hour crowd, definitely not a normal pattern for him. He was agitated.

Despite his restless mood, as he emerged outdoors on city streets, up from the underground tubes of the World Trade Center, he couldn't help but notice what an absolutely perfect day this was in New York City. Yet, as he walked under the cloudless skies of lower Manhattan to his office, even such a glorious morning could not temper his deep anxiety.

His boss had presented chilling economic warnings and detailed recommendations to protect the nation's economy to the executive committee at the Federal Reserve yesterday morning. The entire presentation was based on his own meticulous research, findings and conclusions in a report highlighting hidden risks in the nation's banking system. The report was dismissed wholesale and it alarmed Reed.

Now, at his desk, the day after the meeting, he started re-reading his analysis on the impact of a growing trend in the financial services and banking industry regarding credit default swaps and the proliferation of synthetic derivatives. His report was a fact-based forewarning and chilling documentary putting a dire warning on a practice that was becoming widespread within the industry.

It was not an impenetrable warning as Alan Greenspan's "irrational exuberance" was nearly six years earlier. Instead Clarkin's report provided clarity to systemic changes needed to be made to protect the banking system. He was re-reading his bosses report that he authored again this morning for one reason. Why was it rejected summarily the day before?

Reed Clarkin was a 44 year-old Stanford University trained economist. He was as brilliant in his diagnosis as he was in his prescriptions to alter events in the future. He rarely lost a battle in his efforts to master and control events in his senior role at the New York Federal Reserve, better known to bankers as just The Fed. But yesterday, he lost and this morning he was in early trying to figure out why? What had he missed? What didn't they get? Don't they realize how important this is? He was deep in concentration when a colleague opened his door, rushing in startlingly and unexpectedly. His colleague, Jim Dwyer, leaned down planting his hands on Reed's desk and stared straight into his eyes.

"Listen very carefully, OK?" Dwyer said slowly yet forcefully and deliberately, staring into Reed's eyes. Taken by complete surprise, a stunned Reed could only nod yes. Dwyer continued: "We have an emergency. We need to get out of the building fast. Do you understand me?" Reed raised his hands up from his desk and asked confused: "What's happening?"

Dwyer again looked straight into his friend's eyes. "Two airplanes just hit the World Trade Center. Look behind you, all you can see is smoke. We've got to get out of here. Now."

Reed turns and looks out his office window. Jim isn't joking. He had a grand view of the World Trade Center earlier this morning but not now. All he could see in the moment was smoke. It was so dense and black that it made it nearly impossible to see anything out his window on the seventh floor of the FED Building. He wondered if an airplane crashing into the World Trade Center could cause so much smoke as to envelop the endless deep caverns of Wall Street and literally hide the sky?

Reed didn't comprehend what was happening yet, but when he swiveled back around from his window to his desk, he looked back up at Jim and keenly understood Jim's sense of urgency. He started to gather papers on his desk to put in his briefcase when Jim pushed his briefcase aside and grabbed Reed's arm and said again forcefully: "No time. We've got to go now!" With Jim nearly pulling him out from his chair, Reed jumped up, grabbed his suit jacket from the couch, and followed Jim quickly out of his office.

As they entered the seventh floor elevator together, Reed noticed that there was virtually no one left on his floor. As they reached the lobby and slid their passkeys through the security gate, the security guards told them the subways had been closed and to be careful out on the street. It was mayhem. At least that's what Reed thought they said. Just before they exited the building, they could both see throngs of people running in the streets. Jim stopped and grabbed Reed by the shoulders.

"Come home with me. We'll be safe there." Dwyer lived in Brooklyn Heights, just across the East River and over the Brooklyn Bridge, walking distance from their office. Reed replied: "I can't. I must get home." His home in New Jersey was just across the Hudson River, but he couldn't walk there. He needed to take a train. "That might be impossible. Come with me 'till we know what's going on," Jim insisted. Reed couldn't comprehend what was happening, but he knew he needed to find a way home. "Thanks, but I've got to try."

Jim let go of Reed's shoulders. "Be careful." Jim replied. He turned to leave turning back to Reed just before he left the building. With his hand in a telephonic gesture, he added: "Have Jennifer call me when you get home, OK?" When he saw Reed acknowledge him, Jim exited the building into a startling sea of smoke snaking through the streets.

New York University
Greenwich Village
8:59 AM

"Hey Sara, look at this," Cody whispered, pushing his new Nokia mobile phone so she could read the text on its face. He sat on the left side of Sara Walsh in a first period class, about three seats up and center in the tiered seating of the classroom. He had to reach towards her, but doing so as not to attract the attention of the professor. Sara shrugged indifferently and didn't look toward him or his new phone. "Annoying," she thought to herself. He was insistent, however, pushing his mobile phone again at her.

"Hey Sara, you've got to see this!" She glanced quickly. The little text the Nokia could handle on its face read simply, "Plane Hits WTC" On top of the text a digital clock displayed 8:59 AM and the date 9/11. Sara looked up immediately at Cody and whispered back, "What the hell?" and immediately raised her hand and interrupted the class. "Does anybody know what's going on? A plane just hit the World Trade Center." A buzz ripped through the classroom.

The Twin Towers were a visible landmark backdrop to Washington Square, in the center of the NYU campus. The fear of a terrorist attack loomed large inside a campus of college students attuned to world affairs. Sara used her own mobile phone to call her father Scott, on his mobile phone. The line was busy. She tried his office. That line too was busy. The professor called out to calm the students, but Sara was already up and gone. Her father's office wasn't far. It's on the 79th floor of the World Trade Center.

New York Supreme Court
60 Centre Street, Foley Square
Lower Manhattan
9:01 AM

"I know, I know," James confirmed trying not to sound alarmed. James Walsh could sense the panic in his younger sister. "I'm pretty sure all the phones at the Trade Center are dead, but that doesn't mean anything more than that. I'll keep trying to get through to Dad though." Sara replied quickly, "We've got to go there. I'm on my way to get you. You're at work, right?"

"Yes, I am. Let's think about this." James countered trying to be rational. His sister was insistent. "I'm going there. Are you coming with me?" James didn't hesitate, "Of course, meet me at the front of my office building. I'll be waiting." James said it reassuringly holding back any hint of the real danger he knew was lurking. His office had already been put on alert for a terrorist attack.

Federal Reserve Bank of New York
33 Liberty Street
9:09 AM

Neither Reed nor Jim Dwyer knew that the city was already completely shut down. Yet, when Reed slipped out of the revolving doors at the Fed to the street, the shocking reality of the situation became clear, despite that he was quickly draped in smoke and ash and visibility was nearly zero. Above him, a gigantic grey cloud was dumping ash over him. In front of him, a frightening stampede of human beings was set in motion. In a moment's hesitation, as he tried to fathom what was happening here, he was forcibly pushed from behind and nearly fell. He moved back quickly against the building to get his balance before it was too late.

As he escaped from the rushing crowd, he stood searching in the limited visibility for his colleague, who was now nowhere in sight. Reed Clarkin panicked. He was not the panicky type. He pivoted from his marble perch against the grand Fed Building and stood motionless and silently with his back flush against the building. He not only could feel his heart pounding, he could hear it. The smoke was starting to burn his eyes making it difficult to see and invading his lungs making it harder to breathe. He didn't just feel the fear. He now could taste it.

He had no idea what transformed this beautiful day into a terrorizing night in just hours on an early morning. So many countless men and women running in downtown city streets, covered in dust and fleeing from something awful. What was happening here? Why are all these people running for their lives? What terrible act had just happened to create such panic? A plane hitting a building, no surely it must be a bomb of some kind? Surely, it must be. What should he do? Where should he go? What must he do to survive?

Reed Clarkin wasn't born deaf but meningitis at three-years old took his hearing away completely. He doesn't remember ever hearing. The silence of witnessing a horrific scene is perhaps even more terrorizing in context. Watching this avalanche of smoke pummeling from the sky, as humans scattered in all directions, was the scariest moment of his entire life.

As accomplished as he was, and as independent as he was despite his handicap, he was frightened by the disorder and for the first time in his life, he didn't know what to do. In total fear, Reed Clarkin simply froze surveying the scene until he saw an officer on horseback staring at him and pointing him to head north. Oddly, it calmed him. A lone officer from the NYPD on a horse seemed to calm the others too, as this apparition appeared within the limited visibility on the ground. It was not an illusion, however, and all of a sudden the bedlam stopped and everyone began to walk, almost in an orderly staged march. Reed stepped away from the building and slid into the gathering masses as they tread north on Broadway.

As he walked with so many hundreds of others, perhaps thousands, he thought of his wife and his children. His fear turned to anxiety. He is in the middle of something terrible. Would he ever see them again? He knew that he would never miss them this much again.

He walked in absolute silence and solitude among masses. His mind raced with memories. He wished that he had not run out of the house this morning trying to catch the train without telling his wife that he loved her. He wished that he had kissed her goodbye. Doesn't he always? Instead, he was walking in a cloud of a dust rain from some unknown event downtown headed uptown to what?

This march uptown began at a slow pace because there were so many people in front of him, so many flanked to his side and countless others behind them. Yet, the pace seemed to pick up as the crowd became seamless, as one. They marched in concert north from Wall Street uptown in throngs so deep and expansive that the wide avenues of the city had become narrow lanes.

The paradox of Reed's silent view of terror to the deafening screams of F-16s flying low overhead above the smoke-drenched high-rises downtown spared no one from the gripping fear of a new age of terror. There was no practice run for 9/11. No one foresaw such an ignoble, inhumane, unimaginable attack on America's homeland. Perhaps, no one could? Sirens encapsulated the scene. Emergency vehicles were racing downtown. People, injured or just afraid, were screaming. But Reed never heard any of this. Yet he could sense it, see it, feel it and actually smell the fear unleashed on New York City this morning.

As he reached Times Square, he stopped dead in his tracks. He knew that tragedy had struck his city, yet he was still stunned to see replays of passenger planes crashing deliberately into the World Trade Center on the giant electronic video billboards of 42nd Street. It was jolting and surreal. The words crawling around the building filled him in on what was known so far and what the city was doing in response.

He looked back downtown. He had never looked back during the hour-long march it took to get only this far uptown. He was now frozen in his step, partly in fear, partly in wide-eyed disbelief. He couldn't hear the havoc in the streets but he was an integral part of a chaotic human mass exodus in midtown. Downtown had become one giant black, billowing cloud rising and spewing out over the entire southern horizon. 42nd Street is nearly four miles from ground zero, yet at the moment, the World Trade Center was nowhere to be seen. The scenes of the Twin Towers collapsing on the massive video billboards in Times Square, juxtaposed against actually witnessing firsthand the devastation unleashed downtown, didn't make it any more believable to Reed. In shock, he only accepted this frightening reality.

Scrolling emergency information streaming across Times Square wraparound billboards allowed Reed to understand that the city had completely shut down. Manhattan is an island and he was stuck in the middle. Standing alone amongst thousands of other dislocated humans, he watched the scenes developing on the sidewalks of the city of New York. They were teeming with people walking warily and perhaps aimlessly now to the north, while the streets of the busiest intersection in the world were nearly bare. No taxis, no buses, no limos, no cars, no vans or delivery trucks. Just a perpetual intermittent parade of police cars, ambulances, fire and rescue trucks all set amidst a sight he had never witnessed before in the heart of the city: Humvee military vehicles with US troops.

The electronic billboards kept advising citizens that there were no subways or trains running. The bridges and tunnels were closed. New York City was an island under siege. Shut down. There was simply no way to get home to New Jersey. He needed to devise a plan immediately for his own safety and shelter.

He didn't know anyone who lived in Manhattan except his sister-in-law, Susan, and her husband, Brad Tennyson. He had been there several times on holidays. He decided to find shelter with them.

The events of this morning confused him. He knew they lived in a doorman building nearby, somewhere right on Central Park West. He could remember their view like it was yesterday peering over the wide expanse of Central Park, but just couldn't remember the name of the building. Right now, he couldn't remember the address or even what cross streets intersected their home. How could he forget where they lived? He left his address book in his briefcase, back in the office so his options were limited.

Undaunted, he continued his journey up Broadway to Central Park West. He stopped at the first doorman building next to the Trump Tower on Columbus Circle and asked if Brad lived there. The doorman had a hard time understanding him. Reed saw a cardboard placard on the doorman's concierge desk and he asked if he could use it. The doorman still didn't understand him, but didn't object when Reed took it. Reed wrote the name Brad Tennyson with a question mark across the blank side of the placard and held it up to the doorman. Now, the doorman understood that this man was deaf. He nodded his head no.

Reed held his placard bearing his brother-in-law's name to every doorman on Central Park West on Manhattan's Upper West Side to no avail, until he reached the Orwell Building on 86th Street.

"You looking for Brad?" was the doorman's response as he surveyed this survivor from downtown with the name placard, who was cloaked in dust. Reed read lips proficiently and felt a rush of relief. "Yes," Reed nodded his head repeatedly. "Your name?" asked the doorman in an almost apologetic manner.

Reed pulled out his wallet and gave the doorman his business card. The doorman looked at it carefully and kept looking straight into Reed's eyes, with an acknowledged sadness.

"You just came from there?" The doorman said sympathetically, reaching out to Reed and dusting off his dust-laden shoulders on his suit jacket. Reed nodded. The doorman continued without hesitation: "Brad's out of town. He left last night. But I'll ring Susan for you, right now." He calls Susan and talks with her briefly. He comes around from his station counter and takes Reed's arm, guiding him to a plush leather seat in the lobby. "Susan is on her way down. Here, take a seat. You're gonna be OK here. Trust me, you're gonna be OK now." Brad sits down. "Thank you," he replied. "I'll get you some water. OK?"

"Thank you," Reed said again. For the first time this morning, he took a deep breath.

New York Supreme Court
60 Centre Street, Foley Square
Lower Manhattan
9:15 AM

James was especially good at hiding his emotions. When his sister, Sara, arrived at the steps of the Courthouse, in shock, his demeanor helped calm her down. Sara was frightened and confused having just witnessed a second plane exploding into the World Trade Center, just as he had.

"Oh my God?' Sara shouted. Crowds were beginning to develop in the area. James said nothing, grabbed his sister's hand and led the way. As they pushed their way through the crowd, they kept looking up at the Trade Center spires, now spewing black smoke and ash. When they realized it was too dangerous to go any further, Sara asked: "Do you think Dad will make it out of there?" James turned to his sister: "He made it out the last time. He knows that building. If anyone can find a way out, you know he can. C'mon, let's go. We've got to find out."

Dana Point, California
St. Regis Resort & Spa
The same day -- 6:00 am Pacific Standard Time

Brad Tennyson spent most of his adult life waking up in hotels. Not by choice, strictly by occupation. He flew nearly half a million miles annually. Even though he was ferried to airports by limousine, enjoyed first class cabins or private charters, and stayed in luxury suites while in the capitals of culture worldwide, the travel eventually wore on him. He had learned the secrets to getting sleep on airlines and in hotels a long time ago. Nevertheless, he still woke up nearly every morning never really knowing where he was. Sometimes that is frightening. Today was no exception.

Brad was sound asleep in his Penthouse suite atop the all-new St. Regis Monarch Beach, California when his bedside phone rang at 6:01 in the morning. It startled him half awake, more as an annoyance at first, until it grew louder and disturbing. He didn't know how long the phone was ringing before he picked it up.

He reached out and put on his glasses from the bedside table, sat straight up bracing himself against the headboard, took a deep breath, cleared his throat and answered the phone. "This is Brad." He actually punched his name out trying to make the caller think he was already up, attentive, and in command. As he was doing this, he felt tense, almost paranoid. Why was he pretending to be up? What was he bracing himself for?

He looked again at the digital clock on his bedside table as he spoke and realized it really was only 6:01 in the morning. Not a dream. He knew this call, at this hour, could not be good news. But what happened next could not have been worse. There was no reply on the other end, just loud, terrifying, painful crying. A woman's voice to be sure, but who?

Whoever it was, she was sobbing in absolute fright. Brad was clearly anxious as he cleared his throat again: "Who's calling?" He is trying to sound authoritative, as if doing so would immediately elicit a rational response, an explanation. Instead, no reply again, other than the continued spine-chilling sounds of fear heard on the line. The call was becoming even more distressing for Brad with each second punctuating the panic on the phone. He pleaded now to the caller: "It's Brad, please let me help you?" He emphasized, "Please," which sounded more like a plea.

Still no response as the sounds of sobbing saturated the line. Brad's mind was dashing frantically trying to determine who was calling, why she was calling him, and trying to make some sense out of this conscious nightmare. He makes a calculated guess without knowing it and whispers instinctively: "Kate?"

No reply, but the sobbing subsided. Kate was a project manager at his company travelling with him. He whispers again, almost as if reaching out and calming the caller: "Is that you, Kate?" He was sure it was. But what is so terribly wrong? Finally, a pause on the other end, a pregnant pause of dead silence, then Kate's first words came in a restrained voice: "Turn on the TV."

Brad had no idea what he was about to see, just a forewarning that it must be too scary to speak about or too disconcerting to humanly describe? What could possibly be so disturbing on TV, at this ungodly hour?

For some unknown reason, just before Brad reached for the remote, he looked to his right side, at the sliding door just a few yards from his pedestal bed. Last night, he remembered noticing that the door had been opened when he entered the bedroom. The curtains had been swirling out towards the sea, blowing haphazardly outside the door, yet leading and almost daring him to go to the outside balcony, to see the power of the Pacific and peer into the future. He never closed those doors last night after having been seduced by the sounds of the sea, silhouetted by a magical sunset, and thoughts of how good his life had become. He never saw the undercurrents that betrayed this tranquil scene.

All he noticed this morning was that those same curtains were now still. He looked out again at the ocean. At this hour, when night transforms back to day, dead calm calcified the powerful Pacific. If darkness seemed to hover over this bottomless still ocean, danger seemed to begin blowing over it. Only panic on a telephone line and a premonition of unknown horror on TV hurtled him into a strange new dawn.

Brad released the telephone clenched to his fist and dropped it from his ear after Kate said turn on the TV. He fumbled around the bedside table searching for the remote. He picked up the phone again and cradled it to his ear subconsciously, as he stared at the digital clock again for no apparent reason. He just did. It now read 6:03 as he found and picked up the remote control.

He turned on the TV.

On the screen, vivid live coverage of the World Trade Center in New York appeared, with the top quarter of one of the Towers engulfed in flames, surrounded by a thick shroud of billowing, black smoke. It was surreal, yet still terrifying.

He moved to the edge of the bed and dropped the phone to his lap. Images from the TV cast shadows of flickering light, like lightning flashes against the midnight dark of the cavernous bedroom suite, only adding to the angst of waking up in fright. He put his hand over his mouth.

Charley Gibson and Diane Sawyer of ABC News were live reporting from Good Morning America in New York City. It was 9:03 am on the east coast.

Gibson: "We are going to show you a replay of the second plane…hit the world Trade Center from the other side…So this is obviously or what seems to be, I'm dealing in speculation, seems there is a concerted attack against the World Trade Center underway…"

On the screen now is a replay, in slow motion, of the second plane hitting the second Tower at the World Trade Center. As the plane hits the Tower, you could hear "oh my God." in the background by producers and production staff live on the studio set.

Gibson: "This is terrifying, awful…" Sawyer: "To watch powerless… is a horror…"

Brad sat motionless, becoming slightly nauseous waking up to 'live' images of an explosion and sheer horror happening in real time of a passenger jet slamming into his office building in New York. His employees were in peril at their offices on the 79th floor of the World Trade Center.

His wife and child uptown, were they safe? He couldn't process it, how could he?

He watched, in a trance-like state, an attack on America in real time by an unknown enemy using commercial passenger jets. Passenger planes filled with innocent human lives used as weapons of mass destruction? It is impossible to fathom such terror. Chaos catapulted into the city. No one knew what to do or what to expect next? The image of a United Airlines passenger jet deliberately soaring straight into the World Trade Center jolted the brain. It was traumatic watching it in real time. Replays of the crash didn't make it more real, just more intense.

Humans are not hardwired to comprehend such madness. Brad succumbed to shock. The events unfolding before him paralyzed him.

For Brad Tennyson, this was deeply personal. His office was located in the World Trade Center. He was taking in images unimaginable, an airliner crashing into his company, flames leaping out of windows where he knew his colleagues and co-workers were working, where he normally would have been. Perhaps should have been? Why wasn't he there with them? His boss, Scott Walsh, had called him just yesterday morning asking him to postpone his meeting in California to attend the management meeting, but he told Scott that was impossible. The meeting in California was high profile with a car client and required his attendance. So here he was. And Scott was there.

Shock set in. Fear began to overtake him. With his hand still covering his mouth, disbelief turned to despair. What's happening here? Were other planes to follow next? Is all of New York City now under attack? Who's doing this? Why are we not responding?

John Street & Broadway
Two Blocks from The World Trade Center
9:32 am

Sara and James finally hit a roadblock. It was a police barricade. One lone officer stood outside his patrol car next to the barricade: "You can't go any further – you need to go back. Head north and move as fast you can." Sara wasn't looking at the patrolman. She was looking at what appeared to be people falling from the Towers. "Oh my god, James. They're jumping. Oh my god!" Even the patrolman turned. You could hear multiple, unrelenting thumps. James knew it was bodies hitting the pavilion and streets. He grabbed his sister by the arm and they both ran past the barricade heading to the towers. The policeman let them go.

Dana Point, California
St. Regis Resort & Spa
The same day -- 6:33 am Pacific Standard Time

The barrage of nightmarish images coming at Brad from the television would eventually anesthetize him. Or perhaps later it would be the liquor. Yet, in the moment, he picked up the phone from his lap instinctively and put it to his ear. He could find no words. He just held it there staring at the TV.

The woman on the other end too was still in shock, yet physically still crying, as if that would somehow ease the pain. It was as if she had no control of her physical self. Brad too felt himself shaking. It was like his nerve endings were being jump-started by faulty cables to a car battery, intermittent electric shocks and sparks jolting his brain. His mind just couldn't grasp what was happening and the physical reaction was involuntary. He held the phone only to watch his hand tremble uncontrollably. Nothing he could do would stop it.

His fear only heightened when he imagined what his colleagues in the center of the firestorm, in the largest skyscraper in downtown Manhattan, were doing right now. His fear magnified when he thought about his wife and child in the city, where were they? What was happening to them?

He sat at the edge of the bed completely incapable of motion. The only thing he did know for certain from watching these horrible events unfold in New York was that everything was not going to be all right. The fear of not knowing what was going to happen next felt to Brad like getting the wind knocked out of him. He felt like he was drowning. Gasping for air.

The images on TV kept vigil on the horrifying events still unfolding in New York, at the Pentagon, and in the skies over Pennsylvania. It is out of control. Brad continued falling into a deadened trance, but certain words and phrases stood out as he sat frozen in front of the TV: "The city is going into what is called archangel operation, a code name for locking down the city; Oh my god, people are jumping from the top floors of the World Trade Center; as much as 50,000 people could be in those buildings; American Airlines Flight 77 crashes into the Pentagon; United Airlines Flight 93 crashes in Pennsylvania."

World Trade Center
9:55 am

Sara and James reached the end of the line to access the World Trade Center. There is a secure ring around the perimeter of the buildings with a wall of NYPD blue police cruisers and firefighter trucks and rescue vehicles. Hundreds of brave policemen, firefighters and first responders are working, trying their best to confront and control the most horrific event of their lifetime. Their training is recognized as the best in the world, but it never included confronting something as evil or unimaginable as this, or on this scale. Yet, here they are running into danger, improvising, using the skills and expertise they have as New York's finest with all the courage they can muster.

"Can you tell us where they are sending the wounded?" James asked an NYPD officer. The officer looked at them and responded: "St. Vincent's. Do you need help?" James replied: "No, thanks. We're OK," James quickly replied and added, "We're trying to find our Dad." Sara said, "He works here." The officer said with a sense of urgency, but with surprising empathy: "I'm sorry. You can't go any further..." when they were interrupted by an unearthly noise and then the entire silo of the South Tower collapsed in front of their eyes. It is followed by a tsunami effect of ash rolling in all directions smothering them further in a deadly smoke and ash. The NYPD Officer yelled loudly to James and Sarah: "Get out of here now. Run – run north."

———————————

It was 9:59 in the morning when the South Tower collapsed.

At 10:28 a.m., so did the North Tower.

Soldiers are seldom seen on horseback in the 21st Century. Yet, New York's finest, high on saddles, on Ground Zero, appeared as the dust avalanched through the caverns of Broadway in lower Manhattan. Like centurions, these brave men on horses calmly directed civilians' en masse in chaos to safety. Safety? It was only the ninth month of a new administration into a new century and terror had just come full term.

America was no longer safe.

Multiple airlines with passenger manifests showing full boards were hijacked in the Northeast corridor of the United States during the early morning commute of September 11, 2001. Two planes, United Airlines Flight 175 and American Airlines Flight 11 slammed into America's twin icons of towering glass and steel architecture, piloted by terrorists from a stone age – Al Qaeda. Thousands were pulverized in the crushing, collapsing humiliation of Twin Towers that once stood gallantly 110 floors, as high as the sky. These were not just ordinary office buildings. They were spectacular spires representing the soaring heights of World Trade and capitalism in a bold and brash, swashbuckling, melting pot called New York City.

As the news of the day only got worse, as the images of each horrifying and incredible event was shown live by the minute, as the telephone calls remained unanswered, and after the first pictures of yet another plane hitting the Pentagon was shown on air, Brad and millions like him, were only trying to get their brains around it all. A tragedy was unfolding on such a massive scale, and on a stage so big, that trying to comprehend all this horror was impossible.

As the day turned to night, every American knew that for all her might, America was vulnerable. Without warning, the United States of America had just sustained a massive surprise terrorist attack from an unknown enemy. The tragic events recorded the largest loss of life ever on its own soil from a foreign attack. It became a day in which fear displaced optimism about the future of the country.

What was the most powerful nation in the world doing?

CHAPTER 6: AMERICA UNDER ATTACK

Washington D.C. - The White House
The same day - 10:28 am

Exactly 35 seconds after the Twin Towers collapsed, Dick Cheney picked up his phone in the White House bunker, Area 7, five stories underground. He had never used this underground fortress before. No one ever had. Protocol is to use this secure bunker only when all hell breaks loose.

Less than an hour earlier, secure mobile lines were changed and reactivated by design when an American Airlines passenger jet slammed intentionally into the Southwest side of the Pentagon at 9:37 EDT. Donald Rumsfeld, Secretary of Defense picked up Cheney's call on his mobile phone on the first ring: "Rumsfeld."

"POTUS is airborne. I just reviewed the assessment. We need to meet." Cheney was short and to the point, without any display of emotion. "On my way." Rumsfeld replied looking toward his secret service agents and nodding his head. Rumsfeld was attending to injured staff in the courtyard of the Pentagon. The triage of bodies, the smell of death, the plumes of smoke and incessant sounds of sirens did not betray the emotional toll of the scene, a surreal mix of abject fear and nightmarish fantasy.

As chaotic as the tragic scene was at the Pentagon, calm prevailed with soldiers and citizen staff working side by side with fire and rescue personnel to extinguish blazes and rescue friends and colleagues trapped inside. The death toll was unknown. Rumsfeld's secret service detail had received orders following Rumsfeld's call from Cheney to escort him to the White House, Area 7, without delay. Air transport was on its way.

The two Secret Service agents were already at Rumsfeld's side, helping him attend to the wounded, that were being brought out by the hundreds outside of the now burning icon to America's national defense. Tim Early and John Noonan, agents assigned to the Secretary of Defense, talked to each other after acknowledging the orders they had just received.

Noonan moved closer to Rumsfeld and said something that Rumsfeld nodded in agreement. Noonan and Early then led him outside of the courtyard to an open area, about 75 yards away from EMS vehicles, where a Blackhawk Marine helicopter appeared above within seconds of their arrival. The chopper dropped deliberately from the sky picking up Rumsfeld and his secret service agents before lifting off again and disappearing over the burning Pentagon.

Seven minutes later, Rumsfeld was exiting the helicopter on the grounds of the White House. On the chopper, Noonan had informed Rumsfeld about the collapse of the Twin Towers. The terrifying events were spiraling out of control. He sat silently hearing the awful news. He wondered what shoe would drop next? Yet, he remained sanguine about prospects to put a lid on the disasters before the day ended. He now knew who was responsible. America's response was already being planned by the Joint Chiefs in the 'tank' -- a secure, intact location deep under the Pentagon.

Rumsfeld was ushered to the West Wing by three heavily armed Marines detached to the White House. Once inside, he was lead to a top-secret secluded area known only to the security team at the White House as Area 7.

Inside Area 7, behind a false wall, there was an underground silo, which looked strangely like a space deportation center. Rumsfeld entered the chamber. The entire chamber locked down instantly and went dark. Midnight dark. A laser light ran down his head to toe and back again. The chamber floor seemed to fall out from under him as soon as the laser light dimmed. Rumsfeld knew that he was descending at an incredible speed yet it was momentary, not overwhelming. Despite the horror of the day, he began to realize that he knew very little of the secret workings of this government, other than his own Department of Defense, which was vast. What lay ahead? Dead stop.

Five stories underground, Rumsfeld exited the dimly lit chamber alone. Two Marine soldiers in full battle gear awaited him. Armed to kill, the lead sentry motioned visibly and silently to Rumsfeld to move down the hallway. No words were spoken. As he walked, more Marines became visible. Multiple cameras followed every motion. As he walked past them, a familiar figure surfaced. It was Craig 'Skip' Locke, Cheney's chief of staff. Rumsfeld knew him well. It did not comfort him.

"Mr. Secretary. The Vice President is waiting for you. Follow me." Rumsfeld didn't reply. He simply followed.

Inside Area 7, five stories under the White House, sits a series of state of the art conference rooms with each seat facing its own built-in computer station, communal dining areas, kitchens, state rooms, a library and what seemed like a dozen or so bunk rooms, bedrooms and baths. It is a fortress city designed for efficiency and for the ultimate safety of its occupants. Yet, it is also designed with sympathy for its survivors with architectural augmentations from lighting effects to décor and design deliberations that make living five stories below the earth almost seem normal.

Rumsfeld is led through this labyrinth until he reaches a conference room labeled only: Situation Room. Inside, seated at an oval conference table surrounded by a panoramic video wall is Cheney. Skip Locke enters the room with Rumsfeld. "Mr. Vice President, the Secretary of Defense." Skip leaves and closes the door before any words are spoken. Cheney gestures to Rumsfeld to sit down. He wastes no time or words.

"How bad is it over there?" Cheney spoke with gravity but looked at Don, his friend of many years, with sympathy. Don replies quickly trying hard not to show any emotion. "The deaths and casualties are mounting. It's sickening. How the hell did this happen on our watch?"

Cheney stares at Don understanding the rhetorical question. Don continues: "The Pentagon is still on fire but it's controlled. The command center remains intact. We're operational and I'm not closing this building. We can handle this." Cheney nods as Don keeps going. "Our Ops Deps all survived. They're in the tank making plans against al Qaeda. We've been hit hard, but our retaliation will be swift and merciless."

Cheney nodded again knowing the 'tank' is a classified underground, fortified command center five stories below the Pentagon building. If it was reassuring to know that his commanders in the military survived the morning's attack and were fast at work on America's response, he didn't show it. Instead he picked up a file before him and handed it to Rumsfeld and replied dryly: "Read this. Tell me what you think?"

Don doesn't speak. He takes and opens the file. The file reads: TOP SECRET: OPERATION HAWK'S NEST.

It takes Don just a little over four minutes to read the file, examine the photos and comprehend the mission. In this room, at this time, even four minutes seemed like an eternity. He looks up at Cheney.

"This is interesting. Frankly, I don't think a college professor's fancy for black ops is something I'd want to hang my hat on right now. It's one hell of a long shot, maybe worth a proverbial college try, but what does this have to do with me?" Rumsfeld asks calmly, yet quizzically. Cheney looks straight into Don's eyes and speaks just as calmly: "The nation needs a visible sign that we're back in control. Osama Bin Laden wants war. Putting his head on a fucking platter will quench the thirst of a nation seeking revenge. This plan..." Rumsfeld interrupts: "I still don't..." but Cheney forcibly speaks over his interruption. He speaks now with absolute authority and certainty. "This plan is not the only option we're deploying. This is not an army we are going to war with, or a country, or even an ideology. It is the Devil himself. I need every option available to the President deployed immediately and simultaneously. Yet, the secrecy of this one mission, above all others, is paramount to its success."

"I understand," Rumsfeld says sternly. "I'm planning for this war right now. What I don't understand is my involvement in this Special Op?" Rumsfeld points to the file and asks almost incredulously. "Why isn't this CIA?"

Cheney responds as a friend: "Dammit, Don, I don't have any confidence in them right now. CIA has moles inside Afghanistan and not one of them warned us today. We wake up to passenger jets being used as weapons of mass destruction. And guess what? Not a fucking peep from our intelligence sources. Not a fucking word!"

For the first time in their discussion, Cheney looks furious and raises his voice. "We're at war. We need solid Intel fast. I can't have Tenet or Crumpton overextended as we ramp this up right now. They have eyes on the ground in Afghanistan that better not fucking blink now."

"Understand. Do they know about this Op?" asks Rumsfeld. "No and they won't ever know. The President is the only other person that knows. If Scott Walsh accepts and accomplishes this mission in this timetable, this war is over before it starts. If he fails, we may be looking at the longest and costliest war in America's history." There is a pause. "What are the odds?

You know something I don't?" Rumsfeld asks. Cheney dismisses the question, not happy with Rumsfeld's arrogance with the question. Instead he replies: "This assignment isn't coming from me. It is a direct order from the President."

Rumsfeld sighs but not visibly, looks down at the file, and then stares back at Cheney. There is a pregnant pause before he says: "Understand. Who do you want to run Scott Walsh?" Dick Cheney folds his hands together and his tone is calm again, steely calm: "When the dust settles at the end of today, we've got to get this right. I need you to oversee this op. You will understand soon enough. I have a pro to run Scott Walsh. Her name is McClure, formerly CIA. She can make this happen."

"McClure?" Rumsfeld asks. "Do I know her?" Cheney replies, "Possibly, but you've certainly heard of her reputation. She's the Black Widow." Rumsfeld nods with a wide-eyed surprise acknowledgement. "Keep that in strict confidence. Her official title is White House staff attorney, but it's strictly a cover. She's the Director of a top-secret Presidential Unit. She has the authority to run Special Ops for POTUS by signature codes. McClure and her Presidential Unit are classified, known only to NTK [Need To Know]. You are now on the top of the list." (He pauses and then pushes a button on his console). An attractive blonde, early fifties, enters the room as if on cue.

"Mr. Vice President, Mr. Secretary, " She begins as she strides in and shakes Rumsfeld's hand firmly before Cheney cuts her off and gestures for her to sit.

"Don, meet Leigh Ann McClure. She'll run Walsh day-to-day. She's also the contact that introduced me to Dr. Hislop, from Georgetown University. This op was Hislop's concept developed just after the first World Trade Center bombing back in 1993. That's how long this scenario has been brewing. Leigh has been on an operational watch solo since then. The Clinton team never took any interest in it, but it never was officially stopped. Leigh, please fill Don in." Leigh looks at Don and begins briefing him on OPERATION HAWK'S NEST.

"Big picture first. New York, Washington D.C., Miami, LA and Chicago were the five cities on our radar screen for this operation. We isolated ten candidates from each city using criteria matching the specs for the type of former Special Forces operative we needed."

She pauses momentarily to switch gears in her delivery. "Background. Dr. Hislop, a Middle East scholar at Georgetown had formed a theory immediately after the 1993 World Trade Center bombing. He surmised that Osama Bin Laden and his terrorist organization, Al Qaeda, would attack the United States in an unprecedented way, either on a subway, bridge, tunnel, airport or other major venue in one of these cities. He was also of the opinion that it was highly likely that Al Qaeda would attempt a repeat attack on the World Trade Center. His thesis was that the attack would happen despite our precautions and security; mass casualties would occur, and fear would set in across the country. His concept was based on an assumption that the U.S. government could not stop every terrorist attack."

Rumsfeld interrupts: "Hislop? What's his connection to DOD [Department of Defense]? Did he predict terrorists would use passenger planes as weapons?"

Leigh shifts in her seat and answers immediately. "I'm getting there, sir. But no sir, no one predicted use of passenger planes as bombs. What's important to know at this point is that his concept was reactionary to an event of terror not precautionary. But here's the big idea. While the government plans on stopping or preventing the next terrorist attack, they must also plan on getting hit. Not just to recover from the disaster, but to retaliate quickly. Hislop's plan was the execution of a clandestine black op to assassinate the head of the terrorist organization successfully within weeks or months after the attack."

Rumsfeld nods as he taps unconsciously at the file he had just read. She continues: "Strike back fast and strike at the head and heart of the terrorist organization. The plan was based on an odd, yet simple premise worth consideration. How many people get caught in a maelstrom and in its midst find a way to escape, not just the horrible event, but escape from their current life? Hislop found that there are always several people listed as missing and presumed dead in the aftermath of every national disaster whose deaths are premature. Some escaped never to return. The motivations may be different but the result is the same. These survivors used the calamity to their own devices, some just to collect insurance money fraudulently others simply just to start their lives over as someone else. A second chance, a do-over, as you will."

Rumsfeld is listening intensely as Leigh puts her hands together and pauses with her index finger raised. She went on: "Hislop put that premise to a far bigger test with a sobering twist for national security. What if a terrorist attack happens and someone who was supposed to be in the disaster zone was plucked from the scene without a trace? Or, perhaps he actually wasn't in the attack zone -- yet no one was the wiser? What if that person had past Special Forces military training? What if the government had identified and targeted that unique former soldier and followed him for years in anticipation of a terrorist attack on a suspected public site like the World Trade Center?" She pauses just long enough for Rumsfeld to grasp it, but moved on quickly enough so not to be interrupted by questions.

"Imagine knowing the target's whereabouts 24/7, so closely monitored that the target could be plucked out from the mayhem alive and without a trace? What if we recruited that former soldier back to government service on that very day? It would be a service so secret that he would have to relinquish his identity forever and be trained quickly to hunt and kill the mastermind behind the madness. Dr. Hislop's theory 'from the ashes' presents the opportunity to create America's phantom assassin. Hislop concludes that to assassinate the head of a terrorist organization, like Al Qaeda, would be impossible, unless the assassin was either planted inside the terrorist organization (highly unlikely if we were attacked by surprise), invisible, or a totally nonexistent threat. An assassination on a terrorist organization as insular as Al Qaeda would have to be triggered immediately after an attack and completely by surprise for it to succeed. Hislop's theory was that the only way this can happen is if the assassin simply doesn't exist."

Rumsfeld interjects rhetorically then follows up with a question: "America's phantom assassin. From the ashes… Interesting. What authority do we need to go forward?"

Leigh continues at a faster pace now. "This is already black op status from the prior administration. We're activating it now as an operational TOP SECRET. Scott Walsh is the candidate. You've seen Scott Walsh's file. He was supposed to be in his office at the World Trade Center this morning. He wasn't. We know that because we have been watching his every move since last February."

She hesitates and looks at her watch. "We are picking up Walsh as I speak. He's at a private lake in upstate New York. FBI agents are observing him. He's in an area so remote that no one else knows he's there. So remote that he's unaware of the events of today. They'll pick him up and escort him to West Point. That's where you and I will brief him. We'll depart Washington today at 1300 hours. Scott Walsh will remember me from missions we completed together decades ago, despite that we never kept in touch. After you get him onboard, I'll take him from this meeting to Arizona to prep and train him for the mission. We'll get you back to DOD by 1500 hours. This Op is classified TOP SECRET codenamed 'OPERATION HAWK'S NEST'. If our plan works, Osama Bin Laden will be assassinated within 30 days. Any questions?"

"You've got to be kidding." Rumsfeld replies without hesitation and skeptically adds: "This is the guy you picked to take out Osama Bin Laden? You realize how old he is? This is crazy." Rumsfeld says exasperated. "No, it's more than crazy. It's absurd." Cheney interrupts for the first time. "I certainly wasn't expecting that outburst as your initial response. But I understand it. Look, it's not perfect. But it's also not as crazy as you might think. Go ahead Leigh. Show him."

Leigh passes a photo sheet to Rumsfeld with pictures of ten men on it. Each man identified by a number. Scott's photo is shown as #7. Leigh doesn't waste time: "Scott wasn't our first choice, nor our second or even third. You are looking at all of our choices in New York by priority. #7 is the only one left after today's attack." Cheney interrupts a second time: "For the record, every name on that list is capable of taking out Bin Laden. Including #7."

Rumsfeld looks at Cheney quizzically. Leigh jumps right back in: "We vetted every operative on that list. Scott Walsh is fully capable, despite his age. We are going to customize training for him before the mission starts. He will be ready."

Rumsfeld, still not looking optimistic, decides to move the briefing forward asking: "Assuming Scott Walsh buys into this ill-fated mission, don't we still have a problem?" Leigh puzzled asked, "I'm not sure what you mean?"

"Hislop? How do we control him?" Rumsfeld asks. "That's my job," Leigh responds. "As is this entire mission. Complete secrecy is the only way we can go forward. I have absolute authority to do whatever is necessary to make this mission successful." Leigh continues, as Cheney nods in agreement. "One last item. There will be no further briefings until the mission is completed." Leigh punctuated this point. "Understand you to a point, yet you'll provide me classified progress reports," Rumsfeld interjects. Leigh cuts him off in mid-sentence. "No sir. No reports of any kind, sir. This concept only works if no one knows about anything, but I can support Scott if he needs it. When he needs it. If Scott survives, you will be the first he sees when he gets back. As far as Dr. Hislop is concerned, I know him. I also need him. He can be trusted."

"Trust no one, isn't that how these channels work best?" Rumsfeld retorts, "Doesn't Hislop add another outside connection to this chain that could jeopardize the mission?" Leigh answers his objection, "He has the highest security clearance. He also has connections and access to information that I may need." She pauses, "I will not leave anything to chance."

A buzzer on Cheney's console goes off alerting him. He picks up a phone from the console and listens, then replies: "I'll be there in just a few minutes." Cheney looks at Don. "Are we done here?"

"One last question," replies Rumsfeld. "I understand the mission. With McClure taking charge, why am I involved?" Cheney responds immediately and dead serious: "We need to show Walsh we mean business. Your position qualifies that. We also need to sell him on what well could be a one-way ticket for his country." That statement by Cheney was followed by a deafening pause in the conversation.

No one spoke until Rumsfeld said reservedly: "I understand. I do. But from what I just read in his file, he doesn't particularly like our politics.

Why are you so confident that I can convince him to do this?" Cheney stands. He looks fatigued yet speaks with an air of confidence. "My friend, you're our best bet to make a connection and demonstrate gravitas. Scott Walsh's father saved your brother's life in Italy during World War II. His father was a decorated war hero and died when Scott was just a kid. You may have even known his dad. Like your brother, he was in the last cavalry in the United States Army."

Cheney moves towards Don and puts his hand on his shoulder: "You'll meet Scott Walsh within hours. Our world is upside down. We need him onboard – and now it is up to you." Cheney removes his hand from Don's shoulder and continues: "I have to go. Good luck and Godspeed." He nods to McClure who exits with him, not before she shakes Rumsfeld's hand firmly again acknowledging their joint assignment. No other words are spoken.

Skip Locke enters the room and escorts Rumsfeld back to the elevator. As he is about to enter, Locke asks Rumsfeld: "Aren't you forgetting something, Mr. Secretary?" Rumsfeld looks confused by the question, but then realizes he still is carrying the TOP SECRET file. He hands the file back to Locke. Just as the elevator closes, Don whispers to himself: "God help us."

CHAPTER 7: REPRISAL

The Pentagon
September 11, 2001

"Circle 'round," Rumsfeld said, circling his index finger and looking down. "I want to survey the damage." The pilot of the Blackhawk chopper nodded as he pivots the helicopter downward for a lower and slower approach to circle the Pentagon. The gaping hole in the Pentagon's core surrounded by fires, smoke, and hundreds of emergency red lights flashing from trucks of the EMS crews and fire brigades left an indelible impression from the air. For Rumsfeld, it was a moment of reconnaissance that was deeply personal. The landscape of death and casualties below him included friends, soldiers, and dedicated staff. The images only projected the horror of the scene; the names connected to the faces of lifeless and wounded comrades in the triage lines made it tragically painful and real.

The Pentagon building spans nearly 30 acres, with more than 5 acres in a central courtyard. Yet the landscape below of the vast courtyard was now his focal point. The pilot seemed to sense it and hovered for a few minutes over the containment area. It was filled with stretchers and triage tents, a makeshift military field hospital in a modern day war zone. How many were dead? Injured?

This building was never meant to be a war zone, not in the middle of the nation's capital. Just hours earlier, American Airlines Flight 77, took off from Washington Dulles International Airport heading to Los Angeles. This same Boeing 757 was hijacked en-route and purposely flown straight down into the heart of the Pentagon. Now, just hours after the attack, flying stationary over this vast complex, Don Rumsfeld was taking in the events of a single morning that would change the lives of everyone who survived it, and contemplated how it would affect the lives of everyone else who witnessed it around the world. Ironically, he thought, today marked the 60th anniversary of the groundbreaking of this historic landmark building housing America's military elite. This is the headquarters of the greatest military machine in the world.

He knew what was to come next. The heat of the attack on the Pentagon would only pale in comparison to what was about to be unleashed in response by the Armed Forces of the United States of America, under his command.

Rumsfeld's aides met him as the helicopter finally set down at the South Parking Lot, the staging ground for EMS choppers and rescue vehicles. They briefed him as he walked into a still burning Pentagon. He went straight to the inner Courtyard. The scene was still sickening and yet there was a resilient confidence about the aides and first responders dealing with the fires and injured. He spoke to a few injured men and women before leaving with his aides to the basement, which led directly to the Pentagon's own version of Area 7 at the White House. In this basement was an elevator much like the one he used earlier in the White House. The entrance to the DOD bunker was not as sci-fi as the White House. Nor were the accommodations as large or luxurious, yet it was army functional and still electrifyingly high tech.

Don met first with the Joint Chiefs and held a series of brief secure conference calls with NSA, CIA and FBI. Central command had been shifted immediately after the first attack in New York to NORAD (North America Aerospace Defense Command) in Colorado to shut down air space and control the skies with forward war planning then centralized in

Tampa, at CENTCOM (U.S. Central Command). Now, underground, the Ops Deps were developing operational plans for America's first war of the 21st Century. The walls were panoramic video and computer screens, relaying live streams of data, maps and dramatic close-ups of enemy faces and fortresses. Amidst chaos in the country aboveground, a futuristic high-tech war planning room projected calm and confidence underground. America was preparing to strike back. The objective is clear. Plans to go to war against Al Qaeda in Afghanistan were being drawn up in this very room for a POTUS briefing by morning. Being caught by total surprise by such a significant assault by a terrorist organization this morning stung the Pentagon. You could sense the urgency to take control and crush this new enemy.

Rumsfeld's personal office at the Pentagon was intact after the explosion. He decided to keep every corridor and office operational, despite the damage, as the military complex was ripped wide open on its southwest side. America was now 'unofficially' at war with Al Qaeda and Rumsfeld was charged to develop and coordinate the war plan with NSA and the CIA.

Despite the chaos and carnage, Rumsfeld almost felt comfortable with the charge at hand. Codename: "Operation Enduring Freedom" was already hours in planning by the Joint Chiefs assembled in the bunker below to counterattack. Yet, Rumsfeld's confidence in war planning was simultaneously haunted by a deep brief on Scott Walsh, a classified priority Black Op Codename: "OPERATION HAWK'S NEST".

Several hours later, at 1300 hours, Rumsfeld was taken from the still burning Pentagon back to the chopper that delivered him in minutes to a private runway nearby, where his DOD C37A Grumman Gulfstream G5 awaited, ready for takeoff. On board were two pilots, an Air Force flight attendant and a single passenger, Leigh Ann McClure. Within minutes, they were airborne. Destination: Stewart AFB, West Point. Flight time: 42

minutes. Once airborne, two F-16 fighter jets appeared and escorted the flight. It was the only flight from Washington to New York on the afternoon of 9/11. There would never be a record of it. This was the infancy of a clandestine black op, where a planning phase is never recorded.

Don sat across from Leigh. They nodded to each other. Immediately after takeoff, the flight attendant poured coffee for both passengers. Leigh provided the original TOP SECRET briefing file on Scott Walsh back to Don. He reviewed them again, this time focusing on how he was going to approach this man that he needed to recruit for a mortal mission. They sat in total silence.

As the events unfolded throughout the day, Rumsfeld felt confident that the anarchy that ensued after daybreak had finally passed. The aftermath was no less horrific and it was sobering and humbling to be in charge of America's national defense. He knew that his command officers quickly identified the terrorists behind the attack and were firmly back in control. He knew they would be ready by dawn to map out the offensive counterattack. The Generals under his command were getting ready, fully operational, and highly motivated to lead the effort required to take on America's newest enemy: Osama Bin Laden and Al Qaeda.

Revenge is perhaps the most potent elixir for men at war. The planning had begun. America would waste no time to strike back hard, fast, and with ferocity to exact a toll on terrorists anywhere on the globe. Operation Enduring Freedom was in the capable hands of the Joint Chiefs just hours after the World Trade Center was attacked. General Tommy Franks was selected quickly to lead the combat operations in Afghanistan. With the plans for immediate action under development, Rumsfeld turned his attention to the confidential file before him: "TOP SECRET: DOD – FOR SHOTPUT ONLY". SHOTPUT was Rumsfeld's Top Secret DOD codename.

Inside the file was the classified dossier on "OPERATION HAWK'S NEST". Don bypassed the reports and pulled out the photos of Scott Walsh and started studying them. His first impression was that this guy ages well. He was surprised to see that photos of Walsh, taken when he was in Special Forces in the 70s, were almost identical to those taken decades later. That was what Rumsfeld liked most about the military: attention to detail.

Inspecting these photos close-up, he could immediately detect creases under Walsh's left eye, although almost negligible, but they weren't wrinkles really, they were clearly cuts or possibly shrapnel scars. Another scar noticeable on his left cheek. Definitely shrapnel, he thought. There was something else just underneath and to the right of his right eye. Like a dimple but no, it was like a tiny particle of his face cut off. Yes indeed, he thought, he is missing a piece of his skin and bone just to the right of that eye, definitely not shrapnel this time. Clearly a bullet caused that deformation by his temple. Underneath his chin, he also detected a slight long line; maybe a knife wound that never healed properly. You would think, Rumsfeld wondered, that this many marks on any man would be somewhat disturbing to look at. Yet with Walsh, it seemed only to dramatically call attention to his strength and rugged profile.

His nose was long, large and yet perfectly proportioned on a face that personified strength like a rudder to his soul. Maybe too, the profile of his nose distracted attention to the unruly, unkempt shaggy wild eyebrows that helped frame it, yet somehow it also dramatically demonstrated that he was clearly unaware of his looks. Perhaps, he couldn't care less about what people thought of him anyway? His lips and mouth, although thin and wide, defy detailed description but they too, Rumsfeld believed, said something about the confident character of this man. His hair, jet black without even a speck of gray, was speaking to Rumsfeld too as he tried to get to know Walsh from the photos. He had a full mane of hair somewhat on the longish side but stylish without fuss, avant-garde, perhaps for a man his age?

Rumsfeld believed in picking up clues about people by examining their faces. He liked what he saw in this guy, Walsh. He was of Irish descent yet his dark complexion, black hair, and facial features allowed him to blend in equally as well as an Afghan. He started to move the photos around not to organize them but rather to see a random, fuller, more extemporaneous profile of the man. Study the stance, it tells all, he thought.

Walsh was tall and broad and not surprisingly, some twenty pounds heavier than he was in the 70s. How would that affect his performance on this mission? Yet, whether in a suit, casual clothes or in uniform, his masculinity was easy to notice. The twenty pounds he put on since then only made him look more formidable, not a trace of fat discernible on his body, as the lines of his body traced a physique of powerful force. The other thing that struck Don was not a single photo was posed. How unusual? Every shot captured the candor of the moment and he realized that he had an almost unlikely opportunity to see, actually see, the real Scott Walsh before him. In every shot, at every angle, the photos did not lie: this man was physically fit, confident and poised. He pushed the photos aside and opened the summary report.

Profile: Scott Walsh
Male, Age 53 Born at Fort Dix, NJ 1948
Height: 6'2"
Weight: 225 lbs.
Eyes: Blue
Religion: Roman Catholic
Widower: Wife Amy Jean – MSW Fordham; Psychotherapist; deceased 1951-1998
Children: two
James: 26 (Lawyer, Law Clerk to Chief Justice Frank McKinney, NY Supreme Court)
Sara: 22 (Graduate student, New York University)

Education: Regis High School, NYC 1965
United States Military Academy, West Point 1969
Wharton Business School, University of Pennsylvania 1982

The file would reveal that upon graduation from West Point, he was selected for elite special ops, the Green Berets. He was commissioned as a second lieutenant in the last flight school for the U.S. Army in Alabama. He was trained to fly the Mohawk in combat operations and specifically trained to fly this armed military observation and attack aircraft in Vietnam. He was then assigned to rare classified Intel high tech Special Forces training, based in Southern California before he was assigned Army Intelligence training at Fort Huachuca, Arizona. Having completed that training, his case files were transferred to highly classified black ops as he was assigned and trained for sixteen additional weeks in an experimental special ops training that exceeded both the Army's Green Beret and Navy Seal's rigorous readiness.

He was one of only sixteen people from all the services to receive this elite top secret classified training conducted by Navy Seals, Green Berets, CIA and for the first and only time in history Great Britain's SAS. These training exercises were conducted throughout the world.

At the end of his training, he was assigned officially to the United States Army to fly the Mohawk on combat operations in Vietnam out of Da Nang. He arrived on Christmas Day 1971 in Vietnam. Officially, his file shows 77 combat missions and he was shot down on one mission but rescued. Unofficially, he was taking orders directly from a new Unit assigned to the office of the President of the United States. He operated under this Unit on missions in Cambodia, Germany, Morocco, Turkey, Afghanistan, Iran, Libya and Nigeria. Only those with the highest security clearance are privileged to see these TOP SECRET files and then only by the authority of the President of the United States.

He resigned from the Army abruptly in 1979 with an honorable discharge, two bronze stars and a silver star. Scott Walsh went on to graduate school for management studies and graduated from Wharton at the University of Pennsylvania in 1982. He started his own marketing and security business specializing in large scale live events, and film and show production including the Olympic events that required comprehensive security details. His company initially won the management and execution of the Olympic torch relays and since then his firm has grown in size and reputation. His company is Atateka Productions located on the 79th floor of the World Trade Center in New York City.

Scott Walsh is a widower. Three years ago, his wife Amy passed away from breast cancer. Her death changed him and he appears to have gone into seclusion since losing her. He has two grown children. Both live away from home. Home for Scott is relative right now. He officially lives in a 35th floor apartment at the Trump Building on 68th Street on the west side of Manhattan. He spends much of his time now, almost in self-exile in semi-retirement, between his lake house in upstate NY and his winter home in Fort Lauderdale, Florida. He no longer is fully active in his business, but attends management meetings on the second Tuesday of each month and still participates in major proposal concepts and presentations for new business only. He still sees existing clients on rare social occasions.

He was scheduled to be at his office at the World Trade Center this morning. Yet he did not show. He didn't cancel either, but didn't show up there for some unknown reason. He is confirmed alive, alone, in seclusion in the Adirondacks. FBI confirms his seclusion and exact location. His emails, mobile phone, and home and office telephone records have been searched and there is clear evidence that he was planning to attend the meeting at his office on the morning of 9/11. Phone records indicated he spoke to his children on Sunday night and spoke to his secretary at the

World Trade Center on Monday morning. These transcripts verify that all of them expected him to be in his office at the World Trade Center on Tuesday September 11th.

OPERATION HAWK'S NEST is now activated. Greenlight began at 1030 hours on 9.11.01 with Walsh under surveillance team 3. He is completely cut off from outside communications and is unaware of the terrorist strikes. FBI agents Pat Reese and Gary Moylen are now in the vicinity tracking his movements waiting for orders to pick him up and escort him to West Point. That order will be sent at 1100 hours. Once he is picked up, Agent Fred Stobaeus will secure his summer residence. Walsh will be briefed en route only of the terrorist attacks and his upcoming meeting with DOD at West Point.

Rumsfeld closed the brief for a minute. He looked out the window, as if searching for something. Leigh noticed but left him to his thoughts. After just a few minutes, Rumsfeld reopened the file. He looked back at the photos that he put aside earlier. He wondered how a 50-something year old former soldier could handle such a Herculean mission? He lifted his coffee cup slowly as he focused on the photos again.

Leigh sat across from him watching intently. She knew the personnel briefs could never fully reveal the truth that you really wanted to know about an operative. It has been years since she last saw Scott, yet she had handpicked him for this assignment, even as it was in the hypothetical stage.

Leigh knew Scott was a soldier with adroit killing skills. He was a soldier that chose a battlefield instead of an office in his youth and she understood his deep motivations. How does one win honor of a father he would never know? How can a man seek approval of a father where none was ever going to be given? How can a man close a hole in his heart that would never heal?

There was power in Scott's search for eternal truths, yet the lack of answers never dragged him down. He still had the power and persona to make you confident in his leadership, but he could make you laugh; feel good about yourself and others. He had this uplifting charisma and a way with words that made you understand his depth of feeling. If you really got to know him, you knew that Scott was a soldier by birth but a romantic underneath all the armor. He was Shakespeare in a military theatre of war. Perhaps it was this depth in his psychological makeup that made him the kind of leader that his soldiers would say brought out the best in them.

She understood that better than most. She knew he had brought out the best in her. She fell in love with him only never to see him again. So many years ago... How could she possibly know him after all those years?

When she was selecting former Special Forces soldiers for America's 'Project Jackal' back in 1998, she had interviewed Brad Tennyson, a VP at Atateka Productions, to learn more about its president Scott Walsh. She needed to know if Scott was still capable of the courage he would need to succeed. She needed to find a way to engage Brad Tennyson without his knowledge of her intentions.

On a flight from Los Angeles to Tokyo, she took her seat next to Brad in Upper Class on a Virgin Airways flight. It was no coincidence. He was already settled in his seat, with his executive leather portfolio with the Atateka Productions logo on the workspace next to his armrest. He was enjoying a drink and reading a novel. She could see it was The Pillars of the Earth by Ken Follett. As she got settled into her seat, he looked over at her and smiled.

"Are you a Follett fan?" she asked him. "Without a doubt," he said. "He is a constant companion on my travels. Do you read him?" Leigh answered with a smile, "I've only read one of his. It's the one you're reading now. I'm somewhat of a history buff so I found it fascinating."

"I just started reading it," Brad replied returning the smile. "You know, it's really quite a departure from his past novels. Yet, I'm really finding it hard to put down." Leigh understood and said, "Oh, please go back to it then. I didn't mean to interrupt." Brad replied quickly, "Oh no, I didn't mean to come off that way," he said. "Allow me to introduce myself. I'm Brad. Brad Tennyson." He extended his hand for a handshake. "Nice to meet you, Brad," Leigh replied smiling and shaking his hand. "I'm Tess August."

"Can I get you a drink," the Flight Attendant interrupted. "Not right now, thanks," replied Leigh posing as Tess. "I'll have a vodka on the rocks, two olives," Brad told the flight attendant. He looked back at Tess. "You sure you don't want anything?" She pushed her hair back and said politely to the flight attendant, "Sure, I'll have what he's having." The flight attendant said she would return in a few minutes.

"So Tess, are you from LA?" Brad asked. "No, I'm not. Just connecting flights to Tokyo. How about you?" "I'm a New Yorker," Brad said, "You do business in Tokyo?" he asked. "I do," she answered. "I'm an attorney with Chadbourne & Park. I'm based in Washington D.C. And you?" she inquired.

"I work with a production company in the city," he answered. "This is my first trip to Tokyo. Have you been there often?" "I wouldn't say often," Tess replied. "But I started going a few years ago for my firm so I make 4-5 trips a year now." Brad laughed, "That's often to me. I hope you don't mind if I ask you some questions about Tokyo?"

Brad put his novel aside and he and Tess spent a good part of a very long flight talking about Japan and just about everything else. He had no idea who Tess was nor had any idea that she was interviewing him about the character profile of his boss Scott Walsh. He found her fascinating.

She found that Brad wasn't shy talking about his boss. In the end, she learned that Scott really hadn't changed much – still a little full of himself, yet still a bold and charismatic leader. She found it interesting too that he was admired in business for the same reasons his soldiers admired him. He brought out the best in them. She also learned how much he loved his wife, who he lost suddenly and tragically to breast cancer and how he felt like such a failure to his children after her death. Listening to Brad talk about his boss, with such uncomplicated ease about his complicated life, made her realize how much he must be loved by the people he worked with.

In Flight to West Point

She was still deep in thought when the smell of fresh coffee sifted through her senses and brought her back to the present moment. The flight attendant appeared and poured her a second cup of coffee. Leigh watched Don fidget across from her as the flight attendant then poured him a fresh cup too. She could tell that Don was tense so she decided to interrupt him.

"You look worried. I know this man. What troubles you?" Rumsfeld repositions his staring eyes from the photo to the woman he had only just met this morning. "What worries me?" He momentarily looks down to close the file before looking back at her. "I only wish we had the time for that conversation. You say you know this man. Tell me why he is our guy for this mission?"

"Fair enough," replies Leigh. "What if I told you that if I could select someone thirty years younger, fresh out of Special Forces to enter the lion's den in Afghanistan, I would still choose Scott?" Don tilts his head and cups his hands with a sarcastic gesture to please, by all means, proceed. She sits back comfortably in her seat. "In my line of work, some things are prerequisite: Top physical condition, mastery of weapons and tradecraft, competency with several languages and dialects, the mental toughness to make mission critical decisions in split seconds, and finally, a killer instinct. Scott not only passes all those tests, he is proven in the field." Don interjects, "Proven? He is in his 50's now, he hasn't seen any action for twenty years." "Granted." Leigh replies. "If Scott lacks anything because of age it is simply reflex, but his experience, even outside of Special Forces, make him more worldly, more cunning, to take on a modern day monster."

Don looks puzzled. "What does that mean? Worldly?" Without flinching, Leigh continues: "It means maturity. It means it extends beyond the mandatory military theater of war. This guy has walked in these lands before not just as a soldier, but also as a man. Think of it like this, he can think in several languages without translating the words. Do you have any idea how difficult that is to do? And he has cultivated, in his line of work, that rare ability to size up people in a room. Scott can light up a room or remain invisible instinctively. He not only understands the culture of the lands he travels in, he knows how to fit in those cultures. Do you know how important that will be where he is heading right now?"

The flight attendant interrupts again to ask if they would like anything else? They wave her away politely. Don continues the conversation about Scott, "I get it. Yet, he doesn't seem to have handled the loss of his wife very well. That concerns me. He is going to experience tragic loss in volumes today and we don't know about his kids' safety yet either. How much danger are we putting him in under these circumstances? How much risk does that play for us in going ahead with this plan? Is he going to melt down emotionally when he finds out what happened to his people today?"

"Who the hell knows? We play the hand we are dealt." Leigh replies, then pauses, and looks away. Don doesn't say a word. He just keeps his eyes directly on her. She knows it, can feel it, and takes a deep breath before looking back straight at him.

"Maybe you are right," she ponders aloud. "Perhaps he still hasn't come to terms with his grief? But I think I know him better than most. Because what happened today is so personal to him and what we are proposing will jolt him squarely back into reality. Frankly, from what I know about Scott personally, he's been lost without his wife." Suddenly she gets animated using her hands as her voice now punctuates her sentences. "He needs purpose. We are putting purpose on a silver platter for him." She pauses again. She looks out the window, for an instant, then turns and leans towards Don, attracting his undivided attention.

"You asked me at the beginning of this conversation why Scott is the right guy for this mission? Here's my take: This is a guy who has suffered loss. Unimaginable loss. Of his father, his wife, and brothers on battle-fields. And today, he will lose everyone he worked with at the World Trade Center. I'll bet that his kids are safe and if they are, he will have his own mission well defined. Protect them from evil. Today's loss was at the hands of terrorists and he will be given a mission to hunt and kill the mastermind behind it." She pauses as Rumsfeld listens attentively.

"He will see it as something he can control. This mission gives him a purpose to avenge the deaths of thousands of Americans, including the ones that were closest to him. Most importantly, it will give him a license to protect his children." She sits back and then continues: "It's not that our guy lives for danger. Or revenge. But he doesn't run from it. Scott's one of those rare men amongst us, a patriot with a will to win at any cost, unafraid to lay down his own life to save others. I chased down terrorists with this guy before. Few know him the way I do." Leigh stops talking and now physically leans in towards Don, staring at him straight in his eyes. "Two things I promise you: Scott will hunt Bin Laden down. And then, he will kill him." She sits back facing him, finished.

Don nodded his head and returned the file back to Leigh. He sat back in his seat and appeared to close his eyes for a moment, almost reflectively. He was impressed by what he just heard. For the first time today, he felt a level of confidence that Operation Hawk's Nest might actually succeed despite impossible odds.

Within seconds, his thoughts were abruptly interrupted. The captain announced they were flying over the Hudson River passing New York City on the right side of the aircraft. He looked out the window and could see the smoke billowing east from lower Manhattan, as did McClure.

Where the World Trade Center once proudly stood.

CHAPTER 8: TWIN PLUMES OF SMOKE

The Adirondacks
9/11

Scott Walsh found peace in the Adirondacks. He had driven up from Manhattan this past Sunday, a four hour drive up the winding Taconic Parkway, and through the mountains on the Adirondack Northway. September 9th was the third anniversary of the day he floated his wife ashes, in a biodegradable urn wrapped in a wreath of multicolored roses, down the Hudson River. It was on a favorite spot that he and his wife, Amy, walked to every summer. He drove up on the 9th to feel those feelings again, despite the sadness that came with this personal mecca, a journey that was now becoming an annual tribute to his lost love.

Scott loved to drive. Long distance driving was perhaps an adequate form of therapy for him. His car provided a confidential cabin to ask hard questions, cry out in pain in absolute anonymity, and actually listen to his thoughts. It allowed him to talk one-on-one with someone he loved, who is gone. Scott lost his wife Amy to breast cancer. He knew it still was too soon to know if this pain would ever subside. On the road, from Manhattan north to the Adirondacks, he knew where he was going, but with every mile, he was beginning to realize that he was still totally lost.

He was planning to return to work on Tuesday, but on Monday evening he felt a powerful force to stay longer. On this day, the 11th of September, which would soon become to be known only as 9/11, he was on his way back to the memorial site of the only woman he ever loved. He was still in awe of how she faced her fate with such courage and grace; as much as he understood to be loved by his wife was a very precious love. She was his first love and the love of his life. Her death was so abrupt it haunted him. Like his father, Amy had never said goodbye.

Some days he still wakes up feeling like his life with her was only a dream, as if it unfolded in one of her many books. His apartment in New York City, his vacation home in the Adirondacks, and his winter retreat in Florida, were filled with libraries of books, mostly Amy's. In the past several years, many said his life with Amy was like a storybook romance. Part Camelot. Part Shakespearian drama and tragedy, where they would share an everyday life filled with trials and tribulations, joy and sorrow, victories and defeat, humor and tragedy, the deepest love and an agony that can only come from seeing people you love suffer. Never did they share a single day that was mediocre or marginal. Their love was romantic and real, magical and spontaneous. However, between the laughter and the tears, thunder and lightning struck once too often.

Unafraid, Amy had lived her life to its fullest. It was cut short. Only now was he finally coming to terms that she would have wanted him to continue living his. What was not a mystery to him now was that this life they had shared together was real. If it was any consolation, it helped Scott accept her death. Although, he knew he would never understand it nor ever make sense of it. There is never closure to a hole in your heart.

Today, at sunrise, on his dock at the Atateka, he planted his fishing rod, tackle box and thermos of coffee into his sturdy Old Town 16 foot wood canoe. He checked his waterproof fishing vest to make sure he placed his sausage and egg sandwich in its protective pocket, and a paperback he had started rereading again after 30 years, "A Farewell to Arms" by Ernest Hemingway. Another pocket held his flask of peppermint schnapps, a fishing ritual on the lake. He also patted the familiar left breast pocket that used to hold his pack of Winston's. He quit those a few years ago but the gentle pat reminded him of days gone by.

All systems checked, as the sun rose over the mountains, dispersing light through the morning fog, rising above the shallows of the lake. Scott ushered his bearlike black golden doodle, Ollie Girl, into his canoe before shoving off.

It was daybreak at the Atateka dock located on the eastern shore of Friends Lake, not far from the lake's dam at the northern end. Scott paddled south. At the end of the three-mile lake was an estuary, more like a narrow canal, that got very shallow before connecting to a tributary of the Hudson. It took Scott about thirty minutes to reach the lake's end. It took another fifteen minutes navigating his way through the shallow marshes of the estuary that fed the lake before his canoe was linked in and spirited down the Hudson River. Scott needed only to use his paddle, as a rudder, to guide the canoe in the light but swift rapids downriver. His canoe glided over the rapids a little more than a mile before he would reach a wide bend, where the rapids subsided, and which would be his final destination. As he looked ahead to the eastern banks of that final bend, he noticed something odd, unfamiliar. He knew every rock, every tree, every blade of grass and flower at this site on the Hudson shores from memory. It had been the very place he selected to cast away his wife's ashes three years ago.

Yet, on this morning of September 11th, something was strikingly different. Like an apparition, two plumes of white smoke appeared like twin towers. The first plume rose straight up from the azure waters of the Hudson to the sapphire, cloudless sky rising up from the very spot where he last saw Amy's wreath of multi-colored roses set sail. The second plume rose up from the lookout ridgeline just above prehistoric rock formations. It rose straight up to the sky from on top of an elephant-sized rock that served as his pedestal every time he visited this place. It was here that he looked down upon his late wife's burial site.

It was like they were eternal campfires marking her memorial. As he guided the canoe closer, he began to realize it was probably an optical illusion, just fog rising from the river, but in perfect vertical ascent in two distinct silos. It made him feel even more connected to this site and more attuned to a supernatural presence this morning. He could feel his wife's presence strongly and it now seemed to him that every time he visited here that something extraordinary occurs for a reason. As if she was announcing her presence, guiding him forward, protecting him from harm.

He reaches his destination pulling his canoe up the bank of the river. Ollie made her ritual dance when they got onshore and waited for Scott to set up his fishing gear. It didn't take long and Scott cast out his line to the middle of the river against a light wind from the west. When the bait hit the sparkling waters, Ollie meandered up the banks to the river's path to do some exploring. From on high, she would watch over Scott as he sat on his favorite rock taking in an unseasonably warm wind for an early autumn morning in the mountains. He was pouring a cup of coffee and getting ready to settle in for a morning medley of meditation with a good book and the hunt for a few hungry fish. He came here every year to talk to Amy again, clinging to a hope that she would someday talk back to him.

If the plumes of smoke had vanished, Scott thought, why did he smell smoke without telltale signs of a campfire? This bend on the Hudson was his place to visit Amy and perhaps for her, he thought -- a final resting place. While tides from the Atlantic Ocean compel the Hudson River to flow north, its origin is at Lake Tear of the Clouds, just north of this spot, which actually pushes the currents south. Here these rocks predate the history of mankind, the local Indian tribes called this river: "Muh-he-kun—ne-tuk", meaning "the water that moves both ways". A fitting resting place,

Scott thought, that flows freely north and south. Especially for a woman that sought two things in life, truth and love: absolute truth and unconditional love. Scott knew that Amy knew the truth was always hard to find. Yet she exemplified self-awareness. As much as she realized that you don't find love. Love finds you. He realized that his love for her would not end here on the banks of this mighty Hudson. He knew now that he had not driven aimlessly up to the lake in search of answers again.

Friends Lake is a small, three-mile private lake with few homes and many, like his own, were secluded. He spent this weekend thinking about the past. No longer needing answers. Perhaps thinking about the past was fortifying. Perhaps thinking about the future was too terrifying?

Today was September 11th, 2001. He had marked it on his calendar to be at his office for an important meeting this morning. The meeting, at his office on the 79th Floor of the World Trade Center, started precisely at 8:30 this morning. Scott planned to be there. He had never missed one in three years. But, he stayed at the lake instead. Why? What was he fishing for in the Adirondacks?

Certainly not what was about to happen to him? He left his gear and canoe and took Ollie up the bank to a path that ran along the Hudson shores for her morning walk. As he walked the path between the tall Adirondack evergreens on the east bank of the Hudson, two large men in suits could be seen approaching him. There was no one else on this passageway between the pines. He knew that the suits approaching him didn't belong here. He had a sense that a beautiful sunny morning was about to get dark. Ollie, now back at Scott's side, sensed ominous warning signs too. She bent her head in Scott's direction to make sure she was in step, her tail dropped and she walked deliberately now in almost an attack stance. She looked straight at the approaching men and growled in a sustained warning.

"Good Morning, Scott. She won't bite us, will she?" said one of the suits.

"Should she?" said Scott. "Do I know you?"

"No sir. I'm agent Pat Reese from the FBI. This is agent Gary Moylen." They both flash their credentials at Scott, while Ollie stood guard waiting for Scott's reaction to these strangers on their path. "I take it you don't know what happened at the World Trade Center this morning?"

Scott was good at sizing up situations. He knew immediately that something terrible must have happened. His office was in the World Trade Center. He had no idea why two FBI agents are in the middle of the woods confronting him. "Not a clue. What's up?" He was bracing himself for bad news.

Reese shot a distressed look at Moylen. Moylen just nodded his head. Reese delivered the news of the morning of 9/11 in a stereotypical FBI 'just the facts' manner: "At 8:46 this morning, the first of two passenger jets slammed into the twin towers of the World Trade Center. When the second plane hit a little after 9 am, it was clear that America was under attack by terrorists. Almost simultaneously, a third plane hit the Pentagon and a fourth crashed over Pennsylvania. It is now 11 am, both towers have collapsed, New York City and Washington D.C. are under siege and all planes have been grounded nationwide. The death toll is unknown but will be staggering." Scott looked stunned and did not react immediately as he was in a state of total disbelief. Moylen jumped in as Reese caught his breath, as if a moment of silence would be inexcusable. "I know this is a shock. We don't have details yet. We were instructed to find you, pick you up and deliver you to the U.S. Military Academy at West Point. To a classified meeting with the Secretary of Defense, Don Rumsfeld."

Scott feels his stomach clenching as he fathoms the gravity of what he just heard. Words spill out spontaneously almost unconsciously, almost in a whisper of incredulity: "I was supposed to be there this morning. I have friends and co-workers there," he said before raising the volume in his voice demonstrably: "What the hell is going on?"

Moylen replied quickly and almost somberly: "Just this, all hell broke loose. We're waiting for details. As soon as we know, you'll know too. Hopefully, we will hear something on our ride to West Point. But we need to get started. We've got a car waiting, let's go, OK?"

"Give me a minute." Scott leans down and pats Ollie's head, trying to comprehend what he just heard. Ollie looks up at Scott sensing his anxiety, her tail between her legs, then shifts and sits panting heavily by his side. As Scott slowly processes the moment, he wonders why the FBI is picking him up. He stands back up and looks at the agents: "Look, even if this incredible story you just told me is true, why would the FBI be seeking me out to meet with Rumsfeld?

Moylen answers: "Classified, sir. That's all I know."

"Classified?" Scott shot back reflexively. "You've got to do better than that. You sure you have the right guy? Why would Rumsfeld want to meet with me?" Moylen answers again: "Sir, we don't know. We've got orders to bring you to West Point. "

"Really?" Scott wants answers and he's showing it. He's angry now and talking fast: "I'm not going anywhere until someone starts talking some sense here. I'm standing here in the middle of nowhere being told an incredibly wild horror story? Do you really think you're taking me to a classified meeting at West Point without telling me what it's about?" Reese, the larger of the two FBI agents, spoke out now in a commanding, no nonsense tone. "Sir, maybe you aren't listening. The shit has hit the fan. Our country is under attack." Reese said sternly. "You have friends in those Towers? So do we! We don't have a fucking clue of what's going on right now any more than you do. So listen up. Today more than any other, if you wear the red, white and blue, you do what you are told. And then you hope to God that you played your part to make America safe again. Our orders are to get you to West Point ASAP. You must be one very important SOB if Rumsfeld wants you. So let's go. You coming?"

Scott's eyes widen. Even Gary flinched at the tough stance from Pat, but without hesitation, Scott replied getting Pat's drift, "Ok. Let's go." All of a sudden, Scott liked this guy Pat Reese. He knew how to throw a punch with a heavy dose of reality.

As they walked, Scott's mind could not fully process what he just heard, but Reese jolted him forward with a sense of urgency despite not knowing what comes next. His mind raced to locations where his children might possibly be this morning; trying to visually figure out if they were safe. He pulled out his mobile phone and started to call his daughter first. Moylen saw the phone come out and motioned to Reese but said nothing.

His daughter's phone was busy. He tried his son. Busy. For the next five minutes, as they walked, he kept frantically redialing. The lines were constantly busy. Finally, Moylen broke the silent procession: "Don't bother calling, sir. All mobile phones in the city are dead."

"How do you know that?" Scott replied. "All the cell signals emanated from the top of the Towers. The Towers collapsed," Moylen answered. "This is a lot to take in. Just want to reach my kids, how can I do that? Moylen quickly answered, "We're already on that detail. I promise you as soon as we locate them, you'll be the first to know. Hopefully we'll hear something soon."

"Do you know if they are OK?" Scott asked. "No sir, not yet," Moylen replied with empathy. "It's still total chaos downtown right now." Scott didn't say a word. They continued to walk through a path in the woods to a parking lot nearby, as Scott let the agents lead the way. He knew it was about fifteen minutes away from their present location. He punched in the speed dial for his daughter and put his cell phone to his ear. Soon enough Scott found out for himself that his mobile phone was indeed useless, after dialing his daughter, his son and his office multiple times. Moylen was right. The lines were dead.

Frustrated and confused, Scott was trying now to fathom what was happening in the city. He started to think of his colleagues at work, on the 79th floor of the South Tower, and suddenly his stride faltered. Faces, all he could see in front of him were faces. The faces of all his employees, one by one, traveled in front of him. They were the faces of the dead. Like a marching beat of the drum, these faces marched by one by one.

He was still in shock, like he remembered too many a concussion in his time. The news hit him like a baseball hitting his temple at 90 miles per hour. He was knocked out cold but could still see and hear everybody. Paralysis must be nature's way for bracing the brain from severe trauma? Here he was. His sanctuary and his solace disturbed. He blindly followed the agents to their car, after they reassured him that the FBI was in the process of reaching his children and would relay their safety to him immediately, hopefully soon while they were in transit. They would also relay information to him on the status of survivors at his company in the South Tower, World Trade Center. But how could anyone have survived?

They finally reached the parking lot where only one car was in the lot. Scott started to get in the back seat of the FBI's black Lincoln Town Car. Ollie jumped in first. Long distance driving would not be his friend this day. Ollie sensed it and leaned her body next to him and with her dark penetrating eyes stared into Scott's. He put his arm around her and patted the head of this big and gentle giant to let her know under the most false pretenses: "It'll be alright, Ollie Girl."

CHAPTER 9: ANTIDOTE TO TERROR

Over Manhattan
9/11

Spiders weave complex webs. Nothing is more feared than the black widow.

Leigh McClure sat silently across from Don Rumsfeld looking down at the massacre and massive carpets of smoke enveloping lower Manhattan in real time contemplating the calamity, its consequences, and the critical mission that lay ahead. Not only was Leigh uniquely qualified to lead 'OPERATION HAWK'S NEST,' a clandestine mission to retaliate against Osama Bin Laden, she was destined to orchestrate what would become the most secretive operation ever to be run in the modern world. Seeing the devastation from 30,000 feet above Ground Zero confirmed her belief in the mission and added a heightened level of purpose. She said a silent prayer – for the victims, for her country, and for her team designated to get in and out of Afghanistan before a ground war with a single purpose: the assassination of Osama Bin Laden. She said a separate prayer for Scott Walsh knowing that if he succeeded, he may never return home.

Across from her, Rumsfeld took in the catastrophic scene below. The face of evil is now exposed. From this day forward, he knew that whatever he had envisioned his role would be in the next four years, as Secretary of Defense, it would now and forever be altered by the sheer magnitude of the terror unleashed on America's homeland on 9/11.

What happened earlier today in New York City was now in full view of two people charged with the enormous task to retaliate and defend the nation. As they looked out from their aircraft, they looked down at an open grave of untold thousands of innocent human lives. Passenger planes used as weapons of mass destruction. Insanity. How does one defend a nation when it seems what really is needed is to put the earth back on its axis.

Rumsfeld was processing a day like no other. He bore the weight of a larger war to come. He tried to focus back on 'OPERATION HAWK'S NEST.' He thought that he knew enough about Scott Walsh now to sense that he was capable to take on a mission as incredible as this one. He was also impressed with the woman who sat directly across from him. He wondered what made her tick?

What he knew about her intrigued him. She was born in New York City, this city now under siege, as the only child of a wealthy Ford dealer. She attended the best prep schools the city had to offer and graduated from Trevor Day School at age 16. She received her college degree from Oberlin, a master's degree from M.I.T. in aerospace engineering, and a law degree from the University of Michigan. She had just started working as a Law Associate at White & Case before the CIA recruited her in her late-twenties. She was recruited just a month after her husband's tragic death, not by coincidence.

Her husband's death would define her future. Rumsfeld understood this after reading her file back at the Pentagon before they boarded this flight to West Point. As he sat across from her, he wondered how often fate brings people together, especially for missions impossible. They were about to embark on a clandestine op of outsized proportions and almost limitless powers that would not only impact history, but could result in extreme danger. He stared at her when she wasn't looking as she sat straight across from him facing him. "What do I see?" he said to himself.

He thought back to when they first met, earlier this morning, in the underground bunker at the White House. She exuded a fearlessness, when none was required; nor expected under the circumstances. When she spoke, her voice was resolute, with just a slightest of a rasp, yet solid and self-assured.

Physically, Leigh was tall. OK, he wasn't, he thought. But she was Amazon tall, almost six feet. Even sitting across from him, he could sense her height. Blonde, surely that's what he could see, but really? There were traces of what was that, grey or white, in her roots? She certainly wasn't concerned about it, he thought. Buxom, hmm, he surprised himself going to this characteristic of her appearance so fast. Something about how she didn't button several buttons on her blouse that drew you in, stealing a stare at her well defined cleavage. But considering where they were, what they would be discussing, and how it could possibly shape world history, why was he thinking of her sexually now? She simply possessed a seductive power. He figured that she knew it and she didn't much care, except that she used it only if she had to. She was after all, a woman in a hurry, all business in a business of danger everyday on a global theater. She was one of those most rare human beings dedicating their very existence to a single American pursuit: to serve and protect.

He glanced into her eyes. They were like magnets. She was perhaps the most beautiful woman he had ever met. He had walked amongst the most powerful and beautiful women in the world and what he saw across from him eclipsed any woman. It was hard not to stare. Spellbinding.

She was a woman in a man's world yet she dealt with the most powerful men in the world as an equal. She earned her reputation for intelligence and fearlessness. It was not hard to fathom how even extraordinary men would melt in her presence. She was simply so persuasive, so commanding. Charismatic.

Her hair was thick and full and fell to her chin. Her face was soft and round, with blue eyes that appeared swollen because they were so large to her face. They were deep blue against a perfectly proportioned nose that perched above her full lips. Yet, her beauty didn't overwhelm, because her body and the way she moved it defined a grace and an athleticism that exuded strength and confidence.

Leigh sensed Don staring at her right now. Don didn't notice or stop. She allowed him this moment by pretending she didn't sense it. He kept sizing her up. He thought if it wasn't for the severe scar next to her right eye, she was sinfully perfect. He couldn't see the scars underneath her black pants suit borne under torture in a Libyan stronghold; but he knew about them. He did spot the scuff marks on the sides of her stylish boots that showed her good taste and hinted at her constant state of being rushed, hurrying around in her high couture boots on heels that would leave her slightly off balance. He turned his attention back to her profile. From head to toe, Leigh was a woman borne of grace and guile, beauty with brains, and a woman who would always keep you off balance. He couldn't help noticing how she didn't use makeup at all and it didn't matter. A woman like Leigh, he thought, probably doesn't even think about such vanity because she is so preoccupied with more important things.

He shifted again in his seat and looked out the window. He didn't want to appear to have been conspicuously staring at her. He knew the circumstances of how she was recruited by the CIA years ago. Yet, he couldn't help wondering what would make such a talented, gifted and beautiful woman give up everything to serve her government in such a dangerous occupation? And to do so under the guise of a government civil servant, willing to make the ultimate sacrifice with plausible deniability from the very government she protected?

His thoughts shifted to the teaming of Leigh and Scott on this mission. Would Scott sign on? Was he still capable of such an incredible mission? Did Scott trust Leigh?

He knew that Scott and Leigh had a history. They first worked together when Scott was in Special Forces and Leigh, a young yet decorated CIA field agent in the Middle East. They were assigned to find and kill a lone bomber targeting the USA Athletes at the Munich Olympics in 1972. They did so. Just in the nick of time.

It was one day before the Israeli Olympic athletes were taken hostage and before eleven of the Israeli athletes were massacred shortly thereafter. No one ever knew of the lone bomber from a PLO terrorist organization involved in a plot to kill the American athletes at the same Olympics. No one ever knew because the bomber's name would only have been revealed had he been successful. Walsh and McClure made sure he was not. Scott Walsh killed the bomber, with a single bullet to his brain, just as the terrorist was getting ready to detonate the bomb.

Scott and Leigh found themselves back in action together again in 1976. This time in an operation to find and kill terrorists who were attempting to culture the Ebola virus during its outbreak in Zaire. The hunt took them from the Mediterranean to Morocco before a final confrontation in Istanbul, Turkey. The mission was completed. They captured the virus intact and avoided the consequences of the virus becoming a biochemical weapon. Yet, this mission was not without problems. In the struggle to obtain the virus, all five terrorists were killed. By doing so, it was never known what terrorist organization was actually behind this sinister plot.

Countless other TOP SECRET dramas played out in the lives of Scott and Leigh on subsequent missions during the Seventies. They are too highly classified for a summary briefing. Yet, they crisscrossed twice more on separate missions inside the Soviet bloc. Only Scott and Leigh knew those stories. Highly guarded secrets in this clandestine world sometimes always remain so.

But the most highly guarded secret in the world of spies was the identity of the world's most feared special agent: The Black Widow. She was given this moniker because of the way she disposed of her victims. When police would find her victims, there was a black widow spider weaving an irregular web inside of the open mouth of her victims. There was also something else curious about the Black Widow deaths. The victims were always notorious criminals and the venom of the spider bite, 15 times stronger than a rattlesnake, was merely a calling card, not the cause of death.

Each victim's head and heart was pierced with a 4mm exploding bullet from the chamber of a rare lipstick revolver. Only the CIA and MI5 had such a cold war, high tech toy. Yet, in spy circles, this lipstick device equipped with such precise, compact and deadly bullets was considered the MO of a special agent of Israel's Mossad, a woman using an alias of Erika Chambers. This was precisely the propaganda that the Black Widow used as cover.

There were probably only five men alive in America who actually knew the true identity of the Black Widow. They guarded this knowledge with their lives. The Black Widow deaths became legendary in spy circles. Whoever she was, her precision and elusiveness were highly respected. In fact, the very first Black Widow victim was also perhaps, the most talked about and most heinous in these circles of spies. The victim was Ali Hassan Salameh, AKA The Red Prince -- the known mastermind behind the Munich massacre of eleven Israeli Olympic hopefuls and the feared leader of Force 17 and Black September. He had managed to elude the manhunt by Israel's Mossad after the massacre, but fell victim to the bite of the Black

Widow on a cold January evening in 1973 in a hotel room on the Paris Ritz, Place Vendome.

Salameh's diabolical plan during the Summer Olympics of 1972 was to kill the Israeli Prime Minister, Golda Meier, on the Olympic world stage in Munich. The plan was foiled but not without incident. The ensuing massacre of the Israeli athletes was witnessed 'live' on television for the entire world to see. Ali Hassan Salemeh, the cruel mastermind behind this plot, became the Mossad's number one enemy.

Knowing he was being hunted down did not deter him in his fanaticism to assassinate the Israeli Prime Minister. She escaped in Munich. She had been the principal target in Munich but she never arrived at the Olympic Villages as scheduled. Her survival was, as many believed in CIA circles, somehow connected to Walsh and McClure aiding the Mossad in protecting her on arrival in Munich, while the hostage crisis and subsequent murders ensued later that day.

Salameh made a vow that Golda Meier would not find a way out next time. He crafted a new assassination plot almost immediately after those 1972 Olympic Summer Games. It was designed around a historic upcoming meeting between Pope Paul VI and Golda Meier. It would be the first meeting in history between the leader of the Holy See and Israeli's Prime Minister. It was scheduled for January 16, 1973 in the Vatican. He planned to assassinate her on her arrival in Rome. This time, he made certain to include a failsafe mechanism. She would not get away this time.

Ali Hassan Salameh arrived in Paris on January 15, 1973, the day before the assassination was planned. When he checked in at the Paris Ritz, he received a coded message via telephone that 'Operation Pontiff' was underway. The next 24 hours in Rome were critical. Conditions were perfect. The operation could simply not fail, unlike the first assassination attempt in Munich that ended badly.

Yet, Ali Hassan Salemeh would make a fatal mistake that day that ended up thwarting his assassination attempt. A woman CIA field agent on assignment in Paris found out accidentally that Salemeh was in town. She acquired this guarded information by a high-class call girl that was scheduled to meet Salemeh at his hotel that evening. That agent, Leigh Ann McClure, switched identities with the prostitute and met Salemeh for his final encounter. Upon arriving at his hotel room, she stripped, standing naked in front of him as he stood a breath away. She held only her lipstick in her hand and teasingly asked him to stand still directly in front of her as she slowly started to apply the lipstick.

He obeyed her instruction. He never saw nor heard the muted shot come from the lipstick pistol as the 4mm bullet hit him squarely between the eyes. As he dropped to the floor, she reloaded the chamber of the lipstick revolver, and then aimed a bulls-eye to his heart. She knelt, opened his mouth, and deposited one black widow spider from a vial within a diamond locket that she wore around her neck. She dressed quickly, picked up the phone in the suite and dialed the Mossad's field office in Paris. She left the phone open as she slipped out of the suite knowing the Mossad would trace it.

Of course, Rumsfeld knew of this incredible story, except for the role of CIA agent Leigh Ann McClure, until this morning. Like most others around the world in high security roles, he had always believed the woman behind the Black Widow to be an Israeli agent Erika Chambers. Now, as he looked at Leigh, he wondered if the necklace she was wearing contained such a vial? He also questioned himself on how much more about McClure he did not know?

As the jet started its descent into Stewart Air Force Base, Leigh's phone rang. "Yes," she answered. She sat across from Rumsfeld motionless, listening to the caller for less than a minute. She ended the call almost as quickly as it started: "Copy that. Out" as she flipped off her phone. She looked straight at Don.

"We have confirmation. No survivors at Scott's company at the World Trade Center. They're all presumed dead. His son and daughter have been located in the city: safe. They are both together at his son's apartment. There will be continuing surveillance." Rumsfeld sat motionless. There was simply nothing to say. On the flight to West Point, he realized that Leigh and Scott were formidable players on a world stage. They would accept this dangerous mission. They would succeed because he was convinced that they were gods among men.

CHAPTER 10: DUTY, HONOR, COUNTRY

United States Military Academy - West Point
9/11

A Black Hawk chopper lifted off from Stewart Air Force Base in Newburgh, New York at exactly 1337 hours. Five minutes later, racing at 180 mph, it landed on the northeast side of the parade grounds at West Point. McClure was gazing out the window as it slowed, circled wide and gently touched down, as Rumsfeld looked at his watch, impressed by the precision of military operations – Washington to Stewart AFB, transfer to waiting helicopter – arriving precisely on schedule to the minute.

Don Rumsfeld had been to the U.S. Military Academy on several occasions during his career, most recently in his newest position, as the United States 21st Secretary of Defense. He presented the commencement address this past June. He reflected on his words that day addressing the changing needs of a military force in the 21st Century to adapt for just this kind of tactical warfare. Yet, he never imagined the dizzying speed in which a world can change, as it did today.

As he slowly exited the chopper, he could hear Leigh's phone ringing, despite the roar of the helicopter's rotors winding down. She answered the call after dashing under the blades to a waiting car with Rumsfeld at her side. She immediately got in the car with her call still in progress. Rumsfeld stood momentarily by the car before getting in himself taking in the wide expanse of the military parade grounds, some 40 acres about 150 feet above the Hudson River.

Flanking the grounds, he looked out at the monuments to America's greatest generals. At opposite ends of the grounds stood memorials to "Ike" General Dwight D. Eisenhower at the south and "Mac" General Douglas C. MacArthur at the north. On the northwest corner stood the memorial to the "Father of the Military Academy," Colonel Sylvanus Thayer and on the far western edge is the monument to General Tadeusz Kosciuszko, which overlooks the Hudson River for his contribution to the defense of West Point during the American Revolutionary War. Rumsfeld took it all in feeling the weight of battles ahead and then turned his attention to the last monument of George Washington on horseback on the Plain closest to him just outside of Washington Hall. With not a cloud in the sky or a single soldier on the plain, he stared out at the horse and rider seeking guidance and courage.

When Rumsfeld finally slid into the back seat, an attaché closed his door. Leigh has just ended her call. She said "On schedule, Sir." to which Rumsfeld replied "Good." There was a pause before he spoke up again reflectively. "I was here last June. I was given a tour of these monuments to our Generals," he said pointing out to them. " The words of General George Washington during the Revolutionary War ring out as true today as when he spoke them some 200 years ago: 'The reflection upon my situation and that of this army produces many an uneasy hour when all around me are wrapped in sleep. Few people know the predicament we are in.'"

In the silence that followed, they were escorted away swiftly by a security detail of two Delta Special Forces personnel via an armed, unmarked black Cadillac SUV. They sped towards Michie Stadium, a living monument to famed Army football teams of past, which was visible from and not far from the parade grounds of the U.S. Military Academy.

Leigh's phone rang again. It was FBI agent, Fred Stobaeus, calling her from Scott Walsh's summer home on Friends Lake. "No loose ends, as directed. As soon as the target is confirmed secure at the Point, we'll get the dog to a safe house. The car he drove up in will be picked up today and delivered to a crusher in Queens," reported Agent Stobaeus.

"Is that necessary?" replied Leigh. "Why all the way to Queens?" Leigh asked instinctively.

"So it can't be traced," Stobaeus chimed in. "That car would have been crushed in the World Trade Center garage. We have an undercover operative in Queens that won't ask questions about why we're crushing a brand new Porsche 911. That would raise eyebrows up here."

Leigh smiled if only for a brief moment, for the first time since the day began as she remembered Scott's love for speed, fast cars and motorcycles. "A Porsche 911 you say, any other toys in his garage there? You're certain, absolutely certain, that he drove up in that car?" Stobaeus replied, "Yes, Ma'am. Absolute certainty. There's a Mustang GT convertible in there too, and a Ducati, but he drove up from the city in the Porsche." Leigh said, "Good work, you'll have someone in Queens to verify, right?" Stobaeus answered quickly, "I'm on this one personally. I'm driving the car direct to the crusher" "Good," Leigh added, "Anything you need from me?" Stobaeus hesitates then says "No Ma'am."

Leigh sensed the hesitation, "Is there anything else, Agent Stobaeus?" He paused before saying with reluctance, "It's just something in front of me right now. Probably not important." Leigh asked, "What is it?'

Leigh listened as Agent Stobaeus informed her that there was a study at Scott's summer camp and in it was a shrine to his father. The shrine included several framed photos of his father during World War II. Yet what was in the center of the shrine was compelling. Three medals were displayed, a Silver Star occupied the center flanked by two Bronze Stars and underneath it all was the Silver Star citation inset with an inscription.

"It's probably not important," Stobaeus said flinchingly. "It's just that the inscription on the Silver Star medal stood out. On a crazy day like this, I thought you might want to hear it too, before the target gets there?"

Leigh knew that Scott's father had saved Rumsfeld's brother during WWII. She wanted to hear it and thought that this might be good that Rumsfeld hear this now too before meeting Scott for the first time. She checked her watch. They had time. She replied to Stobaeus with a question: "Is that all?"

"Yes, Ma'am," he replied. "Agent Stobaeus, I'm putting you on hold for one minute. When I come back on, read the inscription, and then hang up. Clear?" Stobaeus replied, "Copy that, Ma'am." She puts Stobaeus on hold.

With her call on hold, Leigh alerted Don that he should listen to this message. She put the call on her advanced smartphone speakerphone. "Ready," she said but she did not advise Stobaeus that Rumsfeld was on the line.

Agent Stobaeus read the Silver Star citation verbatim: "This is the Silver Star Citation for: JOHN J. WALSH, First Lieutenant, Infantry, Company K (then Company I) 362nd Infantry, United States Army.

SILVER STAR

For gallantry in action on 11 October 1944, near Campuzzano, Italy

When an enemy position located in a building poured heavy fire on his platoon, causing many casualties, Lieutenant WALSH acted immediately. Gallantly braving the intense fire, he moved up to the building, spraying it with his automatic weapon. After throwing 2 hand grenades, he forced the door and subdued the enemy inside -- 21 men and one officer. Before his men could fully consolidate the position, the enemy mounted a vicious counterattack with superior numbers. Although movement in the position meant exposure to direct observation and fire, for eight and a half hours Lieutenant WALSH fearlessly moved through his platoon, directing fire, aiding the wounded, and encouraging and inspiring his men to such heights by his cool, aggressive leadership that the counterattack was eventually repulsed with severe loss to the enemy.

Lieutenant WALSH'S combat skills and high courage reflect great credit on himself and the Armed Forces of the United States. Entered military service from Brooklyn, New York.

Stobaeus paused momentarily after reading the citation. Then he hung up, as instructed.

There was something important about this shrine and Lieutenant Walsh's bravery that touched them all today. When she flipped off her phone, Rumsfeld said somberly: "My brother was there on that awful day." He paused before he looked at Leigh and added: "Scott's father saved my brother's life." Leigh looked back at him and let her eyes acknowledge his sentiment. He looked away and out the window of the SUV and took a deep breath: "It's a shame that we must meet under these circumstances."

The words hung heavy. There was nothing for Leigh to say. She was conditioned to remain steady and aloof for these types of raw emotions in her line of work. After a moment of silence, Don spoke out again, as if to no one in particular. "Scott was only ten years old when his father died. I wondered, thinking about what's in store for him, how many times he has thought about his dad after all these years?" Leigh looked pensively at Rumsfeld. And then he continued, "After hearing the Silver Star Citation, I now wonder just how often he must think about his father's eight hours of hell that day?"

Leigh continued to look straight at Don and without saying a word acknowledged the sacrifices of soldiers and the emotional toll of war. She was acutely aware that this is what they signed up for. Moments like this are rare among leaders who must orchestrate covert operations and make life and death decisions to protect America. Yet, it is these rare occasions that remind them of their awesome responsibility and the frailty of human judgment.

Their thoughts are quickly interrupted as they enter the tunnel at Michie Stadium before the car stopped. They were ushered out of the car quickly and headed down a corridor towards the locker rooms. Sentries were posted before the tunnel and straddled deep inside the tunnel. The security detail took them almost directly to the doors to the locker rooms but altered that direction to an unmarked doorway in what seemed to be a false alley. Inside this door, was a chamber passageway that opened only after the Delta chief keyed in an electronic password followed by putting his palm over a recognition device on a panel embedded in the wall.

Inside the chamber, Rumsfeld remembered being briefed of this bunker with the others under his purview at the Department of Defense. The descent in the chamber is fast and without sensation. When they reached their descent five stories below the ground, they were taken down a hall to a briefing room.

Inside the briefing room, Leigh opened her laptop, but did not connect it to the center ports for projection. Instead, she attached a component piece from her briefcase to her laptop and tested projection of video direct to the screen. She had the two videos loaded that Rumsfeld wanted to show to Scott Walsh. Rumsfeld needed these videos, as much to set up his discussion with Scott, as to visually display the horror of today. There was no better way to do this than to show the terror in real time with video footage. The first video was a newsreel compilation of exactly what happened today, much easier to show rather than trying to explain it to Walsh. The second was a classified CIA video brief on Osama Bin Laden and his Al Qaeda terrorist organization, including the latest Intel tracking his movements.

Leigh began setting up her own equipment. Her phone made three short sound bursts. That was the code that Scott Walsh was in the bunker. She turned to Don and finally spoke breaking an uneasy silence in the room.

"I'm all set. I'll play these videos on your cue. Scott's here." Rumsfeld asked almost rhetorically, "What is the running time on these videos?" Leigh replied as she looked at her phone. "Three minutes each. I'll play the newsreel first." She paused, "I received the alert. They are coming down the corridor now." Rumsfeld didn't say anything but Leigh noticed that he took a prolonged deep breath.

Within minutes, Scott Walsh stood before Secretary of Defense Don Rumsfeld and Leigh McClure inside a secure high-tech conference room, built for waging war underground, at West Point. War was imminent.

"Thanks for coming Scott. Don Rumsfeld," Rumsfeld introduces himself and shakes Scott Walsh's hand firmly and long. He turns to introduce Leigh. "This is Leigh Anne McClure." Scott lets go of Rumsfeld's hand as his eyes divert quickly to Leigh. It has been decades since he last saw her. As crazy as this day was, Scott was caught in a moment of colliding emotions. She was just as beautiful as he remembered and all he wanted to do was embrace her. Yet, the danger that always lurked in the background in her presence was omnipresent again in this isolated room, deep underground at his alma mater. He suddenly knew instinctively that the mystery for being summoned here was about to be shockingly revealed. His past was about to shake him into the moment and rudely awaken him to the grim reality of this day.

"Please take a seat," is what Scott heard, but the moment was becoming surreal and he was unmovable. Rumsfeld was speaking: "I would ask you to listen to what we have to say before asking any questions. I assure you that all of your questions will be answered." Scott is still standing, still shaking hands with Leigh yet nodding acknowledgement as Don speaks. Then abruptly, Scott breaks away from his stare at Leigh, lets go his grip on her and interrupts Rumsfeld in midsentence in a measured tone.

"Mr. Secretary. I don't mean to be disrespectful, but before we get started, I need to know that my kids are safe."

Without blinking, Rumsfeld reacted calmly: "Of course. Please take a seat." They both sit down next to each other, as Leigh sits across from them. Rumsfeld continues: "The good news is that your son and daughter are both safe."

"Where are they?" Scott says half interrupting Rumsfeld. "They're at your son's apartment. They're safe and we are keeping eyes on them," Rumsfeld says reassuringly. "Thank God. I need to hear their voices. Can I use that phone..." pointing to a star-like speakerphone on the center console on the round conference table. "I'm sorry Scott," Rumsfeld replies, while quickly trying to take over the conversation. "I assure you that they're safe, but that's not possible right now." Rumsfeld turns to Leigh: "I think we need to show Scott what's happening out there before we get started." He turns his attention back to Scott: "This is a lot to take in, but you need to see what's happened today."

Leigh dimmed the lights from the console and played the first film. It was a compilation video of edited news reports from network coverage detailing the tragic events of this morning of 9/11. It ended with a silent scroll of facts known so far, from number of deaths to total injured. It took three full minutes.

Three minutes of video footage would not tell the whole story. Yet, it was dramatic enough to show Scott the grim reality of the danger unfolding in America. Seeing the horror didn't help put the tragedy in perspective.

It only amplified the terror. When the video ended, Scott sat stunned processing the images as Don proceeded, without hesitation:

"We now know who is responsible: Osama Bin Laden and Al Qaeda. He's solely responsible for this vicious attack on America. We will find him; we will kill him; and destroy his entire terrorist operation. We are going to accomplish this mission by using every tool at our disposal, every arm in our arsenal, and every available asset in our vast resources. But this is not an army with a base, nor an organization with a Headquarters. It is a band of terrorists with safe havens, with deep resources, and ample places to hide. Their safe haven is in Afghanistan. We are about to enter a fight with unfamiliarity. Known unknowns. That will not deter us. We know that we are not fighting a country but an ideology dispersed in a region. We will need to fight this war on terrorism on several fronts. You're here because we need your help."

This was the first time a surprise reaction came from Scott. Unspoken, a slight tilt to his head, a grimace to his face, an eyebrow raised and both eyes focused like a laser beam at Don.

Don noticed questions forming so he picked up his pace so as not to be interrupted. "Because of the long Afghan war with the Soviets, we have deep intelligence sources on the ground in the Region. We have birds that can see movement of human targets and hideouts. These resources will be of invaluable assistance to us on every front as we retaliate. Our plan consists of an all-out campaign to crush these bastards with the full force of our military in Afghanistan. Any country harboring these murderers will also be treated as the enemy. We also know that killing Osama Bin Laden, the head of this snake, will save thousands of lives, but only if we kill him quickly." He pauses momentarily and changes from a deliberate to a more ominous tone.

"It is why we have set into motion a TOP SECRET black op, so secret that only the President of the United States, the Vice President, Leigh McClure, and myself know of the existence of this plan. You, Scott, are at the epicenter of the plan. Let me explain."

Scott interrupted explosively, coughing first to clear his throat. "Explain? Whoa -- explain what? All that Intel in Afghanistan and we let this happen? What happened to all the people I work with in the South Tower? What the hell is going on?" Scott was angry and still processing the images he just saw in the newsreel.

Rumsfeld wasted no time in reacting. "We were hit by surprise. That's a fact. The Towers have collapsed. Everyone is dead. They were pulverized." Rumsfeld said with deadpan emotion and absolute stark authority. "We'll have plenty of time to dissect how we missed knowing about it beforehand. But that's not why we are here. Osama Bin Laden is the mastermind behind every senseless death today. You want to know why you're here. Let me tell you." Rumsfeld was no longer empathetic. He sensed Scott's rising anger. He knew he needed to calm him down quickly and the only way to do that was to be blunt and candid.

Scott held up his hand to stop. He slumped backwards into his chair, looked down and took a deep breath. The news of his son and daughter's safety was a monumental relief, yet offset by a pain and loss too incredible to bear right now. Even to comprehend. He knew his company would have had most of its 75 employees in early today, as they always did on days of management meetings. Some monster named Osama Bin Laden used passenger jets filled with innocent travelers to crash into the World Trade Center killing his employees and thousands of other unsuspecting and innocent lives. He was supposed to be at the office with them today. He wasn't. They were all dead. He wasn't. Why? He motions to Rumsfeld holding up his hand: "I just need a minute."

In the silence that ensued, Leigh poured Scott a cup of coffee. She then pulled a flask from her jacket and put it next to the coffee. It was filled with Old Fitzgerald whiskey. She hoped she still knew his preferences. He looked up at her and opened the flask, poured generously from it into his coffee and offered some to both Leigh and Don. Leigh and Don waited as Scott poured them each a drink from the flask. Then, he lifted his cup, drained it to regain his composure and sat back up still overwhelmed. They all sat in silence. They waited for Scott to react first. Finally, after several long minutes, Scott started talking, staring into his cup and in a low and grave tone: "I'm truly at a loss…even confused on why I'm here? How could I possibly help in this hellish nightmare? I went to school here and can't even recognize it. We're what? Some five stories underground in a high tech star wars environment. So much has changed… "

Rumsfeld picked up where Scott trailed off. "Change. You're right about change, Scott. Do you remember MacArthur's farewell address at West Point? He said, "And through all this welter of change your mission remains fixed, determined, inviolable." Scott reached out and filled his cup from the flask again slowly turning to Rumsfeld. "Only the dead have seen the end of war," Scott replied, "You know Mac quoted Plato in that speech too. But really why am I here?" he asked.

"I'm so sorry," Don nodded and continued quickly. "I'm sure none of this makes sense to you at all. Let me cut to the chase. We've designed a Special Ops with you as the sole agent." Rumsfeld motioned to Leigh.

Scott turned to Leigh as she started talking immediately. "Some background first," Leigh started as he sat up in attention. "After the World Trade Center bombing back in 1993, the way we waged war had to change. We built an infrastructure to defend our nation, with facilities underground such as this one here at the Academy, to strike back if our above ground installations were compromised. Other ideas were devised to find creative ways to strike back militarily abroad with a leaner, highly mobile, rapid strike force."

Scott sat motionless, yet listening with a heightened intensity observed only by seeing the squint in his eyes. Like a hawk eyeing its prey.

"The immediate threat was coming from the Middle East," Leigh concluded her comments as Rumsfeld jumped back in. "At the Center for Mideast Studies at Georgetown University" Rumsfeld interjected, "a Dr. Daniel Hislop developed a confidential thesis prepared for the Department of Defense, under Secretary Bill Cohen at the time, after the World Trade Center bombings back in '93. In the report, he warned of new attacks by terrorists like the ones today. It concluded that it would be impossible to stop every attempt at terrorism in one of our major cities. Hislop was just as certain that the government needed to find a way to respond immediately to take out the existential threat – in fact, find and kill the mastermind of such a serious crime against humanity within a month of the attack."

Leigh picked up the briefing from here: "His study focused on attacks by terrorist groups based in the Middle East and outlying regions grappling with radical fundamentalist Islamic groups. Ironically, he used Osama Bin Laden and Al Qaeda as his example. His recommendation was based on a simple assumption that an attack would occur again in the future at the same site, the World Trade Center, no matter what defenses we prepared to defend it. He believed that the government should find, target and follow person or persons of past Special Forces military combat experience working inside the World Trade Center. If they should survive the next attack, the plan is to fake their death and recruit them to become a phantom assassin to kill Osama Bin Laden."

Scott looked incredulous. Rumsfeld jumped in again as Scott leaned in as if to object. "You see only a phantom assassin would have the cover needed to go it alone. The speed at which we could get our assassin briefed, trained and ready would be critical as the prevailing conventional wisdom is that Bin Laden would have to be killed in the first thirty days after the attack. If we failed, after the thirty-day window, we'd have to scrub the op. Because Bin Laden would be able to hide once a ground war started. It will take us thirty days to ramp up for war. And we are going to war. The clock is already ticking." Leigh sees Scott ready to stop them so she interrupts Rumsfeld and picks up the conversation again. "I know you have questions, but first let me show you what we know about Osama Bin Laden and his whereabouts. It will answer many of them."

Scott is stirring in his seat impatiently, but holds back questions. Leigh plays the video classified brief on Osama Bin Laden and Al Qaeda. Scott concentrates on the image of Bin Laden and the terrain in which he operates. When it ended, Rumsfeld could sense Scott's anger rising at the terrorists. He looked straight at Scott and started speaking slowly, deliberately, and carefully.

"America is under attack. The Commander-in-Chief has chosen you to hunt and kill Osama Bin Laden. This is a TOP SECRET covert black op codenamed 'OPERATION HAWK'S NEST'. We will guard this secret. We will train you. We will give you everything you need to succeed in your mission," he turns toward Leigh continuing. "Leigh will run your op. If you choose to accept the mission, we will provide you a new identity and ensure you have the funds for your children's welfare, and protect them for the rest of their lives." He pauses momentarily.

"I am asking you to accept this mission by the direct order of the President of the United States of America. The president is aware of the sacrifice he is asking of you and knows the sacrifices you, and your family, have already made for our country." He pauses again momentarily, allowing this all to sink in.

"I'm here officially as Secretary of Defense, but I'm also here because frankly, this is personal." Rumsfeld continues on, but Scott looked straight into Rumsfeld's eyes when he heard it was personal. "You may not know this, but your father saved my brother's life in Italy during the Second World War." Scott was listening intently and only slightly cocked his head upon hearing this, apparently surprised. "I also know that my brother wasn't the only American soldier your father saved that day. I speak with admiration knowing your father earned the Silver Star on that awful day. Your dad and my brother were commissioned as Officers in the last cavalry unit on horseback in the United States Army before it was disbanded. They shipped out together in the Infantry to North Africa on one of the first ships to transport troops to fight against Germany. Rumsfeld shifts slowly in his seat and now looks intensely at Scott. "Destiny brought us to West Point today to defend our nation. If you accept this mission on behalf of your country, you will officially be listed as deceased in the World Trade Center attack today. You will become a phantom secret agent in the service of the United States. The codename 'OPERATION HAWK'S NEST' is named in honor of your father, better known to his soldiers as "The Hawk". Your codename for the mission is 'Hawk'. All we need to activate this op now is simply your command." Rumsfeld pauses again only for seconds for emphasis. "If you accept this mission, you will leave here to an undisclosed location for two weeks of training and Intel. Once at that location, you will become the commanding officer of this op with full and absolute authority to carry out your mission to hunt and kill Osama Bin Laden. Leigh will run the op providing operational support for you 24/7. Can the President count on you, Scott?"

CHAPTER 11: OPERATION ENDURING FREEDOM

The Oval Office - The White House
THE DAY AFTER 9/11

0600 hours. President George W. Bush is sitting behind his desk in the Oval Office, flanked by his intelligence officers and Vice President. The nation is having a nervous breakdown.

CIA Chief George Tenet is briefing President Bush and Vice President Cheney with National Security Advisor Condoleezza Rice about the origin of the attacks. They are providing detailed and overwhelming evidence proving that Osama Bin Laden and his terrorist organization Al Qaeda, based in Afghanistan, were the masterminds behind the attacks.

The briefing is taking place in the Oval Office for a reason. The Bush administration understood the fear unleashed throughout America yesterday and wanted to portray confidence that the terrorist threat was contained. A functioning White House was set back in motion, despite uncertainty still swirling about security in the nation's capital. President Bush believed the media needed to witness an administration at work, unafraid, firmly in control and returning to normalcy, at least some degree of normalcy, under circumstances that betrayed any semblance of natural order.

The 'how could this have happened' scenario, on their watch from the day before, changed quickly to 'how to retaliate' against America's newest enemy, a terrorist organization with safe havens in a landlocked region within South Asia and Central Asia. The briefing covered what they knew up-to-the-minute, through intelligence gathering, as well as covert operations on the ground in Afghanistan.

CIA sources failure to provide any warning of yesterday's attacks took an emotional toll on Tenet as death counts mounted. Yet he came prepared. His briefing wasn't repentant, instead laden with confidence and extraordinary detail on the eyes and ears he still had operational on the ground in Afghanistan. He showed satellite photos from just an hour earlier of the regions of Kabul and Tora Bora, the alternate headquarters for Al Qaeda. The close-ups from drone cameras were of particular interest. They concentrated surveillance on real-time activity by the enemy in training camps in and near Kandahar and Kabul.

Both Tenet and Rice, despite the surprise attacks, conveyed a surprising morning after confidence to support the planning of the first military conflict of the 21st Century, CODE NAMED: OPERATION ENDURING FREEDOM by the Department of Defense. Every option was now on the table and Tenet outlined how CIA in Afghanistan, under Hank Crumpton, was readying plans to conduct paramilitary covert ops to pave the way for war.

President Bush raised questions throughout the briefing and avoided placing blame on the CIA for his administration getting blindsided by the attacks. Cheney, on the other hand, appeared to be biting his tongue at the beginning, yet remained ominously silent throughout the meeting. Despite no sleep the night before, Tenet and Rice left the briefing session rebounding with a renewed confidence in their intelligence shops. They left grateful that the president didn't bog down the briefing with blaming the agencies for the obvious failure of an intelligence warning of the attacks. Instead, Bush directed his intelligence officers to go forward with an appetite to take down the terrorist network and fast. He expected his Intel chiefs to get their confidence back and to tackle swift and successful retaliation. Rice and Tenet left fully aware of the urgency of their mission, yet unaware of the one military operation already underway: 'OPERATION HAWK'S NEST'. Only Cheney knew. He stayed behind for a private meeting with President Bush after Tenet and Rice left. It was time he briefed the President. Alone.

CHAPTER 12: OPERATION HAWK'S NEST

Somewhere West of Phoenix
Superstition Mountains

Commercial planes were grounded nationwide immediately after the attacks. Airports across America shut down. Yet two short runways on a remote and abandoned airstrip, on the former proving grounds of a now defunct car company, lit up the night sky in desert sands outside of Phoenix, Arizona. What was happening here in such a remote section of America?

In the 24 hours since 'OPERATION HAWK'S NEST' was activated yesterday morning, a small city was being built from the ground up at this remote location outside Phoenix, nestled between an Apache Indian reservation and real estate owned by the federal government. Both runways saw steady traffic throughout the evening; from the moment the last steamrollers flattened and readied the landing strips. By morning, this desert compound would be transformed into a replica city of Kabul, Afghanistan.

An Army Corps of Engineers in Humvees and construction trucks were among the first to drive through the chained gates of this former ghost town to set up operations. Within hours of their arrival, electricity and running water were fully functional and a landing strip was created for air traffic, with makeshift runway lights operational. The construction of staging grounds for a classified TOP SECRET mission training exercise was underway. An elite Special Forces team from the Presidential Unit arrived in Marine Blackhawk choppers from Davis Monthan Air Force Base in

Tucson. Light cargo planes and small jets started to ferry in equipment, props, supplies, food, water, ammunition, and guns to the newly formed Ops Training site, codenamed: Hawk's Nest.

Scott Walsh, now known only as the "Hawk", was a passenger on one of those jets that landed here, a U.S. Army AC37A Grumman G5. He made a fateful decision for himself, his family, and for his country, prior to boarding the Army jet to Arizona from West Point. He had no trouble accepting this mission for himself and did so without hesitation when Rumsfeld asked him. Yet, on the long overnight flight from Stewart AFB to Arizona, he tried to rationalize his decision. What was tearing him up inside was that he was still alive, when perhaps he shouldn't be. Why did he skip the meeting in his office at the World Trade Center this morning? In the aftermath, taking this mission meant never seeing his children again, assuming a life as a ghost secret agent in the business of assassination. A far cry from the simple life he retreated to after losing his wife.

Could he really give up his very identity, knowing his children would learn their father died in the rubble of the Twin Towers, pulverized - no dead body to identify? He recounted the emotions that would be facing his son and daughter in the hours and days, months and years ahead by making this decision. Scott was a soldier and a realist. He knew that his chances of coming home from this mission were slim, at best, so his children's premature mourning would not be in vain. Still, he struggled with the decision. Was this the way he wanted to leave them? Their grief over the loss of their mother just three years ago was still an open wound. He had a bigger decision to make; would he have them bear another hole in their hearts so quickly?

As much as the decision tortured him, he knew he really had no recourse. He was a born soldier. As much as he enjoyed his life as a civilian, he always missed the significance of his assignments as a Special Forces soldier. He knew if he channeled all this hurt, all this pain, all this energy would propel him to find and kill the maniac responsible for the deaths of his colleagues and other Americans. He wanted to avenge their deaths. He also desperately needed to ensure the safety of his children in a city he loved. He felt powerless as a civilian. As a soldier, he could at least protect them. As a soldier, his life had renewed purpose. If that meant giving up his identity and his life to protect his family and his country, it was his duty. He promised himself one thing. He would not fail on this mission. He will bring back the head of Osama Bin Laden. He would be so prepared and so elusive that Osama Bin Laden would never know what hit him. But when he did, he promised to make sure that Osama Bin Laden would never forget him and remember his face everyday in hell.

After sitting four hours motionless without a twitch, Scott stood up and went over to sit across from Leigh. He didn't say a word. Neither did she. The flight attendant approached them. Scott orders a Jameson on the rocks. Leigh raised two fingers indicating she would have the same. They both turned down an offer to get them a light meal.

As the flight attendant went to get them drinks, Leigh spoke first, "Are you OK?" Scott let the question linger, then answered glibly: "I hope that's not a requirement?" Leigh replied, almost penitently: "I'm sorry. That was stupid. I just want you to know that you don't have to do this."

Scott looked out the window. He appeared to ignore her, lost in thought. Leigh's eyes never left his face. She wondered what he was thinking? Several minutes of silence went by before Scott looked back at her.

"It's easier not having an option, you do know that?" He said honestly. "I understand." She replied knowingly. "Leigh," he said staring into her eyes, "I'm all in. Just tell me one more time that we can do this?" Scott replied, more rhetorically than as a question.

Leigh respected that he didn't want an answer. The hint of a smile emanating from her lips and the slight twinkle in her eyes gave him a warm feeling and perhaps a sign – a sign signaling light at the end of a dark and treacherous tunnel.

CHAPTER 13: TWO DAYS AFTER 9/11

The Pentagon
September 13, 2001

The Pentagon had physically been ripped open and was still smoldering days after the attack. Secretary of Defense Donald Rumsfeld met the President of the United States inside the intact lobby of the Pentagon. President Bush came over to the Pentagon this morning to see the damages himself. He also wanted to thank the soldiers and citizen staff at the Pentagon personally for their courage, and for the care extended to the wounded immediately after the attack. His time was limited, the trip ad hoc, and Andy Card, Bush's Chief of Staff, was marshaling the event to keep it on schedule. Rumsfeld's staff arranged an assembly for Pentagon personnel at the last minute in the Army Auditorium in the basement.

Many of the men and women inside the Pentagon were working around the clock. They were manning critical mission jobs ramping up to war making it impossible to attend. Some were deep underground, in a bunker city five stories underneath the Pentagon basement. In one room, a high tech Pentagon conference room dubbed the "tank," sat all of the three star generals of the Army, Navy, Air Force and Marines. They are known as the "ops deps," the operations deputies that prepare the Chiefs of Staff and ultimately carry out the wars. They would not be able to attend the meeting with the president. They were making war plans codenamed: Operation Enduring Freedom.

After a quick tour of the damage done to the building, President George W. Bush addressed the waiting Pentagon staff in a general session. It was an unscripted George Bush moment, doing what he does best, speaking without a prompter from his heart. He was direct, emotional, and uplifting, despite creating several new words in the English lexicon. His words injected passion to an already charged military ready to retaliate against the enemy.

Before the session started, Rumsfeld asked Andy Card, the President's Chief of Staff, to speak with the president confidentially for a few minutes after the session ended. Card wasn't keen on the idea knowing the president, even during these darkest of days, was determined to be on schedule. Yet, Andy Card knew it must be something too important to wait. He told Rumsfeld he would inform the President.

As the President came off stage, Rumsfeld led him backstage to an A/V equipment area, which was the closest space that offered total privacy, at least as much privacy afforded when surrounded by Secret Service personnel.

"Mr. President, 'OPERATION HAWK'S NEST' is underway," Rumsfeld informed the President. "Leigh McClure is running the op. She has absolute authority on this and I need to know more about her other than the file. You know her well."

"I do," the President replied. He thought for a moment before he continued. He understood he needed to get his Secretary of Defense and his personal friend's confidence up quickly: "I understand completely, Don. Here's all you need to know about McClure. Genius IQ. Perfectionist. Fearless Leader. Experienced. Competent. Overwhelming odds, high intensity are her electricity. She is no-nonsense and has gotten every job

I've thrown at her done." He paused before adding with emphasis: "And done right."

The President paused and looked at Rumsfeld square in the eyes: "Why so much energy devoted to her country, you might be thinking? It goes beyond how her husband was brutally murdered. That got her in this business, but it's not the only reason she rose to the apex of her profession." He pauses. "What I really think is that she has chosen this career because she really had no choice. She has seen the face of evil, close-up. She has confronted the devil, more than once. She knows things that we will never know." And he adds: "Or ever should."

The President puts his right hand on Don's shoulder and shrugs his own shoulders. "Doesn't matter what I think. You just need to know that Leigh McClure is the best damn soldier spy ever to wear the red, white and blue. Trust her." Rumsfeld replies, "Thank you, Mr. President. I will. God help us."

The President started to leave, but stopped and turned looking back at Rumsfeld. "Oh, he will, Don." The President replied making it personal. "Good luck and Godspeed." The President passed through the curtain and vanished.

CHAPTER 14: CAMP HAWK'S NEST

Somewhere in the Arizona desert
September 12, 2001

She never slept. Adrenaline rushes through her veins.

Leigh poured a second cup of coffee and stood looking out at an urban landscape created overnight in the desert, hidden safely by the surrounding Superstition Mountains. The sun cast its first light in the Arizona desert creating visible heat waves hovering over the distant mountain range surrounding the camp. The sun was heating things up early. Perfect, she thought.

It also brilliantly lit up a canvass for Leigh, affording her a panoramic view of a city built here within the past 24 hours. If it looked like a ragtag, staging ground for a Hollywood B movie, it could have been. Here, somewhere west of Phoenix, south of Scottsdale and southwest of Sun City, at abandoned proving grounds of a foreign car company, Leigh McClure hastily created a temporary military training base supervised and staffed by her closely knit TOP SECRET Presidential Unit. It closely replicated Kabul in Afghanistan and sat amidst the desert terrain and severe weather typical of Afghanistan's southern region.

She also constructed urban compounds and city streets replicating Kabul's purported hideouts for Osama Bin Laden. Her team had less than 24 hours to create a mock Kabul twin city. They used every minute into the long night to get the job done. Now, at sunrise, mission accomplished. The new city built overnight was codenamed: Camp Hawk's Nest.

This former boarded-up ghost town was transformed overnight into a training ground for a lone soldier to infiltrate an enemy's headquarters halfway around the globe and assassinate its leader. It is a highly sophisticated, TOP SECRET black op spearheading America's first 21st Century war.

Soldiers built this Kabul copy from the ground up, borrowing assets from the Hawthorne Army Depot (HWAD) in Nevada and purchasing props from staging firms in Las Vegas. They used existing abandoned structures from the site, where they could, or modified them. They acquired elaborate props from nearby Las Vegas to simulate everything from fake storefronts to buildings. Guns and munitions were trucked in, as were a dozen stallions from Camp Navajo, outside of Flagstaff. Between tumbleweed and prop alleyways, this urban scene in the middle of the desert may not have been pretty, Leigh thought, but she saw its innate functional beauty. She is pleased with the result, as it was not only functional, but more importantly, accurate to some of the actual dimensions of Bin Laden's hideouts in the city. She knows how significant that will be for Scott to gain familiarity with sites he will operate in before he arrives in Kabul in two weeks time. While this elaborate replication was critical to learning how to navigate and operate within Kabul – it was just as important for Scott to find an escape route out.

The sun was now radiating through the few cirrus clouds that streaked the desert blue sky. It was already 87 degrees and the forecast was projected to climb over 100 degrees by noon. Leigh is confident, enjoying her coffee, excited about the mission, and surveying the scene. She looks at her watch. It is time to prepare Scott Walsh to kill Osama Bin Laden in Kabul.

She knows she has just five days to get Scott ready here because their next stop would be in the mountains at the Marine Corps Mountain

Warfare Training Center (MCMWTC) in Pickel Meadow, California, the nation's most comprehensive training facility for preparing units to operate in complex, mountainous terrain. That part of the training she deliberately saved for last. Leigh is certain that the mountain terrain would most closely replicate the mountains in Tora Bora, where she was convinced Osama Bin Laden might ultimately flee to hide, if he escaped Kabul, his known whereabouts right now.

As revered as Osama Bin Laden was in Afghanistan, Intel showed that his bravado is a façade. In fact, he is a very fearful man and will take extraordinary measures for maximum personal protection. Intel highly suspects, although unconfirmed, that Bin Laden actually had doubles to decoy his movements and hide his true whereabouts. Leigh is certain that he will run for cover, as quickly as he saw the United States military response, which she knew, as he must too, would come soon.

If she is taking Osama Bin Laden by surprise, in either location, she must get Scott into Kabul on schedule. To do so meant ramping up an already rapid training regimen to get Scott ready under grueling and adverse conditions. She knew it wasn't optimum, yet neither was it impossible. She placed her confidence in her team -- the best ever assembled for this special operation. Half of her team were with her at Hawk's Nest and the rest were back in Washington gathering intelligence to give the mission a leg up when the mission went green light in Afghanistan. They were also setting up an op staging HQ in Room 16 underground in the White House bunker.

"Two weeks to train a 53 year old who hasn't seen close combat for more than 20 years?" he said sarcastically, brandishing an oversize coffee mug and suited up in camouflage fatigues. Leigh moved her head back and forth and smiled at the 25 year old Max Leonhardt, known as the Scientist in the Presidential Unit. He didn't look like a scientist. His blonde curly hair, blue eyes, mustache and tanned 6-foot masculine frame betrayed that description. He could have easily been a poster boy for Surfer Magazine. Yet scientist and soldier was his chosen field and admittedly he is now at the top in his field, at only 25. He knows it too. His specialty is designing high-tech tools of special ops tradecraft. In 'OPERATION HAWK'S NEST', he is in charge of optics (drone and satellite surveillance), and technical communications (including all voice communications and eavesdropping). He is also charged with development of lightweight technical tools, especially weaponry for a lone assassin to transport, carry, and use to break into a fortress and carry out the mission.

Two other men from the Unit sat at a lone, steel, breakfast table drinking coffee. Both are highly skilled commandos, who will lead the physical training exercises here in Arizona and next week in California.

One is Nick Anthony, 26 years old, from U.S. Army Special Forces, now a member of the elite Presidential UNIT, a native from Morristown, New Jersey. At 6'2, this former running back at Alabama has dark hair and olive complexion and a visible deep scar on his left cheek. Combat ready.

The other is Bryan Taylor, 25, an African American from Delta Force Special Forces, a member of the elite Presidential UNIT, and a native of LA. A graduate of USC, he was a former track and field star qualifying for the 1996 Summer Olympics in Atlanta. However, he broke his leg in an accident prior to the Games ending a promising track and field career. Mild mannered demeanor yet his chiseled facial features and physical presence are daunting. Combat ready.

Both soldiers are single. They are fluent in Arabic and are part of the Special Forces Mountain Team that trained on horseback. Their military resumes are stellar. They are also graduates of flight training and ranked in the Top 10 military sharpshooters.

There were six other soldiers from the Unit, not present at breakfast, but bivouacked in the urban staging area. They are here to assist in the training, but Leigh wanted them unseen except in a surprise capacity during Scott's raid on Osama Bin Laden's simulated camp. These men all are skilled special ops officers who will role-play as UBL's (codeword for Osama Bin Laden) elite bodyguards.

One other person was present before Scott arrived in the kitchen area. She is a 44 year-old chef from Scottsdale, a Hopi Indian and friend of Leigh named Violet Sinquah. Leigh broke from tradition from past Special Forces training simulations where meals are normally contained only in backpack rations. She wanted to make sure Scott ate healthy prepared meals during his training. He is certain to lose weight rapidly under the training regimen planned and she wanted to ensure he remained strong.

Violet will prepare all the meals, and she will provide instruction after dinner on the types of animals, snakes, and insects Scott might encounter in Afghanistan. When a scorpion lands on you moments before your opportunity presents itself in combat, Leigh thought Scott should know how to handle it. Violet Sinquah knew how to handle creatures of the night. She grew up on the Hopi reservation just 4 hours north of here and knew these night crawlers all too well. She brought along several of the frightening and poisonous creatures for Scott's instruction, shipped direct from a CIA outpost in the Kandahar province, including the world's most dangerous scorpion, called the death stalker and one of Asia's deadliest snakes, the saw scaled viper. Leigh ruled out the Black Widow spider Violet prized and wanted to show and tell, but not because Afghanistan boasts some of the largest Black Widows on the planet. She simply did not want any association with a spider that was her own secret signature in days gone by.

Scott entered the area for breakfast looking rested despite little sleep and the tension built up by the events of yesterday. He looked out at the soldiers who sat staring at him. They all knew why they were here. There are no introductions. He takes a seat next to the soldiers while Violet poured him a cup of coffee. No small talk. The days ahead are going to be grueling even by a Special Forces soldier's standard. Scott knew what he was in for and also understood the incredibly high stakes. Today, and for the next two weeks, the training was intentionally designed to be physically daunting, exhausting, and repetitive to ensure maximum physical and mental preparedness.

After a quick breakfast (soldiers eat in seven minutes flat), introductions were finally made. Leigh introduced Scott simply as the 'Hawk'. Everyone in the room knew that the identity of the man codenamed the 'Hawk' would forever remain TOP SECRET. That's all they knew, except that he obviously was being trained to infiltrate UBL's terrorist organization as a spy. Hawk was clearly CIA; at least that is exactly what Leigh wanted them to surmise.

Each day began with a two hour exercise routine, which included a three mile run, followed by a one mile swim (there was a 25 meter outdoor lap pool already on the facility that was cleaned and filled the night before), and then a specially prepared obstacle course where navigation was timed. The morning's exercise regimen was followed by an hour and a half practice on the shooting range, some of it staged on horseback. Lunch was outdoors in the blazing sun. Leigh's intent was to keep Scott in the sun, as often as she could, to weather and tan his body so Scott to easily assimilate in the Afghanistan region. The afternoon schedules included replicating surprise and sleuth entries into simulated Kabul compounds resulting always in a kill of Bin Laden, then escape.

Different scenarios and obstacles were prepared on each simulation yet the repetitiveness of the simulations was deliberate. Scott is not surprised to encounter faux enemy UBL guards during each simulation. He half expected it. His past training with Special Forces was never lost and the instincts of his warrior past kicked in almost immediately. Scott never missed a beat. His marksmanship improved quickly. He refused rest or breaks. He hardly spoke except to ask questions when a simulated attack failed.

Leigh's only concern after the first day of training was how difficult the resistance from her faux Unit enemy forces became for Scott. She wanted him to experience the demanding and deadly situations he would most likely encounter, but she surely didn't want him injured. She made a mental note to talk with her Unit separately tonight to make sure they understood.

At dinner nightly, Leigh presented visual summaries of success and failures in the daily training activities. Every simulated kill and escape maneuver was dissected in slow motion videotaped replays. These allowed her to show and pinpoint specific areas Scott needed to improve upon in critical situations. Max Leonhardt had strategically placed the video cameras to capture the training simulations as the makeshift village was being built. He also had brought in a Video Editing Suite to edit footage on the fly so they could be used for these nightly briefings. Scott Walsh was being prepared to be America's most important and most lethal secret agent. No expense was spared to give the 'Hawk' an edge.

As the days of training rolled on, Nick Anthony and Bryan Taylor grew impressed with this older guy's ability, stamina, strength, and combat readiness. They knew the 'Hawk's' mission was to spy on Al Qaeda terrorists and that they were going to be his front line assist. When they first met him, they were surprised at his age. It did concern them. Yet, in just a few days of intense training, they grew to highly respect his physical strength and battle-tested experience, especially his extraordinary ability to make split second decisions in high-pressure situations. His age was no longer a factor. They were proud to assist him. They looked forward to making sure he succeeded in whatever special tasks he was being trained for on such a fast track.

After dinner on the third night of the training exercises, Violet took off her apron, undid the clasp in her hair and let her long, dark hair down. She is a classic Rubenesque figure. Her penetrating eyes, combined with the way she gracefully moves her voluptuous body to make points, is especially provocative and seductive. She began tonight what became a ritually staged "show and tell" on what comes out at night in Afghanistan. It was informational, but she made it both entertaining and instructional. There were times that it was just frightening, as well. This was the part of the early evening that appeared to lend itself to some release of the tension and intensity of the training being conducted by day.

What comes out at night in desert terrains is normally frightening, especially if you don't like things that crawl. Scott dreaded creepy crawlers of all types so he watched Violet closely as she handled these creatures of the night without fear. She was the beauty with the beasts. The only laughter this week came when Violet threw a tarantula at Scott without warning. Scott swatted it off his chest spontaneously and sliced it apart within seconds with a Yarborough knife built into a sheath in his right pant leg. As startling as the situation was, everyone laughed.

No one remembers the 'Hawk' laughing though. He had only one real fear in his life: spiders.

Violet would have a surprise every night. Fortunately for the Hawk, spiders only made her agenda once. There was one other frightful night.

Violet picked up a huge snake – a saw scaled Afghan viper from a basket. It slithered slowly around her neck before sliding into her ample bosom. She looked horrified then dropped apparently dead in front of them. As she was faking her death, she quickly got up with the viper in her hands. She let them know that this viper had been defanged. She certainly never tried to throw anything creepy by surprise at the 'Hawk' ever again. She had been petrified by how instinctively and quickly he killed the tarantula then sliced it to pieces.

After dinner nightly, the search and kill raid simulations continued until midnight. Scott is being prepped to operate in day or night conditions. Conditions in Kabul were replicated here in the desert to aid Scott with his familiarity once he gets on the ground. But, Scott and the UNIT soldiers, masquerading as UBL's inner guard, also all donned traditional Perahan Tunbun, the clothing of most traditional Muslims in Afghanistan, during the exercises. The clothing had a significant relevance during the training exercises, beyond merely replicating reality in Afghanistan.

Scott's Afghan disguise obviously required clothing to meld inconspicuously into the Afghan landscape, but this created unique problems for carrying munitions and equipment. He certainly couldn't carry a backpack or have arms visible. Max Leonhardt found a way to hide munitions underneath the clothing by creating a smart tech, wearable arms factory underneath the Arab garments. It was made of lightweight, moisture-wicking spandex underarmor with several built-in sheaths to carry as much munitions, weaponry and high tech devices as the clothing could handle, without impeding needed movement in battle. The form fitting aspects of the design also deliberately disguised any hint of the bulk munitions factory underneath the garment. Yet, it needed to be flexible enough to run in, crouch in, and ride horseback, without exposing harm to Scott or being visible. Max originally designed it with Kevlar bulletproofing, but it proved too bulky so it was dropped from the design. This left Scott vulnerable, yet it was a compromise needed to assure his mobility in action.

The secrecy of this training facility, 'Hawks Nest', with men dressed in Afghan clothing in combat situations, required tight security on land and in the air. For several days, surveillance in the air was not a primary concern, as all airports across the nation were closed. On September 14th, however, air flight resumed at airports across America, despite the lingering cloud of fear gripping the country. There was a single exception made in instructions by the FAA to all airports. Air flight was restricted and forbidden over the Superstition Mountains. Airlines were advised of the "no-fly" zone. It would not draw any suspicion as it had always been a 'no fly' zone, even prior to 9/11, as it was exclusive air space for training pilots on F16s from nearby Luke Air Force Base. What was unique the day after 9/11 was that the pilots at Luke AFB were instructed to stay out of coordinates in and around Apache Junction, the new home of "Camp Hawks Nest." The training op compound was off the grid for intended secrecy.

On September 17th, the combat training simulations shut down in Arizona. The final day at Camp Hawks Nest was devoted instead to learning how to use sophisticated new high-tech weapons designed specifically to give Scott an edge for this mission. Max Leonhardt designed many of them working in collaboration with engineers at Langley on the invention of a first wrist- watch computer phone: codenamed 'Tracker'. It is quite remarkable with state of the art features unseen outside of the Pentagon, including wireless electronic mail, text and voice messaging, sophisticated encrypted GPS and real time video imaging and flip screen to show satellite pictures on one screen and GPS maps.

While the Tracker was Leonhardt's most exciting tool for America's most lethal secret agent, he had other high tech tools in his arsenal to give the "Hawk" a leg up in his mission. Tools like:

Ring detonator remote control -- for detonating C-4 explosives

Pen Pistols – 4mm caliber to hide in a shirt

Glock 9mm and Browning .380 short with palm-print reader, enabling only Scott to shoot it, in case they were ever used against him

Scott found them all fascinating and learned skillfully how to use them all. Yet, he remained in awe of the innovative high-tech Tracker. It is as futuristic as a Dick Tracy wristwatch two-way radio of his boyhood designed and updated for the 21st century with audio/video and laptop computer capability. It is the most impressive piece of technology he had ever experienced. It is a top-secret high tech tool that he understands will be critical for accessing real time assistance from the Unit once on the ground in Afghanistan. He is amazed how an ops command center in some secret location in Washington D.C. could actually see what would be behind virtually every corner he would come up against inside a Kabul compound, and then relay that image to him in real time on a wireless wristband monitor. All this high tech wizardry accomplished from optics on new unmanned flying drones, satellites and other emerging new optics that the CIA was employing in Afghanistan for intelligence.

He only imagined, at this point, how valuable relaying those instant images in real time back to him on this wearable device might prove to be. Using it in simulations demonstrated just how user-friendly and intuitive it is in practice. In a combat situation, the intuitive nature of this technology might mean the difference between life and death.

Scott is impressed with all of Leonhardt's high tech tools. With these clever inventions and the munitions factory now strapped to his body, he was beginning to feel like a 21st Century superman. Leigh knew that he will need to become one too, in order to achieve the ultimate goal of killing Bin Laden in his host country, heavily fortified, perhaps impenetrable in Kabul.

She also knew that the most logical location for his deadly encounter with Bin Laden is most probably not going to be in Kabul; rather the treacherous mountains of Tora Bora. She needed time to get him ready for this other geographically demanding and difficult environment. For good reason, she saved the mountain training for last.

She would bring him to a training center dedicated to fighting in mountainous terrain tomorrow. They would leave Phoenix and fly to the mountains at the Marine Corps Mountain Warfare Training Center (MCMWTC) in Pickel Meadow, California located in the Toiyabe National Forest in the early morning. Pickel Meadow is 21 miles northwest of Bridgeport, California and 100 miles south of Reno, Nevada. The training center was first used for cold weather mountain training for Infantry troops during the Korean War and today Rumsfeld had 1,000 Special Forces soldiers there getting ready to be the first on the ground in the war to come soon. The 'Hawk' would saddle up with them on their first climb in the morning.

Scott had been to these mountains in California before -- for military mountain training back in 1979. It was a backdrop too for his first trip to Afghanistan more than 20 years ago. Back then, a small band of special ops soldiers and CIA agents trained here for a high-risk mission that would send them to the mountains of Afghanistan, prior to the invasion of Afghanistan by the Soviet Union. Code-named 'Operation Cyclone,' Scott and his team were dropped at night in the Panjshir Valley and rode on horseback with Northern Alliance Forces to General Mossoud's headquarters. The meeting created a back channel for communications between the Northern Alliance Forces and the US for the upcoming invasion by the Soviets in 1979. This also began laying a foundation for the CIA to establish a network in Afghanistan, which would grow in size and significance in the years to come. However, that network failed to send warnings about 9/11. Why?

Leigh's Unit in Washington D.C. were acquiring broad intelligence from CIA. They informed her that just two nights before Al Qaeda's coordinated attacks on America on 9/11, CIA's Afghan intelligence network reported that Al Qaeda operatives assassinated General Mossoud, the leader of the Northern Alliance in Afghanistan and an important ally to the USA. This action by Osama Bin Laden just two days before his attacks on America displayed how carefully he orchestrated the events leading to 9/11. General Mossoud would certainly have been CIA's best asset after 9/11. How was this assassination plot to kill General Mossoud missed by intelligence too?

Leigh understood Scott knew General Mossoud. She would report this breaking news to Scott on the flight to California tonight. As if Scott needed any more motivation...

CHAPTER 15: GREENLIGHT

Ground Zero - New York City
THREE DAYS AFTER 9/11

The nation was still in shock yet itching for revenge and retribution. President Bush's spontaneous reply to a firefighter at Ground Zero in lower Manhattan today electrified and unified the country. When a rescue worker cried out: "I can't hear you!" President George W. Bush held his bullhorn high and shouted back spontaneously: "I can hear you! I can hear you! The rest of the world hears you! And the people – and the people who knocked these buildings down will hear all of us soon!"

At 8:00 that same evening, President Bush arrived back in the nation's capital to meet his VP, Secretary of Defense, and Joint Chiefs in the Situation Room. Just three days after America was attacked, President Bush approved the war plan. 'OPERATION ENDURING FREEDOM' is now operational.

The Pentagon began executing logistics and training for the first 1,000 Special Forces from the U.S. Army's 10th Mountain Division as the critical advance force. This elite fighting force would be the eyes and ears to start a bombing campaign prior to a full- scale invasion by U.S. ground forces. Because of the secrecy of their advance mission and the mountainous terrain in Afghanistan, the soldiers will be riding on horses into America's first war of the 21st Century. There had been no training of soldiers on horseback since the U.S. Cavalry was disbanded fifty years ago. These 1,000 soldiers are planned to ride into Afghanistan through the Central Asian nation of Uzbekistan on October 5th. They will lay the groundwork and set the stage for the bombing campaign that will start simultaneously with the President's planned address to the nation set for October 7th. Because on that date, the President of the United States of America will declare war on Afghanistan.

The Pentagon
SIX DAYS AFTER 9/11

Rumsfeld placed a call to Leigh's new secure mobile Tracker device at 2100 hundred hours. Seeing the caller ID Eagle 1, Leigh answered, "Eagle 2. Over." McClure answered using her code name for OPERATION HAWK'S NEST. Rumsfeld was designated Eagle 1. "This is Eagle 1. You have company joining you on the mountain. They're briefed for your agent's access to limited joint training exercises. Stay under the radar. Eagle 1. Over." Rumsfeld spoke with urgency. "Copy that. Can we buy more time? Eagle 2. Over." replied McClure. "Negative. No change to schedule. This window is operation critical. Repeat. The window is critical. Eagle 1. Over." McClure knew the mission was now on priority status to war. She replied: "Copy that. Eagle 2. Over." She replied understanding the timetable is fixed. "Good luck & Godspeed. Eagle 1 out." "Copy that," Leigh replied. "Eagle 2 over and out."

The call she just received was short. Leigh took a deep breath sitting across from Scott on the U.S. Army AC 37 jet en route to the Sierra Nevada. One more week of training exercises left. 'OPERATION HAWK'S NEST' will become an active TOP SECRET op in the field in a matter of days. She knows that war is now imminent when Rumsfeld confirmed that the op must be deployed on time and without delay. 'OPERATION HAWK'S NEST' had a start in field date of September 25th to be mission completed no later than October 4th, as originally planned. She understood Rumsfeld's urgency.

She looked over at Scott, eyes closed, resting -- but not sleeping. Despite the danger dangling before him, she needed to convince herself that Scott would find his way home alive after the mission.

As she watched him rest, she thought back to a different time, a different place. Her last memory of him was his gentle kiss goodbye. The memory of that lasting kiss would replay itself on so many lonely nights since then. She thought how strange it was that their paths would cross again? How ironic that evil was the intersection where their paths crossed years ago and remains the driving force for their reunion now, more than twenty years later. She had spent most of her life, since she lost her husband, suppressing her feelings. Now, her feelings became unleashed again. She knew to keep them in check no matter how intense. Their reunion was no accident. It was destiny against relentless evil.

They sit in silence. He never inquired about her short call. She never mentioned it. Suddenly, the Flight Attendant interrupted their moment of brief peace. For the first time since their flight together on 9/11, they both had a drink. Scott ordered a Jameson's on the rocks. She had the same. Drinks were followed by a salad and lasagna, served with a bottle of Amarone. When the wine was being opened, Scott smiled for the first time since 9/11. He remembered the first time he ever tasted this rich and powerful, but balanced red wine from north of Verona in Italy. It was a night in Istanbul, so very long ago. He was with Leigh. She had ordered the first bottle on the night after a mission they worked on together that ended in a bloody firefight underground in the Basilica Cistern. Their chase of terrorists who had stolen cultures of the Ebola virus in Zaire had ended in Istanbul. Badly.

His memory of the event was vivid, even now some twenty-six years later. Their mission was a joint CIA/Special Forces op to find stolen cultures of an Ebola virus and capture the terrorists alive for interrogation. The entire case was a mystery.

Even the identity of the terrorists that left Zaire with the cultures was a bizarre tale. Two men, of Arab descent, had been captured on video security surveillance at the Tandala hospital in Zaire at the time of the theft. Yet their photos scanned completely unidentifiable from any database search in the entire intelligence community throughout the world. Why and how would two unknown probable terrorists of Arab descent steal such a deadly virus from Africa?

Finding them and the virus was deemed critical because there was a certainty within the intelligence community of the United States that the virus was stolen for use as a biological weapon. It still needed to be aerosolized to be a clear and imminent danger, but several enemies of the United States were believed as having that rare capability or soon to have it. The hunt for these terrorists and the virus became America's number one priority at the order of then President Gerald Ford of the United States.

Because of Scott and Leigh's success together on previous missions in the Middle East, both CIA and the US Army's Special Forces selected them as their first team for this joint assignment. In every mission critical task force in the United States military, there are redundant backup teams at the ready to dispatch at a moment's notice. Failure is never an option. Yet, this was different than any mission before. It would be an unusual joint task force because the US Army would be in command. CIA didn't like it, but the President of the United States intervened in this situation. The Ebola virus was too dangerous to be made into a biological weapon and the administration was developing new strategies for just this evolving type of biothreat to America. The Army codenamed the op: 'Operation Aerosol'.

The events that would follow happened fast within five frightful days in October 1976.

OPERATION AEROSOL
October 1976

Operation Aerosol was activated onboard the USS John F. Kennedy somewhere in the Mediterranean Sea where Scott and Leigh arrived on F-14 Tomcats from two different continents almost simultaneously. They were briefed. Their instructions were to capture the terrorists, but not until they had a positive ID of the virus in their possession.

During the briefing, they were informed that the vials of the virus were safely contained in an oblong telescopic type container, and they handled an exact replica. It was black about 24 inches long and three inches in diameter. With this little information, they were quickly helicoptered out to a small naval ship off the coast of Morocco in the city of Rabat. From there, they were put on a waiting private powerboat piloted by a local CIA operative. Once inside Rabat's city limits, they were provided a private flat as temporary quarters. Their entry into Morocco was at a secluded shore, under cover of darkness.

CIA had uncovered intelligence earlier in the day indicating that the terrorists arrived in Rabat in the morning by private jet. During interrogations of the pilots, a positive ID was made on the terrorists, but the identities were apparently fabricated. Where the terrorists were headed after landing was unknown.

Scott and Leigh never unpacked their gear. They were in a hurry, poring over maps, familiarizing themselves with the geography, and waiting for CIA Intel for a location of the terrorists. Within hours of their arrival, they were handed their first leads. The terrorists had apparently rented a car at the airport and were last seen several hours earlier driving south to Casablanca.

Casablanca is a little more than an hour by car from Rabat so the terrorists would certainly have been there already. A search for the rental car and all outgoing trains, buses and airports was already underway by the CIA on the ground in Casablanca. The search came up empty. It was assumed that the suspects bypassed Casablanca and were headed south by now to Marrakesh, which would add another four hours, at least, to the terrorists' journey.

Despite a lead, no one could get a make on the terrorists. The forged ID obtained from the rental company contract proved useless. The suspects paid cash making it impossible to investigate further. But they had something to work with: the color, plates and make of car, a Peugeot wagon. With the resources CIA had available, they would find it soon. The terrorists were ahead of them by four hours at least. They would be arriving in Marrakesh within the hour, assuming Marrakesh would indeed be their final destination. Satellites were being positioned to try and find the rental car on the road, but the timeframe was tight to make a discovery in time. CIA operatives were dispatched locally along the route to find the car. Scott and Leigh grabbed their gear and drove outside Rabat's city limits awaiting a pickup by helicopter. They were heading immediately to Marrakesh.

The Peugeot wagon rental was found ditched along the highway on the road to Marrakesh. It was abandoned, apparently discarded by the terrorists, suspicious that they were being followed. It was wiped clean of any ID. It meant that the terrorists knew they were being tailed and apparently, they had help inside Morocco. The trail was cold though by the time Scott and Leigh arrived by helicopter in Marrakesh.

Despite the setback and need for fast Intel, CIA still needed to operate anonymously without notifying the Moroccan government of the pursuit. King Hassan II was an ally, however, any leak of this manhunt would spell disaster in their ability to find the terrorists, as a media leak would create worldwide panic. Everyone involved in Operation Aerosol understood the dilemma.

With a dead trail, CIA focused instead on possible motives for why the terrorists were here in Morocco in the first place. The conventional wisdom was that the terrorists were hired guns for a rogue state seeking the Ebola virus. CIA saw the rogue state acquiring the virus needing to sell the toxin to a state capable of aerosolizing the disease as a weapon of mass destruction. CIA further believed that the Soviet Union was capable and willing to pay any price for the Ebola virus. The rogue state, in collusion with the Soviet Union, needed a remote location where Soviet agents could authenticate the stolen virus as an active virus culture before staging the pickup. CIA was convinced that the nation willing to use the virus would take extraordinary precautions because the entire world would stand united against any state that dared to create such a deadly bioweapon.

It reasoned that Morocco was most probably only a confirmation point, not the transfer site. It also assumed that the actual transfer would have been planned deceptively and circuitously, as was happening now, as a means to try and keep the USA and its CIA completely off balance and hopefully out of the way, whenever and wherever the actual transfer of the virus occurred.

The CIA zeroed in on motive and employed assets on its Soviet spies in the region yielding new intelligence that popped up leads quickly. The suspects were seen in a black Mercedes sedan heading northwest, perhaps to Beni-Mallal. They had no satellite feed on the location yet and it would take hours, so the alert was signaled to put Leigh and Scott in active pursuit.

The decision was instantaneous. Leigh stayed in Marrakesh, in case the lead was a false decoy. Scott headed northwest in pursuit of the black Mercedes. The local CIA field agent reluctantly gave Scott the keys to his Ducati 900 SSD Darmah to catch the Mercedes if he could. He also gave him the location and apartment number of his contact inside Beni-Mallal. The motorcycle was super fast, high and strong enough to go off-road, if necessary, and to peer into passing cars to ID the terrorists -- if he could get close enough. It was nearing midnight when he jumped on the Ducati. He accelerated onto what appeared to be a road marked N8 to Beni-Mallal.

N8 is called a highway. Surprisingly, it is a highway made of crushed dirt and sand, unpaved. It proved to be challenging for a nightrider on a motorcycle built for speed. Traffic at this hour was minimal. It took Scott less than three hours to ride the 220 miles into Beni-Mallal. He was hitting speeds between 90 and well over 100 mph despite the dirt road conditions. Only two black Mercedes came across his path tonight. Neither was his mark.

He rode into the city limits and followed the directions he had for his rendezvous here on Rue Essaouira. It was nearly 3:00 in the morning when he walked up the stairs to the top floor flat. The door was ajar. He pulled his revolver, crouched and pushed the door wide open. As Scott entered the apartment, the room was clear, but he noticed two things simultaneously: a stench of death and a light coming from what seemed like the kitchen. He moved toward the light and as he entered the small kitchen, incredibly shabby conditions were illuminated by a hanging lone light bulb, as a sea of cockroaches scurried everywhere by his presence. The room was clear so he headed to the next two tiny rooms, which appeared to be a bedroom and a bath. He checked out the bedroom, clear. Then, he moved quickly to the bathroom. It was the size of a closet, with nothing but a hole in the floor. It was empty except for a dead man hanging. The odor was overpowering.

He took a step back to recover from the stench before going back inside. He checked the pulse of the man dangling from the rope before cutting the chord dropping the dead man to the floor.

He rushed back to close the front door and doubled back to investigate further. There was no ID on the man but Scott trusted the dead man probably was his contact here. He felt the man's face and neck to determine rigor mortis. Nothing had set in yet, so he knew the hanging occurred shortly before he arrived. Scott knew that whoever did this was close by, perhaps waiting for him. This place didn't just smell like death, it was a portrait of the gates of hell. It was so appalling that he thinks out loud. "This is no place to live, and I will not die here."

He bolted out of the hellhole flat and darted inconspicuously across the street to his Ducati, hidden in an alleyway. He didn't want to start it to attract attention but wanted it nearby for an escape, if needed. He rolled it as close to the street as he could without the bike being detected. He stood still in the dark alley, searching for movement of anything at all up and down the Rue Essaouira. Nearly fifteen minutes went by before a black Mercedes pulled out of a hotel garage down the street and turned west. Scott started his Ducati and followed the Mercedes as far back as he could, never turning on his lights, trying to remain incognito. They raced like this for another ten minutes navigating their way towards the city center outer limits.

Scott anticipated they were headed back to 8N until the Mercedes unexpectedly turned off the main road completely. It wasn't abrupt, like an evasive maneuver, so he didn't think he was detected. The Mercedes drove fast down a descending dirt path leaving a heavy trail of dust and finally stopped at what looked like a graveyard for rusted out construction equipment. Or perhaps it had been a construction site abandoned years ago. Scott stopped his bike at the turn and pulled out his night vision field binoculars. He watched them enter the decrepit site trying to determine what could have possibly brought them to this dead end.

He sensed now that he truly had been undetected and from his vantage point, he radioed in to report events so far to Leigh. As they were speaking, a helicopter came out of nowhere and touched down almost on top of the Mercedes. He watched as two men from the car got out and ran to the chopper. The helicopter lifted up. They vanished.

Scott informed Leigh before racing into the site. While he was pulling up on the side of the Mercedes, Leigh had already contacted CIA to track the helicopter's path via satellite. At the site, Scott saw the driver of the Mercedes slumped over the steering wheel. When he got off his bike, he could see that the driver was shot in the back of the head. The car was bare except for a Makarov 380 on the floor behind the drivers seat. He was certain it had been wiped clean. Nevertheless, he picked it up and brought it back with him as he raced back to Marrakesh.

It was almost 7:00 in the morning when he arrived back at Leigh's apartment. He was tired but the rush of riding a Ducati without traffic on such a long stretch of road was exhilarating enough to keep him awake. He had a hunch sleep was no longer an option because when Leigh opened the door, she had a fresh cup of coffee 'to go' for him and she was locking the door behind her. They jumped in a waiting Peugeot wagon and headed directly to the Marrakesh Menara Airport. She informed Scott en route that the suspects had escaped Morocco. They had flown in the helicopter to Casablanca. Once there, they apparently boarded a private charter plane in Casablanca. Their destination: Istanbul.

Scott and Leigh finally arrived in Istanbul well behind the terrorists and were greeted with more bad news. The local CIA freelancers tailing the terrorists from the Istanbul Ataturk Airport apparently got too close. They were found dead floating in the Bosporus strait, their bodies riddled with bullets from a Soviet PPsh-41 Submachine Gun. Fortunately, CIA found them before the local police. The US had prickly relations with the Turkish government. Unfortunately, the trail was cold again.

Two more days went by in Istanbul as they hunted for the suspects without a trace of them. It was highly suspected now that the terrorists would try and make a handoff of the vials to Soviet agents in a crowded square or heavily trafficked tourist attraction, so they circulated around the Grand Bazaar and Basilica Cistern. Finally lady luck surfaced. The terrorists were under observation in the Basilica Cistern, a vast darkly lit underground chamber of water canals, a famous tourist site in Istanbul. It was built between the 3rd and 4th centuries by the manual labor of nearly 7,000 slaves to provide the water filtration system for the Great Palace of Constantinople. When Scott and Leigh arrived, they knew it would prove a difficult place to capture anyone, especially capturing highly trained killers with evil intentions.

Entrance was by fifty-two descending stone steps. Inside was a maze of more than 100,000 square feet with 336 marble columns, each 30 feet high, arranged in 12 rows of 28 columns, each spaced 16 feet apart just to support the ceiling. Catwalks ran alongside the canals between the columns with strategically balanced lighting effects keeping the vast cistern dark with lights that gently guide you, almost dreamlike in quality. Not ideal for this mission.

Inside, behind a Medusa head pillar, Scott and Leigh witnessed what appeared to be an impromptu meeting between the two terrorists that they had been hunting, with yet a new group of three men, apparently Russians. Instinctively, Scott and Leigh knew what was going down deep underground. The Soviet Union had the resources and guile to aerosolize the virus. It was buying the virus from unknown Arabs. Scott and Leigh knew they had to get the virus before the Russians got their hands on it.

They didn't delay. Leigh used a small telescope to zero in on the meeting behind the Medusa pillar. She positively identified the oblong telescopic type container. It was strapped to one of the suspect's shoulders. There was no time to evaluate best options. Scott instinctively reacted to the situation scuttling his plan to capture these terrorists. He told Leigh they had no choice but to attack, kill and recover the virus immediately.

He zipped open his gym bag and dropped it to the floor. They both pulled out loaded automatic weapons from the bag and immediately opened fire on their targets without hesitation. Scott and Leigh rained bullets from their folding automatic machine guns on the group of five, about thirty feet from them straight across a canal. Two terrorists fell immediately to the platform, almost certainly dead on the first volley of bullets as another, wounded, returned fire and crouched behind the Medusa pillar. The remaining two terrorists had jumped into the water at the sound of gunfire and were trying to escape, swimming in opposite directions. Darkly lit, the Cistern was a maze, which made their escape possible only if Scott and Leigh acted fast and decisively. To complicate matters, gunfire echoed dramatically in the cistern underground. The rapid gunfire created mass confusion and chaos. Tourists began screaming and fleeing in every direction. Innocent tourists are now in grave danger; Scott had to determine which one of the three remaining terrorists had the vials, secure it and get out fast.

Scott nodded quickly to Leigh to cover him. Then he immediately pivoted behind the pillar they were firing from and launched a climbing line to a rafter above and near the Medusa. It took. Leigh returned fire on the terrorist across her, while Scott swung clear across a narrow channel of water, separating them from the terrorist behind the Medusa. When

Leigh stopped her covering fire, the terrorist behind the Medusa came out to return the volley. His momentary lapse of concentration, when he saw Scott swinging in before him, cost him his life. Scott shot him between the eyes, dead.

Scott crushed hard against the Medusa pillar and landed upside down against the Medusa head. From the upside down angle, he saw the Medusa perfectly. The Medusa heads were used as plinths for columns supporting the vaulted ceiling. Medusa was the mythical monster of Greek mythology, had snakes for hair, and could turn hapless adventurers to stone just by looking them in the eyes. Snakes were an overpowering menace in the building of the Cistern. The architects turned the Medusa on their sides and upside down during construction centuries ago symbolically, to reduce the Medusa's powers and lessen the fear of the slaves building the underground water system. When he righted himself up, he checked the dead terrorists on the platform. None of the three dead men had the vials.

He swung the line back to Leigh who swung back to him within seconds. The last two terrorists were still in sight. They were pulling themselves out of the water, back on the walking platforms, less than 50 yards off in opposite directions. Another firefight broke out, deafening loud and terrifying. Tourists already panicked, started a full stampede of human flight in every direction. Several tourists were hit by the terrorist's blasts from their firearms. Scott and Leigh knew they had only minutes left to get these remaining terrorists and the vials or a mass bloodbath was on their hands. There wasn't time to go after both remaining terrorists so in a split second, Scott looked to Leigh and she pointed towards one she thought had the vials. They took turns returning fire on him as they ran to him from separate pathways surrounding him. Within 30 seconds, they silenced the terrorist, as they watched him drop dead on the platform. Within a minute, they caught up with him. The telescopic container on his body contained the vials. They got lucky.

That is when they heard the next volley of gunshots from automatic weapons from the opposite direction. The screams from tourists kept reverberating off the caverns. Scott watched as he witnessed the last terrorist return fire now, not on them, but on the Istanbul Police who had arrived moments earlier protecting their flank unknowingly. When the firefight stopped, Scott and Leigh witnessed the last terrorist fall dead in the canal. They nodded to each other instinctively, split up immediately, dropping their machine guns in the canal and mingled in with the streaming, still screaming tourists trying to exit. Leigh had removed her jacket and wrapped the telescopic casing within her jacket to disguise it. They got out safely. Unseen. Unchecked. With the vial secure. Mission accomplished.

Later that night, Leigh gave the vial to her CIA link, Kevin Nichols, on a powerboat in the Bosporus, after telling him the story, most of it anyway. The CIA contact wasn't happy:

"The General Directorate of Security in Istanbul is pushing us hard. He's questioning our involvement or knowledge of the bloody mess at Basilica Cistern today? Five dead bodies, ten more still in the hospital, scores of innocent civilians injured. A major tourist site shut down."

"How badly injured are they?" Leigh asked. "The five dead are the guys we wanted alive. The rest were tourists, a few with gunshot wounds, but most left the hospital with superficial wounds fortunately. Only two remain in the hospital. They are in critical condition. What were you guys thinking pulling off a stunt like that down there?"

"Look, we've all been chasing these bastards since the outbreak in Zaire. They were meeting with Russians and we knew what was going down. When we finally had eyeballs on the vial, we had no choice. We had to go in. You know that," Leigh said deadpan. Nichols didn't like Leigh's response. "Here's what I know. I'm going to get my head blown off when I tell HQ that all five targets are dead. Plus, we have zero proof now to finger the Soviets, even if they are behind it. You get that, right?"

"Keep in mind that you do have the deadly virus. You wanted that, right?" Leigh said sarcastically as she got off the boat, reaching for Scott's hand as he helped her off the gangway to the dock.

After the CIA transfer, Leigh and Scott decided to relax and unwind after a harrowing few weeks chasing these unknown terrorists across the Middle East. They checked into the House Hotel Bosporus in adjoining suites and met for dinner at the Angelique restaurant, just a short walk and elevator up to the rooftop. As they were seated, the rooftop view of Istanbul at night captivated them. There was music playing, exotic music by a group called Mystic Diversions, live under a million stars, eight stories above the sea. Leigh was dressed in a short, sinuous summer dress that caressed her natural curves. It accentuated the way she moved tonight, so graceful, so natural. The blue hues in her dress were no match for her eyes, these two huge sapphires slightly suggesting something sinful was imminent. At least, that was what Scott was thinking when he watched her sit down.

Scott arrived in faded jeans and an ivy linen shirt, un-tucked, as a slight breeze rippled the casual elegance defining his masculinity. His sleeves were just slightly rolled up. His hair was just long enough to suggest his carefree spirit and his sandals gave that away. He acquired a new scar in the fight that day, just under his right eye, when he crashed into the Medusa. It was not distracting at all, thought Leigh, as she sat there immersing herself in his closeness. He was, she thought, the most handsome creature she had ever seen, as she fantasized what it would be like to sleep with him.

Her dream was interrupted. "Would you prefer red or white?" Scott asked her. "Have you ever had Amarone?" she asked in return, flirting. "Never. Is it good?" he asked, returning the spark. "You mean how good, don't you?" Leigh purred. "Let me order tonight."

"Think I can handle any more surprises today?" he said teasingly. She leaned over to him, brushed her cheek against his and whispered something in his ear. As she moved back, he touched her cheek slowly letting his hand fall naturally to her bare shoulder until she was back. The music that swirled around them in this open-air restaurant on top of the hotel was a premonition of a whirlwind that would someday bring these two together. Even for just a single night.

She ordered the first bottle that night. He remembered the taste of Amarone, as he remembered falling for Leigh. They never saw each other again after that night, that evening under the stars at the Angelique. The first kiss. How it lingered. How their bodies belonged to each other throughout the night. The long embrace, the last lingering kiss, before they said goodbye.

The Flight to Sierra Nevada

The flight attendant refilled their glasses. Scott eyes opened wide and nodded in appreciation as reality crashed back in. He realized that a quarter century had passed since the last time he was this close to Leigh. It seemed like a dream back then; was it a dream now, he thought? Here they are brought together again – to serve and protect? They were so young back then, driven by purpose and yet they still found adventure and romance an intoxicating tonic, short lived as it was. He wondered what she was thinking. Life was so different now. Leigh watched him in his deep trance.

She too wondered what he was thinking. Life was going to be so different now. Their lives intersect again and an intricate dance is set in motion. Is it destiny?

CHAPTER 16: HALFWAY TO HELL

Marine Corps Mountain Warfare Training Center
September 20, 2001

The extreme heat of the desert floor in Arizona gave way to the extreme cold elevations in the mountains of the Sierra Nevada. By chance, this September was warmer in the mountains than ever recently recorded. That simple fact may have saved the mission.

On the afternoon of September 20th, in a simulation where Scott was climbing down a mountain, he lost his footing and fell almost 15 feet off the cliff, before grabbing hold of a small growth jutting out from a crevice. It held and miraculously, he held on, despite dislocating his shoulder in the process.

He was able to gain his footing once again and continue the descent. Had it been colder, as was normally the case at this elevation, around 5600 feet, he would have been reaching out to ice, instead of a jutting tree limb, and that might have proven fatal.

His dislocated shoulder was problematic. A soldier in the Unit, who was first at the scene when Scott descended, helped Scott yank it back in place. Scott felt immediate relief, but it was a recurring injury that would find ways inevitably to flare up again.

Leigh took that as a sign that Scott was not quite as invincible as she hoped. With time so short on preparation for the mission in Afghanistan, she met with her Unit separately that night, without Scott, to ensure that they now took every measure available to protect him from any further injury. There were only two days of training left on the schedule. There was simply no valid reason for Scott to get injured this close to mission launch.

Scott too was becoming increasingly aware of his own limitations. After his fall, he became more cautious in the simulated exercises believing that it was necessary to save his strength for the real battles ahead. He was acutely aware that he never would have been this cautious in his early years of combat training, yet he couldn't deny his age, or the accumulation of injuries of past missions. He was fueled by revenge, but smart enough not to peak too soon. He will, going forward, save his best for his final test yet to come in Afghanistan.

Scott sensed the training and testing of his skills in this rugged terrain was more intense than in Arizona. He became increasingly aware that his trainers expected him to master this high altitude training, physically and mentally, before he would set out to penetrate Bin Laden's hideouts. He learned that Bin Laden's obsession with Tora Bora and his mastery of these mountains meant that it was probable that the Tora Bora Mountains might be the more likely stage for their deadly encounter in the days ahead.

Scott loved the mountains but actually hated steep cliffs and the canyons and rocky edges that made you feel like your next step will be your last. It's not that he had a fear of heights, but Sierra Nevada like Tora Bora, was a labyrinth of horse trails that traced the extreme edges of the cliffs and corners of these precarious mountain passes. The elevations were so high and the view so dangerously seductive that horse or soldiers that succumbed to pause and look down, could not fend off the desire to leap straight down, almost as if there was no other choice. A downward spiral to certain death was the only thing that kept you looking ahead as you climbed these impossible terrains, despite the siren's call to give in to the seduction and take a lasting look down the deep divides into a devil's den.

Scott was reminded everyday in training how the mountains here in California were so much more forgiving than the ones he would encounter in Afghanistan. Yet, he knew that these mountains were still formidable to respect. The practice sessions nearly always started with early morning rides on horseback up the mountains of the Sierra Nevada.

Despite the secrecy of his mission, he rode in morning exercises with the brave soldiers from the 10th Mountain Division. They were riding stallions, the official War Horse of Afghanistan. Stallions might be beautiful, but they are not friendly horses. They bite, kick and rear without notice. Many of the soldiers from the 10th Mountain Division had never ridden a horse in their life, adding some amusement to Scott's intensive training here. You also don't trail stallions together or too close because, as some of the first time riders learned, stallions will fight each other. On a cliff, that is suicide.

Scott loved riding horses, a passion handed down from his father. Stallions were among his favorites. They were tough enough to scramble up rocks on a ledge 500 feet high, hooves sparking from the friction without losing their balance. At the end of a long day, he felt reassured that if he was going to fight alone, his war horse would be his only friend.

The final two days of training were afoot without his horse. The training regimen focused on how a single man could climb up steep mountains, locate caves where Bin Laden was considered likely to have taken refuge, and sneak inside without being detected. The Unit team did their best to provide the 'Hawk' not only real maps of Tora Bora with details and instructions, but also selected different areas of the Sierra Nevada that they configured to match the conditions he would have to climb in Tora Bora.

Scott studied the maps, as best as army intelligence could gather, and climbed to simulated caves that matched anticipated Al Qaeda strongholds.

In each climb, he was subjected not only to the dangers of extreme weather at high altitudes but the surprising intensity of the fighting simulations at suspected Bin Laden cave hideouts. It was grueling, yet it strengthened him mentally and physically. His confidence in accomplishing the mission grew steadily.

Despite allotting more time for the mountain training than in the desert, Leigh knew that they were still significantly behind schedule. The final night on the mountain range, September 24th, was spent on training for a simulated catapult escape plan off the cliffs in Tora Bora to a moving helicopter. Instead of actually rehearsing it, she decided in the interests of time and potential injury (that could occur in a training exercise), to demonstrate the escape in video footage instead.

She wanted Scott to know how to open and use a backpack with extension connecting rods that would be his ticket to an escape off the mountains. The rods would connect him to a wire hanging from a helicopter catapulting him off the cliffs and used by the chopper to reel him in to safety. Scott watched the video and witnessed the trauma of being yanked into the sky at such dynamic force. He rubbed his shoulder and wondered if it could take that force? The night finished with a full briefing on the plan of attack that would roll in motion the following morning. Everyone left the room after the final brief, except for Scott and Leigh. She was the first to speak when the room was empty.

"What do you think, soldier?" she asked. "I'm ready to go, if that's what you mean." Scott answered valiantly. "I needed to hear that. Get some rest. I'll see you off in the morning." Leigh sounded like a General. Scott didn't reply. He was tired. He stood up and walked toward the door. Leigh followed him with her eyes, never getting up and following him. Just before opening the door, he hesitated, turned back at her and smiled.

"Leigh…" It was the first time he addressed her by name. "Yes. What is it?" she replied warmly, smiling back at him.

"Tell me one more time. You have my back the whole way?" he said almost teasingly.

Leigh rose up slowly from her chair. She didn't say anything. She ran over to him and when she reached him, she leaned in to him.

Then she whispered something in his ear.

CHAPTER 17: THE ROAD TO KABUL

The Countdown Begins T minus 10
14 DAYS AFTER 9/11

Nightfall September 25, 2001. The flight from the Sierra Nevada's in California to Camp Doha, Kuwait City is uneventful, but not ordinary.

The flight took 18 hours, with one stopover to refuel on the deck of the USS Abraham Lincoln cruising across the Atlantic Ocean. Two F-16 fighter jets escorted his flight. The twin fighter jets were substituted throughout the flight. It made the long, lonely flight more interesting for Scott. He enjoyed the show they seemed to put on every time there was a change of the guard at 41,000 feet. The newest incoming fighters lined up parallel to the jets they were replacing on both sides of his aircraft. In this changing of the air guard, the departing fighters waved their wings before rising up and rolling straight over the incoming new fighter jet to their side as they raced away. It was quite a show and a welcome distraction for Scott, as he contemplated his mission.

Several times over the ocean, Scott also watched as the thirsty jet escort drops down from the sky, one at a time, only to reappear minutes later. He guesses this acrobatic ritual was for needed fuel as they dropped down from time to time, probably to a waiting flying tanker. At 41,000 feet though, even with a horizon of nearly 250 miles, he couldn't see the refueling aspect, as the F-16 fighters dropped down beneath the clouds. He imagined it to be quite a sight. Imagination was all he had as a friend today. He was the only passenger.

Scott sits alone in the cabin of the U.S. government owned Army AC-37 Jet. There are no markings on this aircraft. There will be no record of this flight to Kuwait in the logbooks. There are two pilots and a flight attendant, the same crew that were Scott's escorts in the air since West Point on 9/11. The crew knew that this was the end of their involvement with this mysterious passenger. They also understood that he was precious cargo of the U.S. Special Forces. They could only wonder how one soldier could be so important to warrant a plane of his own and a constant F-16 security force in the air, whenever he traveled.

Leigh had arranged it all, right down to the smallest of details. She had his meals delivered to the plane before he boarded, including pre-ordered lamb chops, a green bean casserole and scalloped potatoes accompanied with a bottle of Chateauneuf du Pape. She knew it was one of his favorite meals and his love of this particular French red wine was an easy call. She knew it might be a long time before Scott enjoyed a wine as good as this one. How had she remembered his tastes? Had they changed? It was so long ago.

Scott had not eaten this well since his last flight to the mountains for his final simulated trainings. Now, as he watched the flight attendant pour his first glass of the "Popes vino," as he recalled his friend Ray from Mercedes-Benz called this fabulous French red wine, he relaxed knowing it was time to conserve his energy before the gate opens to his new theater of war. For the second time during his intensive preparation, he thought about how Leigh would remember everything down to his discriminating tastes for wine. He wanted to think of her and Istanbul again, but then he quickly brought himself back to reality. He was on the most important mission of his life. Think of nothing except the mission ahead. Focus.

Leigh did not accompany Scott this time. 'OPERATION HAWK'S NEST' was now exiting its 4P status toward greenlight. 4P was the stages of training for this clandestine op, Planning, Preparation, Prototype, and Performance. Usually an intensive 4-8 week process SOP in paramilitary circles, Scott's 4P program lasted a mere two weeks. Greenlight was exactly as it sounds: the op was activated for Performance with a start time of September 25, 2011 and stop deadline of October 4, midnight.

Ten Days. The mission: find and kill America's number one enemy. The war would begin after ten days. Once American bombs dropped in Afghanistan, this mission would be accomplished or scrubbed.

Leigh was in flight back to Washington D.C. from the Sierra Nevada's with her Unit. She was getting ready to sit in the controller's seat in room 16. Room 16 was built in the underground fortress under the White House to run Special Operations exclusively for the Unit. No one except the Vice President and Secretary of Defense knew of the activities going on behind the doors of room 16. Although Cheney and Rumsfeld literally had no interest in the details behind these doors, just the results. Leigh knew she had just ten days to make the impossible, possible.

While Scott was enjoying his last real meal before embarking on his hunt to kill Osama Bin Laden, Leigh was on a secure classified access cell phone with Hank Crumpton, a colleague of hers from her earlier days in the CIA's covert operations. Crumpton was the acknowledged authority behind intelligence in Afghanistan. She was aware that he was experimenting with drone technology. She knew because Crumpton had enlisted her own tech specialist, Max Leonhardt, to help engineer the awkward retrofit of hellfire missiles to the pilotless drones and the retrofit was now underway. Max tipped her off to using this TOP SECRET technology for 'OPERATION HAWK'S NEST'.

Crumpton was emerging as a commanding force inside CIA, especially with the build-up to war. He had engineered the CIA's preeminent role using paramilitary forces in places where U.S. military forces did not roam freely. Crumpton knew Leigh was leading a limited ops mission in Afghanistan for POTUS, but he didn't like not knowing her mission. He highly respected Leigh, however, and not only knew her reputation, but had worked beside her on several critical clandestine operations throughout their careers.

Their conversation was brief, yet peppered with detail and nuance. Leigh went into precise detail of her need for Predator drone access and CIA support, especially the new drones equipped with hellfire missiles. She requested top secret codes to access, on demand, predator drones with hellfire missiles for an upcoming mission slated for September 25th - October 5th over Kabul and in the Tora Bora Region of Afghanistan. Crumpton warned McClure that the hellfire missiles were retrofitted to the Predators only recently and had never been tested yet on the battlefield. Despite the warning, he also told her that he had the utmost confidence in the technology, and despite the retrofit engineering, he felt it would prove itself on mission 1.

He told Leigh that he wanted to know more about the mission. She said simply: "Top Secret." He hesitated before he gave her access codes. It was only then that he asked for her confidence: "We're both racing in the same lane here. I'm your sole guidance in Afghanistan. Wouldn't it be a hell of a lot smarter if I knew what your mission is?" Crumpton said it in a polite and helpful manner.

"You understand why we have these protocols." Leigh said sympathetically. "They exist for good reasons." Crumpton didn't want to hear it. His tone changed. "Protocols? You're kidding me." He was getting angry. "The predator is going to change everything on the battlefield. You are on a secure phone with me. You're asking for help with my predator and you want to use it in a part of the world that is my backyard. We're going to war and you want to keep me in the dark?" Leigh took a deep breath. "You'll be the first I call, when I can." She replied curtly. "Why wait. I can help you now." Crumpton said almost in exasperation. "It's not personal, Hank. Take a breath. I have to go." She hung up.

Crumpton did the same and nearly spit. He immediately called his command post deputy director telling him to advise him immediately if the access codes he just gave McClure were ever activated. Crumpton would not interfere with Leigh's op, but he wanted to watch the fireworks if they were going to happen on his watch. Leigh was so tight-lipped about the op that he was certain that his Hellfire missiles on the Predator drone were going to be tested for the first time on a real battlefield. Soon.

Ali Salem Air Base
Kuwait City

Scott's plane touched down effortlessly in the dark at Ali Salem air base, a U.S. air base about 45 miles northwest of Kuwait City. Time: Zero Five Hundred.

As soon as he descended the exit stairs, a standing armed soldier, just as rehearsed during his training, asked him a single question: "Regiment, Sir?" "362nd Infantry" replied Scott. There was no longer a 362nd Infantry Division. It was code, the correct password to get instructions on airfields used in the mission. Rumsfeld had personally selected the codes for this mission. That was done as a break from tradition in the Army. Rumsfeld wanted passwords that tied into the emotions of the codename for the op. The 362nd Infantry Division had been Scott's father's unit during WWII.

"Follow me, sir. Your gear is being collected separately," the soldier barked, under the roar of F-16 fighter jets taking off in formations of three jets wing-to-wing down a runway in pre-dawn training exercises. It was pitch dark with sunrise expected within the hour. The flames from the F-16 engines at takeoff added a lightning effect to a desert storm rising. Scott was ushered into a waiting Humvee M1151, which took him north outside the primary airfield to an isolated barracks, where he was dropped off. The ground shook from the active F-16 exercises being conducted at the air base, amidst a rolling thunder as the fighter jets screamed across the landscape.

Scott entered the barracks. Inside, he found no surprises. It was laid out exactly as described in the training phase with rows of cots, a lone metal table with two metal chairs, and a cooler containing several bottles of water, propped on the table.

Within minutes of arrival, the door to his barracks opened as two US Air Force soldiers entered carrying his gear, a pair of two long steel cases. They laid them on the metal table before saluting Scott and leaving. In one case, he would find his Afghan clothing, faux passport and visa under the Afghan name of Ahmad Sherzai. The other revealed his entire cache of weapons.

He went directly to the weapons case first. He opened it with a voice-activated command. Inside the case, he unloaded its contents onto the table. He then carefully loaded the firearms with full rounds of ammunition, before turning and opening the case containing his clothing and gear for the Afghan mission.

He laid out all the clothing, parachute and gear on a cot and then stripped out of his army fatigues. He began to put on the custom designed body underarmor slowly and began inserting the myriad of weapons in their pre-designed sheaths within the underarmor. He wiped off the sweat gathering around his face and growing beard and put on his salwar kameez (long shirt over pants), lungee (turban) and his chapan (coat). Finally, he checked his parachute a final time and then rolled it back into a specially designed satchel to carry. With his tan perfected in the deserts of Arizona, and the windburns on his face from the snow cliffs in the Sierra Nevada's, he now looked like any ordinary man in Afghanistan.

Scott Walsh was no ordinary man, of course, in Afghanistan or anywhere else in the world. He was transformed into America's most lethal one-man invisible army.

It was 103 degrees. Sweat poured down his face. He picked up a liter bottle of water. He drained it completely, gulping it down to the last drop. Then he opened the door and threw up. He spit and looked up at a predawn desert sky. He said a prayer. He spit again. He knew he was ready. It was go time.

He could see the sun showing its first light over the horizon and he activated his Tracker at exactly 0630 hours. It had a unique new battery and battery charging system enabling the device to run for 10 days without a charge. As soon as he activated it, green lights and an alarm went off in room 16 below the White House. Leigh and her Unit crew swung into action manning their workstations facing a large video screen. "Greenlight is on. This is Eagle 2. Over," Leigh said, as Scott heard her clearly in his earpiece from 6,566 miles away. "Confirming Greenlight. This is the Hawk. Out," Scott replied. "Communications Clear. Out" Leigh answered.

Scott was now ready to go. He exited the barracks, got in a waiting Humvee and rode a short distance to an old relic of an air transport, a most ugly Ukraine Air Force Antonov An-72P, already idling waiting for its Afghan passenger. Destination: Somewhere isolated on a deserted old airstrip near the Central Asian border of Afghanistan, probably in or near Kazakhstan.

He was the only passenger. Two Russian pilots rode up front. They stared at this strange looking Afghan and motioned to him to sit on a pad toward the right side of the plane. No seats in this plane, or safety belts, just a strap to hold on to. Scott knew the disguise was genuine based on their unfriendly stares and eased himself down against the right side of the cabin, as the An-72 taxied to runway 022R. As it took off, the sun was just jutting up on the horizon and Scott could see the buildup going on at this US high tech air base near Kuwait City. So did the Russians.

He knew now that it was just a matter of time before the United States would attack Afghanistan. Ironically, even the Russians were allies. He would have to find his target fast. He concentrated on his anger trying to channel it to keep himself focused. At some point during the flight, the Russian co-pilot called back at his lone Afghan passenger to ask him his name. He yelled out the question in Dari, perhaps the most common language used in Afghanistan. Scott waited to reply, and then staring down the co-pilot, the Afghan replied, "None of your fucking business" in another Afghan dialect, Pashto.

The Russian co-pilot stared back at the Afghan for several long minutes with dead eyes. He didn't speak Pashto but understood fuck in any language. He spoke in his native Russian to the pilot. Then, both pilots broke out laughing. Then, he turned back to the Afghan and barked back again in Dari: "OK then, Afghan.... but remember me. I will see you again in hell."

Scott smiled at the co-pilot but did not utter a single word. Hours later, the plane landed safely. But the landing was not on a runway. The pilots of this An-72P did a great job of landing on an abandoned airstrip, whose runways had long ago been overrun by nature. They landed on an overgrown narrow lane that provided just the right amount of distance for this awkward looking flying machine to stop before plowing into a dense forest. When Scott exited the aircraft, the pilots pointed him towards another bulwark of the old Soviet Afghan war, a Russian MI-24 "Hind" attack helicopter at the other end of whatever this narrow lane of weeds they kept insisting was a runway.

Scott nodded, grabbed his sack, and as he jumped off the aircraft, he turned to his Russian pilots and said in Russian this time: "Thanks for the lift, I will remember to look you up in hell." The pilots both grinned widely and gave the lone Afghan a demonstrative 'thumbs up' as Scott walked over to the waiting helicopter. As he walked, both pilots wondered what he was up to?

It was midafternoon now somewhere in Kazakhstan. The 'Hind', as NATO forces referred to this chopper, was as scary a machine as its designers ever hoped to imagine. It was fast, had long range and could run at treetop levels avoiding radar and it was as deadly and terrifying as the devil himself. In fact, the Afghans referred to this helicopter from hell as "Satan's Chariots". Scott had seen these choppers years before, at the receiving end of its mighty guns. As he walked up closer to it, he knew that this deadly machine was delivering him closer to the devil's den in Afghanistan.

The reason Leigh chose this particular Russian mode of transport to get Scott into Afghanistan unnoticed was simple enough. Its radar escaping virtues aside, it is also a helicopter that was used in certain regions by Afghan's Northern Alliance. The Northern Alliance had pieced several together after the Soviet invasion fell apart. So seeing one, if you were an Afghan today, is not common but not uncommon either.

Scott looked at his Tracker on his wrist and pushed his smartphone device "on" button. In seconds, the Tracker opened the communications directly to Leigh and her eyes and ears team in Washington D.C. One screen on his Tracker was showing his GPS location on a map and another screen was showing a real-time close-up of Leigh across the globe.

"This is Eagle 2. Communications and visual clear, over." Leigh said to Scott from Washington D.C. "Copy that. Communications clear. Hawk Out." This was the code to keep the communications line open now for the rest of the operation. The mission was already operational -- now it is on a code red. A digital countdown in military time blinked continuously on both screens in room 16 under the White House.

Scott boarded the Mi-24 Hind Attack Helicopter that had two new Russian pilots on board in tandem cockpits. Inside the belly, was another passenger and the uniform was clearly Spetsnaz – Russian Special Forces. They asked no questions of him, despite his appearance as an Afghan. The Russian pilots seemed too busy to care, he thought, going through some pre-flight preparations. The Spetsnaz Special Forces soldier across from him did not seem pleased to have company, especially an unruly Afghan. He grunted at Scott, using his AK-47 as a pointer, to sit across from him. He then got up and went back outside the helicopter. Scott could barely see him and he was too far away to hear him. He was speaking to one of the pilots of his last flight, who was now standing next to his An-72. When the soldier returned, he never looked at Scott and went straight to the cockpit. They spoke in Russian. Scott was fluent in their language, unbeknownst to them.

He heard the gunner tell the pilots to hold until the other plane, the An 72 active on the field, turned around and took off on the same runway again, ahead of them. He couldn't hear everything else they were saying. Yet, he was comforted in knowing that the other pilots in the An-72 had said a few things favorable about him before it took off. A little bit of earned trust goes a long way when trust is absent.

Scott watched as the dust rose off the ground and saw the old Soviet transport An-72 barrel down a nonexistent runway in the middle of nowhere roar off into the sky. It exuded pelican power -- as in how could anything this ugly fly. He smiled.

The adrenaline was kicking in. He was feeling confident. He knew he was ready.

As soon as the An-72 took off and the dust settled, Scott and his newest Russian team aboard the Hind Attack Helicopter lifted off. In flight, Scott asked the pilot in Russian how close to the ground could he get at the drop off point without landing? The pilot answered in Russian: "I can kiss the ground." Scott grinned, nodded and told the pilot: "If you're that good, skip the instructions – I'm not parachuting out. Give me warning before you kiss the ground at the drop off point and I'll drop out on your command." The pilot smiled and nodded in return: "I'm that good. I'll give a two minute warning -- on my command."

As they approached the drop-off point in Afghanistan, the Russian pilot gave the waiting Afghan his two-minute warning. Scott nodded his head and felt that pit in your stomach that comes when you get close to doing something that you think you can, but at the last moment aren't quite so sure you can. For a civilian, it's that thing called butterflies. But for a Special Forces soldier, it's an adrenaline rush. He closes his eyes, takes a deep breath, and says his own kind of silent prayer, to his father, to his late wife, to his colleagues who died in the World Trade Center and to every American who died weeks ago on 9/11. He prayed to them to give him strength to carry out the mission. Then, with less than one minute to go, he readied and steadied himself by the open hatch in the helicopter. He could see the ground just feet away. The pilot was nearly skimming the ground, but he was going fast.

Finally, the pilot started a countdown from 10. At 1, Scott jumped and he hit the ground hard, way too hard at this speed. His knees buckled first as he landed jarringly on his right shoulder with his full weight on it, before he started rolling furiously. He rolled nearly a half dozen times before stopping flat on his stomach. It hurt. He sat up slowly, dazed but not confused. He realized quickly that he was intact, no gushing blood. At least, he didn't dislocate his shoulder again. Some consolation, yet an unexpected and perhaps foolish way to start, he thought. He sat up. No broken bones, no cuts, no telltale major tears to his Afghan garb, yet he was pretty unkempt for being in Afghanistan all but several minutes now. Sitting there still a bit dazed, he rationalized that it was best not to parachute out – one less thing to have any Afghan notice even in this remote area -- somewhere between Mahmud Raqi in the Kapisa province and Kabul. He also thought, in hindsight, that it didn't hurt to look a little worn anyway.

Scott righted himself after cursing the multiple unplanned somersaults. He checked his munitions and the multiple sheaves with equipment he carried in his underarmor. Intact. He checked his Tracker on his forearm and saw it too survived the tumble. It was still activated, so he confirmed his landing and location with Leigh immediately. He talked with her briefly. She told him to sit tight there until they downloaded his maps for his ride into Kabul. An old knee injury flared up from the fall. It was killing him. He drank some water from his canteen and popped several painkillers. While he waited for his maps, his impromptu landing reminded him of a story that a Navy SEAL told him during the training exercises about how nothing ever goes as planned, so plan on living with and capitalizing on the unexpected. This SEAL was on a nuclear sub waiting with his team for orders to conduct an amphibious invasion of the island Grenada. It was code named Operation Urgent Fury. The SEALs had practiced the beach landing on a simulated beach for weeks beforehand, so many times, that they knew they could conduct the landing in their sleep. When the order came at night, they landed under cover of darkness, no surprises, just as rehearsed. But when they hit the beach, within seconds, a firefight broke out that was so intense, it shattered any illusion for a surprise attack. When the shooting died down, the Chief of the Navy SEAL Team realized that they weren't receiving any return fire. No one was shooting at them. They were alone on this beach. No enemy in sight. Someone on his team created the firefight. Who? How? When he yelled out "Cease Fire," it became clear that they had been shooting out into the dark unknown, at no one. Why?

It was quickly determined that one of the SEALs was wounded. He had taken a bullet in his butt. Not from the enemy. It was friendly fire. A member of the SEAL team had left his sidearm handgun, strapped to his side, unlocked at the invasion and when he hit the beach, the gun discharged. That single mistake, after all that planning, preparation and simulation, was responsible for the one-sided beach war this evening. Perhaps he probably could have lived with that mistake, albeit with humility, since no enemy was facing them on that beach that night and no casualties occurred, other than his own. However, this is an elite SEAL team with missions that are designed for precision and perfection. Mistakes for this Special Missions Unit are unacceptable and unforgivable. The handgun didn't just go off igniting a firestorm; his own bullet struck him in the ass. He shot himself. His misfortune made the incident a major teaching point for all training simulations in Special Forces training to come, not just for the Navy's elite DEVGRU, Seal TEAM 6 but for CIA's own elite, secret, Special Operations Group (SOG) and the US Army's elite DEVGRU counterpart Delta Force.

Scott knew he couldn't make a single mistake in his solo mission. Within minutes, Leigh got back to Scott on his Tracker and he returned quickly to reality. "Maps loaded, Proceed. Eagle 2 Out." Scott looked at the navigation maps. "Confirming maps. Hawk Over and Out." He headed southwest.

He walked fast in darkness, following the navigation system on his Tracker, about three miles without seeing anyone, nor being seen, until he reached a bend. It was here that he came across four horses, their leads anchored to a tree, each with wooden saddles. No riders, just horses. Scott kept out of sight and surveyed the area. There was no human activity in sight or any on the perimeter. He double-checked his location. This was the exact coordinate where Scott was to find a single horse left for him by a CIA Afghan operative to ride into Kabul. But there was a problem. There was more than one horse. Four horses, in fact. Now what?

It pissed him off. Horse theft is a crime punishable by death here.

Scott aimed his Tracker on the horses and relayed the image back to Washington. That image echoed a surprise reaction too back in the Ops Command Center. No one acknowledged it nor spoke about it. Scott wasn't expecting any response either and checked the saddle of what he thought was the strongest horse. Why are there four horses? No matter, he needed a horse and it was time to ride. In the dark, his navigation system and the full moon would guide him to Kabul. He mounted and kicked his stallion to run. The horse reared up and warned his rider who was boss. Scott smiled. His confidence rose as he rode this defiant, brave stallion south to Kabul.

He rode fast and determined. He thought of another warrior on horseback, his father. He would make him proud. He rode alone into battle tonight. On a War Horse. The whistling of the winds in the wild of Afghanistan replaced the bugle call to arms for the anonymous nightrider of the last cavalry. 'OPERATION HAWK'S NEST' is now in full swing.

He had an hour's ride in the saddle, if he stayed on the road. Tonight, he rode off road, but as parallel to the main road as the rugged terrain allowed. Just prior to entering Kabul's city limits, Scott dismounted and went through a series of checks to make sure he had easy access to the sheaths inside his coat. He is a one-man weapons factory. He carries an arsenal of weapons, including a pistol, silencer, knives, ammo cartridges, two larger sheaths on his chest that contained pieces of a machine gun when locked together, cellphones and golf ball-size grenades. The cell phone and grenades could be triggered by voice-activation on his Tracker or manually, depending on the need for silent activation in the field.

He checked his Tracker on his wrist and started his stopwatch feature. He signaled Leigh that he was ready to move into the city limits of Kabul. Upon that signal, a map on the wall of room 16 underneath the White House in Washington D.C. lit up. It was a satellite live map with GPS guidance to the exact location where Osama Bin Laden was spotted less than an hour ago. It diagrammed every twist, every turn, while simultaneously mirroring the data in real time on Scott's wristband Tracker.

Scott took a deep breath, re-mounted his horse, and entered Kabul. After several hours of hard riding this night, his mission was only beginning. Inside the city, he rode to a designated area for riders and dismounted. Two Afghan men walked past him without suspecting anything out of the ordinary. His disguise as an Afghan passed its first test. As he dismounted, on another large video screen in room 16, Leigh and her team were monitoring real time satellite and Predator feeds of the area Scott would be passing through to find his target. As his feet touched the ground, Leigh began guiding Scott through the city by talking to him directly through his earpiece. She didn't want him looking at his tracker for directions unless they somehow lost communication. She calculated every step for him and he followed her every instruction. She was his eyes and ears right now. He trusted her.

His disguise proves authentic. He mingled in small crowds and walked alone at several turns without drawing any suspicion inside Kabul at night. He drew nearer to the compound where Osama Bin Laden was last seen within the hour by CIA freelancers on the ground. Leigh was soon patching in Predator feeds of the Bin Laden compound activity in real time. It was fascinating as the Predator had infrared eyes to see anything human moving inside the compound. It gave Scott precise real-time information on how many bodyguards were around each corner, each door, and each room. Leigh also had a satellite positioned focused solely on the compound, as backup. It too was streaming in crisp live images. The images were as clear as eyes on the ground. The technology is extraordinary and awesome.

Scott withdrew his loaded Glock 9mm, unlocked the safety and attached the silencer. There are two guards with AK-47 rifles at sentry at the main door of the compound. He avoided it and Leigh talked him around to a side entrance leading into a kitchen area. There is only one guard on duty there tonight. Scott reached the area quickly, carefully pulling out an old cell phone from one of the sheaths in his underarmor. He placed it unnoticed almost 30 feet from the guard door before hiding behind a large storage and waste bin in the opposite direction.

Leigh is instructing him that there is only one person in the kitchen right now, immediately to the left upon entrance. Scott activated the old cell phone remotely across the alley from the guard and it lit up brightly in the night on the ground. It kept blinking. The light was bright, not dramatically so, just enough to attract the guard's attention. The guard looked around before he started to go after it to see what it was. It took only a minute for the guard to realize that it was just a lost cell phone, so he pocketed it and headed back to his sentry post. The distraction was all Scott needed. He already slipped sight unseen inside the kitchen entrance.

The sentry seated inside never saw Scott come in nor heard the muted bullet from a silencer that pierced his temple and his heart in rapid succession. Leigh is now directing Scott to go in the hallway, turn right, and take out two more guards sitting outside another cluster of rooms where Bin Laden was suspected sleeping. But just as Scott was readying himself to spring into the adjacent room, Leigh barked FREEZE. Scott halted. Dead stop.

On the screen in room 16 under the White House, CIA was feeding confirmation of a sighting of Bin Laden in Tora Bora. It also confirmed a simultaneous sighting of Bin Laden in Kandahar. The screen continued blinking sightings now in three locations, including where Scott now hid in Kabul, creating a major discrepancy in the Intel. Osama Bin Laden was now confirmed in three places at once. How could that be?

Leigh didn't hesitate. "Abort." She ordered. She knew if Scott took out a decoy, the real Bin Laden would go into hiding. She started to guide Scott out, but told him to quietly disturb the kitchen area first to fake a robbery in the food pantry, that would potentially provide evidence for the dead guard. After he did just that, he opened the door quietly, and knocked out the lone sentry outside on guard. He took back the cell phone the guard had picked up minutes ago and he slipped back through Kabul escaping to his waiting horse and made the original journey, in reverse.

Leigh explained the multiple sightings of Osama Bin Laden to Scott as he rode back to his extraction point. They both knew now that there were doubles. There was a rumor that a double existed, but they did not anticipate this scenario tonight and it spelled setback. To kill the wrong one now would invite the real one to run and hide.

There was always the risk of Bin Laden going into hiding if he suspected that his life was in imminent danger by assassination. If the guard came to and believed what had happened in the compound earlier was merely a bungled burglary, which ended in the death of the kitchen sentry and some stolen food, he may want to stick to that storyline. The guard knew that if a professional breach of the compound occurred under his watch, Bin Laden would not tolerate it. He would just kill him on sight.

All Scott could do now was hope for the former outcome because if a breach was confirmed, he knew, as did Leigh, that his mission was in peril. If the real Osama Bin Laden felt threatened, he would be compelled to run and hide. If that happened, ten days would not be enough to find him and his security would be even tougher, if not impossible to penetrate.

Scott reached his extraction destination after another long ride on horseback. It was on that ride that a new plan formulated in his mind. He spoke to Leigh on his Tracker. "Track airline short sales just days before 9/11. Find the broker," he continued, "From there, we will find a connection or a direct contact to Bin Laden." Leigh replied with uncertainty in her voice, "I'm not sure I am following you?" Scott responded, "Look, if Osama Bin Laden was brazen enough to plan an attack of this magnitude on America, he might have been just as intoxicated with power to play the same market he wanted to destroy. Shorting airline stocks would be a sure bet, if he accomplished his mission. He did and my guess is that he accumulated a fortune. If he made such a brazen move, he certainly would disguise the transactions under someone else's account that could never be traced back to him."

Leigh replied pensively, "That is an interesting theory. It won't be easy and time-consuming. Is that the best allocation of our resources right now?" Scott did not hesitate, "Unless you have a better idea, the deadline dictates it. We need to find the real Osama Bin Laden and with so many doubles dispersed in the Region, we must find the surgeon to identify the right one." Leigh responded, "I still don't see a clear connection." Scott answered, "My guess is that this surgeon is highly skilled and far from Afghanistan. His services must be sky high. My hunch is that Bin Laden is paying him through a broker he can trust. Find the broker. He will lead us to the surgeon." "That's interesting," Leigh replies, "What happens next?"

Scott laid out his plan. She thought it was brilliant, if only his assumptions were correct. They didn't have much time to assess them. She went straight to work.

Nine days left. It all hinged on Scott's plan now.

Kazakhstan

Back in Kazakhstan, Scott landed safely, despite no real runway or runway lights. A waiting Navy Osprey V22 airplane sat on the abandoned airstrip and turned on its lights illuminating a path for the Russian chopper to land as it neared. The Russian pilots in the Mi-24 who picked Scott up at the extraction in Afghanistan had never seen an Osprey V22 and landed somewhat awestruck by its design.

The Cold War may be over, but pilots on both sides found it hard to trust each other after so many years as enemies. For these Russian pilots, it was also the first time they ever saw a U.S. Navy Osprey close-up. It was all lit up in the dark night sky facing them, with jet engines roaring, and propellers on wings facing upward to the sky. Was it a hybrid flying fighting machine or is it just a science fiction flying machine they heard about? The Russians had nothing like it in their arsenal. The Russian pilots watched as the Afghan boarded the strange looking American craft and kept their eyes on the plane as it flew up and deliberately darted away.

Within hours, the Osprey landed smoothly on the USS Vinson aircraft carrier somewhere in the Arabian Sea. A commando from the Unit met Scott on deck. Scott recognized him from his training days in Arizona. He escorted him off the deck to an officer's lower berth where he could shower, change and get some sleep. All eyes on deck followed the mysterious looking Afghan getting special attention.

CHAPTER 18: TRUTH & CONSEQUENCES

Central Park West - New York City
September 27, 2001

At approximately 6:25 in the morning, two Special Forces commandos in the Unit, disheveled in dark suits, shirt tails partially out, ties loosened, and looking like they have been out drinking all night, barrel into the grand lobby at 145 Central Park West. Their entrance is boisterous and disorderly. They are playing their roles, as drunks, to perfection. This diversion is to distract the doorman at the building and the lone security officer at this prestigious address on Manhattan's Upper West Side. It proves good enough for Leigh and her operative from her Unit to slip in through a side door service entrance, unseen and undetected.

She is here for an unscheduled early morning meeting with a broker from Wall Street. She rushes up the emergency stairwell to the second floor before catching the elevator to the fifteenth floor, while her operative sleuths off to alter the security cameras in the building in the basement.

Coming out of the elevator, she heads south down a long corridor to the corner apartment, where she quickly picked the lock, unlocked the deadbolt with a microcontroller and sneaks in. She made her way inside the apartment guardedly looking for her target. She sees a light down a hallway and follows it, drawing her 9mm Walther PPK discreetly from its holster. The light guides her to the kitchen. She stops to listen for any movement and to assess the scene before turning the corner into the kitchen.

Two pendant lights over a large kitchen counter were the only source of light but she finds it good enough to adequately survey the room. The digital clock on the microwave prominently glows the time. It is exactly 6:32 am. A short and thin balding man with a beak of a nose, wearing only a towel, is standing with his back to her pouring a cup of coffee. She recognized the man. It is her target. Khalib Seergy.

Khalib Seergy is the trader from Goldmark Sterns who placed 'put options' on multiple airline stocks for a single client on September 10th, one day before 9/11. These 'put options' were essentially bets that the share price of airline stocks would fall. On September 17th, the day the stock market reopened after 9/11 these airline stocks hit rock bottom. The 'put options' profits turned into the hundreds of millions. Seergy placed these bets for his client because either he, or his client, obviously knew of the events planned for 9/11. His volume of 'put options' made him an easy red flag catch for Leigh and the financial team she assembled yesterday within her Unit. She deliberately kept the FBI and Treasury in the dark, for now. She needs Seergy for more important business right now.

Khalib Seergy didn't see Leigh coming into the kitchen. He was preoccupied putting a third teaspoon of sugar into his coffee cup. As he started to stir his coffee, she surprised him from behind, pressing the barrel of her gun directly to the back of his head.

"Don't move." She said convincingly. Seergy instinctively froze. "Put your hands on your head," Leigh instructs him. Trembling, he does exactly what she says. "Now turn around slowly," she said backing off him slowly herself, her voice and cadence balanced yet still emitting high voltage danger.

Again, he did exactly what she told him. When he turned around to face her, he had to look up at her. She is tall. He didn't recognize her. But he had no time to think. Fear set in. The woman is dressed in black and pointing a gun directly at his face. He feels faint, fearing that he was about to die a horrible death. But he did not know why? He assumed he was being robbed. Impulsively, he screamed out to her to spare his life: "Please, don't shoot me! You can have anything you want."

Leigh knows that she has Seergy in a heightened aura of fear, but she doesn't want him to faint on her or panic. She needs information quickly so she spoke to him softly yet sternly:

"I am not here to rob or hurt you. All I need is information. Co-operate and you have nothing to fear." She pauses momentarily. "However, if you don't, I will kill you. Do you understand?" "Yes but…" came his frightened reply. She stopped him in midsentence and staring into his eyes said, "Now listen very carefully." She continues with absolute clarity, "Who is your client that you placed 'put options' on airline stocks the day before 9/11?"

"Holy shit?" Seergy blurted out spontaneously without thinking, but his mind was racing forward as to what this was all about. He screamed out: "Who are you?"

"Wrong answer." Leigh replied harshly without hesitation. She pistol-whipped him hard enough to inflict pain and caused a bloody nose but cautiously enough without breaking his nose or knocking him out cold. He fell quickly to the floor. She then grabbed him by the throat and lifted him partially off the ground with one hand. She maintained the pressure of her pistol on his forehead with her other. He became limp, like a ragdoll. He was now in total fear for his life and he demonstrated absolutely no instinct to fight back. Typical of financial dicks, she thought, and she half expected it. So she just dropped him again to the floor.

She pointed the revolver at him bleeding and whimpering on the kitchen floor and asked: "Let's start again. I ask the questions. You answer them. Understand?"

"Yes, yes, yes," He nods. "Please, please don't shoot me," he begged. "I'll do whatever you want," he cried out in absolute terror, blood streaming out his left nostril and falling on his bare chest. "Let's begin. Who is your client? Is it Osama Bin Laden?"

"Nooooooo," Seergy cried out like a wounded wolf. "I don't know what you're talking about. My client is Osman. A Dr. Deniz Osman." He is so out of breath it sounded more like a dying man's last request, he didn't stop: "Please don't shoot me. I can give you lots of money. I can make you rich."

"This Osman. What kind of Doctor is he?" asks Leigh. "He's a rich, highly respected plastic surgeon." Seergy replied fearfully. "Where does he live?" Leigh asked. "Istanbul," he replied. Leigh knew Scott's assumption that following this money trail might lead them to Osama Bin Laden's surgeon but she did not expect to gather this information so quickly or so easily. It encouraged her and she asked, "Do you have a way to contact him right now?"

"I have his number," he said, his voice quivering. "Where's that?" she asks. "I have it in my computer. It's in my study." Seergy is starting to process what the intruder wants from him. Survival instincts kick in. He senses the intruder believed him about not having any connection to Bin Laden. Maybe there may be a way out of this nightmare.

"Is it OK if I get up?" he asks trying to sound rational. She nods yes and throws him a dishtowel hanging over the stove handle. Seergy wipes the blood from his nose, holds the dishtowel to stop the bleeding and gets up. He spits blood into the sink, looks at her and points: "The study is this way."

"Hands over your head. Now Move." Leigh replies following him. As they walk to the study, past the living room with a breathtaking view of Central Park at sunrise, Leigh asks: "Have you ever met with the Doctor in Istanbul?"

"Yes," he stammered, "several times over the last six years." Leigh cut him off and asked specifically: "Have you spoken to him since 9/11?" He responded quickly: " I did. I spoke to him the day after."

"What did you speak about?" she asked. He answered truthfully. "I told him about the airline trades, my specialty." They had reached the study.

Khalib Seergy is in his mid-thirties, short, thin, almost wiry thin, balding with large patches of hair on the sides and each strand dyed black on an oily scalp. He had a pockmarked complexion with beady black eyes, and a large razor sharp nose above what appeared to be a lipless mouth. He was naked underneath a small Turkish terry cloth sarong. This vain prick was selling out his country for money, lots of money, to be sure. And right now he knows that he's in trouble, with his life hanging by a thread.

In his study, he sits at his desk with Leigh standing at his side, her gun still directed to his head. He opens his laptop and pulls up the contact sheet for his client, Dr. Deniz Osman, a plastic surgeon from Istanbul. When she sees it, she said: "Print it." He printed it out to a desktop printer and handed it to Leigh. "Get up," she said after taking the printout. They head into the living room. They sit in facing chairs. She had total control of him now so she no longer needed to have the gun to his head. She withdrew it and put it back in her shoulder holster, beneath her blazer.

For the next several hours, she interrogated him on his activities focused solely on his dealings with the surgeon from Istanbul before shifting to his dealings with Osama Bin Laden or Al Qaeda. Seergy finally began telling the truth and co-operated, detailing everything she needed to know about the surgeon, but never conceding he had any relationship with Bin Laden. He was lying because he knew that loyalty to Bin Laden was paramount to any other interests. He knew that the price for exposing Bin Laden was certain death – not just his own, but also his son from a recent divorce and then his parents and a sister. Lying wasn't difficult for him either, as he was sure that Leigh was going to kill him anyway, despite his compliance. Yet his fear was so palpable that he never once stopped trembling.

Leigh didn't have to press hard to get Seergy to start telling the truth about his connections to a complex financing network that involved the surgeon and his hospital foundation. She also learned how Goldmark Sterns was complicit in the 'put' calls on airline stocks the day before the 9/11 attacks with the surgeon. She knew that Seergy was lying about his connection to Bin Laden, but she isn't here as a financial cop. Seergy claimed he had no knowledge about 'doubles', but he did have privileged access to Dr. Deniz Osman to arrange a meeting on financial dealings. The information Leigh gleaned was enough, at least for now. She had the name of a plastic surgeon in Istanbul, who appears to be connected somehow as a front man to Bin Laden, through a hospital foundation.

She instructs Seergy to place a call to Dr. Osman. She tells him to set up a meeting with the Doctor at his residence in Istanbul for tomorrow morning. He is to use the 'put' calls on airline stocks as the reason for an emergency meeting so they are not traced back to Osman's hospital foundation. She further instructs Seergy to have Dr. Osman understand that this meeting has to be done in person and immediately because of the highly sensitive nature of the transfer and the enormity of the windfall profit. She told Seergy to project absolute urgency, so much so, that

Goldmark Sterns has scheduled the company jet for departure to Istanbul for arrival for a meeting the next morning.

Seergy understands he has no choice and is fully compliant. The call is made. Dr. Osman's secretary patched an apparent urgent call through to him at approximately 4:45 in the afternoon in Istanbul.

Dr. Osman picks up. "Yes." His secretary tells him: "I'm sorry to interrupt. I have a caller from New York. Khalib Seergy, your broker. He said it's urgent." Dr. Osman replies, "I'll take it." She puts the call through.

"Hello, Khalib. How are you?" Dr. Osman said cordially. "I'm fine, thank you." Seergy announced looking wide-eyed at Leigh for approval. "I'm calling about the airline trades we discussed on my last call." Osman looks puzzled as Seergy keeps talking fast, nervously. "We urgently need to mask these transactions for your protection. Can we meet in the morning?" Dr. Osman is caught off guard, not knowing what to say. "I'm not sure I quite understand? Is there something wrong?" the Doctor is perplexed.

"No, no…Doctor. Rather quite the contrary. I'm calling because we must meet to get your signatures on some paperwork and it can't be done electronically." "Why do we need to meet in person? Can't you just overnight them? I can't get away right now."

"You don't need to, I'll fly in and be there in the morning. Please let me explain. There really is no trouble." The call went on for another five minutes. When the call was finally over, Dr. Osman knew trouble was brewing across the Atlantic. He also suspected, despite all the talk contrary, that these transactions he had nothing to do with may put his life in jeopardy. He had always known that working for Osama Bin Laden was going to end badly someday, just not this way.

This was the second call from Khalib Seergy this month. On that fateful first call, Seergy informed him on the day before 9/11 that he placed a series of transactions called 'puts' on his own hospital funds account. He said he had no choice because it came from orders of his boss and that of Osama Bin Laden. The irony in the conversation at the time was that Dr. Osman had no idea what he was talking about, forget that he did not even know what a 'put option' was in the first place. He was totally surprised that Osama Bin Laden and his own trader were making trades on behalf of his hospital foundation funds, without his knowledge, much less his permission. He certainly had no idea what Al Qaeda had planned for 9/11 and now knowing, after the fact, was far more than chilling. Seergy had told him then not to worry, that the deals could never be traced back to Bin Laden. Yet, the call today certainly shifted the consequences squarely back on him. Either way, this is a nightmare scenario.

Why, all of a sudden, Dr. Osman wondered, is it an emergency to meet and sign papers? Why did Seergy sound nervous on the phone call? He didn't show any sign of nervousness ever before, even after calling him the day after 9/11. If Seergy's firm was really seeking a way to keep their complicity under the radar screen then perhaps Seergy's reasoning wasn't as unfounded as it seemed. However, Seergy tried to disguise that very plausible intention by telling him that the profit is so staggering on the transactions that some safeguards were required to ensure that the payout could not be traced. Maybe so, he thought, but an emergency meeting face-to-face to sign papers? When he questioned Seergy on that issue, Seergy insisted his firm required a personal meeting to ensure the parties involved were onboard with the new moratorium clauses for payout. It was essential, he demanded, to ensure no parties involved attracted the attention of the Feds with payout transactions for a prolonged period of time. Seergy also said it was the sole reason for his absolute necessary and immediate visit tomorrow.

Dr. Osman didn't like what was happening here. He knew his suspicions are valid. Once again, he was frightfully reminded that his fortunes were not only tied to Osama Bin Laden but that his life now hung in the balance.

Yet Dr. Osman was as much an opportunist as a realist. Despite all his qualms, when Seergy told him how staggering the profit was, nearly $200 million dollars, he lapsed into a false dream, even momentarily, rationalizing that maybe this was the score he needed to get out from under the radar of Osama Bin Laden. Perhaps this was the windfall that will help him escape from the control Osama Bin Laden had on him and his business. It proved to be a very temporary lapse because the outsized fear that followed the call from Khalib Seergy dispelled any such illusions, just as quickly as he thought of it.

He has no choice, but to meet with Seergy and his associate from Goldmark Sterns tomorrow. In his gut, he knows he will need to run and hide as soon as they left. He has little time to figure out where to hide, how to move cash out of his accounts to someplace safe without creating suspicion, and how to safeguard his children, one who lived in Ankara and another in London. Fear is fast settling in. He knows there is not enough time.

Leigh is running out of time too. She has no concern regarding the illegality of the Goldmark Stern trades, but needs Khalib Seergy for one purpose. She needs an introduction to the surgeon ASAP. She needs to know everything about these doubles fast. How many? Where are they? (If even he knew?) She also needed to find out just as quickly how this Doctor might be able to get an audience with the real Osama Bin Laden?

The rest of the day was spent planning the events to take place next at the Doctor's residence on the secluded Soyakadasi Island in Istanbul.

Leigh escorted Khalib Seergy out of the apartment building via a back entrance unseen by any staff. The security camera tapes were surreptitiously confiscated immediately after Leigh left the building by the operative inside the building. The same Unit Special Forces agents (still dressed inconspicuously in suits) in the apartment building lobby earlier met them on Columbus Avenue in a black SUV. They sped off to Aviation Field in Newark, New Jersey.

At the airfield, Seergy was detained in a private room, while Leigh and her team started preparations. She activated a Navy SEAL team (on standby to the Unit stationed in the Persian Gulf) to secure the island. She was planning on shutting down the island's operations temporarily shortly after midnight to enable Scott surprise access to Dr. Deniz Osman inside his mansion on the hill pre-dawn. Scott would arrive about an hour after the SEALs secured the island. She would arrive to the island with Seergy from the States early the next morning.

A heavy fog delayed their takeoff from Newark International later that evening. Leigh sat behind her hostage on the flight, Khalib Seergy, wondering if this gambit would work. She got up and spoke to the flight attendant privately. After their brief conversation, Leigh went into the pilot's cabin and closed the door. Within moments, she came back into the main cabin. The pilot confirmed that they would be taxiing soon for takeoff and that they could easily make-up the delay in the air.

At 10:03 in the evening, at Butler Aviation field in Newark, New Jersey, an unmarked U.S. Army AC 37 Gulfstream G5 quietly barreled down runway 24L. Destination: Istanbul, Turkey. Only two passengers were onboard, Leigh Ann McClure and Khalib Seergy. If you checked the logs for that morning, however, this flight never existed.

USS Vinson
Somewhere in the Adriatic Sea
September 28, 2001

At precisely 2200 hours, a futuristic aircraft emerges from the hangar bay to the carrier deck of the USS Vinson. Scott stands nearby, in his Afghan disguise, with two Presidential Unit commandos Nick Anthony and Bryan Taylor in black unmarked commando uniforms, equipped with weapons for a raid. When this space age aircraft appeared from the hangar bay, all three of them looked at each other with astonishment. The plane looks like a flying saucer from science fiction magazines. It sits high on wheels, eerily quiet making a strange whale-like noise, lights blinking for takeoff.

A navy crewman on deck motions to them to head towards the strange-looking aircraft. They ran toward this odd shaped, sci-fi flying machine. As they drew closer to it, a ramp opened and they climbed aboard. Inside two pilots are peering out a wide, narrow window on top. Just below them are five seats set in an U-shape configuration facing forward towards the cockpit. There is a built-in table equipped with computer monitors and headsets for each passenger. The monitors visually display the outside of the aircraft from every angle. They took their seats. Immediately, a four-point safety belt rapidly and automatically strapped them in. Lights that were blinking steadfastly upon entering dimmed out. A brief whirring sound erupted and suddenly they feel hurtled off the carrier deck, moving rapidly skyward. Surprisingly, it was not a jarring experience. It felt smooth, unlike a takeoff from anything they had flown in before.

The captain of the plane sat in the center seat, flanked by co-pilots and gunners. He spoke to them immediately after takeoff. "Welcome aboard the US Air Force X2000. This is your captain speaking. You have the next one and a half hours to get some sleep. Your seat can be adjusted into a bed by the controls on the right side of your seat. Use it. Sleep. If you need water, press the water icon button on your console. It will pop up from your consoles at will. We will wake you fifteen minutes before we drop you off at your destination." He pauses then continues: "You will not be parachuting. We will touch down to let you off." The Captain pauses again, this time changing his tone. "Please do not touch the controls on the computers in front of you. They are for battle purposes only. Now just one more request from the flight deck: please keep this aircraft a secret. No one knows the Air Force has something this advanced and frankly, we'd like to keep it that way." Scott and his crew looked at each other. Eyebrows rose, fascination with the unknown, a quick smile. The captain continued: "One last item, soldiers. We know you don't always have to fly with the U.S. Air Force. We want to thank you for flying with us today and hope you enjoy your flight and come fly with us again. Now, from the flight deck and speaking for the entire United States of America, we wish you good luck on your mission, soldiers. Hooah!" In unison, the soldiers yelled out their own "Hooah" and it felt good. They remained silent from that point on as they each adjusted their individual seats, as each pod unfolded seamlessly into a bed. Lights dimmed and out. The soldiers slept. As if they could only sleep on command.

Somewhere over the Atlantic Ocean

Leigh sat across from Khalib Seergy in a plane over the Atlantic. She stared at him but he was clearly not on her mind. Her thoughts were focused on how a surgeon in Istanbul could lead Scott to Osama Bin Laden? She needed to find answers fast because when they would meet, there would only be seven days left to find and kill him.

CHAPTER 19: INVASION

The Soyakadasi
September 28, 2001

The Soyakadasi is an impenetrable fortress. A high tech militia of twenty full-time armed security forces protects the island 24/7.

Any private island that has a security force of this size signals something important is worth guarding. When it houses a highly specialized and secret medical facility, and not one, but two separate helipads, complete with a luxury Airbus Eurocopter EC155, perhaps this private army on the Soyakadasi is guarding more than facilities?

The island is manned at four main locations this night, according to a satellite scan just minutes prior to the US Navy SEALs amphibious invasion. Four sentries are located at the primary seaside docks; two more guards were sighted at the main entrance of the hospital itself; and one stationed at the rear entrance. Reconnaissance also showed an additional two more guards stationed at the guest quarters below the mansion on the hill by the sea, where Dr. Osman's personal boats are docked. A tenth man, a lone sentry, stood guard on top of the hill at the mansion itself.

Earlier in the day, satellite photo's revealed a duty shift change and exposed a barracks, behind the hospital. Recon after midnight showed only the night shift active, so the additional ten security personnel, presumably the day shift, were still on the island. The planning for the invasion presumed the day shift was hopefully sleeping comfortably in their barracks. They also had to find the island staff and confine them. If this wasn't complex enough, their mission instruction included orders to secure the mansion on the hill, without waking its occupants on the second floor.

At 0100 hours, The SEAL Team, landed at the island beaches at three unprotected points in F470 Combat Rubber Raiding Crafts (CRRC's), launched from a nearby US submarine. They landed undetected and moved quickly to their assigned positions and attacked. They secured the entire island in less than an hour, without a single incident or a single shot. No easy feat considering that in addition to capturing an armed militia group, they had to find and confine an additional island staff of twelve, including medical assistants, housekeepers and maintenance staff. Fortunately, most were asleep during the raid.

At the time of the invasion, none of the SEAL Team knew of the lone Al Qaeda elite bodyguard asleep in the underground sector of the hospital. Fortunately, the Al Qaeda bodyguard was also unaware of the lightning fast occupation of the island by the Navy SEAL Team. In the wee hours of morning, nobody noticed that an invasion had occurred at all. Except for ten unsuspecting and now embarrassed security staff in handcuffs being marched to their barracks, where ten other comrades were already hand-cuffed, gagged and shackled. They were not alone. Inside the barracks, the SEAL Team had also moved the additional twelve island staff. They had been found bunked together in living quarters by the hospital. For now, the base barracks became the temporary makeshift holding cell on the island.

Shortly after the SEAL Team had taken control of the island, Scott arrived on schedule, disguised as the Afghan, with two commandos from the Unit, Nick Anthony and Bryan Taylor. Anthony and Taylor were in black commando uniforms with no nationality insignias. They arrived on the island at 0230 hours aboard the US Air Force experimental X2000. It hovered almost silently above the waiting SEAL staging area at the compound, at the helipad closest to the hospital. A single, powerful beam of light lit their way down an open ramp, as they marched down it slowly toward the waiting Seal Team. As they emerged from the aircraft, the unusual shaped aircraft hovered quietly and effortlessly above the ground. The normally subdued elite commandos of SEAL Team 6 exploded in chatter:

"Dude, you seeing this? Is this for real?"

"What the hell is it?"

"These dudes coming out humans? Or aliens?"

"Yeah. Looks like a spaceship?"

"Dudes, how come we don't have one?"

As quick as it started, the chief of the SEAL Team broke it up. "OK, settle down SEALs. Listen up. Take a good look at the men coming down that ramp. They are friendlies. The first, the Afghan, is now in command of this mission. We are support only. Let me make that clear. He's from our Northern Alliance ally in Afghanistan. From this moment on, we are taking orders directly from him until we get off this island. Is that clear?" In unison, the SEALs answered, "Yes, Sir."

"I can't hear you. Is that clear?"

"Yes Sir!" came a resounding voice in unison from the SEAL Team.

"OK. Take a good look. The two commandos at his side are under his command, as well. If you have any questions during this op, you ask me only. Is that clear?" In unison, the SEALs answered again, "Yes, Sir." The Chief commanded, "Attention!" and the SEAL Team lined up in tight formation as the aircraft that looked suspiciously like a spacecraft, practically invisible and almost dead silent, took off almost as fast as it arrived. The SEALs then met the odd trio that just came down the ramp to join them. No introductions were made. Orders were given.

Two SEAL team warriors and the Chief escorted the trio to the mansion, after a brief tour of the complex and its hospital. Two other SEAL Team soldiers were already waiting for them at the mansion. They stood on guard.

Earlier, they had secured the mansion. There were only three people inside. They awoke the butler in his room on the first floor and left the occupants in the Master Bedroom upstairs asleep, as directed. When they woke the butler of the house, they provided him instructions that, if followed, would assure his survival. He was petrified yet quickly accommodating. He would be of use in the morning at the mansion and then would unknowingly join his fellow staff in the barracks holding cell.

Scott, as the Afghan, with Nick Anthony and Bryan Taylor, along with two SEAL commandos entered the house and went immediately upstairs as planned. They quietly entered Dr. Osman's master bedroom around 0250 hours unnoticed. The Afghan used a magnetic jet injection device to drug the sleeping Ayda Osman with a small dose of sodium thiopental in her neck. Nick and Bryan carefully and silently removed Ayda Osman from the room and had the SEALs take her to a pre-designated room in the guest quarters down the hill. Scott, as the Afghan, sat in a chair next to the sleeping Dr. Deniz Osman.

CHAPTER 20: MYSTIC DIVERSION

The Soyakadasi, Istanbul
September 28, 2001

"Wake up," the Afghan said loudly in English as he tapped the forehead of the sleeping man with the barrel of his handgun. It is 2:55 am in the bedroom of Dr. Deniz Osman.

Dr. Osman's eyes opened fully, but his body never moved a muscle. He looked straight at this stranger in his room (Scott in his Afghan disguise) now sitting in his chair at the side of his bed, a lamp lit providing enough light to expose a pistol aimed clearly at his head. He moved his head slowly to check on his wife.

When the Afghan saw that Dr. Osman was waking, he wasted no time: "Dr. Osman. Don't move and follow my instructions carefully. You and your wife Ayda will go unharmed if you cooperate fully." Dr. Osman realized his wife was no longer at his side and he heard the stranger, an Afghan, clearly. He didn't panic, but he abruptly sat up looking around the room. He was searching for his wife. Where was she?

How could he lose the woman he loved at his side without knowing it, feeling it, hearing it? How had passionate lovemaking and gentle kisses from just hours ago turned into this cruel waking nightmare? He scanned the entire room with his keen surgeon's eye. She was nowhere to be seen. He stared with dead eyes straight back at the menacing Afghan intruder and shouted out coolly and unafraid: "Where is she?" He did so in perfect English.

Scott laughed. He already knew Osman's English was good, but doing so as he woke under duress, demonstrated that he was dealing with a man with incredible intelligence and strength. Scott knew the Doctor could not speak Dari or Pashtun so he spoke to him in English with his Afghan disguise. When the Doctor replied in English, he knew the Doctor recognized he was an Afghan and might recognize English over his native Turkish tongue.

Scott, as the Afghan, lit a cigarette just for effect. He crossed his legs and sat comfortably while staring at Dr. Osman in his bed. He held his firearm casually, not in an immediately threatening way. He blew a perfect smoke ring slowly in the air and then looked straight at the Doctor and said calmly yet in a most commanding tone: "I told you not to move Doctor. I can see you don't follow orders." He continued, "If you want to see your wife again, I suggest you do precisely what I say. Do you understand?" The Doctor replied immediately and unafraid, "Understood."

"Good," The Afghan replied coolly. "Now, get up. Get dressed. Meet me in your study quickly. We have business to discuss." The Afghan paused, snubbed out his cigarette in an ashtray on the table by his chair and stood. "I promise you that your wife will not be harmed." As he started to walk to the bedroom door, the Doctor asked calmly, almost professionally: "May I ask where my wife is? And what business will we be discussing?"

The Afghan stopped and turned facing the Doctor directly and replied sternly: "Do not test my patience, Doctor. The phone in your room is dead and I have your mobile. Your security team is no longer operational. My own militia is now in charge of the island. I'll see you in your study in a few minutes. Get dressed. I take it that you want to see your wife alive again. I don't have much time." The Afghan went out the door.

Dr. Osman jumped out of bed, his mind racing for answers to this waking nightmare. As soon as the Afghan left, he quickly picked up the phone, only to find it dead, as promised. He dressed quickly and paused only to look into the bathroom mirror. Not to be vain, as he surely was, but simply to make sure he is awake, verification that this nightmare was really happening. Not a dream. He knew that today had ominous warnings. Seergy from Goldmark Sterns was due early this morning. But it's not even 3:00 in the morning and now his wife is captive to whom? Who is this Afghan that speaks perfect English?

He dressed quickly in pressed white denims and a blue striped starched shirt with a white collar from Brooks Brothers and a lighter shade of blue blazer from Paul Stuart. He didn't think about what to put on, this is how he dresses daily when not in surgery. Under six feet by several inches, Deniz Osman never appeared small. At 62, he was still in excellent physical shape, poised, accomplished, and strikingly handsome. Even under pressure, even the type associated with events spiraling out of his control, he never loses his composure. But none of his personal attributes matter much now. He is acutely aware that he is in very serious trouble. He peered out the second floor window before heading down the stairs cautiously. It is pitch dark out. He sees nothing out of the ordinary. How did this Afghan penetrate the security on his island? What has he done with Ayda? What the hell is going on?

He enters the study, passing by two strong men in black military fatigues, surely part of the Afghan's crew. Scott, in his Afghan disguise, was sitting in a chair casually drinking coffee.

The Afghan rises like a gentleman when he sees the Doctor. "Doctor Osman...(gestures for him to sit and a waiting cup of coffee sits before him.) We don't have a lot of time and I believe you know why I am here.

(Osman sits as the Afghan points to the coffee cup next to him already poured) that's two sugars and cream, right?"

Dr. Osman nods, wondering how this intruder knows this? The Afghan continues seamlessly: "Who I am doesn't matter." He pauses. "Why I'm here does. Let me begin by saying that picking up the telephone in your bedroom was a mistake. You need to start trusting me if you want to see your wife and your children again. Do as I say, if you ever want to see any of them alive again." Osman felt a pit deep in his gut, the kind you feel just before you throw up. When the Afghan added his children into this yet unknown visit, it unnerved him. Yet his steely resolve didn't fail him. He didn't flinch, nodding yes, holding his deadly stare at the Afghan.

"Good. We understand each other. All you need to do is to provide me information. So please no more games, Dr. Osman. Are we, how you say, simpatico with that?" Dr. Osman nods approval. "Let's proceed," The Afghan continues. "I know you have made decoys, or should I say, doubles, for Osama Bin Laden. Is this not true?"

For the first time, Dr. Deniz Osman's feigned confidence cracks. He looks like he was just punched. He is terrified. Caught? His hand shakes and spills some of his coffee. "Walk me through it," continues the Afghan clearly seeing the visible signs of fear now on his captive's face. "Just give me the cliff notes version. I don't care when or how you met him. I only need to know a few things. How many doubles have you created? How do you deliver them? Is there any way we can differentiate a double from the original?" He pauses to let the gravity of what he is asking to settle in. "Finally, how much contact do you have with Bin Laden himself? Can you arrange a meeting with him?"

As the Afghan delivered multiple questions calmly, Dr. Osman breathed deeply. He was doing his best to regain his composure while sizing up his formidable opponent. While he still half-expected to be beaten, threatened, and knocked senseless if he didn't provide the answers this Afghan wanted, he also believed they would kill him anyway. He knew any hesitation in his answers would be suspect.

He was used to processing life and death decisions quickly in surgery. That decision-making skill now was in full throttle. He quickly tallied up the scenario. He is impressed with this Afghan's rather cool demeanor and exceptionally good English. Certainly, he was not an ordinary Afghan. He was highly educated. He surmised that he must be a senior officer from the Northern Alliance. He knew that he really had no option except to cooperate. For a fleeting moment, he wondered how his island security force had collapsed. He came back to reality in a second and rationalized a new scenario with cooperation. The Afghan holding the cards is calm, intelligent, and perhaps is seeking resolution to a problem mano to mano, without violence.

For that single, brief second, he felt relieved. This Afghan, who held his wife hostage, is not a brute. Perhaps, he could reason with him.

For the next hour, between several cups of Turkish coffee, he answered the questions of his interrogator. The Afghan found his subject interesting. Dr. Osman was as exacting in his speech as he was precise in his surgery. He delved into his secret operations and relationship with Osama Bin Laden. It was cathartic for the surgeon, in a way, as Dr. Osman was desperately seeking for a way out of his ties with Bin Laden. Suddenly, cooperating with this Afghan from the Northern Alliance in the leather chair of his study, with his wife as a hostage somewhere nearby, might well prove prescient. At least he thought so.

He began to understand what the Afghan really wanted from him, access to Bin Laden himself and probably assassination, so he knew how to negotiate the limits of this reality and navigate the expectations of this bold conversation.

He walked the Afghan through a very quick history of his relationship with Bin Laden as far back as 1992 and the completion of his first of four doubles for him that started back in 1993. He was already in the business of surreptitiously making doubles and that is how he was introduced to Bin Laden. It was emancipating, in a strange way, like a confession to a priest.

He never mentioned the high he got from duplicating a human being so perfectly, just the facts. He was forthcoming in most details. He carefully mentioned how an insider, a traitor within Bin Laden's own camp, killed the first double. He skipped over Bin Laden's traitor's fate and told instead how Bin Laden came to this island shortly thereafter, in the mid '90s, to meet him personally. He came to this island to discuss the production (as Osama Bin Laden called it) of several more doubles.

"Perfect Doubles." Said Osman. "Perfection. That was most important to him. He did not want to spare any expense to reach it. Perfection was all that mattered: …in his own likeness."

Dr. Osman talked about how this small island was originally purchased and transformed into this insular specialized remote Medical Center Resort, under his name, for private patients only, one at a time, for reconstructive and plastic surgery. He described briefly how the blueprints for a resort complex that contained a luxurious specialty private hospital for plastic and reconstructive surgery was designed for individual attention only: one patient at a time, a privilege for the wealthy. It was designed from the onset as a front for making doubles for Osama Bin Laden. He elaborated and explained how a secret underground elite surgical high tech operating room was developed under the boutique hospital with long-term patient recovery rooms designed exclusively for Bin Laden's personal interests.

It was also built with a magnificent mansion on the hill, where they were sitting right now. It was designed for the Doctor and his family's pleasure with panoramic views of the sea with additional ultra-luxury guest quarters nearby for any visiting medical staff. A large guesthouse luxury cottage was added adjacent to an Olympic sized pool that was situated right on the bottom of the hill of his private residence and bordering the Sea of Marmara. The plans were prepared by Dr. Osman and his architects and reviewed and approved by Bin Laden himself, as the benefactor.

Two more doubles were created by the year 2000. The Afghan interrupted only once during the conversation to clarify that actually three doubles had been created by 2000 with one of those killed in Bin Laden's own camp by a traitor. The Doctor said that was correct. He talked about how one of those was set up as a decoy in 1999 in Tora Bora to test the CIA's use of their new predator drones. They made the Osama Bin Laden decoy clearly visible and well advertised his position knowing the CIA would attempt a drone flyover. They did. They sighted him clearly. They knew. But nothing happened.

It wasn't because CIA knew it was a decoy double. They had no idea. It actually surprised Bin Laden that the United States would use the drones, but not act with the intelligence they were gathering. They had a chance to kill him and chose not to. Why? It somehow reassured him of what he called "The Great Satan's weaknesses" using such high technology, but afraid to use it to fight and kill. Dr. Osman said that the inaction emboldened Bin Laden and his deputies.

What Scott learned next was truly significant. The Doctor told the Afghan that he had always personally delivered the double to Bin Laden himself and that a Bin Laden elite guard always escorted him and the double to Osama Bin Laden at Tora Bora. The guard was assigned to transport the double to and from the island. It was always the same bodyguard. This guard had been a resident more or less on the island in Istanbul since 1993 to protect the doubles while in production. He was here now, in fact.

About that time is when the Doctor asked the Afghan how he was able to get on the island compound with all the security in place? The Afghan skipped over his comment and asked instead: "Did you just say that Bin Laden's guard is here right now?"

"Yes," said Dr. Osman, realizing that the Afghan was surprised at that revelation. "What's his name?" The Afghan rattled off this question intuitively. "He is Omar al-Faruk," replied the Doctor, sensing the name would create greater surprise by the Afghan. "Omar al-Faruk. He is here, now, on this island?" The Afghan asked. Scott, in his Afghan masquerade, knew well of al-Faruk's notoriety in Afghanistan. He is the fearless and ruthless bodyguard of Osama Bin Laden. So, he was indeed surprised to hear this news. He replied, "I thought he never left Bin Laden's side?"

"I don't know about such things. I can only say that he's here." Osman said calmly. "Where is he?" Scott's urgency was evident. "At this hour, I suspect asleep in the underground quarters in the hospital, close by the double." the Doctor shot back responding to his urgency. "Why is he here now?" asked Scott. Osman replied, "He actually transports the double to the island for the procedures and he stays on guard until the transfer back in Afghanistan. He is my personal escort to Bin Laden in Tora Bora when the surgical recovery is complete."

"I see," the Afghan replied trying to hide his surprise as the Doctor kept talking.

"I'm sorry if I wasn't exact," the Doctor responded. "You see, we have a patient in recovery at the moment – the fourth double, as I mentioned, but this time the surgical requirements changed."

"I'm sorry to interrupt, I'll just be a minute." The Afghan got up and went into the parlor. He met with the Seal Team Captain providing him instructions to capture Omar Al-Faruk.

The Afghan had rejoined Dr. Osman after his briefing with the Seal Team Commander. "You mentioned something about how the surgery on the double was different this time. Proceed," the Afghan queried. "Yes. You see Osama Bin Laden wanted a double this time who would have an exact voice match to his own, in addition to an exact likeness." The Afghan looked up and said, "Interesting? Is that even possible?" He asked as much in amazement as a spontaneous reflex. "I believe it is possible and now I am close to finding out. I am most confident." The Doctor went on. The Afghan interrupted abruptly. "How soon?"

"That is problematic. You must understand that I am confident the surgical precision will yield absolute perfection. I worked for the past six months on this patient brought in from Pakistan. His likeness is now perfect, but we don't want the patient to try and speak for another few weeks. So to answer your question, we will have results soon, but Bin Laden is growing impatient. We are late on delivery by a month already and he is pressuring me daily through his contacts to make this process go quicker." The Afghan seemed to be growing impatient too: "That's understandable. How far are you from a result?" The Doctor seemed to guess. "Weeks, maybe less…"

"You don't have that much time. You must know that by now," The Afghan said without any need to emphasize the importance of speed right now. "I do, but it is certainly not desirable." Dr. Osman seemed perturbed by the Afghan's strident comment on urgency yet went on without missing a beat. "Doesn't anyone seem to understand the difficulty here? Even though we have matched Bin Laden's vocal chords in the patient, we have to make sure the patient does not speak until the vocal chords are healed from the procedures. You see, speech utterances are like snowflakes – no two are exactly the same. This is true even in the same person. If you repeat the same word, it will sound different each time. Our objective is just a tad simpler in making sure the speech pattern of the double will 'match' that of the original, not be exact. Our experiment is to record the voice pattern close enough to fool voice match identification machine technology. For the record, it has never been accomplished before. We failed with another subject, prior to readying this latest patient for the procedure in our hospital now. We've made the necessary adjustments. I am convinced that the outcome this time will yield the result we are striving to achieve. It will be a miracle, of sorts, you know."

"I imagine so. Think carefully now," the Afghan said: "How do you plan on getting this double here now to Bin Laden?"

What he told the Afghan next was incredible. "The system of delivering the double has always been exactly the same. So the process is easy to communicate," Dr. Osman explained. "Bin Laden had a separate line installed at my office for direct and discreet communications. It is my understanding that it can never be traced. I was never to use it except to notify him that we were ready to transport the double."

"Interesting," the Afghan said. "Was there a code you used to signal the double was ready?" he asked. The Afghan seemed like he was leaning in to listen more intently. "I don't know really," Dr. Osman answered. "Omar al-Faruk was the one who would make the call. I've never called out."

"Go on," The Afghan said anxious to know about the details. Osman could sense his anxiety, "Maybe it would help if I give you a big picture first?"

"Please..." interjected the Afghan. Dr. Osman started, "It appeared to me that Bin Laden wanted to know with certainty that even his own guards would accept the double as real. So he orchestrated a plan to have me bring the double up the mountains of Tora Bora on horseback each time, always led by Omar al-Faruk. The path we rode up was always the same." The Afghan nodded to continue as he listened with fascination. "He wanted the new double to physically pass through every section of his elite guards he had stationed in different elevations as we passed by. These sentries were clearly expecting Osama Bin Laden to pass by each time." The Afghan interrupted, "Why do you think that?"

"I didn't think it. You just knew by the way they greeted us," the doctor replied. "You could also tell that they thought the double was Bin Laden himself. That was the point of the exercise."

"Each and every time?" the Afghan asked. "Yes." The Doctor said. "It was clear to me that Bin Laden kept the plan for doubles secret to everyone, except for Omar al-Faruk obviously. But he trusted him like no other man. I'm quite certain Bin Laden thought passing this test up the mountain was critical. The double had to completely fool his elite guards up and down the mountain as a test of his doubles viability. So, yes, I can say with absolute certainty that passing the test was contingent upon this mountain pass. It is why we must always climb the mountain for inspection on delivery."

"I see," the Afghan said. "Do you think the guards had been alerted each time that you were coming?" the Afghan's line of questioning was transforming into a more detective line of questioning. "I do, unequivocally." Dr. Osman replied. "It was clear to me that each time we made the journey that the sentries were alerted to Bin Laden's arrival. They were waiting for him and his two man escort, me -- a Turk, with a pastun cloak and turban and his personal bodyguard, known as the most loyal and fearless fighter alongside Bin Laden against the Soviet army, Omar al-Faruk." The Doctor paused as the Afghan did too.

"How many men did you pass? Did they check credentials at any checkpoint?" The Afghan asked. "At least 50 men, I'm estimating. Maybe more. And no, never did they check our credentials." Dr. Osman replied. "The faces of Bin Laden and al-Faruk are ingrained into each member of the elite guard of Osama Bin Laden. There would be no need to check credentials at each sentry post if they recognized these two men together. They revered them and would bow to the Bin Laden double each time. I must confess that I was not surprised. My doubles are perfect. Each and every time we climbed these mountains, the guards never detected anything out of the ordinary."

The Afghan nodded his head for the Doctor to continue. "The climb on horseback was challenging, but it was all about eyeballs on the double for authenticity. What's important to know is that we always climbed to the same cave location. And every time, the real Bin Laden arrived after we were inside the cave after the sentries left. He entered from the rear of the cave somehow. Alone."

"Why?" the Afghan questioned. "I know it's odd, but he always was alone," the Doctor replied nonplussed. "How did you know which cave to enter? Weren't there many? Where on the mountain was it? Could you identify it on a map for me?" the Afghan asked in a flurry. "That's a lot of questions," said Dr. Osman, catching his breath and trying to get the gist of what the Afghan wants. He paused and took several deep breaths. He wanted to answer so the Afghan clearly understood him. He took a sip of coffee and took another deep breath.

"I understand your need for detail. A couple of things you need to know. First, we always went up the mountain on the same path. On horses provided for us at the border crossing." The Afghan nodded following him. "Second, we never went all the way up the mountain. It was about half way up."

"So how did you know which cave Bin Laden was in? Was it marked somehow? Heavily guarded? Would you recognize it the next time?" The Afghan asked in a battery of questions. "It wasn't marked," the Doctor replied. "Just a few guards at the cave entrance point each time, to my best recollection. Maybe four? The cave wasn't marked in any particular way, but each time we reached Bin Laden's cave, the sentries clearly anticipated us and let us know this was the destination. No guards ever stopped us at other elevations or caves along the route. I think I could recognize it next time, but frankly the guards did guide us to it each time, now that I think about it. Once you dismounted though, it was obvious that the location was heavily fortified."

"How so?" The Afghan wanted to know. "There were stockpiles of missiles, rifles, artillery guns and ammunition under heavy camouflage." The Doctor said in awe. "Can you show me these locations on a map?" the Afghan asked and as he did, he made a mental note to interrogate al-Faruk with the same questions personally. "I can do my best, but like I said, I really just followed al-Faruk's lead."

"I understand," the Afghan replied calmly. "We'll get to maps later. Did al-Faruk talk to anyone going up the mountain? Did the sentries ask him or you or Bin Laden's double any questions?"

"No," the Doctor replied in kind. "Not a single question, as I can remember, but al-Faruk instructed the double to say a few things to the guards before each trip. And the double did as he was told."

"What did he say?" the Afghan queried. "He spoke in Pashto. I have no idea. But the guards seemed upbeat when he spoke," replied the Doctor. The Afghan paused. "Now tell me about the cave and your meeting with the real Bin Laden. Think carefully about this question. I am looking for every detail."

The Doctor paused in reflection. "Getting inside the cave is of interest. The lone sentry that stops us always guides us in, as the others stand guard on the outside. It's not an opening to a cave as you might expect. There is a large stone blocking the entrance that is moved hydraulically, or so it seems, when the guard touches it. That leads to a short passageway to yet another stone blocking yet another entrance, much like the one I just mentioned. Interestingly, the passageway between them is lined with sandbags and what appeared to be that cache of weapons that I mentioned. Another wall opened when the guard seemed to push it at one end. It never opened fully, just enough for us to get in. The guard never followed us in. al-Faruk would then push something on the stone again to close it."

"So, the sentry never came in with you?" the Afghan asked. "No. Never." The Doctor replied without thinking. "Did the guard ever see the two Bin Laden's together, the real and the double?"

"No. You know the odd thing about all this is that every time we entered the cave, the series of events were exactly the same. The room inside was empty and we would sit at a long table. We never waited long before Bin Laden appeared. He arrived from the back of the cave, from a hidden entrance. He was always alone. No bodyguards" The Afghan stopped him, "Wait, you said he was always alone? Are you certain?"

The Doctor paused to think before answering. "Yes, always alone." He paused again in reflection. "I never thought that odd before. He always came over to the table as we stood. No one spoke. He always then led the double to the middle of the room and examined him from head to toe. He disrobed the double and touched him. All of him." The Doctor took a breath. "When he finished his examination, he walked over to me and put his hands on my shoulders and told me that Allah was pleased with my work, in Arabic, then turned to Omar and said something in Pashto that I did not understand. Then, he disappeared behind the back of the cave, as quickly as he entered."

"The same sequence? Every time?" The Afghan asked incredulously. To emphasize his point, he repeated, "Every time?" The Doctor answered without hesitation: "Every time. Always the same."

The Afghan found all of this far too predictable. It worried him. The real Osama Bin Laden would enter the cave himself without being detected by the guards - how? Dr. Osman explained that Osama Bin Laden came into the cave from a false wall inside.

Based on his Intel briefings, Scott knew that Osama Bin Laden could very well have entered from inside the cave. CIA had given the Afghan Mujahideen the money and equipment to build this secret headquarters, inside this 13,000-mile elevation mountain, to help defeat the Soviets years ago. The intelligence also reported that Bin Laden killed the architects and construction crews when the construction of these miles of secret passage-ways was complete. CIA had no blueprints so it was an educated guess that this army fortress inside the mountain remained operational for Bin Laden's personal ambitions. No one knew of these passageways inside the mountain except for Bin Laden himself, his sons and Ayman al-Zawahiri, Bin Laden's second-in-command.

"Let me ask you," the Afghan continued, "Why did Bin Laden leave the cave without the Double?"

Dr. Osman replied quickly, "Superstition and paranoia rule Bin Laden's world. He wanted his elite guards to be the test of the authenticity of the Doubles. So he had to have the double leave the cave and head back so the guards would not wonder where Bin Laden had gone. It also was part of what he called his two-part authentication process. If the double passed all the checkpoints down the mountain again, he would be met by Ayman al-Zawahiri and his horseman, usually about twenty horsemen, he estimated, at the bottom of the mountain. That was when they took the Bin Laden Double with them." Dr. Osman emphasized how that transfer of the Double was made. Again, the process was the same every time. After the transfer, he explained how he would be escorted to his rented Mercedes near the border crossing and driven back to the Parachina airport, in Pakistan. It was not an easy ride, he acknowledged, as it was a rough two-hour journey on a highway that has seen decades of neglect.

The Doctor finished by repeating again that the same procedure was duplicated every time. He actually commented that it was that simple. Scott, as the Afghan, made a mental note: and that complex.

Dr. Osman confessed his fear of Bin Laden and how he had no idea at the beginning back in 1992 of his mysterious Saudi benefactor's terrorist intentions. He saw him differently, at first, as a wealthy Saudi who became a patriot for the Afghan cause against oppressors like the Soviet Union. But when the first World Trade Center bombing occurred in 1993, he knew differently. There was just nothing he could do to end this madness. He became resigned to carry out the charade. There was, quite simply, no other option. Dr. Osman elaborated without being prompted. "You see, I didn't have any remedies to my situation. Being scared is not what I do. My only option was to cooperate with the Saudi and so I did. I did so on my own terms. Each double from that day on was marked for my own protection."

The Afghan was shocked, "Did you just say that you marked the doubles? Why? Wouldn't that put you at risk?" Dr. Osman clarified, "No, not at all. I surgically placed a slight V marking on the inside of the wrist that would not attract any undue attention. This way, I would have something to barter for, if my own life was put in jeopardy. I was not going to be caught in the middle."

The Afghan said somewhat sarcastically and dead serious now: "I am not so sure you are caught in the middle, Doctor. You are aiding and abetting a criminal, but I am not the police. You may have something of usefulness for me. However, as you say, if we are now bartering for your life, I will need to know more than how to recognize them. Frankly, I need to know where they are hiding? And how I can get close to Bin Laden?" The Afghan was tiring of the conversation and displayed anger.

For the first time, the Doctor felt this Afghan's teeth. "I can and will help you. But sir, not without conditions, you must understand." Dr. Osman believed that both he and the Afghan could walk away with what they both needed. He surprised the Afghan by telling him, "I read about the assassination of the 'Lion of Panjshir' [Ahmad Shah Mossoud, leader of the Northern Alliance]. You must believe me that I will help you avenge his death. In any way I can."

Scott knew his Afghan disguise was authentic, but he found it most interesting that the Doctor thought this raid on his island home was accomplished by the Northern Alliance. The Doctor was insightful sensing the Afghan was gathering intelligence to kill Osama Bin Laden, all in revenge for the suicide bombing assassination of Ahmad Shah Mossoud on September 9th, two days before 9/11.

It was difficult to discern whether the Doctor's willingness to help or that his sympathies were real. Frankly, it didn't matter. Dr. Osman was now a willing accomplice to whatever Scott, as the Afghan, wanted and he only needed to know what the Doctor wanted in return. So he asked.

Then he listened.

About an hour and a half had gone by at this point when Scott, as the impersonating Afghan, told Dr. Osman that was enough for now. They agreed on a deal. He told Dr. Osman to get ready for his meeting with his stockbroker, who would be here in a few hours.

"Have your meeting with the broker from New York and when you are finished (he hands him a pen) just click it and I will enter the room. I will need no introduction. After our meeting, I will ensure the safety of you and your wife, as we discussed. I must go now."

The Afghan disappears from the study just as swiftly as he entered the island, like a phantom. But not before putting his hand over his heart and nodding slightly to the Doctor.

CHAPTER 21: MOON SHADOWS

The Soyakadasi
September 28, 2001

Somewhere around 0430 hours, after Scott's hour and a half meeting with Dr. Deniz Osman in the study, and a security huddle with the Chief of SEAL Team 6, Scott took a long solitary walk down the hill to the sea. He had the uncanny ability to formulate plans quickly, simplify complex plans and communicate the big picture. But he was still formulating his plan to take out Osama Bin Laden and it was filled with logistical complexities. He needed time to get it right. Time was not on his side.

He found himself on the bottom of the hill by a pool staring out to sea. He checks his Tracker for the time. He still has about an hour and a half before Leigh arrives with the stockbroker from Goldmark Sterns. He is completely alone and looks at the pool. He stripped bare, relieved to be out of the heavy custom-fitted body underarmor underneath his Afghan robes, and stood over the infinity-edged pool bordering on the Sea of Marmara. A slight wind rushed over him. It was a warm wind, almost 78 degrees Fahrenheit, still hours before daybreak. On the horizon, the night sky was bright. The moon was full. A cloud passed over it as Scott dove in and began to swim laps.

As he completed his first lap, he looked up at the sky to witness a band of clouds, now shaped in a perfect halo, surround a mystical moon. It was as wondrous as it was eerie. The band of clouds seemed frozen, never losing their halo formation around the moon. They grew larger in size with each lap, in a straight line that seemed to deliberately isolate a single beam of radiant light on the pool.

Scott sensed someone watching over him. The rest of the world was in darkness as he swam in a protective ray of light. Moon shadows.

With each stroke, his mind raced back to images of the hospital that he toured on this island with a Navy SEAL prior to his meeting with Dr. Osman. He focuses on one section that resembled a laboratory, of sorts. In it, he saw what appeared to be human masks on top of sculpted heads. It triggered something as he was formulating his plan. Between laps, he processed a plan of action.

Swimming had a way to help Scott focus and relax. When he was ready to get out of the pool, he raced freestyle with his head submerged for 25 meters in a record pace reaching the far end of the pool without a single breath. He stopped, lunging up for air. As he exhaled, he moved his muscled arms up and on the edge of the pool and rested. He looked up at the moon and its halo continued to expand. The moonbeam now shone directly on him. He sensed that his late wife, Amy, was directing the light to guide him. A peace swept over him. He looked up to the moon and whispered something to her above.

CHAPTER 22: SECOND CHANCES

MISSION COUNTDOWN: T MINUS 7
September 28, 2001

Istanbul. 0600 hours Hezarfen Airfield. Two passengers exit down the folding stairway off a plane idling on the tarmac to a waiting black sedan. The car speeds off, as the plane engines whine back up again, and taxies to the private jet aviation hangars.

At the same time, at the Soyakadasi, the Afghan saw his Tracker flash in the darkness. He had just pulled himself out of the pool to get dressed and reached over to pick up his Tracker. He was expecting this call. He spoke into it: "Hawk to Eagle 2. Over." "Eagle 2 has landed. Over," replied Leigh, perturbed that she couldn't see Scott. Leigh was using her own Tracker device. There were only three Trackers in existence. The third was on the wrist of Max Leonhardt back in the underground control room in Washington D.C. Why were Scott's visuals turned off?

"Proceed as planned. We are ready. Over." Scott replied confidently as he finished strapping on the Tracker and giving Leigh visuals now too. "Copy that." She can see Scott now too. "ETA Zero Six Forty Five." She paused then continued, "TD [code for Tracker device] is critical for VM [Visual Monitor]. Is there a problem? Over." Leigh replied sternly. "Copy that. No problem. Over." Scott replied. Leigh sighed before signing out. "Eagle 2 is on the move. Out." Leigh ended the call abruptly, clearly critical in tone that he had taken off his Tracker. She knew that she couldn't help him if she couldn't locate him.

"Over and Out." Scott replied feeling a tinge from the reprimand yet knowing that turning off the TD was a foolish mistake, but not a costly one.

He took an admiring look at his high tech phone now strapped firmly back on his arm. He started the arduous process of getting back in his armored gear in his Afghan clothing and disguise. Leigh will be here soon. But first, he needed to meet with the Seal Team Captain.

The Afghan climbed up the path to the mansion. He first met with the SEAL TEAM Captain. He had briefed the captain earlier on the secret quarters underneath the hospital where Omar al-Faruk was in hiding, and gave him a mission to capture him alive, and hold him in an operating room.

"How did it go?' asked the Afghan. "Mission accomplished, Sir. He's unconscious but alive." The Captain answered. "Great job, Captain. Was there any injury to his head or face?" queried the Afghan. The Captain looked surprised at the question and replied: "No, sir. It happened fast and we took him by complete surprise and overwhelming force. He tried taking his own life so we had to sever his right hand to stop him. He lost a lot of blood quickly and fainted. But he's alive, stable now and no, sir, his face and head are without trauma."

———————

Leigh and Khalib Seergy sped off the tarmac in a black sedan headed for the marine terminal. Leigh had just finished her call with Scott when they arrived at the docks of the airport's marina. The driver leads them to a yacht. No ordinary yacht. It was Dr. Osman's elegant new speed yacht, TRANSFORMER, piloted by Leigh's Special Forces commandos in the Unit, Nick Anthony and Bryan Taylor. Not by coincidence. She winked at both of them.

The former Turkish pilots of this luxurious high speed 108/05 Super Yacht, designed by Studio Bacigalupo and Stefano Righini, had been sleeping soundly in their quarters on the vessel hours before Leigh landed at the Soyakadasi. The Seal Team, by then in control of the Soyakadasi, found and awoke the yacht's pilots during their takeover of the island earlier, handcuffed them and brought them to the barracks, where they joined the growing makeshift prison population on the island. About an hour prior to Leigh's arrival, Nick Anthony and Bryan Taylor manned the yacht to pickup Leigh at the Hezarfen Airfield marine terminal.

The Sea of Marmara was rough this morning yet the luxury speed yacht sliced its way back to the Soyakadasi with relative calm. Just as the sun began to announce a new dawn, Leigh and Seergy were escorted off the high-speed yacht at the private residential dock of Dr. Osman. Bryan Taylor escorted them up the hill to the Doctor's private residence.

The full moon still commands attention, despite daybreak. It illuminates a path from the sea to the hilltop residence of Dr. Osman. The halo surrounding it had vanished, as had the Afghan.

The walk up to the mansion from the Soyakadasi dock, took about five minutes, passing through tiered manicured rows of bountiful gardens. The landscape unveiled an exotic paradise, multi-colored rose bushes set amidst the towering Cypress and Olive trees while Mimosa trees with their fiery yellow flowers lined up against a backlit waterfall cascading down the footpath. As they reached the mansion, parallel paths of the waterfall come together dramatically to a single wooden footbridge over an oval reflecting pool. Tropical fish, of myriad shapes and vibrant colors, parade in the pool as if to welcome visitors to the exclusive mansion residence of Dr. Deniz Osman. As Leigh and Khalib Seergy reached the entrance door, a butler opened the door and took them to Dr. Osman's study. Dr. Osman welcomed them to his home. Coffee was waiting for them, although Khalib Seergy looked like he needed a much stiffer drink.

Seergy didn't waste any time for small talk. He spoke rather abruptly, his nerves on open display. He began outlining why he needed to come here today and thanked Dr. Osman for seeing him so quickly. Before long it was clear why.

Goldmark Sterns knew the 'puts' placed on shorting airline stocks prior to 9/11 would at some point come under scrutiny by the Feds in the USA. His firm needed to hold the funds on the windfall profits for the airline 'puts' that they placed in the Doctor's name before 9/11 to avoid obvious suspicion. The firm also needed legal cover, in writing, from Dr. Osman himself to justify these transactions and to cover up any hint or trace to the real investor – Osama Bin Laden. This was not news to Dr. Osman except the moratorium for payouts. After all, Seergy called him the day after 9/11 informing him that he will be rewarded for this cover-up netting him a handsome cut of the profits – anticipating nearly $20 million dollars.

The NYSE (New York Stock Exchange) had shut down after 9/11 and did not reopen until September 17th. When it did, the market fell 684 points, setting a record for the biggest loss in exchange history for one trading day. American Airlines stock suffered a 39% decline while United Airlines dropped 42%.

Seergy was sweating when he finally said he brought along his associate needed to witness an agreement between Dr. Osman and Goldmark Sterns agreeing to the terms under discussion. He informed the Doctor that once these terms and conditions were acknowledged, Goldmark would take and hold the $200 million USD and after the one-year moratorium transfer the sum in a Swiss bank account designated solely for Dr.

Deniz Osman and his hospital foundation. Dr. Osman would then transfer $180 Million USD to a secret al Qaeda Swiss bank account set up by Osama Bin Laden. Seergy laid out the logic for waiting, which all seemed so perfectly rational, considering it was so illegal in the first place. Finally, he asked Dr. Osman to sign the agreement. What he didn't tell the Doctor was that Goldmark's lawyers had buried legal jargon, inside the 150-page legal document, with specific clauses claiming Goldmark was simply an agent for the transactions requested by the client. The clauses also claimed that Goldmark had advised the hospitable foundation that the transactions were unsafe instruments. This was done simply to provide plausible deniability for the firm in any FBI investigation.

None of this mattered to Dr. Osman. His world was falling apart. He had no choice and now had his own motives. He motioned to Seergy to bring the papers over to his desk in the study to review them. He got up and moved to his desk. He started to read it slowly, at first, and then took out his own pen and simply clicked it. On cue, the Afghan entered the room.

The Afghan was not alone and Seergy took notice, with an audible gasp, jumping out of his seat, standing at attention. Osama Bin Laden, the mastermind behind the 9/11 attacks was standing in the room with the Afghan. This face of evil, broadcast daily on these days following 9/11, was no longer a face on a TV screen. He was present.

Except for Seergy, everyone in the room knew that it was Osama's double. But Seergy's reaction confirmed that the double was indeed convincing. The Afghan told Seergy to sit down. It was then that Osama Bin Laden walked over to Seergy, stood in front of him, stared down at him and said something in Arabic that Seergy understood, but did not dare to reply. He was so frightened that he couldn't speak or hardly breathe. Osama Bin Laden stared menacingly at him in absolute silence. Whatever he had just said to Seergy, he wanted it to sink in. Seergy's heavy breathing stopped. Time stood still. Breaking the stillness, Osama's double turned and whispered something to the Afghan. Then just as quickly as he arrived, he left the room.

"Mr. Seergy," the Afghan spoke after Bin Laden left the room, "All eyes are now upon you. Do as you are told and you will live another day. Understand?" Seergy nods affirmatively several times, like a nervous, cowering, retreating dog. The Afghan now hands him a 3x5 card. It has a 212 area code. New York City. "Mr. Seergy" he says again with dramatic emphasis. "I'm going to ask you to call the number on this card. Before I do, I am going to give a series of instructions. No matter what I say, don't interrupt. Do you understand?"

Seergy is too frightened to reply. His silence angered the Afghan who pulls out a knife from beneath his clothing lunging its jagged edge towards Seergy's neck. He grabs Seergy's head by the little hair he had left and places the knife skillfully touching, but not breaking the skin on Seergy's neck. "Even a slightest hint of hesitation," the Afghan continues. "I'll cut your throat. Pay attention, because I am giving you these instructions once and only once. Understand?"

Seergy no longer hesitates. He nods yes very carefully against the knife several times. As scared as he is, he is trying to concentrate, trying to think how his life can be saved from this horror. He only hopes his heartbeat isn't as loud as it feels, pounding so fast and so hard in his chest. He doesn't want to telegraph his absolute fright, but absolute fear is impossible to hide.

"Good. Let's start over." The Afghan said calmly. "When I tell you to call that number on this card, a woman will answer the phone. I want you to ignore her and ask for Lloyd Ballantyne." Seergy's eyes widen, he fidgets, but feels the blade breaking his skin slightly, wanting to interrupt, but maintains his silence in fear. Blood now trickles from a slight cut to his throat from the movement. Lloyd Ballantyne is the CEO of Seergy's firm. The Afghan notices the cut and Seergy's reaction, but he continues on with the instructions.

"She will say he isn't there. Tell her who you are but don't engage with her. Tell her that there are hidden cameras throughout her house. Tell her to hand the phone to Lloyd now. That it is a matter of life and death." The Afghan pauses and removes the knife from his neck and lets go of his head. He slides his fingers delicately down the sides of the knife, as if to sharpen it.

He continues to talk in a matter of fact manner. "When Ballantyne picks up, he will be angry; he will berate you personally. Tell him to shut up and listen. Tell him that you're a hostage and that you just met with Osama Bin Laden. Tell him he's going to kill you both, if he doesn't follow the instructions." The Afghan hands him a second 3x5 card. "This card has the instructions to provide Ballantyne. They are simple. Just read them off to him." The instructions on the card read:

> Transfer $10 million a day for the next twenty days to 20 different Swiss accounts.

> Instructions for the transfers will come via an email to his mistress's email account.

The Afghan pauses for Seergy to read the card and get ready for the call. "Any questions?" asks the Afghan.

Seergy doesn't answer. He's part paralyzed in fear yet trying to concentrate and remember everything about the call. The Afghan seems to understand and puts his knife back in the sheath under his garment. Seergy watches the knife slide back into the sheath as if it were being done in slow motion intentionally. He blurts out unconsciously: "Lloyd Ballantyne is the CEO of Goldmark Sterns." It comes out creaky and weak. He coughs and speaks it out again: "Jesus. Lloyd Ballantyne is the CEO of Goldmark Sterns. I'm nobody. He won't listen to me. I think you need to make this call."

"You think so?" says the Afghan in a threatening tone. "You don't get to think. Your life is at stake here, you do understand that?" Seergy stammered: "Yes sir, I do." The Afghan replied, "Good. One last and important item: When you finish giving him instructions, tell him don't expect any further communications. Tell him if the first transfer isn't completed by noon today, and everyday by noon thereafter, Osama Bin Laden will kill you both within the very hour that the transfer was missed. Then, hang up. Is that clear?" Seergy nods his head yes several times in a very jerky fashion.

The Afghan tells him to make the call now using the phone on the desk. Scott has played the role of the Afghan perfectly. Seergy is primed to make this call. Scott also knows from his interrogation with the Doctor earlier that the phone on the desk can't be traced.

Khalib Seergy heads over to the desk and sits down. The small amount of blood that trickled down from his throat had dried up already. It was just a superficial wound. He takes the cards with him. He looks at the first card, takes a deep breath, picks up the phone and begins the call. His hands are trembling.

At the same time, Leigh is sending the Swiss bank account codes to the personal email of Ballantyne's mistress, Concetta Andolini, from Seergy's laptop computer using his Goldmark's email account. She mentally adds up the sums. Scott is ransoming Goldmark Sterns to the tune of $200 million dollars. Interesting, she thought, the direct amount of the profit for selling the airline shorts.

In New York, at a mansion master bedroom on West 76th Street, a brownstone owned by a Concetta Andolini, but bought for cash for 6.6 million dollars by Lloyd Ballantyne two years ago, a phone rings just before midnight. Concetta is Lloyd's 28-year-old mistress, divorced and mother of two. She had been an assistant to Manfred Drew, a bond trader on the 40th floor at Goldmark Sterns until she met Lloyd. That fateful meeting with Lloyd was almost three years ago, when she accompanied Manfred to Lloyd's opulent summer home in Southampton.

Lloyd was spellbound by her beauty and decided that he must have her. Why not? After all, Lloyd was a short, bald, middle-aged baron of Wall Street. He had been a ruthless, unscrupulous trader and now was chief of the company that was the most influential trading house on the planet. He was what Tom Wolfe would call a self-proclaimed 'master of the universe.'

Lloyd Ballantyne was married, had a trophy bride, Valerie, and one child, now grown, a daughter Adrienne. His wife married him more than twenty years ago in an arrangement, of sorts. Valerie was an aspiring actress, looking for a break in the business. He was a rich bond trader, at the time, looking for a beautiful wife to help him make it up the ladder on Wall Street. Her beauty and acting skills were what was needed to fulfill his blind ambition. He didn't propose marriage; he made a deal. She bought it. Since then, she did what she had to do to help Lloyd with his career and nothing more. That was the deal they made years ago.

Lloyd had everything the world had to offer, but he was always wanting more. This is, after all, a man who didn't need to be loved nor ever expected it. He only loved money and power. He loved money because it could buy power. Power bought the prestige he craved. He didn't care that his wife Valerie wouldn't touch him, since their child was born. He knew that she couldn't care less who he slept with or even where he found it. Just not from her and never in "her" house. She detested him and his lack of loving his only child and his alienation from them repulsed her. They both were trophies, a means to an end, nothing more.

He spent his nights lately at Connie's. He had become tired of the long parade of prostitutes that serviced him at his suite in the Waldorf and was actually getting a bit concerned lately about a young District Attorney in New York, Eliot Spitzer, that appeared to be trying to make a name for himself by cracking down on call girls at the time. Not that a DA would think about targeting a master of the universe like himself, but when he saw Connie for the first time, he felt it was the right time to walk away from his escort services, at least for a while.

Concetta used Connie as her nickname. Lloyd didn't love her, but she was his favorite toy of late. She could easily be mistaken for a young Sophia Loren, in the eyes of Lloyd Ballantyne anyway. She had jet black hair, long, lustrous curls, black pearl-like eyes, with long lashes, an olive complexion with a small mole set to the left of her cheek and perfectly shaped nose. She was tall, almost 6 feet in heels and a body perfect, untouched by the cosmetic artistry of a plastic surgeon. Breasts full and heavy yet proportioned and positioned as much for pure art as pleasure. Her cleavage is the first thing men notice about Connie and never forget. Her waist was narrow to the touch until your hands fanned out against her full, round, feminine hips that arched up high over graceful lines leading around to her shaved supple mound in front. Shaved except for a single short line of closely trimmed hair stemming to and from her clitoris, as if pointing there for the uninitiated or simply an exclamation point. As Lloyd would soon find out, she was built for pleasure. Her legs were thin, long and elegant, smooth leading to veinless and seemingly boneless feet decorated in shining red toenails to finish her incredible beauty.

Her supple body mesmerized him and her curves were what Lloyd was thinking about when the phone rang tonight. Connie was in the process of giving Lloyd his favorite sex. She sat on top of him, a vixen of voluntary surrender, caressing his throbbing manhood with her hands and hips in slow and sensual movements of a woman who knows how to give as get. She alternated the rhythm of her strokes by occasionally swinging her full breasts slowly up over his chest and into his face sliding back sinuously to kiss what he wants kissed and nibbles at it to heighten his pleasure without hurting him. She had just started when the phone rang, startling them both. Who calls at this hour? She finally pushes away from him and answers the call on the fourth ring, as Lloyd looks clearly annoyed by the interruption. She says hello and then quickly and irritably raises her voice: "There is no one here by that name. Do you know what time it is?" She then looks ashen.

Lloyd notices and sits up on the bed staring at her looking unsettled. She listens further and then says: "Hold on." She cups the phone for privacy and ever so softly, yet in a shocked tone, tells Lloyd: "It's someone saying his name is Seergy from your office. He's saying it is a matter of life and death. He even said that someone is watching us right now." She pulls the sheets up to cover her breasts. Lloyd grabs the phone taking it away from Connie and yells with utmost authority on the line: "This had better be a fucking emergency. I..." when he is cut off and interrupted by Seergy. Within minutes, Lloyd looks like he just had the wind knocked out of him. He just stares out in space as he listens. Then Seergy hangs up, never giving Lloyd a chance to react. When he does, he throws the phone across the room and erupts.

"Fuck. Fuck. Fuck! That fucking idiot. That fucking idiot!" is all he can muster, at first.

He jumps out of bed like a madman, frantically getting dressed while barking commands at Connie like she is his lapdog. "Call for my car right now, goddamnit. Pour me a Jameson's. A double. Then get me your fucking laptop and put it in my fucking briefcase. Fuck. Fuck. Fuck!" Then he slams his fist on the dresser.

Connie was used to his outbreaks, his foul mouth, and bad temper. But she never saw an outburst like this. If he was throwing the F bomb out this flagrantly, at this rapid tempo, she knew something dreadful was happening. "Jesus, Lloyd, what happened?"

"Just shut the fuck up and do what I said. Can't you fucking do anything right?"

"Ok, Ok, but is this really about me, honey?"

"Fuck," he bellowed out slowly like a wounded animal, changing his angry tone of voice for the first time since the call came in. "I'm sorry, Connie," He pulls her close to him and looks into her eyes. "But this is serious, fucking bad news. I need to get to the office fast." He sits at the edge of the bed, face now buried in his hands, breathing fast and furiously. "Don't worry. I'll calm down. Just help me, goddammit. OK?"

Connie senses the urgency well enough to know not to ask questions. She gets out of bed, throws on her robe and glances around the room searching for a video camera. Seeing none in sight, she calls for his limo, while Lloyd gets back up and continues to get dressed. After making the call, she goes to the study, directly to the bar, and pours two Jameson's, both doubles.

Lloyd is calling Leo Dinkins, his head of security at Goldmark Sterns. Dinkins picks up after four long rings, as Lloyd's blood pressure keeps rising by the ring. "Pick up, godammit," Lloyd keeps repeating.

"Dinkins." Finally, Leo Dinkins answers from a deep sleep. "We have an emergency. Meet me in my office in fifteen minutes." Lloyd replies with a heightened urgency in his voice. Dinkins shakes the cobwebs from his interrupted sleep. "Anything you want to tell me now? Dinkins asks. "It's a matter of life and death, Leo." Lloyd said it with a graveness that Leo had never heard before from Lloyd. "Understand. I'm on my way." Leo replied.

When Lloyd hangs up, Connie is at his side with his whiskey and his briefcase and a look that shows her concern. "Did you put your laptop in my briefcase?" he asked. "Yes," she replied. "Why do you need that?" she asked. "It's not important," he said, but sensing her fear of involvement, he paused and then told her. "Part of that call was that they had a camera in it, recording us, so I need to get both of our laptops debugged." That was an easy lie. He already knew her password so he did not need to ask for it. "Of course, darling," she said buying his lie. He took the briefcase, downed his whiskey in a two gulps, took a deep breath and left. He did not kiss her goodbye. He never did. She went to the bar and grabbed her drink. She sighed, thankful that this madman is out of the house.

The Soyakadasi

As soon as Seergy hangs up, the Afghan signals Bryan Taylor to take him away. He escorts Seergy back down the hill to the yacht. Seergy is noticeably frightened, uncertain what happens next. He's not asking any more questions this morning. He's resigned to following orders. Resignation is what happens when you are in fear of your life constantly in a 24-hour period.

As soon as Khalib Seergy is out of the room, and despite the tension in the room, Dr. Osman asks calmly: "Can I see my wife now?" The Afghan reassures him: "Soon. You will be with her tonight," the Afghan replied. "We are working on elements of the plan we discussed earlier and they are all within the realm of happening quickly." The Afghan paused. "But first, I have something for you to do immediately."

"I don't understand," said the Doctor. "Let me explain," the Afghan countered. He then told Dr. Osman that he needed a mask made right away, a perfect mask, so that he could masquerade as a double for Omar al-Faruk. He asked: "How quickly can that be done?" Dr. Osman was only beginning to see where this might be leading. The plan he discussed with the Afghan earlier called for planning an imminent rendezvous with Osama Bin Laden and the transfer of the double. But making a mask of Omar al-Faruk was clearly a new angle. While not understanding it all, he knew to listen carefully and follow instructions. He replied: "Since Omar al-Faruk is here, I could make his mold in the next hour if he cooperated but frankly, I don't see that happening. Even if he did, I would need several more hours to sculpt it and mold it to your face."

"I can assure you that he will cooperate," the Afghan replied confidently. "Time is running out, we need to get started. Your timetable to arrange the transfer of the double also needs to be moved up. We need to meet with Bin Laden in Afghanistan now."

"When?" asks the Doctor knocked off guard. "Tomorrow," The Afghan replies. "Whoa..." the Doctor moans. "I'm only now beginning to understand your plan fully. Please I want to cooperate. But, I don't think you fully understand how all this works," the Doctor answered. "Allow me to explain. Please?" The Afghan was curious. "Go ahead."

Dr. Osman took a deep breath. "Thank you. You see after the mold is made, I still need to surgically transplant hair and skin surfaces to the mask to make it perfect, then I would need 48 hours, at a minimum, to sculpt it, dry it and make it fit perfectly to your profile. This is required so the neck extensions fit perfectly and hold up to both hot and cold extremes," the Doctor said in almost a clinical tone, as if he was more comfortable talking about surgery than the details of his escape from all this madness.

The Afghan cut him off. "You need to realize the sense of urgency here. You have 24 hours. Do I make myself clear?" the Afghan was losing his patience.

"I'll do the best I can," Dr. Osman said reluctantly feeling the danger and pressure coming from the unknown Afghan. The Afghan didn't appreciate Osman's tone and responded sarcastically and with authority: "I'm sure you will, Doctor. Make it perfect if you want to come back alive. 24 hours. The clock is ticking." The Doctor got the cold and deadly message. "It will be perfect. That's what I do."

"Good. We'll leave as soon as the mask is ready." The Afghan said more calmly now. "It is time to call your contact to arrange the transfer." The Doctor's head was spinning, "Please, I totally understand your sense of urgency. But if this plan is to work, that's too soon to have Bin Laden inspect the double. The double should not speak yet, it could destroy his new vocal chords..." The Afghan cuts him off mid-sentence. "I'll just be a minute," and leaves the room.

The Doctor is getting nervous. The Afghan returns with Nick Anthony and Osama's double. The Afghan, speaking Arabic, tells Osama's double to speak. The double speaks, also in Arabic, saying "Dr. Osman. How do I sound? Is it a perfect match?"

Dr. Osman stands, a smile spontaneously appears and he puts his hands on the double's shoulders, looking into the eyes of the double: "Perfect, it is perfect." He then puts his fingers on the double's lips: "Please do not speak again until we go back to Afghanistan. Your vocal chords are still recuperating. Understand?" The double nods his head. Dr. Osman turns next to the Afghan and exclaims: "This feat has never been accomplished before. Let us not squander such a victory in medical science. Bin Laden will expect a voice match test on-site."

"I have no intention of failing," replied the Afghan. "But time is not our friend." The Afghan motions to Nick to bring Osama's double back to the outer room. "The timetable is non-negotiable. I need you to make the call. Right now," The Afghan tells the Doctor. They discussed the best way to explain to whoever answered the phone why Omar al-Faruk was not making this call and why Dr. Osman was instead. The Afghan realized the danger that this deviation from the norm might cause. But he has no choice. His mission deadline is approaching. He has no time left.

Dr. Osman tries to shake his nervousness and makes the call, in Arabic, to Bin Laden's deputy from his office, on the red secure phone on the side of his desk that has a direct connection to UBL; there is no dialer. The Afghan and Leigh took notice of this unusual phone that had some unique wiring to an odd device. Dr. Osman told them that it was installed that way so that there was no way for a call to be traced. Neither had ever seen anything like it before. They sat beside the Doctor listening in on the call, as best they could. When Dr. Osman got off the phone, he filled them in on his conversation. Bin Laden's deputy didn't seem concerned that the Doctor was calling instead of his trusted bodyguard. It fortunately never came up. The deputy confirmed the rendezvous in Tora Bora: 1500 hours September 30. A little more than 38 hours from now. Scott had a suspicion that Osama Bin Laden wanted expediency as much as he did, for different reasons.

The rendezvous with Osama Bin Laden is now scheduled. It fit the schedule perfectly, perhaps too perfectly. Perfection was sounding all too neat for the Afghan, Scott.

Dr. Osman sits precariously at his study processing a very scary start of a new day, and it was only beginning. He felt his life spiraling out of control. He needs to go into surgery next to make a disguise while still awaiting a promised reunion with his wife. Was she really alive? Can he trust this intruder from the Northern Alliance? Is this plan crazy? But then what are the options?

He wondered if his life would end here in Istanbul today or on a mountaintop in Tora Bora in the days to come. Even as he contemplated his uncertain future, he was puzzled by and did not know the woman still present in the room with the Afghan. She was introduced as an American associate from Goldmark Sterns. No name was given. Who was she, he thought? Why was she here? She never spoke. He never asked. He wondered though. She came with Khalib Seergy, but if she is his associate, why didn't she leave with him?

He suspected she is CIA. How else could the Afghan guarantee that he is to be placed into a witness protection system in the USA after the transfer? The whole thing sounds ridiculous, he mused, assuming if he survives whatever this Afghan is planning during this next body double transfer to Osama Bin Laden. He wasn't even too sure what a witness protection system meant. Yet, somehow he knew it included a new identity, living in the USA with his wife and with a promised 10 million dollars in the bank. At least, that was the inherent promise made by the Afghan from the Northern Alliance. It certainly wasn't etched in a contract, yet it was a far better option than the only one he had left: run and hide. What other choices did he have anyway to get his wife back and safe? And what choice is left that also can assure his children's safety? Safe, he thought, what a crazy notion that was in the first place. This is crazy. Staying alive, protecting his family is good enough for now.

Nick Anthony returned to the study, informing the Afghan that the guard Omar al-Faruk was captured alive and is now stable in the operating room ready for Dr. Osman. The Afghan turned to Dr. Osman and told him to go with Nick. Nick and Dr. Osman left immediately.

Scott, in his obviously perfect disguise as the Afghan, turned to Leigh. He sighed and exclaimed: "That was exhausting." Leigh laughed. "I'll get you another cup of coffee. I've got the maps with me. We have a lot of work to do." Scott smiled at Leigh, "That sounds good. This plan is actually coming together. It just seems too damn easy, don't you think?" Leigh doesn't hesitate, "Easy? Let's pray it is. You get one day's rest and then you leave for Afghanistan."

During the next several hours, Scott and Leigh hammered out the plan to assassinate Osama Bin Laden. Everything is moving fast. Once the plan was agreed upon, planning shifted to the escape plan. The priority was proof of death, getting the evidence package back to the States. They also needed to coordinate a Predator drone attack with CIA to take out 20 horsemen who would be waiting to transfer the double at the end of the series of mountain caves bordering Pakistan. Based on his conversation with Dr. Osman and assuming he can trust him, Scott believed that Ayman al-Zawahiri would be one of those horsemen waiting for the double. This will be a prized bonus kill to Osama Bin Laden's death. Yet both Scott and Leigh understood that this part of the plan was a secondary objective.

With time running out, Scott and Leigh pored over maps, locations and exact coordinates, especially where the horseback regiment of Ayman al-Zawahiri might catch up to Scott for the transfer of the double. The hazards and complications were many and particularly bound to the aftermath and residual effects of the Drone attack on Ayman al-Zawahiri's twenty horsemen. So too rests the unanswered questions to a yet unknown series of events impacting from the success or failure of the mission. How many others might be watching? How many others will hear about it? How fast might it be reported? With the number 1 and number 2 Al Qaeda leaders assassinated on a single day, will a communications meltdown occur on the mountains of Tora Bora? How to assure that the evidence of Bin Laden's death be secured and get safely back to the USA? What is the best method for escape? What happens next?

Leigh agrees with Scott's overall plan, despite the calculated dangers, but sees flaws with two critical elements: First, his reliance on the Predator Drone with hellfire missiles for an escape plan. These hellfire missiles on the Predator have never been tested on the battlefield. What if they failed? With that as a real possibility, she felt if Scott succeeded in killing Bin Laden, that he needed to escape with the evidence of the kill far more quickly, even before he descended down the mountain. The evidence of Osama Bin Laden's assassination is tantamount to convince the world of this victory. So to Leigh, Scott's escape back with the evidence is the #1 priority. Frankly, she didn't care if the Doctor or the double made it back. Second, she didn't like Scott's insistence not to kill Osama's double, in the first place. Scott had promised Osama's double safe haven in Pakistan and a $10 million Swiss bank account if he cooperated. Why had he done that? Scott is convinced that hiding the Double in Pakistan is important because the Double might yet prove to be a rare asset for future missions. Leigh loved his optimism, but she wasn't thinking about future missions when this one still seemed impossible.

In the end, Scott and Leigh discussed her conditions and alternatives and finally hashed out their differences. With some compromises made, the plan to assassinate Osama Bin Laden was now agreed upon. Plan A was revised and then set in stone. Leigh will head back to Washington D.C. immediately. All systems go.

There is no plan B in this business, just rare second chances. Osama Bin Laden will be dead before sundown on September 30th, if all goes as planned.

CHAPTER 23: ALL SYSTEMS GO

September 29, 2001

The plan to kill Osama Bin Laden was set in motion. What had seemed impossible just days ago, now looked increasingly possible.

On the plane back to Washington, Leigh began engaging operational codes on her secure laptop, and opening up lines of communication with the CIA for the use of an all-new weapon system: Predator drones, equipped with hellfire missiles. When she completed this task, she made the first of two important calls.

The first call en route was to an old friend of Scott's, Axel Andersson, in Gothenburg, Sweden. She needed to find a safe house for Dr. Osman and his wife, until the witness protection system could relocate them safely to the States. Scott had informed Leigh that Axel could be trusted to provide safe haven.

She made direct contact with Axel at his summer home on a West Coast archipelago. It was a few hours north of Gothenburg, Sweden. After a brief introduction, Leigh made her unusual request, ending with a question. Axel didn't reply quickly and there was a long pause in the call. Leigh knew she laid out a complicated request that might raise more questions than she could answer, but she had no choice. Finally, Axel spoke: "I was notified of Scott's death on 9/11. We were close friends. You must know that I would do anything for him. But how do I know that you are, who you say you are?"

"Because words are easy, like the wind; faithful friends are hard to find," Leigh replied quoting Shakespeare. Scott had told her to use this quote as a credential with Axel. He would know upon hearing it that she could be trusted. "Go on," he replied.

Leigh briefed Axel over the phone. She had never met him, but she did so without reservation, yet never revealing that Scott was still alive as a secret agent. When the briefing ended, Axel added that he would protect the confidentiality of her request to his own death, after he knew the secrecy required of the request. Leigh never needed to advise Axel of the danger of harboring the Doctor and his wife. She never asked him to protect the confidentiality of the request either. Axel was all in for his late friend. Scott knew his friend well.

It was morning, about 0912 hours, on a Saturday in Sweden when the call ended. Axel put down his mobile phone on the kitchen counter, picked up his coffee mug, looked out at the North Sea and sighed. His wife, Monika, asked him who was on the phone so early this morning? He broke his stare at the sea and turned to Monika. "A Ghost," he said. He picked up his mobile phone and slipped outside to walk on sands that so often found him solace and balance. Monika walked out to the porch, as Axel was already on the path to the sea. She sensed imminent danger. She whispered to herself: "God help us."

Leigh moved on to her next task tying up loose ends. She needed to find a permanent hiding place for Osama Bin Laden's double, and at the same time, turn him back in Al Qaeda's custody without any trace to an American intelligence operation. This complicated the whereabouts of a safe haven for the double and made her job of keeping tabs on the double that much more complicated long term.

Her next call was to Fran Tiefenthaler, a former CIA agent who had vast experience in the region. She had previously been stationed as a field agent in Pakistan, until being made in charge of tradecraft on her Unit team. Fran was already entrenched in the ops command center underground at the White House. It was 0300 hours in the White House when her call came in.

Fran would be one of many who are awake at work at this ungodly hour protecting and serving the United States of America. There were some things Fran needed to know. There were things Fran must never know. Leigh, restless and without much sleep, still felt ready enough to walk Fran through the details that she needed to know. She carefully outlined what she wanted Fran to do next.

The CIA recruited Fran Tiefenthaler several years before Leigh was inducted. She became a candidate based on circumstance. Fran had married an Iranian student while she and her husband were students at Princeton University. She dropped out of college when she became pregnant in her sophomore year. After having the child, a boy, in New Jersey, her husband brought them all to Iran for the summer. He decided at the end of summer that they should stay in Iran permanently. Fran wanted to return. He would not permit it. They argued about it. He became physically and verbally abusive.

She was nearly killed in 1968 after a vicious beating that occurred when he found plane tickets, hidden in her drawer, for her and her son back to the United States. That near death experience didn't scare her or stop her. She was dogged in her pursuit to get her child out of harms way. She kept plotting a way to get home to America, despite the difficulties and personal danger, in trying to get her son out with her. Her life became a living hell. She suffered emotional and physical beatings daily by her husband. Finally, her plotting ended one night when her abusive husband not only beat her to a pulp, but also tragically killed his son in a wild rage. It was just two days before Christmas in 1968.

Despite her weakened and bloody state, she managed to escape from her husband fleeing to the U.S. Embassy that night before reporting the murder. Fran was provided asylum at the U.S. Embassy receiving medical treatment until she was healthy enough to return to the United States on Christmas Day. The Ambassador's attaché, who finally found her safe exit out of Iran, was also an undercover CIA field agent. He recruited Fran to the CIA the following year. Fran became one of the CIA's best field agents in the Middle East and had recruited more spies within Iran and Iraq and more recently, in Pakistan, than any other agent during her thirty-two year career. She was a ruthless operator and her spy network was not only impressive in size but by the amount of credible intelligence she continually gathered.

She was called upon early in her own career to recruit Leigh McClure to the CIA's clandestine service back in October 1970. Leigh's recruitment was no accident. It came immediately after Leigh's husband's senseless death as a passenger aboard TWA Flight 741 on September 6, 1970 from Frankfurt International Airport, Germany destined for John F. Kennedy International Airport in New York. That plane never made it to New York. Instead, it was hijacked by the Popular Front for the Liberation of Palestine.

September 6, 1970 was a harrowing day in flight history, as another four more flights to New York from Switzerland, Amsterdam, and London were part of the hijacking master plan. Before the day ended, TWA Flight 741 and Swissair Flight 100 diverted to Dawson's Field in Amman, Jordan with 310 hostages.

On the very next day, the hijackers in Jordan held a media event. They told the international press that they had renamed Dawson's Field to "Revolution Airport" and in front of the cameras, lined up hundreds of hostages on the sand facing the hijacked planes on the tarmac. They announced they would return these hostages for the release of all their political prisoners jailed in Israel. Seeing her husband lined up in the sand on TV live, Leigh, like so many other relatives of hostages, had scant hope that she would ever see her husband again.

Surprisingly, most were freed after September 11, 1970 because of a hostage deal made by the British. Leigh's husband was not among them. One of the freed hostages later told her that the hijackers didn't believe that her husband was an American so they tortured him in an attempt to have him confess that he was an Israeli soldier. No one knows what happened next except that these terrorists simply beat him to near death before publicly beheading him. Leigh was broken.

Months later, after her husband's body was retrieved, flown back and his funeral was held, Fran reached out and recruited Leigh to the CIA. Leigh joined the CIA without hesitation. She found purpose in her life with a career that could avenge her husband's death. She maintained a close relationship with Fran from that day forward.

No one ever really knew how special that friendship grew over the years at CIA. Yet those at CIA who knew them ever doubted the indelible bond they shared. While their careers crisscrossed the Middle East on assignments over a thirty-year span, their contact was minimal.

That is the official story. With their past as prologue to their lasting friendship, rumor within CIA rank and file also has it that they actually worked on special assignments together in the then Soviet Union bloc during the gallop to glasnost. It was during the height of the Cold War that Leigh and Fran forged their friendship and where a professional bond between two super agents for the CIA became so personal.

In the inner circles of this clandestine universe, it was no surprise to some that during the Hostage Crisis in Iran in 1979 that Fran's ex-husband, who was never prosecuted for the death of her son, was found killed in his home in Tehran. When the police found his body, they discovered bullet holes to his head and heart apparently shot in close range with 4mm bullets. It was also rumored that there was a black widow dancing in his mouth at the crime scene.

Leigh continues her conversation with Fran while airborne en route to Washington D.C., somewhere over the Atlantic. "I understand my mission," Fran said after being briefed. "How much time do I have?" There was a pause before Leigh replied.

Fran calculated the time she needed to find a Pakistani ISI agent [Pakistan's Inter Services Intelligence agency] in her book that could be bribed and secure a long-term hideout to hide a double of Osama Bin Laden.

"24 hours, give or take," Leigh replied. "The timing sucks," Fran said calmly. "But understand the urgency here. The amount of the bribe helps. It is large, which is good and bad. But I need to be on the ground in Pakistan to make this happen." Leigh knew this aspect of the overall mission might be impossible, because of the time constraints, yet she had no option. "I have a plane waiting for you at Andrews [Air Force Base]." Fran replied with a question, "Do you know when and where the transfer occurs yet?" Leigh answered, "The transfer will occur at approximately 1600 hours Sunday afternoon at Parachina Airport, inside the aviation hangar on the west side. Are you familiar with the airport?"

"All too well," Fran said. "Sorry excuse for an airport. You want me there for the transfer?" Leigh replied, "I do. Your guy can board the plane inside the hangar for the transfer. It is an unmarked Gulfstream G5 identi-fied on its tailfin with the alpha numbers: JJF44. You got that?"

"Copy that." Fran replied. "Your contact can board alone and check the account access online onboard if he doesn't trust you. He can call from the plane to verify access to funds and the transfer." Fran commented, "I like that." Leigh added, "Bin Laden's double will be disguised for transport to a safe house. "

"Really? Disguised as what?" Fran asks. Leigh replied, "As any Afghan. With papers identifying him as Omar al-Faruk." Fran laughs, "Any Afghan?" she pauses. "He's Bin Laden's strongman," Fran replies excitedly. "So what else are you not telling me?"

"That's all you need to know for now," Leigh said. "Got it. I'm on it." were Fran's last words. "Godspeed." were Leigh's, as well.

It was 0315 hours in Washington DC, on Saturday September 29th when Leigh completed her call with Fran from her flight from Istanbul. Istanbul time was 7 hours ahead of Washington, DC, so everything was now in play for zero hour to begin tomorrow at dawn when Scott leaves Istanbul for Tora Bora to fulfill the mission.

Leigh arrived back in Washington surprisingly rested. She learned early in her career how to get restful sleep on planes during intercontinental transit. She is picked up at Andrews Air Force base in a White House black Lincoln Town car sedan, with two Marine guards attached to the White House as escorts. They drove her straight to her apartment in Georgetown and were told to wait. She unlocked the door and went straight up to her second floor bedroom. She has no time to rest. She jumps into the shower and let the steaming jets of hot water try to peel off the stress of the past few days. She took the time to shave her legs, apply a touch of makeup, and dry her hair. She then packed just enough clothes for the remaining mission days ahead.

The Marines double-parked in front of her townhouse. The driver watched the front of the townhouse; the other walked to the back through a small alleyway to guard the rear exit. When she came back out about twenty minutes later, the Marine out front notified the one in the rear. He grabbed her bags and put them in the trunk as she slid into the back seat. The Marine from the rear was now back and he jumped into the front passenger seat. They took off and arrived at the West Wing of the White House at around 1600 hours. Within minutes, Leigh is sitting in her make-shift temporary special ops headquarters Room 16. It is five stories underground the most powerful office in the world.

At the Pentagon, Rumsfeld was notified of Leigh's return from Istanbul. He wanted to call her for an update, but he knew that was out of bounds. He waited for her call.

Max Leonhardt walks into Leigh's new makeshift office and walked her through an 83-point checklist, right down to the logistics still being finalized for the escape plans for Scott, the double and the Doctor. Max and Leigh both have photographic memories so he knew he didn't need to slow down his presentation of the facts at hand. He saves one piece of important information for last.

"Goldmark Sterns made the second deposit to the Swiss Bank accounts promptly at noon today. All systems are go," said Max. Leigh did not say anything and she didn't look pleased. "Is there a problem, boss?" Max asked curiously.

"I don't know. This is looking all too neat," Leigh replied. "Just because a plan works as planned doesn't mean there's a trap somewhere," Max said to downplay Leigh's anxiety. "I don't mean that," Leigh explained.

"The plan was hastily conceived. We haven't played out all the contingencies. What are we missing?" Her anxiety was wide-open.

"What are we missing?" Max replied repeating the question. "There's nothing missing. Not yet anyway." He went on: "In fact, I'd say we have an incredible advantage right now that none of us could have imagined a few days ago. Stop worrying."

"I'm not worried," Leigh snapped. "We have no contingency. I just don't want us to miss anything now that we're on the move." Max jumped in, "This is the UNIT," he reassured her. "We do our best work when we are on the move. Get some rest while you can." Max was right. She knew that. Everything was nearly in place for the execution of the plan as is and agreed to by Scott and Leigh earlier today in Istanbul.

She left Max and headed to a private bunk down the hall outfitted with an alarm and direct phone to room 16 if they needed her. She did not undress. She lay down, closed her eyes, not to rest but to visualize the plan for tomorrow. She is trying to see what parts of the plan might need changing or modification. She replayed in her mind her private planning with Scott prior to her departure from Istanbul. She focused on what she considered loose ends and she narrowed it down now to the fates of Khalib Seergy, Omar al-Faruk and Dr. Osman and his wife.

Was Seergy a liability? Leigh recounted what Seergy knew and didn't know. All she needed to do with Seergy, at this point, is hold him captive until all the deposits were accounted for from Goldmark Sterns. She knew he was terrified, and that he is convinced that Osama Bin Laden will kill him if he misses a step. It gave her the confidence she needed to send him home alive from his guarded exile in an Istanbul hotel once the last deposit is made and accounted for. He will be in a lot of trouble with his boss, Lloyd Ballantyne, when he returns, but neither of them could possibly compromise her mission nor could they ever identify Scott. They both also might prove useful for another mission down the road.

The fate of Omar al-Faruk took care of itself. Scott informed her of how he was taken hostage by the SEAL Team. Following the mask of his face being made, Scott said Omar al-Faruk would become the first casualty of war to welcome Osama Bin Laden to hell on Sunday, September 30.

Finally, she turned her attention to Dr. Osman and his wife. His wife, Ayda, was in detention at the Soyakadasi guesthouse under the guard of the Navy SEAL team. Dr. Osman had proved to be a helpful partner today, with plenty of motivation to be sure, and with limited options, if any, but Scott sensed something else about this man. He seemed to have been tormented about his relationship with Bin Laden over the years and was coming to terms with it, now knowing that he might be an integral part in killing him. Dr. Osman proved to Scott that he was fearless, intelligent, and could be an asset to him in the mission ahead, as well as, a resource in missions to come, with unique surgical skills to add to his resume as an agent for clandestine services for the USA. Scott outlined a plan to keep Dr. Osman on their team indefinitely, offering him asylum and protection under the USA witness protection program. Leigh discussed the risks with Scott, but his arguments were too dynamic to dismiss. She reluctantly agreed and now she was second-guessing that decision. She also realized that it was a needless distraction in the scope of what drives the mission.

She cast her concerns away now ready to move forward. It had been a very long day, witnessing a sunrise and a sunset on two different continents in a single day. Tomorrow was Sunday September 30, 2001. It promised to be the longest and most significant day yet in 'OPERATION HAWK'S NEST'.

CHAPTER 24: DEATH INSIDE A DEVIL'S DEN

Tora Bora
September 30, 2001

19 days passed since 9/11. Osama Bin Laden remains a free man after killing 3,000 unarmed and unsuspecting helpless men, women and children on American soil, with impunity. That was all about to change.

At exactly 0600 hours, Scott, disguised as the Afghan, and Dr. Osman met four SEAL Team soldiers in the mansion in the master bedroom on the Soyakadasi. The SEAL Team delivered two surgical practice cadavers, as instructed, from the laboratory in the underground hospital, while Nick Anthony and Bryan Taylor simultaneously delivered the corpse of Omar al-Faruk. Before anyone was to leave this island this morning, an elaborate faux murder/suicide is being staged before the mansion is to be burnt to the ground.

Dr. Deniz Osman was reconnected with his wife yesterday afternoon, after agreeing to terms. She had been held hostage inside the guest residence by the pool. It is where they both stayed together last night. This morning, Dr. Osman is the architect for the scene of his own faux death and that of his wife. It is all part of a plan designed to leave no trace of this Op on the island and to verify the deaths of the Doctor and his wife, so they can assume new identities. A detonating device on the mansion is designed to trigger the fire later this evening.

In his master bedroom, Dr. Osman has the SEALs lay out the male and female cadavers side-by-side on his bed placing their heads in positions to his specific instructions. Dr. Osman then instructed Nick and Bryan carrying the corpse of Omar al-Faruk to the end of the bed in a standing position. While they held his corpse up, Scott carefully placed a Baikal IJ-70 (Makarov) pistol in Omar's lifeless hand, then aimed and pushed al-Faruk's index finger squeezing the trigger on the Makarov shooting the two cadavers in the bed directly in their skulls.

Scott had already put a bullet from this same gun to Omar al-Faruk's head yesterday afternoon, after his mask was completed to Dr. Osman's satisfaction. It was at point blank range to his temple, as if Omar al-Faruk had shot himself, an apparent suicide. Now in the mansion master bedroom, Dr. Osman instructed Nick and Bryan to drop the corpse, let it fall from its own weight. When they did, the dead body of Omar al-Faruk slumped hard on the edge of the bed, with the weapon still frozen in his hand. The scene not completed, Dr. Osman poured vials of blood (taken from himself and his wife yesterday) strategically under the cadavers on the bed. He engineered the spill from the vials to ensure that the blood appeared to race from their heads directly from the bullet holes in the skulls. He did the same with vials of blood he extracted yesterday from Omar al-Faruk. The male and female cadavers were carefully prepped this way so a blood analysis could be done later to identify the dead bodies as his wife and himself. Once this murder/suicide was successfully staged, Nick and Bryan poured kerosene throughout the room. The plan was to set fire to this room when the mission was complete. Authorities in Istanbul would anonymously be tipped off to the fire after the mansion was burnt to the ground. Nothing was left for chance. There would be no trace to who invaded the island and no mistake to who killed the Doctor and his wife.

Before the SEAL Team would cease operations at the Soyakadasi and depart the island, two members of the SEAL Team transported the Afghan, Dr. Osman and his wife, and another person looking just like

Omar-al-Faruk (the Osama double now in al-Faruk's mask) along with Special Forces soldiers Nick Anthony and Bryan Taylor back to the marine terminal at Istanbul's Hezarfen Airfield. They boarded this group on Dr. Osman's yacht, the TRANSFORMER.

When they reached the air terminal, the Afghan, and his new entourage were taken by limo directly to the private plane hangar and boarded Dr. Osman's Gulfstream G-IV with the alphanumeric markings JJF44. Nick and Bryan immediately entered the cockpit. They were already dressed in flight pilot uniforms for private commercial aviation pilots from Turkey. They began their checklist for takeoff. The others all took their seats. There were no flight attendants. No food. Just bottled water for this flight. Bryan taxied the jet out of the hangar and made a right turn heading to runway NC24R. Flight 801 was cleared for takeoff at exactly 0731 hours on Sunday, September 30, 2001. Destination: Parachina, Pakistan. Flight Time: 4 hours 28 minutes.

Because there is a three-hour time zone difference between these two cities, the entire world city clocks in the ops command center in room 16 underground the White House automatically recalibrated to Pakistan time. Just for the mission. Underneath the large digital time clock on all four video walls in the ops command room sat another smaller digital display, which would initiate a mission start time starting at zero running to the side of the date marked: 9/30/01. That clock began running at takeoff.

OPERATION HAWK'S NEST was now activated in its final sequence. At the same time, the new pilots of the speed yacht TRANSFORMER, from the Navy SEAL Team, received notification of the Afghan's takeoff from Istanbul's Hezarfen Airfield. They were racing out to sea at nearly 55 knots, full speed for the TRANSFORMER since they left the Afghan at the marine terminal in Istanbul and were now about thirty minutes shy of their rendezvous with the U.S. Submarine Scorpion, a phantom sub believed to have been sunk during the Cold War.

Pakistan
Sunday, September 30, 2001

1459 Hours. The Gulfstream jet screeched to a touchdown at the Parachina Airport, near Peshawar, Pakistan. The jet taxied to a worn private jet hangar that has seen better days. A fleet of seven black Mercedes-Benz S sedans, V12 and V8 equipped, some with considerable mileage, others outfitted exclusively with armor, stood at glimmering attention in neat rows inside the hangar. They were available by reservation, with or without a driver. Scott had told the Doctor about these unusual fleet rentals. The Doctor had made the reservation for an armored car the day before and when they exited the aircraft, he went to the fleet desk and came back to the group with a set of keys, for the armored car.

Nick Anthony was the designated driver. He had studied the maps thoroughly en route on the flight. He is driving the Afghan (Scott), Osama's double (still masquerading as Omar al Faruk), and Dr. Osman to a designated drop off point on the Pakistani border with Afghanistan. It is an uncomfortable ride on rough roads outside Parachina, a border town to Afghanistan, taking about 2 1/2 hours. As Nick left the hangar, he felt a surge when he stepped on the gas and realized he was driving a V-12 factory armored car from Mercedes-Benz, as probable B7 standard, built to withstand Military Spec automatic rounds, grenades, and landmines, long enough to get the passengers out of harms way.

Nick pulled over at a predetermined coordinate on the map and let the Afghan and his passengers out. They walked by foot several hundred yards into a narrow horse trail up in the mountain ahead where they found three horses, with wooden saddles and empty saddlebags, except for Scott's, which contained an odd, worn knapsack. It was just as planned. Two Pakistani freelancers with the CIA, who were further up the mountain watching them with binoculars, had delivered what they needed, as instructed. They were also instructed to leave immediately after they dropped the horses, which they decided foolishly not to obey.

They watched as the Afghan and his party got ready to ride up the mountains ahead in Tora Bora. They immediately recognized Omar al-Faruk but neither of the two others. They looked at each other in fear though when al-Faruk took off a mask he was apparently wearing only to reveal his true identity as Osama Bin Laden. They had no idea that Bin Laden was a double. Then they observed one of the other men take the mask of Omar al-Faruk from Bin Laden, clean it, and fit it perfectly now onto the unknown Afghan's face, masquerading him as Omar al-Faruk. None of this made sense to them. Something was up. They would need to report it immediately.

The CIA local freelancers could not believe their eyes as they watched the scene unfold below them. They sat there frozen in time before getting up to leave the scene and report it. They were being observed, as well. Nick Anthony sneaked up from behind them. He killed them both instantaneously using just his knife and force to cleanly cut their throats.

The Afghan (now disguised as Omar al-Faruk) moved his party out. About a quarter mile ahead, as they rode on horseback, they encountered the first and only border checkpoint where Pakistan ends and Afghanistan begins. When the guard saw Osama Bin Laden, he bowed fervently and spoke in Arabic: "Sallallahu 'alayhi wasallam", meaning Bless and Give Him Peace, known also as a prayer upon the final messenger. The faux Osama nodded as the three horsemen continued their journey north into the mountains of Tora Bora through the first checkpoint: unchecked.

Throughout the next hour and a half, the real Osama's militia on the mountain range would cheer and hail their leader as the faux Osama passed their multiple sentry points. These men knew that war with the Americans was coming soon. He would stop occasionally and encourage the mountain men to stand resolute against the enemy. They would stand together and yell praise in unison every time he told them in Arabic "I will remember this day and the sacrifices you make with me."

Clearly, the faux Osama was a compelling and credible double; even his closest guards who covered one of his many hideouts in the upper elevations were jubilant to see him and his bodyguard Omar-al-Faruk. They were completely fooled by the scrupulous attention to detail of Dr. Osman's surgical skills on Osama's double and Omar's disguise.

Tora Bora is not a mountain, rather a section of the White Mountains. The jagged points can reach an altitude of more than 14,000 feet. The mountains stretch about six miles long and six miles wide across a myriad of narrow valleys, and snow-covered ridgelines. Caves dot the entire landscape and while not a modern fortress, it is a labyrinth of cave strongholds, ammunition dumps, fuel depots, war rooms, makeshift field hospitals, mess halls, and escape routes, some excavated and constructed with rough roads. It was designed to be a mountain military base, first for the mujahedeen, then further enhanced as a Headquarters for Osama Bin Laden and his terrorist organization, Al Qaeda. It now was equipped with limited electricity and running water, in lower parts.

At about 5,000 feet up the mountains, Omar al-Faruk, the Doctor and the faux Osama were directed to a landing on the edge of a ridge with a single cave entrance by four sentry guards, heavily armed with side arms,

AK-47s, grenades and visible behind them Stinger missiles. The climb up on horseback was treacherous and Scott masquerading as Omar al-Faruk made sure he kept the stallions several horse lengths behind each other. The Doctor confirmed they were at the same rendezvous location as previous treks up this mountain. They had reached their destination.

Clearly, this was no ordinary cave entrance. Nor was it natural. Behind the sentry was a rock wall and it opened hydraulically by one of the sentries. It was only when the wall started to slide open did you realize that this was not an opening to the cave. Instead it opened to an inner narrow core passageway, about 20 feet, covered by rows of stacked sandbags, leading to another inner cave opening, about 3' deep and 5' tall made of concrete. It was on a very restrictive hinge that allowed only a slight opening to enter. Fat mans revenge.

As they entered the cave, these strange images were being broadcast live on the main video wall in room 16 underground in the ops command center at the White House from Scott's Tracker device, complete with clear audio transmission. The clock reads 1659 hours. The next 15 minutes would become the most compelling video footage ever in the TOP SECRET classified files of the United States Government.

Inside, a rather plain cell-like square stone and dirt structure revealed itself, no larger than 25' long and 12' wide. For all the ducking required just to enter this cave, it was surprising to see so much head room inside, nearly 8 feet and the room was fortified by steel beams. The sentry led them in and hit a switch, which flooded the room brightly with light, under two electric ceiling fluorescent lights that spanned the entire length of the room. There was no one else in the room. The sentry bowed to Osama's double, as if he were authentic, and left the room. As he did, the heavy door groaned and closed shut.

Scott, masquerading as Omar; the double, surgically perfect to be an impostor for Osama Bin Laden and wearing Osama's trademark camouflage jacket; and the Doctor, dressed in Afghan clothing but playing himself, immediately sat down on chairs set to a rectangular steel conference table situated on the right side of the room. The table, 14' long with 10 steel chairs flanking it, four on a side and seats at each end, appeared to be bolted to the floor. It was odd. Afghans sat on the floors not seats. Perhaps, Scott thought, they were wired, like electric chairs? A map of the region covered the wall behind the table. The floor was carpeted almost completely with an oversized Afghan rug on a dirt floor. On the left side of the cave, shelving units covered the entire facing wall, which appeared to house a pantry for food, water and supplies. There were few modern conveniences. Yet, it was pleasant to be inside, away from the stinging, damp cold outside. No one else was inside this cave nor was any hint of any secret inner doors leading to any other rooms evident. The sentry who had just left didn't appear to be expecting anyone either.

As they were getting acclimated to the room, an inner panel of the back wall slid forward a few feet and from around that panel appeared Osama Bin Laden. The visitors all stood as if to greet someone important. Bin Laden did not greet them. Instead, he went immediately to his double and with two hands guided him to the middle of the room. He stared at his face.

No one moved as Osama Bin Laden viewed his body double like he was looking in a mirror for several minutes. As he was doing so, Scott was inconspicuously pulling out his Glock 9mm and attaching his silencer underneath his coat. It is also when he noticed a mark on the right side of Bin Laden's right hand in a tiny shape of a V. The same mark that the Doctor had told him he had made on each double.

Scott reacted instinctively, his toes and stomach clenched, and his entire body flushed with adrenaline. He placed his Glock on the table as he quickly pulled out a dart pistol from a sheath underneath his garment. It was already loaded. The first shot hit Bin Laden in the neck. Scott ever so swiftly turned and without any warning shot the next dart at the faux Osama Bin Laden he brought up the mountain. Both of the Bin Laden's fell, as if dead, to the floor. The darts contained non-lethal doses of a powerful knockout drug on impact.

Scott motioned to the Doctor to get down as he dropped his dart pistol and picked up his Glock. He rushed to the hidden panel towards the back of the cave wall. With his weapon held firmly between both hands, he leaped into the unknown alleyway behind the wall.

A bullet ripped through his left shoulder, pushing him back against the cave wall in excruciating pain, while another hit his pistol and threw it several feet away. Other bullets rained past him, as he rolled trying to recover his ground quickly. He saw see three men coming at him. Two were apparent bodyguards as yet another Osama Bin Laden was shielded behind them. He must be the real Bin Laden.

He realized the bullets weren't hitting him, just keeping him in place. They saw he was now unarmed. They weren't trying to kill him. They wanted him captured alive. This was a tragic mistake on their part. They had no idea of the adroit killing skills of the man masquerading as Omar al Faruk this day.

Within seconds, despite his own wounds, he shot and killed both of Bin Laden's bodyguards, each with a single shot. They did not see him shoot from underneath his cloak with another weapon and had no time to react. Osama Bin Laden did. He took aim and unloaded his pistol in rapid fire. Scott rolled and as pain now ignited from his shoulder and legs, he still summoned up enough strength to take aim. He shot the pistol right out of the hand of Osama Bin Laden, who had just stopped to reload.

He should have aimed directly at Bin Laden, but chose instead to take out Bin Laden's gun. He didn't want the real Osama Bin Laden to die without knowing his true identity. But he also didn't have the time to admire the best shot he ever made in his life, when his own life was depending on it, because he summoned the strength to bound up and start running at Osama Bin Laden.

Osama Bin Laden reacted instinctively and fled. Scott caught up to him and tackled him with a failsafe throw down technique that he learned, but had never mastered at West Point, until today. He had the real Osama Bin Laden firmly in his grasp, on the ground, in an alleyway inside the inner core of a secret cave 5,000 feet up inside the center of Osama Bin Laden's Headquarters in Tora Bora.

He wasted no time. He sat up on and over him and despite his own heart pounding like it was going to burst, he realized that Osama Bin Laden wasn't fighting him. In fact, Osama was unexpectedly limp. He didn't expect to be able to kill him this closely without a struggle. He certainly didn't expect the mastermind behind 9/11 to be such a coward. He stared at Osama Bin Laden after deliberately checking Bin Laden's right hand. No mark. He had his man.

Osama Bin Laden shouted, "Omar. Why are you doing this, Omar?" Scott immediately rips his mask off. "Omar is dead," Scott replied in English now pointing his Glock between the eyes of Osama Bin Laden. He gazed straight into his eyes and whispered ever so slowly and distinctly in English: "I'm Scott Walsh. US Special Forces."

Osama Bin Laden's face looked ashen. He immediately broke down, pleading pitifully for his life. He began promising great riches in exchange for letting him go. Yet, he had to know that this was his fate. He began visibly to sweat profusely, with tears streaming down his face.

Scott couldn't believe it. Was this how the Devil destructs? No remorse, no sorrow, just pitiful pleas for self-preservation?

Without hesitation, Scott shot Osama Bin Laden dead with one shot. Point-blank with the muzzle pressed straight into his forehead. Scott got off him and stood up, looking at Bin Laden. Blood gushed from the head. He took one more shot to be certain. Point blank to his heart. Blood oozed slowly from his heart.

Osama bin Laden is dead.

Despite the darkness in the cave, Scott's Tracker device captured the kill in real time on the video wall back at the underground ops command center. The digital clock under the White House read out 1705 hours in Afghanistan; 0835 hours in Washington D.C. The digital calendar read September 30, 2001. It was like time stopped inside the Ops Command Center under the White House. Scott Walsh assassinated Osama Bin Laden four days ahead of mission schedule.

Applause spontaneously burst out in the ops center, despite all the danger they all knew that Scott had yet to navigate. The Devil was dead.

The Doctor had now cautiously and fearfully entered the alleyway. He heard multiple gunshots. His fear and curiosity lured him in. He saw several dead bodies and a single body standing, bloody yet alive. It was the Afghan.

As he went to aid the Afghan, he saw the dead bodies. The man on the ground below the Afghan was unmistakable. It was Osama Bin Laden.

Blood was everywhere. It took him only a minute to realize that the Afghan too had been shot, probably multiple times. His left shoulder looked the worse of it. He reached out to the Afghan to check his shoulder and said, "Let me check that?" The Afghan pushed the Doctor's hand away and then bent down and lifted Osama's right hand, showing it to the Doctor. "There is no V. It's confirmation. Conclusive, right?" The Afghan was clearly in pain and impatient. "My god, yes. But how...?" the Doctor is interrupted in mid-sentence. Scott was picking up the mask of Omar el Faruk. "Put this on for me. Check to make sure there's no blood on it." The Doctor checks it, "I need to clean it and your face."

"OK. Not now. We have lots to do. Follow me." The Afghan ordered as he started walking fast, back towards the cave. When Scott and the Doctor made their way back inside, the Doctor grabbed the satchel and pulled out a soft bag that contained his medical equipment and supplies. Inside he grabbed a device that looked like binoculars, of sorts, or even an old viewfinder, except larger and all in one piece. As the Doctor was examining the contents of the satchel, Scott was taking the pulses of the two faux UBL's he drugged earlier. The Doctor insisted Scott stop and sit down so he could administer to the gunshot to his shoulder. The bullet had ripped through his clothing so the wound was open without Scott needing to remove any clothing. The Doctor could clearly see that the bullet had torn right through the top of his shoulder, ripping apart muscles but missing his bones.

"The bullet passed straight through the shoulder. You got lucky." The Doctor advised Scott. "Let me clean it and put a few stitches in and..." The Doctor was cut off fast by Scott. "Clean it up fast. No time for stitches. We've got work to do."

The Doctor quickly cleaned the wound, as Scott grimaced in pain, and used large compresses to stop the bleeding. Using gauze, he wrapped it around the compresses and around his shoulder several times, so they could make the journey down the mountain without attending to it again. He knew he would have to cover up any sign of injury to not attract any attention to the wounds by the guards. As soon as he was finished, Scott jumped up and went straight over to the faux Osama, lying limp, that had come into the room earlier from the alleyway behind the cave. He told the Doctor to grab his bag and device and help him drag this body back into the alleyway behind the cave. When they finished, he told the Doctor to start the forensics that they rehearsed in Istanbul on the real Bin Laden. Scott reached down at the body they just dragged in and removed his own coat, which was torn and bloodied, and replaced it with this clean one, on this body, that was under the camouflage jacket. Then he pulled out his gun, already equipped with the silencer, put the gun right to the heart and shot this faux Osama dead.

The Doctor was so startled when he watched the Afghan kill the double that he froze. Scott grabbed him, shook him by the collar and slapped him hard in the face: "We've got a job to do. Snap out of it, Doc. Let's get the forensics done. Now." Scott was losing patience and was feeling anxious and overwhelmed. Blood started pouring from the faux Osama. Scott grabbed the odd-looking device that had come from the satchel that looked like binoculars. It was actually a handmade, handheld biometrics recorder that could take iris scans, fingerprints and facial scans and store them in a disk port no larger than a fingernail. This was Max Leonhardt's invention, a contraption that all hands on deck in the ops center found spellbinding at the moment, as they watched Scott use it. If connected to a computer, it could relay the images back to the ops command center who could identify and cross match Osama's DNA within hours. But there were no computers, no scanning equipment here in the caves of Tora Bora. Scott would need to bring back this evidence to the States.

As Scott was taking the iris scans, the Doctor finally jumped into action himself. He was in the process of drawing blood vials, in units, from the real Osama's dead body. It took nearly fifteen minutes for the Doctor and Scott to finish their pre-planned gathering of forensic evidence on the body of the real Osama Bin Laden. Under the circumstances, it seemed like an eternity.

Physical evidence was next. Dr. Osman surgically excised an eye, part of the inner cheek, the right index finger and an ear from the corpse of Osama Bin Laden. He placed these body parts in separate premade safety gel paks that would keep these parts frozen until opened. Scott opened his new coat exposing his underarmor. He placed each sealed body part in compartments made specifically for them, one by one, in his unique, form-fitted body underarmor. The Doctor stared silently at Scott's body underarmor, the sheaves built in it and the weapons it concealed with awe. The Doctor realized that no one knew this Afghan's name, not a single person asked, including himself, over the incredible events of the past few days. Yet everyone knew he was in charge. For the first time, he also grew aware that this Afghan was not an ordinary Afghan. In fact, he wondered now just who the hell he was?

They both stood up. The Afghan stopped momentarily and handed Omar's mask to the Doctor. The Doctor inspected it and cleaned it. "Come here," he told Scott. He washed Scott's face with cleansing pads and inspected his face for cuts or open wounds. There wasn't any – just blood that splattered all over his face. He gave the mask back to the Afghan who started pulling on the mask as the Doctor made the necessary adjustments. After all this, the Afghan looked just like Omar el Faruk again.

The Doctor asked, "How did you know that it wasn't the real Bin Laden at first?" The Afghan replied, "When Bin Laden first walked in, I sensed something wrong. I looked at his right hand and noticed the V; the mark on the hand that you told me signified a double. I shot both the doubles with drug darts so they are unaware of what happened out here." The Afghan added, "Do you think the guards in front of the cave heard any of this?" The Doctor said without hesitation, "I don't think we need to worry." The Doctor went on to say, "I could hear the shots inside. They were muffled though." He said, adding: "I don't think it carried enough for the outside guards to hear it. The wall must be thick enough to dull the gunshots too." The Doctor sputtered all of this out quickly, but lacking the confident tone he carried in Istanbul. The Doctor still sensed peril in this misadventure as he looked back at the alleyway. Behind this wall was a long, narrow hallway leading to other areas, but no one was going to find out today where it led. Scott, as the Afghan, was clearly only interested in procuring proof of Bin Laden's death and escaping. Fast.

The Doctor and the Afghan started cleaning up the carnage. Before they left the scene, Bin Laden's dead body was now bunched and folded up in a canvass sack they put him in, resembling a heap of garbage, with missing body parts, next to the other exposed dead and bloodied bodies.

As they left, Scott searched for a control switch on the wall that would move the inner faux wall back in position, closing the entrance to this alleyway where they would leave Osama's dead body. He didn't find any switch before realizing that it must move hydraulically somehow. He kept pushing on small section of the beams and finally something triggered motion and the wall slid slowly back into position. He motioned to the Doctor to get back inside the main room as it was closing and he followed the Doctor after pushing the part of the partition that had triggered its closing.

Back inside the main cave, they sat at the table. They waited for their own fake Osama Bin Laden to wake up from Scott's drug-induced dart. The Doctor knew about this aspect of the original plan. It was the only part of the plan that actually happened as planned. This made the escape plan increasingly more dangerous, he knew. Had Bin Laden or his bodyguards radioed for assistance? If it weren't for the Afghan's cool demeanor after all this mayhem, he would have surely thought his own death would be imminent. This Afghan, whoever he might be, still looked intensely strong enough and smart enough to get them all back to safety.

About five minutes went by. The Afghan and Doctor sat in silence. Only the Doctor moved occasionally as he checked the drugged body several times for a pulse. Finally, the faux Osama woke up, got up off the floor slowly and sat down next to the Doctor and Scott.

"What happened?" he said in Arabic. The Afghan answered in Arabic: "The guard drugged us all. No one remembers what happened. But we must leave now. Are you ready to go? Do you remember the plan?"

"Yes, that's all I remember," Osama's double said as he was slowly shaking off the effects of the drug. "That is all you need to remember for now. Remember, be cool, you're Osama Bin Laden now. Let's go."

They got up and headed out exactly as they entered. As they got to the passageway, a sentry led them out. The sentry bowed deeply showing respect to the faux Osama, looked around carefully, saw no one other than the three who entered, then led them out past the other guards to their waiting horses. The gunfight inside the cave apparently was unheard outside the cave entrance. As they left on horseback, the faux Osama told the guards, as was rehearsed back in Istanbul: "Stay alert. Stay strong. I'm here beside you. I am always asking about you guys."

About an hour and a half later, past several more Al Qaeda militia sentry posts, they passed the same guards they encountered earlier without incident. At each checkpoint down the mountain, Scott felt more assured that the real Osama Bin Laden or his bodyguards never signaled an alert before they were killed. Their escape from Tora Bora was working, as planned. Yet the assassination did not go as planned. He was injured and the path ahead was still filled with peril. It worried him. They kept proceeding down the mountain.

At a predetermined coordinate, near a remote edge of the mountain, about three-quarters through the descent, Scott stopped, dismounted from his horse and gave his final instructions to the Doctor and the faux Osama. He also removed his Omar-al-Faruk mask and gave it to the Doctor, who placed it in his saddlebag. They were splitting up at this descent point to facilitate the escape from Tora Bora. Scott sent them back down the final elevations of the mountain without him and began his own jaunt to the facing edge of the mountain alone.

After they left, Scott opened his saddlebags on his horse. In it was water and a hybrid backpack. He offered some water to his horse first before drinking the rest of it all in swigs, as if he just crawled off the Sahara desert. Scott was breathing heavily. Sweat dripped down his torso despite the frigid air that hung in these altitudes. He was experiencing difficulty breathing. A fever was setting in, his arm and shoulder ached, and blood started to seep slowly through the compresses. He looked down at the odd-looking backpack and got dizzy, and slumped to the ground.

Back in Washington D.C., all eyes watched Scott drop to the ground and not get up. Leigh alerted Nick Anthony. "Eagle Two to Eagle Four. Stand by, Over." she said. "Copy that, Eagle Two. Eagle Four Out," Nick replied. He knew the backup plan. He waited for the coordinates and the order.

The Doctor and Osama's double were already on their descent off the mountain, too distant to see the fall. Fortunately, Scott never fainted when he fell. As much as he wanted to just lie there and rest, he knew he had no time and that eyes were on him. He had injured his left knee again, the same one that took a heavy hit on the mountains during his training in California. As if reaching out for a reserve tank of gas, he grabbed the knapsack, stood slowly and hoisted it on his shoulder with his good arm. Only the closing of his left eye suggested that he was wincing in pain. He mounted his horse and was on the move again.

You could sense the relief in room 16 underground the White House. Without missing a beat, Leigh contacted Nick Anthony. "This is Eagle Two to Eagle Four. Stand Down. Repeat. Stand Down. Hawk is on the move. Over." Nick Anthony received the message. "Standing down. This is Eagle Four to Eagle Two. Repeat. Standing Down. Out," replied Nick, sitting in his Mercedes in Pakistan, on the border of Afghanistan. Nick only felt a slight sense of relief. The mission was still in progress. In this part of the world, he knew danger still lurks around every bend. "Eagle Two to Eagle Four. Copy that. Out."

Scott, as the Afghan, began following specific instructions that his Tracker device GPS system was now sending him in real time. He knew to remain radio silent until he escapes. The illuminated map guided him to the mountain's edge on the eastern border.

Some fifteen minutes later, upon arrival on a mountain ledge, he dismounted again and took off the backpack expecting to feel some needed relief from the stabbing pain of carrying it this long. Instead, even just the slightest movement near his shoulder introduced severe and throbbing pain. There was nothing left to do, but open the backpack. Inside were instructions for assembling a rather unusual device that wired in and around the backpack itself, which was then attached to a titanium-telescoping rod.

It wasn't until he assembled it completely did he recognize it as the device he had trained to assemble in the mountains of the Sierra Nevada's for rapid air escape. Scott finished the assembly, put on this weird back-pack, took off his headband and stood up surveying the valley.

He looked across and then down, straight down as if glancing down at a gargantuan open grave. With the weight of the world keeping him still, as the winds whipped wildly around him, he waited to escape with this unwieldy and weird-looking tool that rose high above him and dangled over the cliff from his backpack.

From a mountain peak across the valley, a young Al Qaeda soldier on guard spotted the profile of a lone Afghan perched high on a mountain ledge. He did not use binoculars just a scope on his sniper's shotgun, a Barrett .50 Cal with a maximum range of 2600 meters. He focused in on the errant Afghan who he thought possibly was lost, because he certainly should not have been on this ridgeline on this mountain today. That is when he noticed something strange about this picture. Below the point on the mountain where the Afghan stood, he saw a Russian "Hind" attack helicopter climbing straight up the cliff at a high speed just underneath that lone Afghan. The huge helicopter was so dangerously close to the cliff and rising upwards so fast, it hypnotized him. When he saw it yank the Afghan off the ledge and pitch high and east, he realized the fast moving distraction made him derelict in his own duty. He dropped his high-powered rifle to load his stinger surface to air missile to take out the helicopter.

CHAPTER 25: HELL FIRE

Tora Bora, Afghanistan
September 30, 2001

It was the first time Scott ever saw a Predator drone in the sky. It was gliding silently through the mountains until it lurched violently to its left launching a missile from its underbelly. When he heard the impact of the hellfire missile on its target on the ground, he knew that whoever named this missile had certainly heard it first. There was just no other word to describe it. Hellfire.

When he looked down and witnessed the pinpoint explosion at the base of the Tora Bora mountain range, he clearly understood that this new Predator drone is going to change the face of modern warfare. The missiles plume reaches 1,050 degrees Fahrenheit at its hottest and the explosion is thunderous. Its wake rises up the fury of hell itself.

Thunder is the sound created by lightning, so if thunder can be heard, lightning is near. Not so with the Predator. There is no thunder, no flash, no warning. It strikes almost silently, and it rocked and shook the entire mountain range. Scott knew the Doctor and Osama's double had to be awfully close to that attack. He wondered how they could escape from such a swift and deadly unseen killing force?

In that split second, completely by surprise, his own escape off the mountain was triggered. He is whiplashed right off his feet from a ledge of the mountain. He had purposely positioned himself on this ledge for just such an escape from Tora Bora. Yet, he just isn't prepared for how absolutely jolting it is. Out of the blue, and from underneath his ledge on the mountain, a Russian MI-24 "Hind" attack helicopter swept up and then over him, literally hooked the cable rod connected to his backpack that was purposely positioned to connect this way, and in the process literally jerked him off the mountain ledge without warning.

He never heard the huge helicopter, and never saw it until it was too late. He was distracted by the blast below. But it caught the rod connected to Scott's backpack and yanked him off the mountain and up towards the helicopter at what seemed a dizzying speed.

As Leigh watched this violent scene develop from room 16 in Washington D.C., she cringed. Too bad there wasn't time to rehearse this daredevil escape in California. Scott was obviously learning the hard way.

Hanging precipitously from the belly of one of "Satan's Chariots," Scott is not feeling the exhilaration of a daring escape, but rather sheer fright, even for a highly trained Special Forces soldier. Nothing prepares you for the real moment. Especially when it hurts.

As the Russian MI-24 "Hind" attack helicopter flew north and east at a controlled but escalating speed, Scott is ever so slowly reeled in on the winch from his 36' foot cable toward the inside safety of the chopper. Scott struggles to breathe at this altitude and speed yet managed to maintain stability despite a shoulder that now felt ripped apart and dislocated by the jolting motion made when the connection engaged abruptly. He hung on when all of a sudden, in the distance and towards the area that the Hellfire missile destroyed its prey, he saw the actual Predator drone for the second time. It flashes by him at about 100 miles per hour underneath his feet.

It was dusk. Yet the drone was visible, as clearly identifiable as if it flew by in the light of day. It too, by itself, was a toxic and terrifying sight.

Even at some 100 miles per hour, it seemed to creep – even eerily unbalanced -- the slow motion effect of a machine built for death.

Back in Langley, Virginia, a pilot was literally flying this Predator drone (nearly 7,000 miles from Afghanistan), from remote controls and computer screens inside an air-conditioned ops command center at CIA Headquarters. He was also photographing everything the drone had just destroyed in its path. He was getting ready to turn the drone to return to finish the job, if needed. The Predator carried two hellfire missiles and it had only used one. Operators inside the command center in the same room were evaluating not only the optics of the drone equipped with hellfire missiles in its maiden flight, but observing the balance of the drone in flight after shooting one of its missiles. The missiles are heavy. They were added as an afterthought to the initial design of the drone, in response to a need to take out targets quickly after pinpointing locations. Right now, the results are nothing short of incredible.

The drone dragged significantly after firing off one of its heavy missiles losing its balance. Its speed dropped by almost 30%, a direct result of this weight imbalance. Yet it did not decrease its battle-ready performance in any other way. While it may have looked a bit silly for such a sinister system in the skies with a hanging missile on one side of its belly, its performance was not hampered at all. The drone's ability to roll or change directions, to locate targets and fire the remaining hellfire missile with precision was confirmed. In its maiden mission, the Predator became an instant stunning victory for the CIA.

What Scott did not understand yet is that the attacks by the drone were designed to be almost surgical in precision in its efforts to take out human targets. He has nothing to fear about the doctor or the double being in harms way, as long as they followed his instructions.

Leigh recorded the entire operation off of Scott's Tracker and simultaneously projected the video of the event on a large plasma screen in her command center, flanked by video images being relayed by an encrypted satellite feed and the Predator drone. The Tracker device proved to be the scientific breakthrough audio/video wireless communications innovation it claimed to be. The clarity of the video was crystal clear.

When the Predator drone did its fly-by recon of the attack site, Leigh witnessed the Doctor and the double escaping on video relay, just as planned. It would soon be confirmed by Nick Anthony, who was waiting a few miles from them in a bulletproof Mercedes-Benz to drive them back safely to Pakistan. The escape from Tora Bora to the Parachina Airport would still be unpredictable and perilous, as the impossible road conditions would hinder a quick getaway, especially if they needed one. Any delay to the scheduled departure could still jeopardize their safety.

Events unfolding in real time in Tora Bora were dramatic. After the missiles aftermath and explosion cleared, the number of horsemen could no longer be confirmed because they were vaporized. All that remained were scorch scars on smoldering earth. In the distance, some two miles to be exact, satellite imagery and drone optics showed what appeared to be four Al Qaeda men exiting from a Mercedes-Benz SUV escaping on foot to a cave opening close by. Ayman al-Zawahiri was identified as one of these men.

Just as these images were relayed, reconnaissance simultaneously picked up a retaliatory surface to air missile strike launch by Al Qaeda against the active Predator drone. It pinpointed the location of the surface to air launch from further up on the mountain.

The instruments onboard the Predator alerted its pilot 7,000 miles away, who analyzed it in seconds, then triggered the drone to instantly release a candle, a heat sensor decoy from its rear panel to attract the incoming Al Qaeda Stinger missile. As it did, the pilot also swung the drone around quickly enough to take the offensive. He fired directly at the location on the mountain that had a sniper readying yet another surface to air missile targeted at the Hind helicopter, where the Afghan, Scott, just entered safely.

In an instant, two things happened lightning fast: the Al Qaeda shoulder launched missile aimed at the drone took out the candle decoy as expected, protecting the drone. That explosion was muted by another explosion that happened seconds later. It was so violent that you could see chunks of the mountain disgorged by the Predator's remaining hellfire missile. The Hellfire missile was so precise that it hit the sniper directly as he was still readying to launch a surface to air missile at the Hind Helicopter -- before his finger engaged the trigger.

Within seconds of an explosion in the sky and on the mountain, the drone made a wide circle for a second recon look. It sent confirming pictures back to Langley before it too escaped the area intact. The drone was piloted back to its base at a temporary CIA paramilitary air base somewhere highly classified on the border of Afghanistan.

This was America's first strike ever in military history by a Predator drone equipped with hellfire missiles. There was euphoria at CIA on its maiden mission, despite its failure to kill Ayman al-Zawahiri, its primary target amidst the horsemen. Al-Zawahiri apparently was not one of the men in this Al Qaeda horseback brigade that was eliminated. Instead, he was apparently escorted to Tora Bora in the SUV that the drone recon now showed abandoned. By pure luck, arriving behind the horsemen today saved his life. The secondary mission, however, defending the Russian Helicopter out of Tora Bora, proved to be a total success. The helicopter, unharmed, raced back to a secret runway somewhere in Uzbekistan, to drop off Scott before heading back to its base in Russia.

Crumpton received the initial orders to launch the first ever drone attack in Afghanistan, equipped with retrofit hellfire missiles via secure signature codes from the Unit, headed by Leigh Ann McClure. He was not privy to the mission the Unit was undertaking. It was an op run by POTUS and classified FOR SHOTPUT ONLY: TOP SECRET. All Crumpton knew was that the DOD had access so why was CIA being shut out? After all, the Predators fell under his jurisdiction in Afghanistan.

Crumpton's curiosity wasn't going to be satisfied on this day. Yet the Predator's role in the op was extraordinary, just as he predicted. It confirmed what he already suspected about the military efficiency of his lethal drones with hellfire missiles strapped to the underside of their bellies. The precision of the Predator drone, with retrofitted precision missile capability, proved to be a stunning success for the new drone technology. It was also a major accomplishment for Hank Crumpton at CIA, who pushed for just this type of technology to support missile carrying capacity on the optical drones.

Still, his inquisitive mind sometimes got the better of him. What kind of op was Leigh deploying in the heart of Al Qaeda country in the build-up to war? How did she know the whereabouts of Ayman al-Zawahiri when he didn't? Crumpton liked to be the provider of such intelligence not the receiver, so he was curious as to what assets she had in gathering such coveted intelligence. He wondered too if Ayman al-Zawahiri had been tipped off somehow? Why wasn't he with his horsemen, as planned? His secure phone rang interrupting his thoughts. The Caller ID showed it was Leigh McClure.

"Crumpton," he answered. "Did you have time to watch it?" she asked. "I did." Crumpton replied as if uninterested. "It was impressive. Thank you," she said keeping the thanks measured, following his lead. Crumpton did not reply. Leigh continued: "I understand this was Job 1 for the Predator with the retrofit. Tell all your people: Bravo!"

"I'll do that. Looks like we missed one of the bad guys though," Crumpton couldn't let al-Zawahiri's escape go without comment. However, Leigh wasn't going to change the positive tone intended as the purpose of her call: "Part of the plan, perhaps?" she replied. "Anyone that near a Predator will be scared to death, don't you think? Might be good to have a bad guy knowing our new prowess in the sky?" She paused briefly. "Awesome performance Hank. I have to go. Godspeed." She hung up.

Hank Crumpton sat still, reflecting on the events that just occurred in Afghanistan. It was indeed an awesome display of power in split seconds by a pilot sitting comfortably in seats inside a temperature controlled command center at CIA headquarters in Langley, Virginia. Neither he, nor the Predator drone pilot, had any idea that they had just saved Scott's life and those of the Doctor and the double for another day. It was a different type of mission for this pilot, a mission within a mission, with no strings attached. Nor did he know that he just assisted in 'OPERATION HAWK'S NEST', on the very same day that Osama Bin Laden was killed.

Hank Crumpton didn't know any of this bombshell information either, but he decided not to pursue trying to uncover the details of Leigh's mission right now. He let it go, something he is unaccustomed to doing. He had his own war to fight with his own impossible deadline looming.

He continued organizing CIA paramilitary assets supporting the infiltration of Special Forces into Afghanistan, who would be on the ground in just five days. He had no idea that before the drone attack, Osama Bin

Laden was assassinated. The time of Bin Laden's death occurred at exactly 1705 hours on Sunday afternoon, September 30, 2001 in a cave at Tora Bora. The helicopter that his predator drone protected carried the assassin.

The mission was successful. The escape with proof of Osama Bin Laden's death was underway. No one anywhere in the world knew about the assassination. Yet.

CHAPTER 26: ESCAPE

The Long Road Home
September 30, 2001

Osama Bin Laden is dead.

Proof of death is with the Afghan, Scott, known only as the 'Hawk' in the UNIT. He successfully escaped from Tora Bora and is en route to the USS Vinson onboard a US Navy Osprey before heading to Washington, D.C. The fate of the Dr. Osman and Osama's body double is still yet unknown. Had their escape simply not been reported yet? Had the Pakistani ISI agent arrived in Parachina? Or did something go wrong?

Leigh did not want to contact Rumsfeld until she confirmed all loose ends. She needed to know that Scott had made it safely to the USS Vinson, with the evidence still in hand. She needed to know the status of the body double of Bin Laden with the ISI agent and the location of the safe house. Finally, she needed to know that the Doctor and his wife were safely in the air with Nick Anthony and Bryan Taylor -- destination: Gothenburg, Sweden.

She was anxious, despite the significant success of the mission in its final stage. Did the Doctor and Bin Laden's body double make it down the mountain safely? Did Nick Anthony make their rendezvous? If he did, she knew it would still take Nick hours more of driving on rough roads to get to the Parachina Airport in Pakistan.

She wanted to contact Bryan Taylor at the hangar in Pakistan to find out what was happening on his end. Instead, she followed her professional instincts, stuck to protocol and waited for his call.

Bryan Taylor had stayed behind at the Parachina Airport during the mission to ready the plane for a fast escape and to safeguard Ayda Osman, the Doctor's wife, who remained on the plane. He was busy refueling the jet, stocking the plane with snacks, meals and drinks from a kitchen in the terminal. He also studied maps and loaded the flight plan for Gothenburg. Their next destination was 4,111 miles away, flight time 5 hours 54 minutes.

He had also spoken with Fran several times regarding the details of her arrival with an ISI agent in a separate jet and plans for transferring Osama's double, who will be disguised as Omar al-Faruk. Her plane arrived on schedule and was idling just outside the hangar. When her plane arrived, Bryan Taylor taxied his jet out of the hangar and positioned it next to her plane, engines idling. Bryan had been contacted by Nick Anthony alerting him they were close and to standby for takeoff.

Nick Anthony finally pulled into the Parachina Airport. He was tired, hungry, and couldn't wait to get out of this hellhole. He was not used to playing backup as a commando in the UNIT. But he just spent nearly five hours of waiting in unfriendly territory. His drive out to the Tora Bora region was longer than expected and the road conditions were atrocious (If you could call this a road, in the first place). Almost as soon as they arrived, he had to take out two CIA freelancers before the Afghan and his party started up the mountain. Then, he waited anxiously for the Doctor and the double of Bin Laden (now disguised as Omar al Faruk) to return. He had hidden and camouflaged the Mercedes, near the drop off point on the border of Afghanistan, and spent the next 4-5 hours in the forest hiding and waiting. They were late coming back to the rendezvous coordinates.

There was nothing he could do about it. The op was in play and required a blackout in communications.

Yet, when they finally returned, he was glad they finally made it back alive. He could see that both men were happy to see him but also recognized that they both had just been through something so terrible that they couldn't talk. They took the long and bumpy ride back to the Parachina Airport in total silence. He wanted to know what happened up there, how the Afghan fared, did he get out, too? After all, he was put on standby at one point ready to engage himself in the op. When he was told to stand down, he wondered what had happened. But right now, he knew to keep his mouth shut and all he wanted was to get the hell out of here fast. He rode as fast he could on the rough road back to the airport.

At the airport, Fran had already arrived. She had been sitting with the Pakistani ISI agent [code-named Campy] on the Pakistani Government plane waiting for Bryan's call to make the transfer. While she waited, she replayed the last 24 hours of her own life.

She was initially concerned that the ISI agent she recruited seemed almost too eager to take this high-risk venture, even though the bribe was substantial -- $10,000,000 Dollars USD. Yet her most dependable freelance Pakistani CIA agent and closest friend in this Region convinced her that the ISI agent recruited for the job could be trusted on two counts: First, the ISI agent believed he was helping Osama Bin Laden himself, who he revered. Second, this was a vast sum of money, so large that he would respect and honor the agreement in its entirety. Still, Fran had enough experience to know the fragility of this plan. Dealing with deceitful and dishonest people makes guarantees impossible to gauge. Because of the timeframe, she really had no choice but to make this deal.

The deal guaranteed the ISI agent a fortune. But to enjoy this fortune, he had to be smart about where to hide Osama's double and how to get him safely to the hideout, a safe haven. Fran told him that the Osama's double will be transferred to him disguised as Omar Al-Faruk. The disguise would give him cover and easy mobility, without attracting anyone's attention as he delivered his package to a safe haven.

The ISI agent needed to find a safe haven. Senior military personnel in Pakistan were a primary source. He had friends in high places at Pakistan's Military Academy in Abbottabad that could easily have such resources and welcomed bribes, but few who he could trust maintaining such a secret long term. There was only one stationed at the Academy that was a close and trusted friend. He reached out to him.

His friend, a Colonel stationed at the Pakistan's Military Academy, upon learning of the scheme, thought it preposterous until learning that he could walk away with a million US dollars. He said he could help. He would provide a safe house, a virtual mansion fortress about 800 yards from the Military Academy itself. It was undergoing repairs and was unoccupied at the moment.

Of course, the Colonel wasn't about to rent the property to such a high profile target seeking such privileged and private sanctuary. He was naturally fearful of the deal in the first place. He wanted the money, yet wanted no trace of being connected to it, other than security arrangements.

He offered to "sell" the safe house to the ISI agent for a transaction fee of $1 million in U.S. dollars and a security fee of $1,000 in U.S. Dollars monthly. The sale could be arranged so as not to identify either of them personally in the transaction yet the dollars could be transferred to a Swiss bank account for the Colonel.

That was a ton of money to ask even by the unscrupulous Colonel's standards, but he felt he could get away with it because the deal was so highly confidential and hiding a double of Bin Laden by orders of Bin Laden himself made it so dangerous. Besides, he knew it would be negotiated down, as everything in this Region of the world is negotiated.

He made the offer. It was accepted immediately. There was no negotiation. It surprised him and he felt he didn't ask for enough. It wasn't until he raised his price that he realized he made a big mistake. Nevertheless, the original deal held and the deal was made in the early morning hours, despite the house not being made available to the ISI agent for several weeks.

The transaction would be made through a middleman. This is the standard practice of business dealings in the Region, so bribes need to be spread around. This added to the complexity of confidentiality. The Colonel's price was exorbitant, yet the Colonel knew if this safe house were truly meant to become Osama's hidden Pakistan HQ, the price would not be an issue. He was right. In the meantime, the Colonel would put up the double, in disguise during transit, at a safe house until the mansion was ready.

Fran knew this Pakistani ISI agent had a history of taking bribes and proved trustworthy for keeping his mouth shut whenever implicated in past cases. The fact that the ISI agent believed he was dealing with Osama Bin Laden directly was critical too -- as that fact alone -- would insure he would keep this transaction a highly guarded secret. In fact, that was the only reason Fran decided to keep him alive once the transaction was completed.

Fran sat on the plane waiting for the call from Bryan Taylor to make the transfer. She was impressed how the ISI agent so quickly found a safe haven. She looked at him wondering if he could pull it off? The ISI agent sat across from her impatiently waiting for the transfer to take place. No money would change hands until that occurred. Waiting in this business is never a sign of good things to happen. Fran looked out her window when she saw a car pull up to the jet idling next to theirs. She watched as the Air Step descended while Nick Anthony, and two Arab men climbed aboard. Within minutes, her phone rang two times and then went silent. It was the signal she waited for. She told the ISI agent: "Let's go."

They departed their jet to the other waiting jet with the markings JJF44. Fran spirited up the steps with a Pakistani in a military uniform. Onboard, Bryan Taylor welcomed them and pointed to two seats in the back. The ISI agent sat down next to a computer already open and blinking to insert a Swiss bank account number. He reached into his pocket and pulled out a piece of paper with a number. He entered it and the screen lit up as he watched a real time transfer of $10,000,000 placed into his account. When it was completed, he shut the computer down. He looked up at Fran.

"Thank you. Let's go." Fran acknowledged by nodding and turning to depart the jet. Bryan Taylor already had Osama's double ready to depart with them, disguised as Omar al-Faruk. The ISI agent looked at Osama's double. "Can you speak English? Osama's double replied, "I do." The ISI agent smiled, "I will get you to safety. Now, we must go." Fran, the ISI agent and Osama's double departed the aircraft for their own. Fran was the last to depart. She winked to Bryan before she left.

Bryan headed to the cockpit and took his seat. Nick looked at Bryan, "What was that about?" Bryan just shook his head and said "Later, man. As soon as their plane taxis to the runway, we'll follow them." Bryan picked up his phone and punched in numbers.

"Eagle Three to Eagle Two. Over." It was Bryan Taylor to Leigh McClure. "Come in Eagle Three. This is Eagle Two. Over," replied Leigh.

"Mission accomplished. Oscar Mike. Over." Taylor confirmed success. Oscar Mike meant that they were now on the move to the next destination: Gothenburg, Sweden. "Copy that. Report status of Campy? Over." Leigh confirmed that Nick Anthony arrived safely with the Doctor and Osama's double. She wanted to know the status of the transfer of the double to the ISI Pakistani agent, code-name: Campy.

"Mission accomplished. Repeat. Mission accomplished," and then he added enthusiastically, "It's all good. Over." Bryan Taylor's reassuring voice gave her instant gratification that the mission was a complete and total success.

"Thumbs up Eagle Three. Bravo. Eagle Two Over and Out." Bryan smiled and looked at Nick: "Copy that. Eagle Three. Over and Out."

Bryan put his phone away. Nick looked at Bryan, "Let's go. Fran's plane is on the move." Bryan put his runway lights on and steered the jet toward the runway behind Fran's Lear jet, property of the Pakistan ISI agent. Fran's flight barreled down the runway and lifted off. Destination: Islamabad International Airport. Within minutes of their departure, Bryan spoke to the Parachina tower and taxied to the sole runway at 2212 hours. Flight 19 to Gothenburg was cleared for takeoff, although the logs book would show a flight plan with a different destination: Istanbul. Mission accomplished.

The jet roared down a dark runway lit only by torches and lifted off. Bryan and Nick looked at each other as the plane leveled off at 38,000 feet. They both knew that they had been in the belly of the beast in the run-up to war against Al Qaeda. They survived. They just didn't know if the Afghan was still alive – the Afghan they knew only as the Hawk.

"Ever been to Gothenburg, Nick?" Bryan asked. "Never been to Sweden. How 'bout you?" Nick replied. "No." Bryan said reflectively. A few minutes went by in silence.

"I hear that the women there are the only real blondes in the world." Nick broke the silence. Another full minute went by before Bryan answered, "Really?" Nick shot back, "That's all you got, Bryan? Really?" then they both laughed. It was the first time either of them had laughed in a long time.

It was fleeting. Within minutes, Nick as navigator spoke up again: "Tora Bora -- on your left." Nick and Bryan looked out towards the Tora Bora mountain range before turning back towards each other in acknowledgement. It was too dark to see anything in the distance. There was not a single light shining throughout the mountain range to indicate any sign of life, although Al Qaeda's large fighting force were stationed here. Neither Nick nor Bryan said another word. Perhaps words failed them because they both had too many questions left unanswered.

Since 9/11, they worked every day on special assignment with a special agent, the nameless soldier, the Afghan known only as the Hawk. While always unsure of his mission, they knew theirs – to train and support the Hawk in his mission. Their final responsibility in this mission now was to deliver the Doctor and his wife, Ayda to Gothenburg, Sweden. Upon arrival, Axel Andersson would meet him at the Gothenburg International Airport, coordinate logistics on the ground and provide the final instructions as to where to hide and shelter the Doctor and his wife.

The mission with the Hawk ended here at Tora Bora. The Hawk wasn't coming home with them. They were told only that his escape plan was coordinated with other assets and not to get involved. Yet as they flew over Tora Bora, they also knew that many of their questions must remain unanswered because of the classified nature of their operations. So this man "Hawk" must remain a mystery too. But still they both wondered, as they flew over the White Mountain range, if the Hawk made it out? They had no idea yet that they had just assisted the "Hawk" in killing America's number one enemy: Osama Bin Laden.

CHAPTER 27: MISSION ACCOMPLISHED

A Soldier Returns Home

Proof of the assassination of Osama Bin Laden was in Scott's specially designed sheaves inside his body underarmor. He was airborne in a Navy Osprey V22 as the sole passenger. Back in Kazakhstan, he had landed safely in the 'Hind' attack chopper courtesy of his Russian crew. He boarded the Osprey and was being flown to the USS Vinson aircraft carrier, somewhere in the Persian Gulf. He was in need of immediate medical attention.

The pilot of the Osprey was quick to radio in medic support needed on deck when they landed and advised of the specific injury to the Afghan on board. As the Osprey touched down on the carrier, Scott arrived in pain, and jet-lagged. He was met on deck by a medical team, headed up by a Special Forces commando assigned to the Unit. Scott recognized him from the training simulations in Arizona, a Dr. Jay Medeiros from Texas. He saluted the Afghan as they put him on a stretcher, as much as Scott said he didn't need it and could walk on his own.

When they got inside his quarters, the Doctor was first to speak: "Let's take a look at your wounds." Scott started to undress and replied, "The only injury is to my shoulder." The Doctor looked at the large blood-stains on his pants too and said sympathetically, "Yes Sir."

As Scott undressed, the medic couldn't help but be surprised at the munitions factory strapped to his torso and upper thighs. "Let me help you with that," the Doctor said as he tried to take over. Scott waved him off.

"No, please. I am not removing this." The Doctor asked, "Are you sure?" Scott nodded yes.

The Doctor began to examine Scott and his wounds. As he cleaned them, he noticed that Scott was in duress. He readied a syringe and warned Scott that he would feel a pinch, but he wanted to give him some immediate relief from the pain.

He continued evaluating his wounds. "You got lucky soldier," The Doctor said. "A single bullet ripped through your shoulder clean. It didn't take too much of you with it. The bullet went straight through you -- pretty damn lucky except you lost a lot of blood. Has that shot given you any relief yet?" Scott replied, "Yes, sir. Thank you." That's good because I need to get your shoulder back in place. You dislocated it. Give me your arm."

"I don't know, Doc. Is this necessary right now?" Scott replied. "Don't worry. I'm really good at this, soldier. I'll be quick." The Doctor reached out and took Scotts arm. "You'll feel so much better. Promise." The Doctor slowly rotated Scott's arm several times and then, without warning, jerked Scott's arm hard and let go saying, "That's it." Scott's shoulder popped back perfectly in place and it instantly felt better.

"Wow – Oh my god, that feels so much better. You're damn good at this, Doc. Thank you." The Doctor replied modestly: "Don't mention it," as he started tapping another needle immediately. "Now, I'm gonna give you a cocktail of pain killers to help you heal and sleep on your way home. Ready?"

"As long as you have something to chase it with," said Scott, as he winced demonstrably in pain as the Doctor stuck the needle straight into his shoulder wound. He blurted out during the shot: "Jesus, Doc, did you need to stick that right there?"

"Yes, sorry soldier, but you'll thank me later. That was loaded with painkillers." Scott winced and replied, "Yeah, make sure you remind me later, OK?" The Doctor smiled as he readied yet another needle for injection. "OK, One last shot. Good stuff - antibiotics. Give me your hip -- won't hurt. Promise. Are you ready?" Scott nodded yes closing his eyes. As soon as the injection was finished, the Doctor said, "Not so bad, was it? Good news. No more shots. However, I need to put in a few stitches to make sure we stop that bleeding for good." The Doctor paused looking at Scott to make sure he was OK. "You good, soldier?" the Doctor asked.

"About that chaser…could use a whiskey to be honest," Scott replied. The Doctor laughed, "Me too." Scott answered with a smile, "That's comforting, you sure you're a Doc?" The Doctor laughed, "I just don't think it's polite to let a hero drink alone."

"Oh, I'm no hero, Doc," Scott replied quickly. "So, what are you saying soldier? You don't want me to drink while I'm stitching you up?" the Doc replied in jest. "You drive a hard bargain, Doc," Scott replied. "How about before you begin stitching that we enjoy a whiskey first?"

"Coming right up." The Doctor smiled and retrieved a bottle of Jack Daniels and poured two glasses. He raised his glass to Scott and made a toast: "To your health, soldier!" They clinked glasses and the Doctor finished cleaning loose bullet shrapnel from Scott's shoulder and several areas in his thigh, knee and calf. He kept referring to his patient as lucky. "Whoever cleaned the shoulder wound and put compresses on stopped a good part of the bleeding. He knew what he was doing. You could easily have bled out." Scott just kept thinking that this doctor had no idea just how lucky he really was today.

The stitches, 37 of them on his shoulder and another dozen or so in his leg and side, seemed excessive to Scott, as he was completely unaware of fragments torn into his right leg. It took well over an hour and several shots of whiskey by Scott for Dr. Medeiros to finish the job. When he finished patching Scott up, Dr. Medeiros said: "We're done for now. A few things you must know. I had to leave in some bullet fragments because they were too deep to incise them out. They were so deeply embedded in your tissue that they could cause nerve or muscle damage if I kept digging."

"Understand, Doc. But what are you saying?" Scott asked thinking he might have a serious problem. The Doctor looked intently at Scott. "Look. You're going to be ok. It's just that you will be carrying around a bit of lead inside you as a reminder to where you've been. I'm giving you these pills – they're painkillers and I already loaded you up with antibiotics with that shot. You need to see a doctor as soon as you get back in the States. But you are going to be fine. You just need to get a lot of rest." Scott took the drug packet, smiled at the Doctor and shook his hand. "Thanks, Doc." He got up to dress and leave.

As he got off the table, the Doctor said: "I don't know what you did today soldier to earn these stitches. Nor am I supposed to know. I know you don't want to be called a hero, so I won't go there. So just let me say, Thank you soldier. It's been an honor. Godspeed."

"Thanks again, Doc," Scott replied asking, "Share a final drink with me before I leave?" Dr. Medeiros smiles and without hesitation pours generously from the bottle of Jack Daniels. Within minutes, without words, they clink glasses and drain their glasses.

"Do you know how much time I have before my departure?" Scott asked. "Your plane is on standby," the Doctor replied. "We have a change of clothing for you in one of our Officers Quarters. A hot shower will help you sleep on the long flight back to the States. Take as long as you need. How does that sound?" Scott smiles. "A hot shower is welcome. Thanks again."

Scott starts to dress. "Let me help you," The doctor starts to assist Scott. When Scott is ready, he escorts him to an Officer Quarters on deck.

As Scott showered, shaved his beard, and put on civilian clothes laid out for him in the officer quarters, the thought of putting his dirty, sweat-covered body underarmor back on wasn't pleasant, but necessary. He had tried to air the underarmor out in his cabin while showering but it was heavy, wet with sweat and dried blood, and carried the weight of formidable forensics evidence of the death of Osama Bin Laden. He had no option except to put this on first before the clean clothing. But before he did, it was not before checking each sheath and assuring that the contents were securely contained inside each section.

Putting the underarmor back on with his shoulder injury seemed next to impossible. The pain pierced into his shoulder, his neck and spine every time he moved it. Even the whiskey and drugs didn't help much every time he moved. He had no choice. After fitting the underarmor as tight to his body as he possibly could, he put on the civilian clothes from his bag, casual jeans and a striped blue oxford shirt with a pair of Frye cowboy boots. Finally, he put on a blue blazer, which fit well enough over his underarmor without attracting any undue attention, considering how much artillery and forensics evidence the underarmor was hiding underneath it all. The blazer had his new passport and identity inside the blazer pocket. He studied these new documents. It all seemed so surreal.

He had one more flight to catch back to the States. It would be on a U.S. Navy Gulfstream III.

As he boarded his flight to Washington, D.C., he realized he was not going home, because he never could go home again. Everything began to sink in. He accomplished the mission and survived. The news would be a bombshell. What comes next, he thought?

He was too exhausted to think of it as he buckled up. The U.S. Navy C20 Gulfstream III taxied to the end of the runway deck for instructions to takeoff down the USS Vinson carrier deck. Scott could not help but notice the hyperactivity on deck and never before noticed so many fighter jets on alert on the deck of a carrier. As his jet rumbled down the deck for takeoff, the sight of the slew of fighters on alert was an awesome image. He wondered how long would it be now for the U.S. Armed Forces to retaliate against Al Qaeda? He wondered if his actions today would in any way impact the direction and final outcome of what was now a certainty: war.

As soon as the plane reached an altitude of 34,000 feet and leveled off, a navy flight attendant, Susan Lynch, went over to the only civilian onboard, also the only passenger onboard. Susan Lynch had never seen this man before, but she knew that this man, all 6'2" blue eyes hunk of him, had to be someone special. He was not only the sole occupant onboard as a passenger, but under the manifest he was listed peculiarly as "OPSEC" – meaning this passenger was on a need to know basis only: Operational Security is classified.

"Can I get you something to drink, sir?" Susan said with a warm and welcoming smile. "Whiskey, neat. Thank you," Scott replied. "Can I get you anything else? A meal? Snack? Susan answered with a slight flirtation in her Southern drawl. Scott replied, "No thanks. I'll probably sleep through the entire flight."

"Should I make it a double then? I'm sorry I didn't get your name." Susan smiled pouring on her Southern charm. Scott couldn't help but smile: "Can't help you with my name," he paused looking at her. "All they gave me was a serial number since I took this job. I'll take you up on that double though." She continued to flirt, "Scotch or Irish?"

"Irish," he said instinctively. "You got it soldier. That's funny about your name," she said playfully. "They did the same with me when I joined the Navy. Serial numbers are a mouthful in a conversation so I still use my former name sometimes on the job." Scott laughed, "What would that be?" he asked, actually enjoying her flirtation. "Susan," she said it softly and dramatically in her southern drawl.

"Susan," he repeated her name just as softly. "A pretty name," he said reflectively while smiling at her now. "Much prettier sounding too with that southern drawl. Where are you from?"

Susan answered, "Dallas, Texas is my home. But enough about me, you all." She said with her wide smile. "Let me get that drink for you. I can see how tired you are."

When Susan came back with the drink, she also brought him a blanket, a pillow and some bottled water. When she finished, he said: "How long is this flight?"

"About 13 to 14 hours overall, depending on headwinds and time it takes to refuel," she replied. "The first leg is eight hours with a pit stop on the USS John F. Kennedy in the Atlantic. Andrews is about five hours from the carrier with time zone changes. I will be checking on you often, so if you need anything, just let me know. But if I find you asleep through our pit stop, should I just let you sleep? You look so tired," she said softly, caringly.

"I am." He replied almost with a sigh. "No need to fuss over me. I'll sleep straight through."

"Goodnight," she said. "Get some rest," she whispered as she reached over him and turned off his overhead reading light and went back to her station where she also dimmed all the cabin lights.

She watched his silhouette take down the whiskey quickly. His arm fell off the armrest as he fell asleep in his seat almost immediately. She waited for a few minutes before going over to him, putting the blanket over him and reclining his seat. He started to stir but never awoke. She picked up his glass. He was breathing deeply, sound asleep. She went back to her station wondering who he was?

She witnessed the high alert activity on the aircraft carrier where they were dispatched to transport this sole passenger back to the States. War was imminent. Her passenger had no name and this flight was on "OPSEC". She wondered if he knew what would be happening in this crazy world next?

Area 7
The White House
Washington, D.C.

Sunday evening September 30th, Washington D.C. Leigh is at her desk in the middle of a telephone conversation with Dr. Jay Medeiros still onboard the USS Vinson. "You are right about that," Medeiros is saying. "The wounds are for the most part superficial. Several shots pierced him. A bullet passed clean through his shoulder, a good thing really. But I had to leave some other bullet fragments inside him. He was in a lot of pain but has meds now. He's a strong guy – he'll recover quickly," Medeiros informs her.

"Thanks Jay. Will he need a Doctor when he arrives here?" Leigh asked. "He's pretty beaten up," Medeiros answers. "I don't see any need for a Doctor when he lands. I do recommend he see a Doctor for follow-up as soon as he can after he settles in." Leigh replies, "Thanks Jay. I hope to see you soon." Medeiros replies, "That will be nice. Quick question. When he departed, his Jet was flanked by F-16s. Can you tell me what his mission was?" Leigh answered, "No can do. Just know that you just helped a real American hero. I've got to run. Bye."

As soon as Leigh put down the call, Max Leonhardt came into her office. "All schedules are updated. Hawk is on the move. You'll pick him up in the morning at Andrews [Andrews Air Force Base]." Leonhardt continued, "Fran called and confirmed the transfer of Osama's double with the ISI agent went without a hitch." Leigh said, "That's great news. What are we hearing from CIA out of Afghanistan?" she asked.

"More good news," Leonhardt answered. "CIA reported no chatter about the drone attack or any other incidents at Tora Bora. They did report sightings of Osama Bin Laden crossing the Pakistan border after sunset. Of course that's our double, they sighted. The answer is that all is quiet now on the Afghan front." Leigh repeated Leonhardt's last words softly, "Hmmm, All is quiet on the Afghan front." Then she added, "Interesting."

Leonhardt then added, "The video recording of UBL's kill is now in Secretary Rumsfeld's hands. And one last item for your follow-up." Leigh said, "Go ahead." "Crumpton wants to hear from you ASAP." Leonhardt replied and added, "Apparently CIA loaned two local freelance contacts to our UNIT in Pakistan yesterday. They were reported missing." Leigh answered slowly, "That was unfortunate. I'll call Crumpton after we finish up tonight."

Leigh and Leonhardt spent the next hour developing a checklist and reviewing details to close down OPERATION: HAWK'S NEST. They also quickly reviewed logistics for tomorrow's pickup of the 'Hawk' at Andrews Air Force Base. When the briefing concluded, she told Max to assemble the team at 19:45 tonight in the control room.

After Max left, she called Crumpton at CIA on his secure phone. "Crumpton." He answered knowing it was Leigh on his caller ID. She didn't mince words. "Your freelance party won't be coming home. There was an accident. The scene is secure."

"Anything else I should know?" Crumpton said sadly, understanding that any op has its risks. "No," Leigh answered. "That wraps up my business today. Thank you, Hank." She personalized it, knowing Crumpton was a big help today and understanding that he was not happy being left out of the loop on an operation in his influence area.

"Someday we should have dinner together Leigh, don't you think? I bet it would be interesting?" "I bet it would," Leigh laughed continuing, "Do you think we'll ever find the time?" Crumpton answered her sincerely: "Let's not let time be the excuse. Do take care." Without hesitation, Leigh replied: "The same to you, my friend." She hung up.

Her next call was to Don Rumsfeld on his secure ops phone. It was late in the afternoon in the nations capital. "Rumsfeld." He said identifying himself. "Good news, sir. Mission accomplished. Agent and hard evidence arrive mid-morning. FYI: Dead Quiet, repeat Dead Quiet." (Dead Quiet was code for zero acknowledgement of UBL's assassination by Al Qaeda.)

"Congratulations, Leigh. Dead quiet confirmed. Casualties?"

"None on our side, sir." Leigh said. "Incredible." Rumsfeld meant it and went on: "Tell everyone in your Unit bravo." "I will, sir," she replied.

"Angler [code name for Vice President Dick Cheney] will want to meet when the agent arrives. Is there a timeframe that works for you?" Rumsfeld asked. Leigh said, "The agent may need follow-up with a medic on arrival. He's ambulatory but recovering from gunshot wounds. Say mid-afternoon?" Rumsfeld answered, "That will work."

There was a long silence before Rumsfeld talked again. "Leigh... are you still there?" "Yes, sir, " she answered. Rumsfeld asked softly: "Is he OK?"

"Time will tell. He has new scars." Leigh spoke from her heart. Another long silence ensued before Rumsfeld spoke. "From what I have observed, he wears scars well. The words of Cormac McCarthy come to mind: 'Scars have the strange power to remind us our past is real.' You deserve Congratulations, Leigh. I will call you with plans for tomorrow after I speak to Angler." Rumsfeld hung up.

Leigh still had hours to go to close down OPERATION HAWK'S NEST. In the evening, she met with her Unit team, passed on Rumsfeld's congratulations, and instructed the team to close the Ops Command Center down and take the day off tomorrow light. Light means stay close to home and make sure you answer your alerts. The Unit was on call 24/7.

Every Unit Team specialist is sworn to secrecy. They serve at the will of the President of the United States. Secrecy is sacrosanct in the Unit and plausible deniability by the government applies to every mission. The team was witness to and active participants in the assassination of America's number one enemy today. No casualties to report. Mission Accomplished. Yet, the brave men and women of the Unit could not celebrate this success. Praise is not for patriots and change was in the wind.

The Ritz Carlton
Istanbul, Turkey
Suite 1228
The day before

Khalib Seergy was frightened as he sat uncomfortably, in a most comfortable chair, in a luxurious suite, number 1228, on the Concierge floor of the Ritz Carlton Hotel. This hotel on the hill had breathtaking views of the city, overlooking the mystical mosques and markets of Istanbul on the sea. Yet, even with such a stunning, panoramic view from his room, Khalib

Seergy could not see the beauty of the city in front of him. He checked in himself earlier with no cash, no checks, no luggage, no mobile phone, no computer and just one credit card after being dropped off by the woman who abducted him in New York a day earlier. Was it just a day? It felt like a lifetime and with each hour prospects dimmed. He still feared for his life and wondered how his life could change so dramatically in just one day.

He was rattled and still thinking deeply about Leigh's last words to him as he was dropped off at the marine terminal, near the bottom of the hill. Her threats became real as he began the steep trek up the hill to the Ritz Carlton Hotel. He was reliving the moment and his mind wandered to a weird circumstance as he was walking to the hotel, as instructed. He was about halfway up the hill, when he could see a burly, unkempt rotund Arab man, armed with nothing but a shoeshine kit, sitting on a park bench. He got up from the bench just before he reached him and started walking slowly in front of him, slower than his own pace, for sure. As he did, he also inadvertently dropped one of his brushes from the kit.

It landed almost directly in front of him so Khalib instinctively picked it up and yelled out to the man to get his attention: "Hey, you dropped something." The burly Arab stopped and when Seergy got right behind him, he turned and forcefully grabbed him by his shirt pushing his fist hard into Seergy's Adam's apple.

"You're being watched. Go directly to your hotel and do not leave your room. Under any circumstances - you understand?" Seergy replied quickly, "But I was just trying to…" Seergy was cut off in mid-sentence.

"Shut the fuck up little man," he squeezed Seergy's neck tighter, "Go to your room and stay there. Do not leave until I knock on your door in ten days. Now, go!" Seergy nodded yes as he stared into the Arab man's eyes of death. Then the Arab man let him go and he watched Seergy hightail it up the steep roadway to the entrance of the Ritz Carlton.

At the entrance, a security team was waiting for him and he checked in. An hour later, after checking in to the hotel, he was still clearly desperate and afraid, still fearful that every move he makes is being watched.

Leigh, whose name he did not know, but who he feared more than any other person in the world, except Osama Bin Laden, told him to check in here at the Ritz Carlton, where Suite 1228 would be reserved for him. She told him to never leave his room for any reason, to order only room service and not ever to make a telephone call outside of the hotel or have any contact with hotel staff. He was told that he was being monitored 24/7 by Osama Bin Laden's secret guards at the hotel and if he did any of these things, he was promised a slow, painful death. If he cooperated fully, and if all the monetary transfers were made, he would be contacted in ten days and he would be free to leave, unharmed. The Arab on the street made her message resonate.

What other choice did he have? Armed only with one credit card that she took from his own wallet, his Black American Express card, he realized he was also personally getting stuck paying for this room, which would become his personal prison cell for the next ten days. That is assuming he stays put and follows her instructions. There certainly was no question in his mind that he would obey Leigh's every instruction. The final words from his female abductor (before he was released on the dock) were that these instructions were coming directly from Osama Bin Laden. He saw the man that directed the 9/11 attacks just hours before and his life was now tethered to his for life. Leigh had leaned in close to him for her final instruction and whispered in his ear, in Arabic: "Do you understand, Khalib?"

"Sallallahu ʿalayhi wasallam," he replied. For the first time in Khalib Seergy's life, this self-anointed master of the universe had no clue what to do next. Leigh did. She had no plans to ever call this asshole back.

CHAPTER 28: SEA CHANGE

Office of the Vice President, The White House

It was certainly not the reaction Rumsfeld expected from Vice President Dick Cheney. Cheney had just one word to say when he was told about the assassination of Osama Bin Laden and Scott's successful escape, aided by the Russians: "Fuck."

The Vice President sat in rapt attention in his office on Sunday night September 30th as the Secretary of Defense briefed him on key aspects of the hunt and kill of Osama Bin Laden by Scott Walsh and Leigh Ann McClure and her Unit. He was reading the TOP SECRET Classified document as Rumsfeld spoke. Cheney's reaction was immediate.

It was followed by silence as Cheney was clearly thinking now. "Let's meet this hero at Andrews with McClure, is that possible?" Cheney spoke, but he was still deep in thought, almost if Rumsfeld was invisible. "Of course. I will arrange it." Rumsfeld said quietly. "The Russians airlifted him. Do the Russians know what we were doing?" Cheney looked up now, as if to see Rumsfeld's reaction.

"Intel scout op is all they know." Rumsfeld replied. "No doubt they think we have a spy from the Northern Alliance under our wing. Al Qaeda is a mutual enemy."

"Is there any way they could know we got Bin Laden?" Cheney asks? Rumsfeld replied spontaneously, "No sir. Absolutely not."

Cheney nods, keeps reading the brief. Several minutes go by in absolute silence. "How many doubles are there now?" Cheney asks. "Including this one we're hiding in Pakistan, just two." Rumsfeld clarifies. "Incredible." Cheney mutters as he strokes his chin.

Rumsfeld sat facing Cheney in quiet again for several more minutes. He knew Dick well enough to know that he was just thinking, but knew too not to leave, as Cheney hadn't dismissed him yet. Cheney sits back now from his desk. He looks straight at Rumsfeld. "Brilliant. Al Qaeda has just lost their leader and they think the Northern Alliance just settled a score over Mossoud's assassination."

"Brilliant indeed. Leigh said it was Scott's plan all the way, after the doubles were confirmed. Still, al-Zawahiri knows we had something to do with it." Rumsfeld replied seeing Cheney was ready to engage. "I bet he does. Hellfire missiles on drones, dammit there's American ingenuity. Still no chatter about all this?" Cheney asked. "Nothing," Rumsfeld replied. We're monitoring reports by the hour now from NSA." Cheney nods.

"Al Qaeda doesn't want anybody to know is my guess. I wouldn't be surprised if Ayman al-Zawahiri is already selecting the double to decoy as UBL himself. That sonofabitch didn't think Bin Laden had the guts to be the leader anyway. Think about it: the mastermind al-Zawahiri now takes over. The decoy UBL is going to be broadcast as the real McCoy on Al Jazeera ad nausea now until we attack. Is that a good thing or bad for us?" Rumsfeld spontaneously replies: "Frankly, I hadn't considered it."

Cheney pauses before making his own guess: "My gut tells me that if al-Zawahiri and Al Qaeda keep the assassination of Bin Laden under wraps, we might consider keeping the lid on it too." Rumsfeld tilts his head inquisitively yet remains silent. Yet another unexpected response from Cheney, he wonders where he is going with this?

Cheney catches Rumsfeld's reaction and continues: "If the past few weeks have taught me anything about this Congress, they would take this assassination as news that the war is over before it started." He sits back and continues: "They just don't get it. There is just such little appetite to fight on the hill. Why no one wants to cast the net over this region right now to demonstrate our power is beyond me. Why they don't want to scare these goddamn terrorists from ever thinking about coming to our shores again is beyond comprehension."

"I agree." Rumsfeld concurs. "I'm absolutely convinced," Cheney continues, "After hearing this news, that we keep it as tightlipped as they do. It allows us two things: First: an advantage knowing that Bin Laden is dead. We don't need to spend any more capital hunting for this monster. Second: We can push harder now than ever on our focus on Iraq. We have an upper hand to sweep all this shit up at once. We may never have such advantage again. What do you think?"

Rumsfeld replied thoughtfully: "This is all very intriguing. I see that. They don't know if we know, so they wait. They think if we know, we will broadcast it all over the world. We don't. They start parading out a decoy as the real thing to see what we do. We do nothing. Perhaps, this is a perfect standoff." He pauses. "Or perhaps, it's too simplistic?"

"Perhaps it presents us another opportunity that we hadn't thought of?" Cheney adds inquisitively. Rumsfeld nods his head and plays it out: "Alright. We know we just interrupted Al Qaeda's planning just days before we launch our ground war. It will be a real advantage attacking when chaos is creeping in their chain of command, especially if Ayman al-Zawahiri has to pretend to take orders from a walking mannequin of UBL and needs to squelch any rumors quickly that the real UBL is dead."

"Advantage yes, but I'm talking about a more strategic opportunity that presents itself." Cheney offers. "I see that too." Rumsfeld concurs and continues, "Congress doesn't know what we know so the threats remain just as real as yesterday. I must agree with you, Dick. During the past several weeks, you had to lobby incessantly for an invasion of Iraq, even as the war planning for Afghanistan was in motion." Rumsfeld paused again as he sees Cheney is listening intently. "Why is it not obvious to them?" Rumsfeld queried. "Why can't they see the need to focus on all things related to terror right here and right now and go massive? The United States must display our military strength on a bigger, worldwide stage as a result of 9/11 to show terrorists we will not tolerate it. It is disappointing that Congress would see the assassination as mission accomplished. After 9/11, our job is now defined. Perhaps, it is our fate. We have an advantage now. Let's see what develops overseas overnight." Cheney doesn't reply right away. He looks deep in thought again.

"Agreed," Cheney says after a few minutes and without any concern in his voice. "I am looking forward to meeting Scott tomorrow. He will need to know why we may need to quiet his accomplishments right now. Assuming that we decide to do that. He'll be useful in future endeavors. How can we make that happen?"

"We have that contingency in place." Rumsfeld says with determination. "There is no precedent really. But this never happened in the first place. Scott Walsh no longer exists. Yet, we now have a ghost assassin as a secret agent in our service." Cheney nods and asks: "We have much to think about tonight. Loose ends?"

Rumsfeld is quick to reply: "If we decide to keep the assassination of Bin Laden under wraps, if that remains an option on the table tomorrow morning, the only variable is Scott." Cheney is just as quick: "Sometimes you surprise me. Scott is the only constant in this whole equation. That is why I selected him for the mission in the first place. He may not agree with our politics, but he will do anything to keep his son and daughter, the only people he has left in this rotten world to live for – safe." Rumsfeld replied,

"But sir, that is exactly what I mean." Rumsfeld continues with an added emphasis: "Scott will want to see his son and daughter. Immediately. They attended his funeral last week in New York. It's complicated."

Cheney pauses, but decisively ends their discussion on a very personal note: "Don, how long have we known each other? I don't believe in complicated. Let's see what develops in the morning and make the right decisions." Cheney stands and shakes Rumsfeld's hand firmly. "Job well done, my friend. Very well done. It's nice to have an early victory as we brace for what's ahead." Rumsfeld nods and leaves and as he does says softly to himself: "God help us."

Georgetown
After dark – same day

Leigh arrived at her townhouse in a White House unmarked staff town car shortly after 9:00 in the evening. She hadn't slept here since September 10th. She bought this townhouse less than a year ago primarily because she was thinking of an early retirement and pursuing a teaching career at Georgetown's School of Foreign Service, within easy walking distance. Funny how events shape your life?

She got out of the car and walked up a small spiral stairway leading to her front door. She loved coming home. She felt at home in her new house too, with an entrance flanked at night by two large gaslights, flames flickering furtively as if winking seductively at her own secretive service. She fumbled through her purse to find her keys, probably the only thing in her life that she always seemed to lose. This is the first home she has lived in that she had yet needed to break into because of lost keys. She fished around the bottomless bag one last time and found it.

She opened the door and froze. Instinctively, she knew someone was in her townhouse. Her reaction was swift and intuitive. She withdrew her sidearm, unlocked its safety, crouched and started to move slowly and deliberately through the foyer. When she came to the open archway leading into the parlor, she crouched and leapt quickly into the room, eyes sweeping the room rapidly with revolver steady to fire at any sudden movement, when she saw someone sitting in a chair.

She aimed at his head recognizing him instantaneously. She lowered her revolver. "Ever hear of knocking, perhaps calling first?" she said sounding peculiarly pissed off, as she locked her pistol and started putting it back in her holster. "I'm so sorry." Don Rumsfeld said as he stood, still in his coat. "I should have called."

"Really, Mr. Secretary?" Leigh said with an indignant formality as she put away her sidearm. "I see I've rattled you. I'm so sorry. Trust me it was not my intention. Have you eaten yet, Leigh?"

"What?" Leigh relaxed. "No, I haven't eaten. Prefer a stiff drink right about now, join me?"

"Keep your coat on," Rumsfeld continued. "You deserve a hero's toast and a patriot's meal."

"Really? I'm exhausted and look like shit."

"I won't take no for an answer." He stood and ushered her back out the door.

Rumsfeld's SUV pulled up and took them to a favorite in this town. At the restaurant, Leigh realized that nothing surprises her anymore. They are dining in a private room at J&Gs, in a room, which she didn't know existed, above the main dining area in the restaurant. The room is small and secluded yet intimate, warmly lit with candles and a spectacular view of the Washington Monument at night. As tired as she is, she is famished.

They had just started on the main course of NY Strip steaks when a bottle of Amarone was opened. Rumsfeld had ordered Amarone calling it the elixir of heroes as they drank to Scott and Leigh and her team's success. She wondered if he knew that Amarone was also Scott's favorite red wine?

What followed Rumsfeld's toast and congratulations disturbed her universe. He briefed her on what he and Cheney were thinking of doing if Al Qaeda was going to try to conceal Bin Laden's assassination. She was dumbfounded. What are they thinking? What is Scott going to think?

They talked about it. Debated its merits, without anger or emotion. Rumsfeld left the topic open-ended unless chatter developed and was discovered by NSA on Bin Laden's assassination by morning. Leigh wondered if Don really wanted her input or if he was trying to sell her on the idea. She trusted Don well enough to give him the benefit of the doubt. Yet she had this nagging concern that there was a rush to war in Iraq for all the wrong reasons.

Their conversation soon focused on keeping OPERATION HAWK'S NEST engaged as an ongoing black op. Donald Rumsfeld is a persuasive man and his attention to detail and sense of urgency are impressive. Leigh is being given absolute authority and carte blanche power to run a phantom assassin op ongoing in the most powerful country in the world. Absolute power, she knew all too well, in this town can be corrupting. Many who have chosen this path have been left to rot in the dustbins of history. If she and her Unit or Scott were ever caught on the wrong side of history, they will be held by oath to deny its very existence, as the government would invoke plausible deniability.

Leigh worried about Scott's arrival tomorrow with this extraordinary turn of events. She was pleased that Cheney would be there at Andrews to greet him. She was relieved somewhat that it would be Cheney and Rumsfeld to brief him on how the government was going to handle the assassination. She asked him if it was possible for Scott and POTUS to meet. Rumsfeld just ignored the question. She didn't ask again. It was when Don started talking about Scott's future, as a special phantom agent for the United States, that Leigh realized that Don was widening her berth to creatively handle issues central to Scott's life ahead – how he could still remain anonymous, yet still possibly be secretly reunited with his son and daughter.

They talked well into the night. About the upcoming war, some politics, but mostly how to protect Scott and reward him for his service. When he dropped her off back at her townhouse, it was close to midnight. His cell phone rang just as she was getting out. He grabbed her arm ushering her back in the SUV. She pivoted and sat back down. Don was answering the phone.

"Yes sir. Let me put her on." He hands her his cell phone as Leigh uses her free hand to gesture a question of who it is on the phone? Rumsfeld ignores her and just hands her the phone. She says: "McClure."

"Good evening Leigh. This is the President." Her eyes widen as she looks to Rumsfeld. "Mr. President, good evening." She replied. "I know it's late but I just met with the Vice President and received the great news. I'm calling because I want to thank you." Leigh said, "I appreciate the call, Sir. It was a real team effort."

"An outstanding team effort to be sure." The President replied and continued, "Let me add on behalf of every American tonight, bravo. Sleep well tonight, Leigh, knowing that America sleeps safer tonight because of what you and your team have sacrificed for your country." Leigh replied, "Mr. President. Thank you. I will pass this on to the team."

"Leigh, one last thing. I am sorry that I don't have the time to thank you or your team in person. But I will soon. Goodnight." Leigh replied, "Goodnight, Mr. President." She hands the phone back to Don and smiles.

"Nice touch, Mr. Secretary. Did that really just happen?" Rumsfeld smiled, "Classified, can't say 'really' about anything much anymore. Goodnight. Get some rest. See you tomorrow."

As Leigh got out of the limo, she turned to Don, "Goodnight, Mr. Secretary. Thank you too for a welcome intrusion." She added smiling back at him, "But seriously, I wouldn't make a habit of surprising me in my home again. See you tomorrow." Rumsfeld salutes her.

When she reached her front door, she dug back into her purse to find her key. This time she was fumbling on purpose and waiting for Don's armored SUV limo to turn down the street. As soon as the car was out of sight, she went back down the stairs and rang the doorbell of an apartment she leases out in her basement. Within a minute, an outside light came on and the door opened.

"Leigh. What a surprise. Haven't seen you in a while. Is everything OK?" an older gentleman said while opening the door. "I'm unsure. I could use your advice." Leigh answered. "For what its worth, please come in my dear Leigh. It's late." He replied seeing she was worried. "I'm sorry it's so late. I promise not to keep you." Leigh said apologetically. "But it's important."

He looked at her sympathetically, "Don't worry about keeping this old man up. You know I hardly sleep. Please come in." As she entered, she said "Thanks, Daniel."

"You look worried. Why don't you pour each of us a brandy? I'll start a fire." Daniel started toward the fireplace. "You're so kind. You sure it's OK – it's quite late?" she said tentatively. "Really. It's fine," he laughed. "Now go get that brandy or I will change my mind."

She laughed with him, "I'm on it. How lucky I am to have you as a friend?" He looked at her saying, "How many times do I have to tell you that luck never has anything to do with it?"

Between conversation of conspiracy mixed with Cognac and a Bailey's Irish Cream, a crackling fire cast calming shadows dancing throughout the cozy man cave that Professor Daniel Hislop occupied under her townhouse. He didn't always live here. He owned the entire townhouse for more than thirty years and just a few years earlier, sold his townhouse to Leigh after consulting with her on moving out. He hadn't fully expected Leigh to buy it but he was so happy when she did. He never wanted to move out, but events made his decision necessary.

Daniel Hislop lost his wife, a former analyst with the NSA, tragically and suddenly almost five years before he thought about selling the townhouse. His wife, Ruth, died from a rare blood clot in her leg that traveled to her heart one night while she was sleeping. Death came in the dark of night without any warning. She was only 57 at her death. He was two years older.

When he was nearing 67, still grieving silently and alone, his children persuaded him to seek smaller quarters, especially one without so many stairs. His daughter, Emily, a librarian in San Francisco, and his son, David, a political science professor at the University of Chicago, convinced him that he didn't need such a big home now and that their visits would be easier for them, if he traveled to their homes instead of their traveling to Washington D.C. to visit him. They understood he would probably never retire from Georgetown University, but it was more difficult for them to visit as they each had small children now. As much as he still loved this house, even he rationalized that his children were right. It was too large to navigate, with far too many steps to climb, especially as he grew on in years. He hated to leave it so he thought that perhaps he could create a separate basement apartment and possibly lease it from a new owner. He had asked

Leigh, as a good friend, if she thought anyone would buy his townhouse if he stayed on as a tenant in a basement apartment. She agreed to help find a buyer.

Daniel invested in a major renovation to make the basement a separate apartment. He had hired the acclaimed architect, Edward Fitzgerald of New York and Santa Fe, to create an elegant yet cozy one-bedroom apartment underneath his townhouse. Fitzgerald created two elaborate entrances, in the front and back. In the front, he tore down the concrete steps leading into the main house and created a descending pathway accessible from two sides behind newly carved archways under a new grand spiral main stairway of his own design leading back up to the main house. Underneath these main stairs leading into the main house in the Townhouse, he designed a rotunda of sorts, unique with its mosaic-tiled dome underneath it and which led almost invitingly towards the basement apartment. This path from the rotunda descended gradually through a short corridor. Fitzgerald had engineered a way to eliminate stairs completely by developing this declining path and he flanked the path with light colored Spanish Colonial tile and mosaics and landscape lighting. Two oversized mahogany doors welcomed you as you came to the end of the corridor. As you entered the basement apartment through this gateway, a visual sweeping view of a sunken living room led your eyes to a north wall ensconced with a grand neoclassical custom fireplace designed by Walter Arnold. Translucent backlit brocatello di Siena panels surrounded the fireplace carved in volcano onyx with brocatello insets. There was an American eagle set into the onyx niche above the mantel. The back entrance was just as unique and brought you in to the expansive country kitchen, via a circular garden entrance with a series of single steps leading to custom French doors. The fireplace in the rear was massive, large enough to handle a cauldron, fitting perfectly in the country kitchen décor.

Leigh entered tonight at Dr. Hislop's front entrance to his basement apartment. The furnishings in the living room were simple yet comfortable and warm. As Leigh now poured the brandy, she remembered how she had been a guest at the house several times before she had bought it from Professor Hislop. She remembered when he told her about his plans for this basement apartment. Until then, she had only seen the first floor and garden so she asked to see the entire townhouse before she gave him an opinion. She loved it and liked the idea of having her now good friend Dr. Daniel Hislop from Georgetown University as her neighbor. He had been trying to recruit her as a professor at Georgetown for some time, which tempted her often to think about retiring from the government and teaching. Without hesitation at the time, she told the Doctor someone would indeed buy it knowing the basement would come with a lease tenant. Just days later, before Daniel even listed it, she bought it herself.

She was glad she bought this house even though she didn't see much of it this past year. It was close to everything she loved about Washington. Her front door was just steps to Dumbarton Oaks and Montrose Park, on 31st Street between R and Q streets. She loved the coffee at Georgetown Cupcake, the eggs benedict brunch at Martin's Tavern on a Sunday morning, and the owner at Filomena's made her feel like she was his best customer. Hardly a Sunday went by, when she was in town, that she didn't also spend time on the lawn at Georgetown University reading and discussing world events with Daniel.

Mostly, she loved just being in the company of Daniel. He was a wise and witty man and trustworthy friend. Leigh and Dr. Hislop shared a fascination of the clandestine world of secrets that transform the world. They also shared a keen sense of history. They also believed that there are evil people that disturb the universe and that it was imperative for righteous people to shape history. What happened in the last twenty days only happened because a proffer by Dr. Hislop was put to its test. Leigh as much wanted to inform him, as she was interested in hearing his opinions, on keeping what happened in Tora Bora a secret. Moral questions and values were always sharply debated in the Doctor's den, none more so than tonight.

"What you are telling me is incredible. My intuition tells me not to trust Cheney. Any of them, really." Hislop told Leigh. "What do you mean?" replied Leigh. "Think about it carefully. He wants Bin Laden dead. He gets what he wants but tries to cover it up. Why?"

"OK, I see where you are going. But the point Rumsfeld made is bigger than that."

"Is it?" Hislop fires back at her. "I am a scholar of Islam and the Middle East. Iraq had nothing to do with this and these guys know it. There is an agenda here bigger than us."

"You are such a cynic. I should never have come to see you tonight."

"A cynic, Leigh? Your logic is indefensible. And you know that. You are so much better than this. You must be tired beyond belief. Can't you see how bad this is going to turn out?"

"Such the drama queen, Daniel, really!" Leigh exclaims in exasperation. "There are truths and consequences to all events and when they are secret, we both know the outcomes are never truly known. So long as men can breathe or eyes can see."

"No. Really, Leigh?" Hislop says in disbelief. "Dare you use Shakespeare in this widening web of deceit? At least quote Hamlet, if you must." He is theatrical in his gestures but he calms down and speaks to Leigh like a trusted friend. "I am now worried for your own safety. To be honest, this hero who just killed Osama Bin Laden is probably the next dead man in this story." He leans towards her, takes a deep breath, and looks straight into her eyes. "That is why you wanted to talk tonight, isn't it?"

That is when the conversation got more intense and interesting. When Leigh left Daniel at around 2:30 in the morning, she knew exactly what to do next.

CHAPTER 29: HOMECOMING

Washington, D.C.
October 1, 2001

Dick Cheney and Don Rumsfeld flanked the President in his daily security brief at 0600 hours. George Tenet, head of CIA; Hank Crumpton, CIA Counterterrorism chief leading the paramilitary war planning in Afghanistan; and Condoleezza Rice, head of NSA were providing specific details and the status of harrowing situations and threats that were happening around the world, as the nation slept. This is how the most powerful people in the world start their day.

Just 20 days had passed since 9/11. These security briefings became lightning rods, and the decisions made here in the Oval Office and later in the Situation Room, will shape a new world order. But if anyone ever wondered why presidents prematurely gray, look no further than starting your day in the backdraft of evil lurking in every corner of the world.

Rice covered what NSA was listening in on from the night before from around the globe. She detailed information being gathered from chatter in multiple 'hot spots' around the world. It was a busy night and her briefing identified serious threats in more than seven countries, including the one country, Afghanistan, where the USA was planning to launch a coordinated attack in just days to come.

George Tenet from CIA led his briefing with a digest of critical information regarding Afghanistan. CIA had picked up information overnight about a propaganda video that had been produced by Al Qaeda featuring a statement against America by Osama Bin Laden. Sources confirm that the video will be aired worldwide on the Al Jazeera network on the day of a U.S. invasion of Afghanistan. He also reported that there were no confirmed sightings or locations for Bin Laden yesterday in Afghanistan, but that a buildup of Al Qaeda fighters was reported in Tora Bora, providing clues to his whereabouts. There was an unconfirmed sighting of Bin Laden by freelance CIA operatives on the border of Pakistan, but it too could not be confirmed as the operatives were found dead hours after the initial reports.

An extensive network of CIA freelance contacts was being actively engaged for Intel throughout the Region. They were in the process of gathering targeted locations of known Al Qaeda terrorists. Tenet unveiled decks of 'Most Wanted' Jihadist terrorists cards with identifying photographs of high target Al Qaeda terrorists for distribution to the troops. Leads were just beginning to come in on locations of several of these targets. CIA was also meeting with the Northern Alliance, in coordination with DOD Special Forces, readying for infiltration into Afghanistan to guide targeted air strikes when the first 1,000 Special Forces hit the ground in the build-up to war.

Tenet requested a separate meeting to be scheduled later in the day regarding intelligence on weapons of mass destruction in Iraq. CIA had more solid information coming in from satellite imagery and from hard interviews with suspects on the ground. POTUS agreed but told Tenet to be wary, not to let anyone stretch the case on WMD in Iraq with war fever so high. He also wants the secretary of State, Colin Powell, in at the next meeting.

Crumpton finished the CIA brief on actions yesterday in Afghanistan. He reported on a highly successful first battlefield deployment of the Predator with hellfire missiles in Tora Bora in support of a

Presidential Unit black op. He could not show a video clip of its success. All video footage in support of a Presidential Unit op is highly classified and filed only in the Unit's TOP SECRET archives. Crumpton knew the strict protocol for the Unit's missions. The Unit Chief briefs POTUS on every op; therefore, he had no business going any further than he already had on the classified subject. Crumpton desired to ask POTUS what the op accomplished and why the CIA was not the central player. However, he stopped perilously short of crossing that interdepartmental line. The lines of command are highly respected in these circles and Tenet's own silence on the matter demonstrated how important these boundaries are to safeguarding the chain of command for our national defense. Yet, it did not deter Crumpton from closing his brief with how the Unit allowed the escape of Ayman al-Zawahiri in yesterday's mission. That touch of insolence irritated Cheney and Rumsfeld but their silence masked any degree of discontent and disguised their knowledge of the op. When CIA and NSA finished their briefing, it was interesting that neither agency mentioned any chatter on any networks about an assassination or even an attempt on the life of Osama Bin Laden yesterday. It did not go unnoticed by Cheney, Rumsfeld and especially, President Bush. When the briefing ended at 0645 sharp, President Bush told Cheney and Rumsfeld to stay behind.

When the Oval Office was clear, the President spoke first: "This may sound a little West Texan to you all, but am I the only one that noticed that no one in the world knows we just killed that son-of-a-bitch Osama Bin Laden, not even our own intelligence community? Can someone please tell me one more time that he's dead? And how do we know this?" The President was clearly baffled.

"It was a clever, fast and stealth operation. We'll have proof and the hard evidence today to review with you once positive ID is made on Bin

Laden's death, Mr. President." Cheney said calmly and continued: "and then we have the most important decisions to make."

"I'm not sure I follow you?" the President said further perplexed.

"As I mentioned last night..." Cheney then took over the meeting and reopened a serious dialogue and debate on the strategy for retaliation against Al Qaeda in Afghanistan, to a more comprehensive strategy that was evolving into waging war against Radical Islam not just in Afghanistan, but also throughout the world. The conversation went far beyond the events that led to killing Osama Bin Laden the day before to a new strategy: establishing a central military base of operation in the Region, preferably in the Middle East.

There was consensus building in the intelligence community, even before this meeting, that toppling Saddam Hussein and occupying Iraq was crucial in carrying out this new war in the wake of 9/11. The evidence was mounting that Saddam Hussein had WMD (weapons of mass destruction) and the threat of a dirty bomb reaching New York or any city in America was more real today than ever. This administration could not let America be caught by surprise ever again.

Yet, President Bush remained cautious and skeptical about intelligence. He just got burned on lack of intelligence on 9/11. The conversation steered clear of battlefield tactics and remained anchored in how to deal first with the assassination of Bin Laden and what to do with the proof and the special agent responsible for the kill returning from Tora Bora today. Towards the end of their meeting, Cheney was emphatic: "We know this much, Mr. President. The country overwhelmingly supports ground troops in Afghanistan. However, we also know that there's no appetite by this Congress for a second front to this war right now." Cheney continues: "With so much at stake, sir, we can't stand for bureaucratic bullshit in the face of evil. We have no choice now but to topple Saddam to keep our country safe. Our homeland must never be taken by surprise ever again. It can never happen again on our watch. It is why this strategy must be implemented. There is no time remaining for debate."

The President listened to the gravity of Cheney's conclusions and turned his attention to Rumsfeld: "Don?"

"I'm in agreement, Mr. President, on keeping the assassination under wraps." Rumsfeld answered. "And on the ensuing strategy, I concur as well."

"You and the Vice President are on the same page here?" The President asked, almost as if he didn't want to hear the answer.

"We have no alternative," Rumsfeld replied confidently. "Our response to 9/11 must crush terrorism in its tracks and send a message about our strength and resolve. We must become the aggressor once we retaliate; shock the enemy, demonstrate from the onset that we have awesome power, resources and guts to eliminate them from the face of the earth. That means unpredictability and fear must become our weapons, no longer theirs." Rumsfeld declares.

"I understand. But how does Iraq fit in this equation?" The President asks. "Iraq serves a critical regional component of our overall strategy to take out terrorism throughout the world," Cheney replies to his question. "Afghanistan is a historical quagmire. We can only kill so many terrorists before they spill out to another safe haven. We can't win this fight or protect the homeland unless we have a military base in the region. Saddam Hussein is a known bad actor. CIA has proof of WMD and he's used gas against his own people. He's closing in on developing tactical nuclear briefcase bombs. It's got to stop." Cheney paused. "We need to take him out and occupy Iraq, while we have a united global outcry against terrorism. We need a base there to control the Middle East theatre, which is a hotbed for jihad," he pauses again. "Something else happens by taking charge of this awful mess in this volatile region. Democracy will be exposed and embraced. " Cheney concludes, "Most importantly, we control our destiny instead of reacting to madmen around the globe. We create a new world order ensuring the safety of our homeland."

"Your argument is compelling under the circumstances," President Bush replies. "But Congress will never approve ground troops in Iraq without hard evidence of WMD. I haven't seen any definitive evidence yet and the 'trust our Intel' isn't scoring any points with me after I got blindsided on 9/11. You're right that Congress doesn't want a two front war. I don't either. At the end of the day, the death of every soldier hangs on my head. I acknowledge your sense of urgency and appreciate your candor. But what you're proposing is the Neocon strategy. We may have no time for robust debate, but we do have an obligation to be very careful and cautious in our assessments. Don, didn't you say you saw a danger in the neoconservative political view?"

"I did," Don joined the conversation again. "That was before 9/11. Their focus was on Iraq as a clear and present danger, not Al Qaeda. Today, terrorism is the clear and present danger of our time. Yet, having a defining defense capability in the heart of Middle East is significant in protecting our homeland. I believe it is essential to containing the threats now facing our nation. I'll add that the acceptance of the democracy concept by the neocons in this region of the world is still a bit of a stretch in my mind. But I don't discount that it can be accomplished, if it had our full and resolute backing." Rumsfeld paused. "Mr. President, the Vice President is absolutely correct. We must never be caught by surprise ever again. We must never be attacked on our soil again. Not on our watch. The invasion of Iraq and ridding the world of Saddam Hussein undeniably takes us in the right direction."

The President did not reply immediately. He sat still, then leaning in to the group, he said: "I find keeping the assassination under wraps quite an interesting development. As far as Iraq is concerned, my position remains unchanged. I need to see more hard evidence before I can consider it. I also hear you and understand we are out of time. So get to the bottom of this quickly," the President said calmly. "One last thing. I know that it's dangerous keeping secrets in this town. What risks are we taking if we keep Bin Laden's assassination quiet?"

"The only risk is if it leaks out from the inside," Cheney was quick to reply. "If Al Qaeda announces the assassination, which clearly would not be in their own interest, we can clearly take credit for it whenever that happened. So, the risk is only if a leak occurs within. And the only people who know about this are the three of us, Leigh McClure and the Unit and the operative Scott Walsh. Process of elimination: Walsh is the only risk."

"Why is he a risk?" The President asked. Rumsfeld looked at Cheney. Cheney nodded for Don to go ahead. Rumsfeld offered: "I think the Vice President was answering your question about risk. We don't have a history personally with Walsh. He might not agree with our strategy. God knows we have plenty of naysayers in Congress who don't share our beliefs in how to forge ahead against this imminent threat either."

Cheney leaned in towards the President: "Mr. President, if Walsh becomes a free agent and leaks this op out, bad things start happening in rapid succession. If that happens, we will not only be set back, but in this hostile political environment, here in Washington, it will cause irreparable harm -- not only to you, but to the country. Everything has changed since we woke up on 9/11. In your best interests and the best interest of the country, I don't think we should even be discussing this any more. You do understand, Mr. President?"

The President stood up and walked away, past his desk and stared out the window for several minutes. The Vice President and Secretary of Defense gathered their briefcases and left the Oval Office in silence.

Rumsfeld exited the White House at 0846 hours to return to the Pentagon. His driver opened the passenger door alerting Rumsfeld to a passenger accompanying him. Sitting inside his limo was an unexpected passenger: Leigh Anne McClure.

"This is a surprise. I wasn't expecting to see you until later this morning." Don said as he looked in. "Get in. We need to talk." Leigh replied deadpan.

Rumsfeld slips in quickly sensing something wrong. "Have your driver take us to the Lincoln Memorial." Leigh told Rumsfeld and didn't make that a question. It became clear to Rumsfeld that Leigh had some troubling news to share. Without hesitation, he told his driver to take them to the Lincoln Memorial, as he also pushed the button on the console raising the security bevel between the passengers and driver.

"What's wrong?" he asked Leigh with obvious concern. "I hope nothing. We'll talk when we get there," was all she said.

They left the grounds of the White House and headed to the Lincoln Memorial. Rumsfeld knew that the car was secure for any conversation that she wanted to have in confidence, but he demurred to her wishes. Whatever she had to say, it needed to be in a secure area where their conversation couldn't be picked up by the roving ears of the NSA. One step forward in this line of work seems always to include a step backward. The silence in the back seat of the car was deafening. Rumsfeld is a seasoned, experienced political and government operative who knew never to second-guess a situation. He knows he can trust his instincts. He worries only when he must so his hand is always steady and his intellect is always razor sharp. He sat relaxed in the back seat with Leigh and would wait until she was ready to explain herself.

They arrived at the Lincoln Memorial rather quickly, as traffic was light. There was a chill in the air contradicting a sun shining brightly above absent of cloud cover. There were no tourists allowed at this hour. Since 9/11, the Lincoln Memorial was closed to the public with no timetable set by Congress for reopening it to the public. These were not normal times.

The sentries on duty at the front entrance recognized the Secretary of Defense and did not check his or his guest's credentials. As Rumsfeld and McClure passed through the entrance unchecked, Rumsfeld nodded and said good morning to the guards as the guards saluted him. He made a mental note to have the guards reprimanded for not checking his credentials and to have a memo sent immediately to all guardhouses to ensure strict credentialing of all who seek to pass through America's guarded gates. No exceptions.

The Lincoln Memorial is one of the nation's most beautiful monuments. Henry Bacon had designed the tribute to Lincoln with a keen eye to the ancient Greek temples. The memorial stands at 190 feet long, 119 feet wide, and almost 100 feet high, surrounded by a peristyle of 36 fluted Doric columns, one for each of the thirty six States in the Union at the time of Lincoln's death. There are two more columns in-anti's at the entrance behind the colonnade. The north and south side chambers contain carved inscriptions of Lincoln's Second Inaugural Address and his Gettysburg Address. Lying symbolically between the north and south chambers is the central hall where Abraham Lincoln, America's sixteenth president, sits in contemplation. The statue of Lincoln took four years to be carved by the Piccirilli brothers under the supervision of the sculptor, Daniel Chester French. The statue of Lincoln itself is 19 feet high and weighs 175 tons. When Rumsfeld and McClure reached Lincoln, Don broke his silence:

"What is troubling you?" he asked. "After we met last night, I've had time to reflect on the decision. I need to know that I can trust you?" Leigh asked intently. "That's outrageous. I can't believe you are asking?" admonished Rumsfeld. "I need to trust you because I need to protect Scott. My concerns for his safety are real. I made some changes to our schedule this morning. We won't be meeting Scott at Andrews, as planned. I'll do that, but I will get him to our meeting, after the evidence has been verified. That meeting must be with the President, in the Oval Office." Leigh was direct yet she was probing.

"That's a big change, don't you think? Is Scott requesting this?" Rumsfeld said calmly, but without disguising his surprise. "No, sir. I am." And then she added: "For his protection."

"From whom, Leigh," Don snapped back.

"Insurance is all I ask. Don't go there. You owe me this."

"Leigh, I owe Scott too. I would never betray your trust. And if you know me, as you say you do, then you also know that I would never betray Scott." Leigh shot back: "Then make this happen."

Rumsfeld turned away from her for a minute and looked up at Lincoln. Then he took a deep breath and looked straight into her eyes. "Done." Rumsfeld almost huffed that single word out, but then quickly regained his composure.

"Understand this." Rumsfeld said somberly. "The decision to keep the assassination of Bin Laden under wraps is now fait accompli. By changing the plan to meet Scott at the last minute, suspicions will only intensify about Scott's loyalty." He looks straight into her eyes. "He is the only one considered as a risk for a leak. You get that, right?" Rumsfeld said in a dead serious tone.

"I think it's utter bullshit, but I get it. But you have to know I'm ahead of that curve already." Leigh said with an air of defiance and a cool confidence. "I get that now. Moving forward, though, you need to trust me. Unconditionally. Can you do that?" Rumsfeld asked.

"Do I have a choice?" Her tone of voice changed dramatically, letting down her guard for the first time. Don sighs. "Let's think this through together. We are planning to conceal the assassination unless Al Qaeda announces it, which we feel certain they won't. They probably think the assassination was carried out by the Northern Alliance, giving more credence to the notion that they will keep this quiet. That means we must prevent any chance of any of this ever leaking out. That puts Scott under a microscope."

"Do you think we need to protect him?" Leigh asked, even though she had already devised a plan to do so.

"By changing the plan, red flags go up. Getting on the President's schedule this late also sounds an alarm. Scott might be seen as a high risk to keeping the assassination confidential."

"This is absolutely crazy." Her anger is back and it shows. "It is." Don replies calmly. "But you are asking me to give it to you straight. Do we need to protect him?" He asks almost rhetorically before addressing it. "The circle of confidants here is small enough to contain but circles widen at the margins. I've been in this town long enough to know that information spills to closest confidants. If Skip gets read in, as an example, you know better than me that I can't do this alone."

"Of course, Cheney will read Skip Lockes in, if he hasn't already." She exhales feeling beaten. "I know Skip better than you, sir. He'll have a hit out on Scott with his own private army: Blackstone. Cheney won't even know about it."

"Perhaps," replies Don quickly. "Then we need to find a way to get him out of the White House after the meeting to a safe haven. Any ideas?" Leigh pauses before saying: "I suspected trouble after we spoke last night. I already have a contingency plan. Here's my plan for getting him out the White House." It took less than ten minutes for Leigh to share with Don an escape plan for Scott from the White House. When she finished, she asked him what he thought of it and could he support it?

Rumsfeld was quick to say: "I would think it's brilliant if I wasn't so sorry that this is the way we have to welcome Scott home. However, I don't understand why you don't want me to speak to the Vice President now to ensure he doesn't speak to Skip? This can all be avoided?"

"I have given that much thought. Now you have to trust me. And you must promise me that you will not speak to the Vice President about any of this until after we get Scott to safety?" Leigh asked earnestly.

Rumsfeld looked surprised. "You have my word. Should I be there with you when you fill Scott in on all this before the meeting with the President?"

"Thank you, but no," she replied. "He needs to know that his life is in danger. It's best that I do this alone. He knows me." Leigh answered pensively.

As they started to walk down the steps of the Lincoln Memorial together, Rumsfeld stopped, took Leigh by the arm, and turned her attention back to Lincoln's statue again. He looked at Lincoln and recited from memory: "The dogmas of the quiet past are inadequate to the stormy present. The occasion is piled high with difficulty, and we must rise with the occasion. As our case is new, so we must think anew and act anew. These are the words of Abraham Lincoln." He paused, just looking at the glorious statue of Lincoln. Then, he turned to Leigh and looked right into her eyes: "I promise you, no harm will come to you or Scott. Not on my watch." They walked down the steps to the waiting car, in silence. When Don opened the door for Leigh, she leaned into him and whispered something.

Andrews Air Force Base
Prince Georges County, Maryland

Idling on the tarmac, Leigh awaits Scott's arrival at Andrews Air Force Base. She sits alone in a White House staff SUV, one designated with blackout windows to protect the privacy of the passengers to the outside world; another thick privacy panel built-in between the passengers and the driver for secure classified communications.

As his plane landed and taxied to the hangar, her vehicle followed it. When Scott got in, they stared at each other but never touched, not even to shake hands. They just stared. Leigh finally was the first to speak:

"Nice job, for an old man…cowboy," she said with a radiant smile.

"Ain't easy being me? I have to admit, you did pretty good yourself." He smiled back.

She leaned into him and whispered in his ear: "Congrats and welcome home soldier. I missed you." She kisses him. He kisses her back. He doesn't let her go.

"It was almost exactly as planned. How often does that happen?" Leigh said after their passionate kiss. Scott smiled, still embracing her, "We got lucky. You know that I couldn't have done it without you and one hell of a team that you've assembled. Any chance that I'll get a chance to thank them personally before I ship out?"

"No way. You don't exist anymore." Replied Leigh. "You'll need to get used to that and I do mean starting right now." He let go of her and they both sat back in their seats.

"Understood." He shifts uncomfortably in his seat. "Any way I can take this body belt off soon? It's killing me…"

"I bet. We'll make that our first stop. How's your shoulder?"

"Hurts like a sonofabitch, but I'm alive."

"What was it like over there?"

"Just like you saw it. Horrible."

"Are you OK?"

"I'll be OK. Just leave it at that for now."

"I hear you."

Leigh lets the conversation end. When she felt enough time lapsed to restart the conversation, she looked at Scott again and said: "We're headed straight to my townhouse. There are some new developments…"

When she finished briefing him about keeping the assassination under wraps, she told him to act like he was hearing all this for the first time when Cheney and Rumsfeld fill him in with the President later this afternoon at the White House. She just wanted him to have some time to process it. She never mentioned that his life was in danger. Not yet.

Scott said that he thought the whole plan of concealing Osama Bin Laden's assassination was nuts, but he had a feeling that no one was asking for his advice. He sensed something else was up?

They went to her townhouse from Andrews, where a change of clothing was waiting, along with a pre-packed travel bag of clothing and toiletries. Inside the bag, he found a wallet containing credit cards, cash, driver's license, health insurance cards and a passport – all under his new identity of Jack Barrett and new address in Palos Verdes, California. The black American Express card stood out in its titanium frame. Hidden in an inside compartment, he found numerous additional fake passports and credit cards with complete documentation for six other alias' for his use with his photograph and fingerprints. He wasted no time in taking off the body underarmor and took out the evidence packs separating the physical, blood specimens, and the biometric recordings. He put them in a package Leigh gave to him for the FBI evidence lab.

He looked carefully at his weaponry and ammunition in the remaining sheaves and decided to keep them where they were. He rolled up the weapons and ammunition in the body underarmor and put it in the bottom of his travel bag. He showered, shaved, and dressed quickly in the white shirt, dark charcoal suit and grey and white striped tie laid out on the bed for him. It fit perfectly. Looking in the mirror, he still saw the Afghan image of himself, but it faded quickly revealing himself as a civilian again. Despite the hidden wounds and newfound scars, he looked like any American man dressed for work.

Just before he picked up his bag, he removed the evidence packs and before closing the bag, he reached down inside it, opened the sheave with the weapons inside and took the Glock 9mm and silencer out. He loaded the pistol, secured the silencer to it, and laid it on top inside his bag. He grabbed the bag and evidence pack and headed downstairs.

He met Leigh in the kitchen and watched her as she was stoking a fire in the fireplace. He placed his evidence kit on the table while draping his suit jacket over a chair. It was dark outside with a slight drizzle falling from the sky. As she stood up and turned facing him the fire quickly roared casting a flickering romantic hew to her large country kitchen.

"I'm sorry I took so long," Scott began to say. "I..." when he was cut off in mid-sentence by Leigh as she walked up to him and placed her index finger on her lips. She leaned into him and whispered, "I wish. I wish..." when he embraced her and kissed her long and lustily. She fell into his arms and embrace as if she was melting. It wasn't until the third ring did she notice her mobile phone was ringing. She moved slowly away from Scott and answered it. She told the caller, "I'll be right there."

"It was the lab. They are coming to the back door now." She told Scott. He handed her the forensics evidence kit from the table. He watched her while she scanned the evidence files and made copies of the disk from a port on her laptop, one for him, one for her. The copies were the size of a fingernail.

Leigh took the forensics kit and casually walked to the back door. She spoke briefly to someone already at the door before closing it. Scott realized that she had placed the disk port inside the evidence package and sealed it as she was headed to open the door. The evidence was on its way to the lab. Her cell phone rang again. She picked it up and answered right away. She hung up without saying a word. Scott noticed it as odd, but said nothing to her. The doorbell rang again. This time, Leigh went to the front door. When she returned to the kitchen, she was carrying food.

"Hungry?"

"Famished, " Scott replied. Leigh opens the package, laying out its contents on plates. "Steak and fries OK? It's from Clyde's." Leigh announced. "Clyde's?" Scott mused, "I remember that place."

"Can you open a bottle of wine?" Leigh asks as she heads over to the kitchen table overlooking the garden in the back and grabs plates putting out the food. Scott looks at the wine rack and selects a Cakebread Cabernet. He opens the bottle and grabs two wine glasses above the rack and heads to the kitchen table where Leigh has everything ready. He pours the wine, handing one to Leigh as he raises his glass to her to make a toast. Leigh waves him off saying. "No toasts yet. Let's eat first," she said "We're heading to the White House next so let me brief you on some breaking news over lunch."

Scott didn't say a word, but he thought: Why do I suddenly sense something wrong?

It was 12:45 in the afternoon in Washington, D.C. They sat in the kitchen by the fireplace, eating steaks and fries and sharing a bottle of Cakebread Cabernet. She started to discuss the new strategy by the White House of concealing Bin Laden's death. He clearly was not in agreement with the plan to keep a lid on the truth. Nevertheless, he felt the arguments were compelling. Not that he had any choice. The White House has cast counterterrorism in a new light since 9/11. The argument about a state or a terrorist organization getting their hands on tactical nuclear weapons was real, undeniable and chilling. What just happened on 9/11 was enough to keep Scott from getting in the way or objecting to the new strategy. Still it did not deter Leigh and Scott from having almost the exact same conversation that she had with Dr. Daniel Hislop the night before.

Warriors with a conscience.

They talked nonstop for an hour. It was more than a bond between brave soldiers. Something was triggering this almost sacred communion of conversation between them. Perhaps it was more than the moral dilemmas of war. Perhaps, it was just insatiable desire at the moment to be next to each other?

It was far more than a conversational dance. What strange twist of fate brought them together again? Widow and widower, soldier and spy, was this a second chance at life and love? Or is it another fateful goodbye?

As intense as their feelings were for each other, Leigh knew that they could not end up in each other's arms. Not today, not tonight. And with the news she is about to tell Scott, perhaps not ever. With this reality all but certain, she dropped the bomb on him: his life was now in danger. He would have to run for his life as soon as he would leave the meeting in the Oval Office.

She explained why, in detail, and gave Scott the escape plan. He sat speechless in abject disbelief. But not defeated. It was nearly 2:30 when she finished and he processed all that was about to come. Nothing was making sense to him. Yet, he did process the situation and instinctively knew exactly what he needed to do next.

The phone rang. Leigh looked at Scott before she picked it up. He knew and nodded yes. She picked it up, then nodded back at him and said just three words: "On our way" before hanging up. The web of the warrior and spy was spinning out of control again.

The White House

Scott had never been to the White House. When they arrived inside the Oval Office, the President was sitting behind his desk talking with Rumsfeld and Cheney. He stood up, walked around his desk and went straight to Scott and Leigh to shake their hands. The next hour was an intense briefing about how the assassination of Osama bin Laden had led to a new underlying top-secret counterterrorism strategy to support the war plans for Afghanistan and wherever terrorism reared its ugly head. Central to this plan was keeping Ayman al-Zawahiri thinking that America does not know that Bin Laden is dead.

Cheney and Rumsfeld also forecast needs for Scott's service ongoing supported solely by Leigh's Presidential Unit on several other fronts, specifically in Iraq, Iran, North Korea and China. They talked about threats and opportunities to keep America safe. The fear of a nuclear dirty bomb was now a primary concern. This is why they needed a phantom agent that could navigate secretly around the world for the United States, unencumbered by bureaucracy, and why the Unit activities were so highly classified.

The meeting ended when a buzzer went off and the President got up and picked up one of the phones on his desk. He listened for a few seconds and appeared to take a deep breath as if he just received awful news. "Understand. Just come in." Andy Card knocked and entered the Oval Office. He looked rushed. Without acknowledging anyone in the oval office, he handed the President a note. The president looked at it and then nodded to Card: "Give us a few minutes, then put him through." Card left, this time nodding to Cheney and Rumsfeld. "I have to take this call," the President said calmly and added: "Are we done here?"

"We are, Mr. President." Cheney advised. Don was the first on his feet. Scott and Leigh stood ready to leave, as did the Vice President. The President stood and walked over to Scott. He shook Scott's hand firmly and leaned into him and whispered something in his ear. Scott smiled and whispered something back to the president, the two still gripping the firm handshake. The President let go and then gripped Scott's shoulder and said openly: "If you ever need anything, you just call me and tell my secretary it's the Hawk. That's a guarantee that I'll personally pick up." Scott replied: "I hope I'll never need to make that call, Mr. President. Thank you."

"No, the country thanks you Scott. Now, Leigh..." The president turns to her and grabs her forearm and shakes her hand. "Not a night turns to day that I don't think of how fortunate we all are with you leading the Unit. These are difficult days. Thank you and Godspeed."

Once outside the Oval Office, Cheney, Rumsfeld, McClure and Scott Walsh stood briefly in a vestibule next to Andy Card's office. Card walked in and stared ever so briefly at the stranger with Cheney, Rumsfeld and McClure. Just as quickly, he said good day to the group and he went straight into the Oval Office closing the door behind him. Rumsfeld told Leigh to stay here in the vestibule until he returned. Cheney was shaking Scott's hand:

"It's a pleasure to meet you. It's not often that I get to walk in the shadow of a true American hero. I hope you understand why we need to keep this confidential."

"Not for me to say, sir." Cheney nods and says "Good luck and godspeed."

"Thank you, Mr. Vice President." Scott tried to hold Cheney back for a second by the way he said thanks, as much as by the way he looked back at him. "You do know that I can be trusted," he said staring into Cheney's eyes. Cheney smiled back at Scott not understanding his odd statement and said, "Of course." Cheney then turned to Leigh, shook her hand and thanked her too. Rumsfeld then motioned to all of them saying, "I need to get something from the Vice President's office. Please wait here. I'll be back in just a minute."

Rumsfeld and Cheney then walked down the corridor. Leigh and Scott watched them until they disappeared at the end of the corridor. Leigh turned to Scott and asked him what the President had whispered to him just before they left the Oval Office.

"He wanted to know how I passed for an Afghan with such brilliant blue eyes, and I replied with special contact lenses. And then and you won't believe this," said Scott, "he whispered 'How do you know it's really me?'"

"No way, he never said that," Leigh said spontaneously starting to laugh. "If I wasn't so concerned about getting out of here alive, I probably would have fallen down laughing myself. Right there in the Oval Office."

"What did you whisper back to him after that?"

"I told him it didn't matter to me. I just hoped we were all on the same team." And then he laughed. "Jesus, Scott. He doesn't know they targeted you next."

"Apparently not. But now he knows me. Who knows? I may need to make that call."

"Not right now, cowboy. Let's stick to the plan."

"Do you think we can trust anyone here?"

"Just me. You can trust me, you do know that don't you?" Leigh said emphatically. "That…I do." He said it slowly, while staring into her eyes, his own eyes expressing that she was the only one in the world he now trusted. Then he cupped her cheek with both hand hands and he kissed her. She embraced him and the kiss lingered until a phone rang just outside the private vestibule, where they stood. She moved back a step and took a big breath.

"You better get hold of yourself, cowboy. All hell breaks loose in just a few minutes." Leigh said concerned. "I know. I just wanted to say goodbye and thank you. A kiss in the White House, how many people can say that, right? So long lives this." Leigh put her index finger on his lips. "OK, Shakespeare, but don't you dare say goodbye to me." Scott smiled, "I won't then. But I think we better get going." Leigh grabbed hold of his arm. "Before we do, if I need to reach you, how will I do that?" she asked. Scott looked serious and was quick to reply: "You gave me a secure mobile phone. Don't ever call that number. I left it in the room back at your place. Instead, run an ad in the New York Times, the one they sell on the bottom of page one. Make it simple. Put a picture of that little girl, Alex, with her Lemonade Stand from Philadelphia with one word to support Alex's Lemonade Stand: Donate and then her 800 number. If I see that ad, I'll call you on your mobile." She made a mental note of it. "Got it. Who is this Alex?"

"No time now to explain it. She's a brave little girl from the Philly area. You'll find her. I see Rumsfeld coming to get us."

Rumsfeld appeared alone heading back in their direction. As soon as he reached them, he said: "Ready?" They both nodded in agreement. He looked right at Scott: "I'm sorry about this. It will end soon." Scott did not reply.

They started down the corridor from the Oval Office heading past the Cabinet Room and towards the Press Briefing Room. Cameras cover movement and space in every room and closet in the White House with one exception -- a small supply closet on the West Colonnade between the Press Briefing Room and the Press Corps offices. That exception was made under the Clinton Administration, in case the President needed to speak confidentially with staff prior to or after leaving the Press Briefing area.

As they walked closer to it, Don handed Scott his briefcase as Scott quickly stepped ahead of them and darted into the supply closet. Within a minute, he was back and caught up with them in stride, now in a tie identical to Rumsfeld's and wearing the exact same type of rimless eyeglasses. They already were wearing the identical suit, not by coincidence.

They reached an exit on the side of the White House where two black town cars were idling, waiting for them. The first car was Rumsfeld's and the driver opened the side door with an umbrella and escorted his passenger to his waiting limo in a slight drizzle. Separately, only seconds later, the other driver was opening the side door of his limo, also with an umbrella, and escorted his two passengers to their waiting limo, following behind Rumsfeld's car to the exit gate.

Two limos left the White House grounds using the same exit gate. They turned in opposite directions.

CHAPTER 30: OPERATION SPYCATCHER

Langley, Virginia
The Same Day

Not far from CIA's sprawling campus at Langley stands a gleaming 10-story tall glass and steel edifice that is headquarters for Blackstone Federated International (BFI). Its proximity to CIA headquarters in Langley is no coincidence.

Blackstone has no known CIA connection or any official paramilitary affiliation with the government in any capacity. Yet the tight security and barbed wire fences around its perimeter indicate that this is no ordinary corporation. Myriad satellite links and telecommunications devices jut out of every corner of the roof.

The fact that the CEO and most of its employees have former high-level CIA field agent credentials and/or Special Forces military backgrounds can almost ascertain what type of business they are conducting. It has been widely suspected in Washington's corridors that this firm is a shadow military for the US Government. Yet, never has there been a trace of evidence to prove it. Nor disprove it.

It is here, on the 8th floor, that Dick Willemin sits in the center of a high tech black box control room surrounded by oversized interactive maps and video walls with multiple feeds, each monitor numbered corresponding to a desk agent in tiered seating facing the massive video wall. Willemin has a greying crew cut, with coke bottle glasses, broad shoulders and slightly tattooed muscular arms. His voice is deep and gravelly and commands absolute authority. He barks orders leading teams, located not only here in Langley but throughout various corridors of the nation's capital, to begin Operation Spycatcher – a classic abduction/elimination op.

Willemin and his team are tracking a limo that just left the White House. In it are Leigh McClure and an unknown male – their target for this op, identified only by a scanned photograph projected on a right center screen. They are tracking the limo on the video wall as it leaves the White House gates in real time. Willemin's orders are to abduct the sole male passenger without any harm brought to either the driver or woman occupant. His orders also made it imperative that the woman in the car, Leigh McClure, a White House staff attorney, should be protected at all costs.

Operation Spycatcher was hastily assembled. They did not have the male passenger's name or identity -- only his photo, unusual for such an op, but that would be enough for Willemin and his seasoned and savvy professional agents to carry out their mission. The photo came up unidentifiable in every government database they had at their disposal, including the FBI's. They were tracking essentially what they call a "ghost" in these circles.

They are tracking the limo via satellite imagery and via human Intel sources on the ground. Willemin has a fleet of high pursuit SUVs throughout Washington D.C. Today he dispatched four of them with trained former Special Forces soldiers assigned to this duty. Two SUVs picked up the vehicle as it left the White House gates with the target onboard and shadowed it, using skilled maneuvers, so as not to be noticed as a tail. They followed them from the moment they turned out of the White House grounds.

Leigh's car headed north on 15th Street NW toward G Street and went left following 2 lanes onto I street. They turned right onto Pennsylvania Avenue when two other SUVs from Willemin's fleet picked up the pursuit.

At the next traffic circle, they took the second exit as the first SUV took the first exit and the second SUV kept on the trail and followed the target vehicle as it exited the traffic circle and remained on Pennsylvania. The limo then turned slightly left onto M Street NW and continued onto Canal Road NW before turning on Wisconsin Avenue NW. The SUV in pursuit stopped at the light. On Prospect Street from opposite directions, two more SUVs pulled up to follow the target vehicle.

Leigh is watching the skillful orchestration of this elaborate tail with four different SUVs, by her count. Had she not been trained in this business, she never would have been any the wiser that they were being followed. Her limo finally turns left on N street and pulled into an alleyway to the rear entrance of Billy Martin's restaurant in Georgetown.

The first SUV to reach Martin's behind the limo stopped just across Martin's on N Street. The agents confirmed the destination and that two people including the 'probable' target exited from the back of the limo and dashed inside. 'Probable" was used because they could not see or identify the faces of the two people who left the limo.

Willemin hated the word 'probable' with confirmations. He smelled a rat.

The rain had stopped and the sun was slowly breaking through clouds even this late in the day. The way the sunlight streaked through the buildings here in Georgetown after a rainstorm created a luster in the sky with shadows that cast curious silhouettes on Billy Martin's unique location on the corner and atop the hill. Part magical, part mysterious, Martin's seemed to have a supernatural spotlight on its front door, which only made the place that much more of a perfect watering hole for Washington's elite. From a booth here, a power player in world events can imagine anything, especially after a few good drinks.

Two of Willemin's agents in suits exited the SUV on N Street and covered the back door at Martin's. They stood next to the waiting limo where the 'target' they were tailing had just exited. The driver of the limo saw them pull in. He acted nonchalant and seemed content in reading a newspaper as he waited for his passengers, providing them an appearance, at least, of not noticing the suits that just appeared. One of Willemin's men lit a cigarette as the two men started a conversation between themselves apparently doing the same charade -- acting like nothing out of the ordinary was underway.

Yet another SUV in the pursuit arrived and eased into a parking spot almost in front of Martin's on Wisconsin. Two more of Willemin's agents jumped out and walked across Wisconsin to Martin's front door. One of those men entered the restaurant, as the other stood guard. Other agents remained concealed behind blackout tinting sitting in the back of the SUV out front. A third SUV from this same team now pulled up slowly in the rear of Martin's, stopping less than thirty yards away from the target vehicle. It is the primary vehicle for a quick abduction from the rear in the alleyway. The two agents on guard, smoking at the rear of Martin's, nod to the vehicle's driver. Something is about to happen. Everyone is now in place.

From his perch in the command and control center, Dick Willemin liked what he saw. He has surrounded Martin's and contained the perimeter. It is time to go in.

He directs this mission with precision, and with bravado much like a conductor in an orchestra. He is the only Director of Operations inside Blackstone that plays music in the control room during an op in progress. He calls out the shots using his arms wildly in orchestration. Today, he was playing end titles to the movie "Glory" from The City of Prague Philharmonic. No one dared asked why. His taste in music during his ops was much like surgeons in operating theaters. The music probably calmed him or gave him the energy needed to keep him on edge.

Willemin's cool and calm demeanor, rich baritone voice, and his commanding presence as an ops conductor made him a favorite in running operations at Blackstone. His proclivity for drama, coupled with his eccentricity, also made him a legend in the control room. His op is now fully operational. He puts his agents on notice to grab the target on his way out of Martin's. At the same time, he is already thinking quickly about a Plan B, in case the target mysteriously slips away from him. He didn't doubt that gut feeling right now either. This was all looking way too easy.

Inside Martin's, Leigh was settling into a booth. Not just any booth, one close to the front of the restaurant with a clear view of both N Street and Wisconsin. The booths in Martin's are named after famous people who were known to have dined, or perhaps, more appropriately, drank the nights away here. She was sitting in The JFK & Jackie booth, where rumor has it, John Fitzgerald Kennedy proposed in this booth, when he was a freshman Congressman.

Leigh is looking for and found not one but two suspect SUVs parked outside Billy Martin's. She is surrounded, just as she expected, and planned for. She sits alone in the booth, pretending to be looking at the menu when the first of the men in the SUVs entered Martin's and headed straight to the bar. The bar scene was already getting cranked up even though it still was early but she was aware of his presence. The man, an agent in a dark suit, surveyed the scene and spoke inconspicuously (a microphone was attached to his lapel unseen) informing the Command Center at Blackstone in Langley that the woman was spotted, but that she was alone in a booth and that the target was nowhere to be seen inside the restaurant.

He told command that he was heading directly into the rest rooms to check on the target's whereabouts, assuming he must be in there. After he reached the men's room and checked out every stall, he relayed to Command that the target wasn't in there either, for all hands to remain on lookout as he headed into the ladies room.

Back inside the command center, Willemin didn't flinch listening to his agent inside Martin's. He had anticipated this possible outcome and had already relayed several orders to his two agents in the rear of the restaurant (even as the agent inside headed into the rest rooms). The two agents outside in the back grabbed the driver out of Leigh's limo and pushed him inside the SUV that was already in the alley. The SUV sat idling in the rear as these two agents then rushed inside Martin's through the back entrance and darted inside the kitchen. At the same time, the agent who had just left the men's room slipped inside the ladies room.

Leigh watched the agent coming out of the men's room and heading into the ladies room, and noticed two more agents race in from the back entrance going straight into the kitchen. She is impressed by how fast, unobtrusive except to her trained eyes, and coordinated these operatives are doing their job. They are highly trained, as she expected. Within minutes, the two men came out of the kitchen about the same instant that the first agent exited the ladies room, but not before a young woman came out before him looking quite upset. Leigh is enjoying the folly of their chase and is finding it hard not to act obvious or start laughing because she finds it so funny. She suppressed that feeling for the moment, as she noticed the agent coming out of the ladies room was headed directly towards her.

Just minutes before, inside the kitchen, the two agents entering from the rear entrance had rushed in announcing that they were government agents looking for a suspect. They held fake IDs high with guns drawn getting the kitchen staff's attention quickly. They maneuvered around the kitchen showing a photo of the 'target' to each member of the kitchen staff. Not a single staff member recognized the man in the photo. It was clear the suspect had not entered the kitchen.

The two agents left the kitchen to stand guard again by the rear entrance after confirming that the target was not found in the kitchen, passing along more bad news from the wait staff claiming the target was not even seen inside the restaurant. There is dead silence in the control room at Blackstone. The agent who left the ladies room was now walking quickly to the front entrance again, passing Leigh this time but observing her close-up as he did, but not stopping. Leigh acted nonchalant, perusing the menu as he passed by her. As he reached the maître de by the front door, he casually but firmly grabbed the maître de by the arm and pulled her, without much resistance at all, to the small vestibule between two doors at the front entrance of Martin's.

(Holding a fake official badge and credential), "We need your help. We're looking for this man (showing her a picture of the target). Did you see him come in?"

"Is he a killer or something?"

"Just answer the question, please. I don't have time?"

"No."

"No? Take a good look again. We know he just came in here. Where is he?"

"Listen. I've never seen this man. Not today. Never."

A couple was starting to approach the front door to enter when the other agent guarding the front door stopped them. It looked like he was talking to them, delaying them from interrupting the interrogation going on inside the entrance vestibule.

"OK, now look at that woman in the third booth sitting alone. Did she come in with a man?" the agent asked. "Yes," she said trying to pull her arm free. "You're hurting me." He let go of her arm quickly and asks politely, "Where is he?"

"He's down towards the end of the booths by the window." She points to him. "I think he's some kind of big shot. I mean I recognize him but can't place him." The agent is trying to see if he can recognize the target without being conspicuous. "He's sitting with the manager of the New York Mets. My boss said his name is Bobby Valentine. Easy name for me to remember, Valentine, and he's kinda real cute too. Hey is that guy with Valentine the one you're looking for? Who is he? Did he do something bad?"

"No, that's the Secretary of Defense, Don Rumsfeld," he said the name clearly to signal and tip off Willemin on his microphone, in the Ops Command Center, so he knew instantly what is happening here. "But that's OK. He's not the guy we're looking for. Thanks for your help."

The agent quickly exited out the front door, and Willemin, having heard their conversation through the agent's live mike, started relaying new orders to the team to abort and head to new locations at the local airports and bus and train stations. Willemin is standing now in his command post thinking about his next move. He realized that the Secretary of Defense and this woman, whoever she was, deliberately foiled the plan. He followed the wrong car. The target obviously must have left in Rumsfeld's car in disguise. How had he not seen that coming? What is Rumsfeld doing here? Why is he part of this diversion? What the hell is going on?

The SUV in the rear now pulls up next to the Limo. The side door opened and the driver abducted from Leigh's limo was dumped back in the street, as the caravan of SUVs sped off in different directions. Leigh's driver, one of Leigh's own commandos, got up dusting himself off and quickly inspecting his knee that hit the pavement hard before getting back in his parked limo. He knew that the planned distraction worked as planned.

Back in Martin's, slipping into Leigh's booth across from her, Don Rumsfeld sits down. "That seemed to work, as planned." He said with satisfaction. "So it did," she replied. "But did you really need to sit down next to Bobby Valentine?" Leigh asked? "I wasn't expecting that move."

"I know Bobby. I couldn't ignore him. What's the matter, you not a Mets fan?" Rumsfeld said jokingly. Leigh waves him off saying, "I'm sorry. It just threw me off."

Don sensed the tension in her voice. He knew something else was in play: "Have you heard from Scott?"

"I wish. Our man just cut loose." Leigh replied. "What?" Don said exasperated. "Scott jumped out of your limo almost as soon as it left the White House." Leigh said without any emotion. "Has he abandoned the escape plan?" Don asked surprised.

"Our plan, anyway. I had a feeling he would, just didn't think he would move so fast." Leigh said pensively. Don stared at Leigh and watched her face looking to see if it said anything about how much she knew of this new turn of events. He didn't detect any clues and asked:

"Are you tracking him, did he make it to the airport?" Leigh answered sadly, "When our man cut loose, that's a signal to me to let him run free. If these bastards at Blackstone are as good as I know them to be, they'll catch him sooner or later. That means we are out of time. You need to get to Cheney now." Don didn't hesitate: "Let's go." He drops a large bill on the table and they exit in the rear.

The limo with Rumsfeld and McClure takes off. It drops her off first, at her townhouse, and then speeds off to the residence of the Vice President of the United States.

The White House
An hour earlier

When Scott jumped in Rumsfeld's car on the side entrance to the White House, he is pleasantly surprised to see Max Leonhardt, from the Unit, as his driver.

"Fancy seeing you here, Max."

"At your service, sir."

"That's good to hear, because I need to make a change in plans. More importantly, I need your confidence. Meaning not a word to anyone about this – even Leigh. You can do that for me, right?" asked Scott. "I report to Leigh. You know that," replied Max.

"I do." Scott replies thinking. "Can you do me one favor? Don't tell her until you get back to your original destination at DOD? She'll understand." Max didn't hesitate: "That I will do for you, sir." Max answers and asks: "Where do you want me to take you?" Scott replied, "JW Marriott Hotel."

"It's literally right around the corner," Max told him. "Great - don't stop in front. Cruise by real slow just before the hotel and I'll slip out when you're moving. OK?" requested Scott. "No problem, sir. There's a travel bag on the back seat next to you. You'll need that. It was transferred out of Leigh's car during your meeting at the White House." Scott replied: "I see it - Thanks." Scott grabbed it, unzipped it open quickly to check on his gun on top. Nothing was disturbed in transit. He zipped it close. The Hotel was in sight. Max gave Scott a heads up: "We're almost there. I'm slowing and staying at this speed for you. Good luck, Godspeed!" Scott looks out the window and waits until he feels he has a clear opening, opens the door and slips out without a trace. When he closed the door, Max thought he heard the Hawk say:

"When the morning comes..."

Blackstone HQ
Langley, Virginia
An Hour Later

Dick Willemin is a man who hates to lose. How he chose a profession with so many chances at failing would be ironic unless you watched him work. In the vernacular of his occupation, 'he always gets his man'. Always -- despite all the challenges every mission throws at him.

He is a master of strategy. Not only is he an expert on counter-intelligence, he is a prince of nuance and hide and seek. He studies his prey and knows how to get inside their heads. He thinks like they think. He's smarter and just a little bit quicker. He knows their next move before they do. And he plots out their moves and deceptions like they are pieces on his chessboard.

Besides the music that surrounds and swirls inside his control room environment, he does actually have an oversized Civil War chess set, on a platform, on display in the front of the room, where he challenges his team in games when the action is on hold during ops. He finds chess games during an op's downtime a perfect way to maintain total focus. He is a master. He has never lost a single game. His concentration is uncanny. His ability to see the consequences of every move is incomparable.

The chess pieces had not been touched in Operation Spycatcher yet. He was losing ground fast. Skip Lockes, Cheney's Chief of Staff, is his client. Skip informed him that the target would be in the limo that left the

White House with the woman, Leigh Anne McClure, so he could have easily blamed him, not himself, for the switch that occurred with Rumsfeld. Instead, Willemin only saw the op as more challenging than when it began. As soon he heard Rumsfeld's name at Martin's, he knew that a switch occurred and that the target had just been given nearly an hour head start without being apprehended.

Willemin doesn't panic. Instead, he concentrates and starts to think like his target. The target must be a high value, highly skilled, cunning former soldier to be on a rogue hit list. He needs to step up his game. What will his target do next?

JW Marriott
An Hour Earlier

The slight drizzle stopped and the sun is beginning to break out, even as the day was nearing an end. Scott slipped out of the limo seamlessly and began walking on the sidewalk in front of the busy McPherson Square Metro station across from the JW Marriott Hotel. He made his way to the crosswalk, crossed at the light and went into the front entrance of the hotel.

A porter asked him if he needed assistance with his bag. Scott nodded him off, but tipped him anyway, and received directions from the lobby to the meeting rooms. Scott walked past the front desk towards the main elevator banks. He stepped in and pushed the button for the 3rd floor.

When he reached the third floor, there is a huge hall leading directly to several meeting rooms and two ballrooms. In between them were restrooms. When he reached the men's room, he ducked in. It appeared to be empty and he made sure it was before selecting a stall nearly three quarters down the row of gleaming porcelain sinks and mahogany privacy bathroom stalls. Luckily, it was late in the day, meetings were over, and there were no porters in the men's room.

Inside the stall, he opens his bag and began changing his clothes. He donned a striped shirt, navy sweater, light-colored blue jeans, and a blue blazer. He replaces his black shoes with tan loafers. He then unzips another compartment in his bag. In it, he finds a stack of phony ID credentials including passports, each bearing his photograph. He stashed these IDs in separate compartments in his new blazer, custom made with compartments for them.

He reaches back in the bag and unzips another liner and takes out two small wads of cash, wrapped in identical markings. Each contained $500 dollars in twenty-dollar bills. He put $500 in his wallet. He stashed the rest in another compartment designed for hiding cash in his new blazer. He reorganizes his bag, a leather bag, with the distinct colors and stitching of a baseball glove. The compartments in the bag were quite ingenious, he thought. Max's doing, for sure.

The Blazer is quite functional, as well, he thought, lots of hidden, inner compartments. As he closes the travel bag, he zips open his fly and takes a piss. When he finished, at the sound of an automatic flush, he opens the stall. He looks around, making sure there was still no one in the restroom, checking every stall. He takes a deep breath and looks in the mirror, adjusting his open collar inside his blazer. He washes his hands, using the linen towel to dry and then brushed his hand through his hair, hair that was ever so slightly too long now and hints of grey starting to show in streaks for the first time in his life. He stood staring at himself for a moment. Then, after taking another deep breath, he winces. Not from the fresh wounds, as much as ones that seemed never to go away. He picks up his bag and vanishes.

Blackstone HQ
Langley, Virginia
An Hour Later

Willemin initiated a manhunt, using a dragnet around the nation's capital. While no one sighted the target, he could have easily changed identities and slipped out of the country by now. Willemin doesn't think so.

His teams, stationed at mass transit bus and rail transportation terminals throughout Washington, had all checked in negative on sightings of the target. No sightings were confirmed either at the two major airports, Reagan National and Dulles International. His agents also reported negative findings from outlying airports at Washington Executive Airport near Clinton, Maryland; Thurgood Marshall Airport in Baltimore; and Stafford Regional in Virginia. There are simply no leads coming in from any source and the trail remains cold.

Willemin knows the target may be well ahead of him but he's convinced that he hasn't fled the area by plane, bus or rail. He knows his target is a pro and will likely use more diversion tactics to make a getaway. The search is now going to be focused on the open road. But where will the target find wheels?

Willemin dispatches his chase cars to the airports and engaged his helicopter teams to track the roadways leaving the capitol district. He orders his control room team to begin monitoring video from tollbooths in contiguous states.

All he had at this point was just a photo of the target, no name, no bio, not even an alias -- not much to go by for a black box operation. He was also at least an hour behind the target. He didn't have any more time to lose so he gave the target a name. He wanted to personalize the manhunt to motivate his team. He named his target -- the Phantom.

It would certainly help if he had more Intel on the target. Especially now that he knows that Rumsfeld is now an integral part of thwarting the objective. Why? He picked up his secure mobile phone and called the Chief of Staff for the Vice President of the United States.

"That was quick," were the first words that Skip Lockes said as he picked up, knowing it was Willemin. "We've got a problem." Willemin announced. "Give it to me straight." Lockes replied.

"Calico 1 created a diversion. We lost the target." Willemin said coolly. A long dead silence hung on the line as Skip tried to process what he just heard. Rumsfeld is on to the op. Skip chimes in finally. "That's immaterial. Can the lost be found?"

"Of course. It's the primary reason for my call. Can you provide me any Intel at all on this ghost?" Willemin is unemotionally straightforward and direct. He is thinking about why the DOD chief is involved and why he is immaterial. "Impossible. That was a given going into this op." Skip's pulse ticked upward. "Understand." Willemin said quietly and then probed, "The pursuit is active. Are there any other surprises I should be aware of?"

"No. Get it done." Skip hung up. He was worried. Calico 1 is the codename for Rumsfeld at Blackstone. Skip Lockes started this op to eliminate the Hawk because he believed his boss needed protection from loose ends in keeping the assassination of Al Qaeda's leader quiet. He wondered why Rumsfeld was complicit in protecting Hawk and how did he know that he was targeted in the first place? Not exactly a great way to end the day. Now he has to worry about what Rumsfeld's next move will be.

Skip pulled a bottle of Dewar's scotch from his bottom drawer and poured liberally into a glass. He peered out the window of his office, took a deep breath and knocked down the drink in a single swig. He is sitting in his office at the Vice President's home at Number One Observatory Circle. There is still enough light outdoors to see the Naval Observatory. Not enough light though to know what exactly to do next.

Inside the control room at Blackstone, Willemin flipped his mobile phone off and walked to the front of the room. Everyone froze and watched his every move. He looked at them staring at him as he flamboyantly made his first move on the oversized chess board in front of the room – a chess board that was also projected on one of the 32 screens that covered the entire front surface of the control room. He smiled and walked confidently and ever so slowly back to his command seat. He wasn't thinking of his next move, he was already thinking of the consequences of his next move. When he reached his seat, he looked out at his entire crew surrounding the room in front of their computer monitors. He looked at each agent, slowly and patiently. They felt his stare and knew he was about to address them. He punched in keys on his keyboard and the face of the phantom covered every screen in the control room.

"Just to remind you all, this is the face of our target. Has anyone discovered his identity yet? Anyone?" Dead silence invaded the room, despite the whir of the electronics overwhelming the confines of the space.

"OK, does anyone know where the Phantom is?" An agent inside the control room, known as the 'worm' for his expertise in hacking inside some of the safest, encrypted areas around the globe, spoke first. "The switch with Rumsfeld was totally unexpected. The town car that supposedly had Rumsfeld obviously had the target inside. We traced that car and it went directly to the Pentagon. No stops. The target is unidentified except by the picture you have on the screen, otherwise he's an invisible man – there's not a trace of his likeness in any database. That's peculiar, but probably no coincidence if he's a spy. Perhaps you aptly named him the Phantom."

"Please tell me that this is going somewhere?" Willemin bellowed. The worm spoke cautiously: "It's a very real possibility that Secretary Rumsfeld is on to our op and actively harboring this Phantom inside the Pentagon. It's a safe haven from us, for sure. All we can do now is to watch the gates at the Pentagon closely."

"Interesting yet a sophomorically simplistic theory," came the sarcastic reply from Willemin. "Why? Their obvious diversion had us chasing the wrong car in the first place." The worm replied.

"Touché," Willemin replied, "but I seem to remember the words of Arthur Conan Doyle as a teaching point here: 'there is nothing more deceptive than an obvious fact.'"

"I don't dispute that. I'm just saying in the interests of time, perhaps there is a quicker way to discover facts?" the worm asked respectfully now underscoring the obvious knowing that the Secretary of Defense is now a factor. The agents expect their boss to call his client to find out why Rumsfeld is involved.

"Tell me something I don't already know." Willemin said lacking the hubris he started with. He knew, as they all did in this room now, that the client needed to provide them more information on the target to solve this mystery now that Rumsfeld is involved. However, Willemin failed to tell them what he imagines to be the truth. That his client may not only be unaware of Mr. Rumsfeld's complicity, but he also may be clueless where all of this might lead.

"This is getting complicated." The worm replied and finally decided to say what everyone is thinking. "Remember when we came up against Gray Fox once before?"

Dick Willemin punched more keys on his computer and released his hold on all the screens on the panoramic video wall. The music was filtering through again and each screen was now showing different locations and running time codes. He rose from his desk and started to walk slowly back to the chess set up front. He said loudly: "Gray Fox."

Gray Fox is a highly specialized confidential DOD Unit (or so they thought) working on secret military missions at the sole discretion of the Secretary of Defense by orders of a single person: the President of the United States. It is the most secretive and most powerful paramilitary force in the world, a completely unknown group of elite commandos and CIA operatives working exclusively for the President of the United States, known simply as 'The Unit'. People in Willemin's line of work have heard about their bravado and expertise, but no one has ever been able to identify the people behind these mission impossible ops. What they do know is that the power of this paramilitary Unit far exceeds even their own expertise.

If Gray Fox had been activated to protect the Phantom, Willemin knew that his op was in peril. So he judiciously let those two words hang inside the control room. He reached the front of the room and looked at the latest move now on the chessboard. The music from 'Glory' was reaching a crescendo. He noticed that one of the agents had already made their move on his chessboard. He studied the board for a minute and made his next move too. He turned to address his team who awaited his orders stunned by the two words he left hanging: Gray Fox.

"Geniuses. Listen up. If Gray Fox is activated, Operation Spycatcher will be shut down. Until that happens, our orders remain clear. Now, stop wasting my time and go find this Phantom. He's no ghost. He's real. Find him!"

He walked slowly back to his seat. He started relaying orders on the telephone to various units in the field. He wished he knew why this target with no name or bio was so important to Skip? He didn't like that he was up against Rumsfeld. Willemin also thought that with the war around the corner that all this was only going to get far more dangerous. He needed to catch this spy quickly before he lost control.

JW Marriott
Washington D.C.
Forty-five Minutes Earlier

It was nearing rush hour in the nation's capital. Scott was quickly perusing cars in the basement parking levels at the JW Marriott, looking for a car that might have a parking ticket left visible to get out of the lot. He was frustrated not finding one quickly until he saw a BMW K1200RS motorcycle, parked close to the exit. He wouldn't even need a ticket to sleuth out of the parking lot. He knew how to get around the security for starting this machine without a key. He didn't like being so exposed on a bike but he figured he could make it to Reagan National from here in less than fifteen minutes, even this close to rush hour. He also believed that he was not being tracked or followed yet, that his exit from Rumsfeld's car went successfully undetected. If he could make it there in fifteen, he thought, he would still be under the radar.

When he reached the bike, he strapped his bag to the back but not before opening his bag, pulling out a windbreaker and replacing his blazer with the jacket. He then quickly picked the lock on the helmet, then hot-wired the BMW, started it on his first attempt and put on the helmet. A good fit. He then maneuvered around the exit gate and roared out on the backside of the hotel, heading to Reagan National Airport.

The traffic is moving, but seemed to be crawling compared to the BMW he stole, as he nimbly maneuvered in and out of high-speed traffic with relative ease. The BMW was a heavy ultra-sports tourer and Scott knew that the stability was superb. He reached speeds up to nearly 120mph on a straightaway on the highway. Scott was a master on any bike, but he had a fondness and appreciation for BMWs and their capabilities, especially at high speeds. The ABS braking system would also help him maneuver safely if he needed it. And need it, he might. If any cops appeared on the highway, he had no plans to stop. He knew he could outrun any police cruiser or motorcycle on this machine.

He pulled into the long-term parking garage at Reagan National in less than fifteen minutes feeling exhilarated. There was always a rush that he got from riding motorcycles at high speeds. It took so much concentration that it relieved him of any other thoughts that had been racing though his head. When he reached the third level of the parking garage, he was cruising slowly looking attentively inside the driver's side of parked cars. He was looking for a car with a parking ticket inside and he was hoping its owner would not be returning for it for days. After cruising slowly down three lanes, he finally found one. The edge of the parking ticket just slightly exposed in the driver's side sun visor. It was a new Volvo S80. He rode the bike down to the 2nd level and left it in a motorcycle parking area, grabbed a screwdriver out of the bike's tool kit, and walked back up to the third level to the Volvo S80 with his bag. When he reached the Volvo, he broke into the Volvo, then jammed the screwdriver into the ignition and started it.

As he exited the gate at Reagan National, he realized he did well by choosing this particular car. The ticket charge was only $2.00; the minimum for any car in long-term parking, meaning this car had only been in the garage for less than a few hours, at the most. No one would be looking for this stolen car for some days, for sure. He exited the airport heading due east towards an airport outside of the Beltway near Ocean City, Maryland. He had just started running yet felt confident he wasn't being followed.

Not yet, anyway.

The Home of Vice President Dick Cheney
Number One Observatory Circle

Dick Cheney was having dinner with his wife, Lynne, in the dining room when he was interrupted by one of his aides. It was the first time they shared a dinner since 9/11.

"Mr. Vice President," Jake started to whisper to Cheney. "Jake, no need to whisper in front of Lynne." Jake apologizes quickly: "Mr. Vice President, the Secretary of Defense is here to see you. He says it is of the utmost importance. I left him waiting for you in the study."

Both Lynne and Dick look up at each other with expressions more of surprise than as if something was wrong. Don Rumsfeld had been a guest at their Washington residence several times and Dick and Don were longtime friends but he never came unannounced. "Get him a drink, Jake. Tell him I will be there in a minute." Looking now at Lynne, Dick said: "I'm sorry, Lynne."

"No need to be sorry, dear. Please invite him for dinner." Cheney walked over to Lynne and kissed her forehead. "I will."

When Dick Cheney entered the study, Don had a drink in his hand, but still standing looking over a diorama on display of a cutaway of the USS Abraham Lincoln, a Nimitz Class aircraft carrier – one of the largest and most feared warships in the world. "I wasn't expecting you tonight. Would you like to join us for dinner?"

"Not tonight." Don replied dryly. "This is quite impressive," he continued pointing to the display. "Indeed," Cheney replied sensing something was wrong. Don looked straight at Cheney: "Scott Walsh is in danger." Cheney looks surprised. "What the hell are you talking about?"

"Take a seat, Dick," Rumsfeld said sympathetically. "I can see you know nothing about this." Cheney sits and Don sits across from him before continuing. "Did you tell Skip about OPERATION HAWK'S NEST?"

"Of course. He's cleared on all my business." Cheney answers. "That is why I am here," Rumsfeld continued. "I'm absolutely certain that he's now off the reservation. He's attempting to close loose ends. You must stop it and stop it now."

"Are you seriously telling me what I think you are?" Cheney is truly flabbergasted. "I'm here for one reason. To confirm it." Don couldn't be clearer. "Are you certain it's Skip?" Cheney asked understanding the urgency of his request. "Yes." Don answered with absolute certainty.

"Goddamn it." Cheney replied with out hesitating, "I'll fix it immediately. Is there anything else?"

Rumsfeld puts his drink down. "No." He stands up from his chair, as does Cheney. Rumsfeld shakes Cheney's hand. "I'll see you in the morning." As Rumsfeld exits the room, he turns back to Cheney. "Goodnight, Dick." Cheney looked at Rumsfeld and gave a simple nod of his head.

As soon as Rumsfeld left, Cheney picked up the phone on his desk in the study and pushed the button marked Chief of Staff.

"Yes sir," spoke his Chief of Staff on the first ring.

"Are you still here in the residence?"

"I am, sir."

"Can you join me in the study. Now?"

"Yes, sir. I'm on my way."

Craig Locke was a formidable Chief of Staff. He's known by his nickname "Skip." He's a consummate Washington insider and power player, a graduate of West Point, a former Army Colonel and highly decorated Green Beret veteran of the Vietnam War. He became a CIA operative under former CIA Director George H. W. Bush before spending the last decade at the side of Dick Cheney. Cheney recruited him when he was Secretary of Defense during the Iraq War "Operation Desert Storm" in 1991.

Craig Locke is a big and powerful man. At 6'6" tall, he was a former basketball star at West Point, and even at 55 years of age now, his daily regimen always began at the gym lifting weights and jogging three miles every morning. He still played basketball with friends twice a week in the evenings. In his circle of friends, he's heralded as one of the few men at their age that can still dunk a basketball without pulling a hamstring. Psychologically, he was a bully on the court as he was on his job. He's an overconfident, clear-eyed and doubt-free Chief of Staff serving one of the most powerful men in the world. The world is his stage and he revels in it. He sees his boss as America's strongest asset in keeping the Unites States safe. He is staunchly devoted to the Vice President and is fiercely loyal and protective of his boss, even if it meant playing outside the boundaries of his own powers.

Cheney admires his loyalty. He often thought the "Skip" as his clearest thinking confidant and an equal. He would joke that the "Skip" was also rude, defiant and hostile mainly because Bobby Knight had been his mentor and chief tormentor. Skip played for Bobby Knight at West Point, and he tells the story about how his coach was so upset about a loss to Navy at Dahlgren Hall that he made his team board the bus home in their uniforms, without showers. It was in the middle of a freezing February winter night. Knight couldn't contain his anger even on the bus ride back to West Point. He got so worked up that he stopped the bus on the New

York Thruway, just north of New York City. Then he forced his entire team off the bus and told the team to jog back to West Point. Perhaps, Cheney joked, Skip picked up too many of his former coach's character quirks in the process.

If Cheney was perhaps the quickest decision maker in the government, "Skip's" prowess in that department is equal. It is as if Cheney and the Skip shared the same brain impulses, as they were always on the same page, with the same rationale, never without reservations about their gut instincts and logic. On issues of America's security, in the positions they commanded, they were a potent, powerful, and dominating force.

Skip knocked and entered the study. He went straight to the bar to pour a scotch straight up. "Don't bother with that. You won't be here long enough to enjoy it." Cheney said from a chair in the study.

The Skip left the bar area and went to sit down next to his boss. He sits on a facing leather chair to Cheney, now knowing that Rumsfeld obviously had contacted him. Cheney looks straight into his eyes and doesn't mince words:

"If you have an op out on the Hawk, end it now. Is that clear?"

"You have nothing to worry about sir."

"Stop the bullshit. I'm going to make this easy for you. If you're involved, stop the op now, no questions asked. If you're not involved, tell me right now and help me find the culprit behind it." Skip replied quickly and self-righteously: "My job is to protect you sir. I think this is the necessary course of action."

"Do you, now? So you decide to play god in my name?" Cheney doesn't raise his voice, but just the way he said these words, Skip knew he had never seen the ire of Cheney so intensely displayed. "And without consulting me?" Skip did not take kindly to Cheney's tone. He replied in kind,

"You have much on your plate, sir. My duty, unfortunately, must sometimes be prejudicial to preserving state secrets, above all else, and to keep the events secret even to you, sir, no matter what course of action is deemed desirable or not. I'm looking out not just for you, Mr. Vice President but, for the sake of the country."

"Duty, Honor, Country." Cheney is now talking with gravity. "You let me worry about my own damn history. You certainly picked the wrong day to fuck up, Colonel." He pauses wanting the weight of his words to sink in before continuing looking straight at Skip. "The Hawk's one of the good guys. Put a stop to whatever you started and do it now. That's an order. Close the goddamn door on your way out."

Skip doesn't take criticism well. Never did. He's a perfectionist with a chip on his shoulder for anyone who doesn't think he's right, 100 per cent of the time. Cheney never criticized Skip in the past so this outburst of anger toward him was especially painful because it was so personal. His boss never treated him this way before. Yet, he has seen Cheney lose his temper with others. He knew it best to leave and get out now.

He got up and walked deliberately to the doorway. Just before he closes the door, he looks back at Cheney but decides not to say a word. Cheney noticed his hesitation and stopped him.

"If you have ever done anything else like this before, speak now." Cheney said in a terse tone. The Skip nods no. Without a word, he exits the room and closes the door.

Wicomico Regional Airport
Salisbury-Ocean City, Maryland
About 8:00 PM

Scott cruised into the Wicomico Regional Airport in the early evening in a black Volvo he stole just hours earlier at Reagan National. It was a long highway drive, some 130 miles from Washington D.C. He got stuck in several tie-ups on US-50 E, due to congestion on the roads passing through Annapolis, and on the Bay Bridge Toll Plaza. It added unwanted time to his escape.

He pulled into the Wicomico Regional Airport, after navigating long stretches of roads with not a car in sight. When he got there, he realized why. This was a small airport where peak travel in and out was geared for summer residents at the nearby shore. It was only thirty minutes to the beach in Ocean City, Maryland. He parked the car after driving through an automatic gate getting his ticket. The lot was surprisingly nearly full for this time of year, with several hundred cars in it. He went inside the terminal, noticing a Courtyard by Marriott passenger van idling in front of the terminal, with large lettering displaying the hotel's telephone number prominently. He made a mental note of it.

Inside the terminal, the ticket counter was nearly empty. There were only two gates, one for Piedmont and another for US Airways. They were the only airlines serving this hub. He saw three rental car agencies, situated at the far side of the terminal entrance. He walked down to their counters and once there, he realized that only one rental agency was manned at this hour.

"Can I help y'all?" came the somewhat discernable southern drawl from the young female Avis agent when she saw him come up to the counter.

"I need a car for a week, preferably mid-size." Scott said with a smile. "Do you have a reservation?" the agent replied inquisitively. Scott replied quickly: "No. Do you have any cars available?"

The agent was friendly. "We do. Let me check for you." Scott said, "Thanks" in a relaxed manner. Just a few quick minutes went by when the agent spoke: "I have a Ford Taurus?" Scott nodded, "That'll be fine."

"OK, sir. Do you need insurance? We recommend it."

"No thanks."

"OK, how about the gas option? You don't need to fill 'er up when you come back; we'll do that for you. It's $3.00 a gallon, just so you know." She raises an eyebrow.

"That's highway robbery" he smiles "but sure. It's convenient. That's fine." Scott said without any drama.

"OK, that's going to total $245.15 with tax and that's with a special discount we have on our weekly rentals, if you bring it back here. How's that work for you?

"That sounds good."

"Ok, I just need to see your driver's license and a credit card." She looks at the ID. "John Palermo. I used to know a guy with that name," the agent said as she was printing out his rental contract. Scott just ignores her like it was a rhetorical question she uses a lot.

"Ok, I just need you to sign here and initial these other areas and you're ready to go."

Scott signs as John Palermo as the agent tells him that the car is in the Avis lot at the side of the terminal in space 17. She gives him the key and a copy of the contract. "Thank you." Scott said as he grabbed his bag and headed out. "Need directions?" she asked, as he walking away.

"No, Thanks," Scott said. "I've been here before."

He pulled out of the Avis lot and drove toward Salisbury in a darkness of foreboding. After driving a few miles from the airport, he was surprised he had yet to see a single car on the road. Nonetheless, he drove several more miles to be absolutely certain that he was not being tailed. He drove through the town of Salisbury cruising at the speed limit trying not to attract any attention.

Salisbury was a small town, population of a little over 20,000 or so in southeastern, Maryland. Yet, still it was the largest city on the eastern shore in this state. The main drag was an unattractive mishmash, busy intersections with several hotels set back off the highway and restaurants and strip malls galore. He saw the Courtyard by Marriott coming up ahead of him and pulled into it. It was dark, the hotel sign the only illumination, except for a dim light coming from the lobby. It was under renovation and did not look inviting. The parking lot was nearly empty, suggesting vacancies.

There was a Mobil gas station next door. He drove into the station and parked next to a telephone booth. He punched in the number he had memorized to the Courtyard from the shuttle at the airport. He made a reservation for tonight only and asked if he could still get the shuttle from the airport in about an hour. The reservation agent confirmed his stay and assured him that the shuttle would be in front of the airport in an hour to get him to the hotel.

Across the street, there was an Outback Steakhouse. It looked busy even at this hour, the parking lot nearly full. He needed to eat. It was late so he drove over and went in hoping they would still be serving dinner. He waited to be seated. He was surprised that the place was nearly empty except for the bar. The hostess finally greeted him and he asked if they were still serving dinner. She nodded and told him to take a seat anywhere in the dining room. She followed him with a menu as he walked into the dining area and sat down in a booth near the back. It was a perfect hideaway for a quick meal. Even the waitress was fast, efficient and almost invisible. The place was dark and in his corner, he relaxed. He had a decent steak, medium rare, and double Vodka on the rocks. He ate quickly, signaled to get the check, paid the bill in cash and left as inconspicuously as he arrived.

As he accelerated out of the parking lot, his rear view mirror became his friend as he kept on the lookout for any visible sign of being tailed. He double backed to the Wicomico Regional Airport, feeling like he was still running free, no signs of being followed. Once back at the airport, he pulled his rented Taurus into the parking lot. He found a space between two other cars and as far as he could distance it away from the Volvo, that he had left there just hours earlier. He grabbed his bag out of the rental car and walked to the terminal again.

This time he did not go in. He walked toward the Courtyard by Marriott shuttle van, which still sat in front of the terminal idling. He knocked on the van's door, as the driver was asleep. Inside the van, he was the sole passenger. The shuttle departed for the hotel in Salisbury, about five miles from the airport. Scott kept a lookout for anyone that might be tailing him.

Georgetown
About the same hour

Leigh picked up on the first ring, reluctantly. "Yes," and her voice trailed off.

Rumsfeld spoke with determination: "The tail has been cut off. "

Leigh hangs up.

Blackstone HQ
Langley, Virginia
Three Hours Earlier

He tapped on the playlist and the room swirled now in Mozart's Symphony No 40 in G Minor. He got up from his chair and walked up to the video wall. With a laser pointer, using it like an orchestra leader's baton, Willemin held it high and pointed dramatically to screen #17. This screen was playing back every car that entered and left Reagan National Airport long term parking between 4:00 and 5:00 PM today. It was playing with a recorded time code rolling under each frame. Other screens on the wall had this same scenario rolling from every airport in the area. But he was fixated on the screen showing the long-term parking lot video from Reagan National. He commanded: "Freeze 17 now. Roll it back to 15:15 to a black Volvo with Virginia plates."

Within seconds, the screen above was frozen with a black Volvo with Virginia plates leaving the long term parking exit gate at Reagan National. "Transfer the Volvo to the main [center large screen video]." It sat frozen in the center largest screen within a second of the command.

"OK geniuses, anyone notice anything peculiar about this particular Swedish specimen?"

"Got Yankee plates?" yelled out one of the techs.

"Not bad looking for a Volvo," another quipped.

"Blackout windows are a nice touch, I might add,'" came another sarcastic remark.

"It entered into the long term lot less than an hour ago with two passengers. Came out with just one," remarked a quiet tech in the far corner known simply as Radar in this control room.

"Very good, agent Radar. Very good indeed." Said Willemin from the front of the room. "Roll it back and let's show everyone in the room what Radar saw. This is how we catch the target everyone."

The video rolls back and in seconds -- in slow motion -- we see a couple arriving in the black Volvo S80 Sedan at exactly 4:21:23 and the same car leaving with a driver only, at exactly 4:59:57.

"Most interesting, a couple arrives to the airport and parks their car in long term parking. It will be days or more before they return, but lo and behold, we see the same car leaving only 38 minutes later. Think we got our man?" a rhetorical, if not sarcastic, question from the leader, which everyone working with Willemin knows. The screen magnifies the driver on the screen. They have their target.

"Finally. Here we go. Listen up. Move all resources to find that car. We are now three hours behind this Phantom. Let's find him, fast!" Willemin walks back to the chessboard. The game is progressing well and he moves his queen in for a kill on a bishop. He knows he is behind in finding the target but he also knows now that he is catching up.

Courtyard by Marriott
Salisbury, Maryland
Two Hours before Midnight

Scott had just finished installing wireless spy cams inside the smoke detectors and fire alarms in room 330, on the third floor, northwest corner room of the Marriott. It is a corner room, as requested at check-in. He left his room and walked down the hall, listening for any activity behind the doors of all the rooms on the third floor. As far as he could detect, only two other rooms on the floor were occupied. He took the fire stairwell down two floors and went through the door. It opened into a corridor towards the front of the hotel and the lobby. He had noticed the housekeeping office was located here when he checked in and that the door was open. Fortunately, at this hour, it still was open. He walked in and accidentally met an older woman in a chambermaid's uniform sitting behind a desk, who noticed him.

"Can I help you?" a heavy woman, looking visibly tired asked the guest in a southern drawl.

"I hope so. How y'all doing tonight?" Scott asked a question instead of answering one, as he does typically when he is stalling for time. He did so in a mild southern drawl, trying to be inconspicuous. He's looking for a passkey to all the rooms and he is visually spying the desk for them. Caught off guard, the chambermaid on the evening shift says with just the slightest hint of nervousness: "Why I'm good as can be expected." she replies. "And y'all?"

He sees what looks like two passkeys on top of each other on the side of the desk and continues the conversation, trying to distract her. "Can't complain, but I've got a bit of a problem. I left my toothbrush at home and was wondering if y'all have any for guests forgetful as me?"

"Why I just reckon we can," She replies kindly, feeling very comfortable now with the stranger. "You just won't believe how many folks forget their toothbrushes and so much more. Now you stay here, sugar," she says as she gets up from the desk. "I'll be just a minute." She ambles back a few feet in a walk-in closet behind her. In no time at all, she was back. She handed him a small travel kit with a new toothbrush and a small tube of toothpaste. "I just can't thank you enough. Toothpaste too. You're so kind. How much do I owe you?" Scott said with a wide grin. "Why it's my pleasure," she said. "And of course, it's complimentary. Is there anything else?"

Scott smiled again saying, "No, thank you so much. Y'all have a nice night now." As he turned and started to leave, the housekeeper smiled back to him, "Y'all have a nice night now too. If you need anything during your stay, you come see me you hear." He nodded and left housekeeping, where there was now only one passkey sitting on her desk.

No one noticed him coming out of housekeeping. He took the inner stairwell again back up to the third floor, the top floor in this archetypical engineered mid-range hotel chain. On the third floor, he walked back to his corner room 330. He went in and opened his travel bag once again to get the device needed that would connect a remote TV to the wireless spy cams he had removed earlier. With the remote device in hand, he left his room and knocked softly on the door across the hall. No one answered.

He wasn't expecting anyone to answer either. He had been observing the room for more than an hour and saw no evidence of anyone occupying the room. He used the passkey he just lifted down in housekeeping and went in. Inside, he fitted the remote device to the rear of the TV monitor and pressed the on button to the device while also turning on the TV. It triggered live video from his remote wireless spy cams in his room 330 across the hall. He tested them several times by turning the TV on and off. The system worked. He went back across the hall back into his room 330 and got ready to go to bed.

Courtyard by Marriott
Salisbury, Maryland
Before Sunrise, The Next Day

Two men, dressed in black suits, quietly slipped into room 330 in the dark of dawn, using a passkey, brandishing handguns with silencers. The digital alarm clock next to the bed was the only ray of light displaying 4:16 am. The man sleeping in the bed was fully wrapped in his covers, with his pillow over his head suggesting a fitful sleep. The first intruder crept up closely and was placing the barrel of his gun next to the pillow by the head of the suspect in the bed, as the second man stood facing the bed from the other side, crouched with both hands on his gun targeted at the man in the bed. Two shots were fired. Pop. Pop. The muted sounds of gunshots with silencers.

Two more shots were fired simultaneously.

Blackstone HQ - Control Room
Langley, Virginia

Hours earlier, shortly before midnight, screen 9 flashed twice and the tech at Blackstone in Willemin's op room in Langley hit the freeze frame and yelled out: "Got him."

"Put it on the center screen," Willemin shouted out. He was already looking at the car in the freeze frame. As the shot on screen 9 moved to higher resolution and was blown up on the main screen, Willemin rose up from his seat. "Look at that, will you?" He's walking up to the center screen with a swagger waving his laser pointer baton shining it on the license plate.

"We've located the bastard again. Bay Bridge Toll Plaza heading east on US-50 at exactly 18:22 hours. OK, geniuses, where's he going?" The chatter from 25 men and women in a single room chasing a single suspect in silence for the last several hours rang out:

"Boog's Barbecue in Ocean City. Love the ribs, man.'"

"Oh no, he headed to the Delaware border on that route. He's gonna steal the Mason-Dixon stone if we don't stop him."

"The bloody bloke is bearing down to Bloodsworth Island. He's a vampire."

"Bullshit, He's gonna turn around when he finds out there's nothing out there."

"I'd put a watch on the Oxford-Bellevue Ferry, could double back?"

"He's going straight to Wicomico Regional Airport."

Willemin shouts out: "OK, Stop." He looks around the room. "Who just said Wicomico?" Radar spoke up: "me, sir."

"OK, Radar. Why?"

"No one on the run would head in that direction unless they were rendezvousing with a boat in Ocean City or catching a flight in Salisbury. I know these parts, spending every summer of my life out there. Boats are visible out there, present more risk if you're running. It's got to be the airport. This guy is good. He probably guessed Wicomico was the only airport near Washington we wouldn't have bothered watching."

Willemin looked at everyone's blank stares after Radar's calculations. "Well, what the hell is everybody staring at? We're more than six hours behind this ghost. Let's go geniuses. Get boots on the ground in Wicomico. Pronto!"

He heads to the chessboard up front. Before he makes his next move he concentrates on what the next move the Phantom might be making at a remote regional airfield. He makes his move and then walks back to his command seat. He puts on his headset with authority. He listens to the chatter of his techs and agents channeling their efforts to get operatives on the ground fast in Salisbury.

A Cessna Citation X, with two Blackstone agents onboard, was fueled and cleared for takeoff at Thurgood Marshall Airport in Baltimore at 12:37 am. As it taxied down the runway, destination Wicomico Regional Airport, security personnel at Wicomico were powering up the runway lights for its arrival.

Wicomico had closed down just hours before and the only visible light from the Regional Airport at this late hour came from the multiple video monitors in the security office. Fortunately for Blackstone, they had a monopoly on the security contracts for all the airports in the USA. In fact, Blackstone had security contracts with every airport, every distribution port, and every hotel chain and power plant in America. Its network was vast, yet no one would ever know that just this one company had such a monopoly, as Blackstone was operating under different security names in every state. The benefits of this powerful reach made such a flight in the middle of the night not only possible, but also impossible to trace. It also allowed the security team at Wicomico to patch their video from their security cams at the airport through to Blackstone's Command Center in Langley. Willemin and his team were watching the tapes looking for the target even before The Cessna Citation X from Baltimore was in the air.

When the turboprop Cessna landed in Salisbury, the agents onboard met with the security staff inside the terminal in the security office. No one on the security staff at the airport recognized the target or ever saw him today. They sat in silence, drinking coffee, just waiting for instructions. The wait was surprisingly short. Blackstone dispatched the agents from Baltimore to the parking lot in front of the terminal before they had time to finish half a cup. Once outdoors, they moved fast trying to locate the vehicle stolen from Reagan National. Within minutes, they broke into a black Volvo S80 with Virginia plates.

Back in Langley, Willemin and his team continued combing through Wicomico's security cams multiple video feeds from locations inside the terminal and parking lots. Willemin was thinking like the hunted and anticipated so much more of the story could be found in the tapes. He had all 25 feeds running with time codes on his video wall, with his highly trained techs monitoring every frame to find the target. His concentration was interrupted when his agents at Wicomico reported back that the target left no trace of identity in the Volvo.

As of 0215 hours, all Blackstone had now was the getaway car. Without a parking ticket, they could not determine what time the target had reached the terminal. While the eyes continued searching inside Langley, Willemin estimated that the target must have reached the terminal sometime after 1900 hours and before 2000 hours. There were only two flights that departed after 1900 hours. His team had already checked the video feeds at the gates for those flights. It was confirmed that the target did not get on those flights. He was still in Salisbury. Willemin thought where?

"Got our man!" shouted a tech in the control room. Screen 19 was blinking and a freeze frame with a time posted of 2012 hours was visible under the photo of the target at the Avis counter. "Move him to center screen." Willemin was up and walking with his laser pointer.

"OK, who's got the feed on the Avis outdoor lot?"

"Screen 22 blinks and a tech running that monitor speaks up: "I do, I'm advancing it to 2012 hours and moving it to center screen now." They all watch it advance until the tech freezes it at time code 2019 when they all see the target open the door to a silver Ford Taurus with Maryland tags. "OK, geniuses. We found the Phantom on the move again. We're still almost six hours behind him. Tech 19, get our agents to find his contract and report back ASAP. OK, the rest of you, talk to me. Where is he now, geniuses?"

The techs always enjoy this part of Willemin's hunts. They participate in unison at will:

"Getting laid by now in the backseat of a Ford."

"Yeah, and he hasn't even driven a Ford, lately?"

"Funny, not!"

"Wonder if he got the insurance?"

"Now that's funny. He's gonna need it tonight!"

"OK, for real now. He's trying to throw us off the track. He's doubling back to D.C.?"

"After he gets laid, I bet."

"Maybe so, but my bet he's off to dinner and a good night's sleep. He'll be back to get the first flight out."

"Bullshit! You don't think he knows we're following him? That's too easy."

"The most obvious is sometimes the best strategy."

"What other options does he have?"

Willemin finally jumps in: "Geniuses, that's what this exercise is. What are his options?"

Screen 12 is blinking again. The tech manning the #12 monitor has been watching the parking lot video feed, the same one that found the black Volvo earlier in the evening. He speaks out for the second time tonight: "Got him again. This time in the Ford. Time code is 2142 hours."

Willemin is excited: "Move it to Center Screen. Then, play it forward." Everyone in the room is watching the target get out of the Taurus and walk out of the frame towards the terminal. Willemin barks out: "Who's got the terminal feed out front? Why do I have to ask for this?" Screen 13 on the video wall blinks and the tech in charge of that monitor forwards his feed to time code 2142 and freezes it as he transfers his screen 13 to center screen. As soon as it lands on center screen, he plays it forward and freezes it when the target is seen getting on a Courtyard by Marriott shuttle van in front of the Terminal. Simultaneously, Willemin gets a call on his earphone from the agents in Wicomico. He tells the room full of techs to listen up while he takes this call. The agents just entered the Avis office shut down for the night and found the contract for the Ford Taurus. He patches their call live through the room on a speakerphone.

"Fill us in," says Willemin to the agents.

"The Taurus is rented to a John Palermo, age 46, valid driver's license from Illinois. Paid via Amex card under same name. It's a one week rental with a return back to the airport." "Copy that," replied Willemin. "We found the Taurus. It's outside in the parking lot on the opposite end of where you found the Volvo. Check it out now. Over."

"Copy that. Over.

"Report back. Out."

"Copy that. Out."

When the call ended, you could sense the energy heighten in a room at the wee hours of the morning. Willemin was excited, he spoke out to the room: "OK, get our hotel security desk to contact that Marriott hotel now. Find out when a John Palermo checked in and his room number. We were six hours behind but geniuses, guess what? We just caught up. We're about to meet this bastard, whatever his real name is. Soon!" Willemin walks back to his command seat slowly, thinking with each step, with each breath. The room is swirling in activity yet it was dead calm.

The techs watched Willemin's every move. When he sits down, he rubs his forehead and yells out. "What's it take to get a cup of coffee around here." The techs look around at each other and smile, suppressing laughter. They know Willemin is getting close to solving this mystery. Meanwhile, the two junior agents working the gopher duty tonight in the command post nearly knock each other down running to get the chief his coffee.

As soon as Willemin gets his coffee and takes a long slow sip, he sits up and talks rapidly again to his techs: "Don't suppose those ID's for the target show anything of interest?" he said.

"Driver's license and credit cards are both valid under the ID's used. They're real, not stolen or forgeries," replied Tech 25. "This guy is obviously carrying credentials for multiple identities that are untraceable and valid on computer checks. He's either a spy from outside or one of our own. No one else could trick the system this perfectly," confirmed the tech 25 in charge of Identification. Tech 25's codename was Moose.

"So we're up against a pro. OK, Moose, how about telling us something we don't already know?" inquires Willemin, as he takes several more sips of his coffee. It's now 3:25 in the morning. The whole Command Center now smells like a coffee house, caffeine the drug keeping the agents at their peak.

"Here's the rundown. He's last seen headed to the Courtyard Marriott in Salisbury at 2142 hours. It's now 0325 hours. There's no flight ticket for any John Palermo, the identity he was last using, for any flights in the entire region for tomorrow. If we get confirmation soon that he actually checked in, checkmate! We've got our man."

"I don't like it. It's too easy. It's a trap." Willemin shot back and just as he started to talk again, Tech 24 interrupts: "Confirmation on Palermo -- checked in at Courtyard by Marriott, Salisbury. Time of check-in 2207, Room Number is 330. Repeat Time of Check-in 2207. Room Number is Three, Three, Zero."

"Nice work," Willemin piped in. "We just caught up with the target. Or did we?" Before he could put the question mark on his sentence, Willemin is alerted to a call incoming from the agents at Wicomico. He does not patch it through for the entire room to hear this time: "Go." Willemin answers.

"The Ford is clean. Squeaky-clean. Same as it was for the Volvo. Over."

"Expected as much. We can now confirm the target is at the Courtyard by Marriott in Salisbury. Room 330. Repeat, the target is confirmed checked in at the Courtyard by Marriott in Salisbury. Room Three, Three, Zero. Proceed to target. Over."

"Confirming. Courtyard by Marriott Salisbury. Room Three, Three, Zero. Repeat, Room Three, Three, Zero. We are on the move. Over."

"Proceed with caution. Out."

"Copy that. Out."

Willemin punched the panel button shutting off his call. He took off his headset, picked up his coffee and walked to the chessboard up front. He looked it over and made his next move. Tech 7 was now making his next move on the same board. Willemin took a sip and made his next move quickly. All of a sudden tech 7 and the chief were making moves within minutes of each other. Tech 7 put this action being taped from a remote cam inside the room to center screen in front for all to watch. As the intensity of the game heightened by the rapid pace of the players, everyone in the room watched. There was nothing left for them to do. Unless something went wrong, unlikely as that may be.

For Willemin, it was all too easy. Something is wrong.

Courtyard by Marriott
Salisbury, Maryland
Before Sunrise, The Next Day

The Courtyard by Marriott airport shuttle van left the hotel a little bit after 5:00 in the morning with four passengers. The driver of the shuttle was almost ten minutes late. The waiting passengers, if upset about the delay, never showed it. They shuffled in the van half asleep. There were few cars on the road at this hour and it was still dark when the passengers exited at the airport about 5:22. The passengers were not travelling together and no one spoke on the short shuttle ride to the airport except for the casual grunt to the driver as they got on and off the van. Inside the terminal, it was more crowded than the bus but still not busy by any stretch of the imagination.

Security personnel were on the lookout as soon as the airport opened this morning for a John Palermo with a description of a male passenger that looked suspiciously like one of the men who got off the Marriott shuttle van. They met him at the US Airways check-in counter. He showed them ID for a Gene Petrone. They had it checked and in a few minutes allowed him to proceed in purchasing a ticket to Charlotte departing in less than thirty minutes. He was not their man.

Willemin stood up raising his fists high in the air in triumph after he made his last move on the chessboard. Checkmate. Tech 7 pushed his King over in defeat.

"OK, geniuses. Time check." "It's 0510 Chief. Still no word from agents in the field."

Willemin begins to think something went wrong at the hotel or that they hadn't made the hit yet because of collateral damage situations. In this line of work there is always a possibility for a delay. He heads back to his desk. He can't call agents directly in the field on deadly mission undertakings at zero hour for abduction and kill. The rule is always patience in the final loop. There is nothing he can do, but wait. He is an impatient man, but he sits and waits. At 0557 hours, the call he was waiting for came in. He took the call in private.

The West Wing
Office of the Vice President
The White House

Craig "Skip" Locke had his driver take him to his other office located in the West Wing of the White House, after leaving a gruff and hostile encounter with his boss at the VP's residence. He sat in his office, with a drink in his hand. A bottle of Dewar's Scotch, open, but still nearly full, sat on top of his desk. He doesn't remember his boss ever reprimanding him before. In fact, he doesn't remember anyone ever telling him that he doesn't know what the fuck he is doing. He was furious. He downed another Scotch, bottoms up. He was getting mildly drunk, something he hardly ever does, considering he is a man that consumes a bottle of Scotch daily without ever a telltale trace, never even as much as a slurry word.

He started working on the stack of papers in his inbox. Work is his sanctuary. He never married, never had a family and he was an only child growing up mostly in army bases throughout the USA. His father had been Colonel Frederick T. Locke, career Army and served in WWII and a veteran of the D-Day invasion, with two bronze stars for bravery and a purple heart, for a bullet he took in his gut and survived. As he dived into his work tonight, he kept filling his tumbler full of scotch. In the early hours of the morning, he slumped his head down on his desk and fell asleep in a half drunken stupor.

At 0600 hours, he awoke lifting his head up from the desk, by a loud ringing. It was his phone. He picked it up. "Skip," He said softly into the phone, as if not wanting to disturb his anticipated hangover. There was no reply just a dead phone. But the ringing didn't stop. As he tried to shake off the cobwebs from a short and drunken sleep at his desk, he realized the call was not coming from his office phone. It was coming instead from his mobile phone.

He picked that up from his desk after locating it under papers. "Skip," Craig said again with authority now as he answered his mobile phone. He saw it was Dick Willemin on caller ID.

"Update. We're getting close." Willemin reported. "Close? Is he alive?" Skip said unknowingly. "He's alive. Not for long." Willemin replied confidently. "Abort the mission." Skip said calmly.

"Did you say abort?" Willemin said completely baffled. "Abort. Are you deaf?" Skip asked defiantly. "I hear you. I'll shut it down immediately. Anything I need to know?" Willemin asked. "Scrub it clean." Skip replied. Willemin hesitated and finally said: "As best we can, sir."

"Whoa. What the hell does that mean?" Now Skip was concerned. "There's been an incident and some casualties," Willemin added. "The target took down two of our agents and the local police got there before we could. There's nothing to worry about, sir. Our agents can't be traced back to us."

"Dammit. How the hell did that happen?" Skip was surprised. "The target was better than we were tonight. You must have known, but you gave us nothing on him. As good as we are, we were up against a ghost tonight," Willemin reported. "A few more hours from now, maybe we could have caught back up with him again and have a different story. But this ends now."

"Yes. It ends now." Skip pauses. "Sorry to hear about the casualties, I know you're close to all your field agents. Are you absolutely certain we are out of the woods on this?"

"I am. We'll be clean and out of the box in a few hours," replied Willemin.

Skip is sitting up straight now, hand behind his head and taking all this in, wishing he had a cup of coffee in his other hand. "Where's the target now. What's his condition?"

"He's alive. Quite the fox." Willemin added. "We're tracking a flight from Salisbury to Charlotte. We think he slipped past us at the airport. He's fully aware now that we have him on our radar screens though. I already dispatched agents at a US Air gate in Charlotte to welcome him at arrival, but we'll abort as soon I hang up with you."

After a long pause with nothing said, Skip asked: "Do you know who he is?"

"No. Jesus, are you telling me that you don't?" Willemin is flabbergasted. "I don't. This guy is a ghost." Skip replied. "No shit," Willemin retorts. "He's a very hot property obviously and must be covert. He's either new to CIA or has some new kind of classification because even our contacts in Langley don't know of him. Even our databases can't get a negligible trace on his identity. Something else: he's an older guy than we expected too, but I haven't seen anyone in the business this good since James Bond."

"You do know Bond is make believe." Skip replies. "As I suspect this guy is too." Willemin answers coyly. "He is. And here is where we must end this. Go shut it down."

"Done," Willemin hung up.

The White House
Office of General Counsel

"Anne Moore from the Times," her secretary notified her before putting the call through. "Thank you," replied Leigh. She had been waiting for her call.

Anne Moore is a reporter for the NY Times, a Pulitzer Prize winner and author of several books about the CIA. Anne and Leigh have a history. The two women became friends while students at the University of Michigan. They were in different schools. Leigh studying in the Law School while Anne was studying for a Masters in Journalism. They met in a Taekwondo program.

Since graduation, they went separate ways, but maintained a friendship that became more professional than personal partly because of their occupations. They traded information about world events from their unique perspectives. If Leigh was sometimes surprised at Anne's reporting of some of these facts, Anne reciprocated with information that had value to the agency. Leigh understood the value of a free press in a dangerous world. Their relationship was a mutually beneficial arrangement.

"Leigh, Hi. I have your request." Anne said, "I am looking at the ad for a charity you want to run on the front page. An ad? I know you, but this is a first. I don't get it. What's up?"

"Can you run it to appear in the morning paper?" Leigh asked. "Not without a fight with the ad boys, this is page one. It's sold out for years in advance. Besides I need at least a better reason than none at all." Anne replied.

"I know how difficult it is, that's why I sent the request to you personally. It needs to be in the morning paper. Can you do it or not?" There is a pause on the line. "Consider it done but I expect to hear from you soon," came the delayed reply from Anne.

"Thank you. You'll be my only call. " Leigh said appreciatively. "Before the first bombs fall?" queried Anne. "Such the drama queen, of course." Leigh laughs. "I've got to run. Thanks again, Anne. Bye." Anne replied, "Remember before the first bombs fall. I mean it. Bye, Leigh. Talk soon."

Charlotte Douglas International Airport
Charlotte, North Carolina
October 2, 2001

US Airways flight 119 from Wicomico Regional touches down at exactly 7:57 am, ahead of schedule. It turns slowly at the end of the runway and begins its short taxi to Gate 18. Inside the terminal, at the waiting area of gate 18 sits a lone passenger reading the morning edition of The Charlotte Observer. She is an attractive young woman dressed casually in jeans and a sweater. Inside the newspaper, she is hiding yet studying a photograph of Gene Petrone, an incoming passenger.

There are only seven passengers onboard. As the passengers exited US Airways flight 262, the woman in waiting watched each passenger go by. She had received the abort order by Blackstone before the plane landed, but she is here on a recon op to take photos of passenger Gene Petrone. She watched each passenger walk off. She counted only 6. Gene Petrone wasn't among them.

Scott, now with an assumed identity as Gene Petrone, slipped out of the plane at Gate 18 unseen using access to the Marriott planeside catering service boom. He lowered himself off it quickly, with his travel bag, and ran into an open service bay in the terminal unnoticed.

He navigated his way inside the terminal, through the belly of beltways in the bowels of luggage handling without attracting attention. He managed his way back into the passenger terminal going directly to the US Airways ticketing counter in the main terminal. He purchased a one-way ticket to Detroit Metro. It would depart in less than 30 minutes.

He took a seat in the waiting area, surveying the scene. The area is nearly empty. He looked to see if anyone is suspicious looking, trying to determine if anyone is on his tail. Within ten minutes, his flight to Detroit began boarding. He boarded last and took his aisle seat in coach, the last seat at the back of the plane. Flight 117 to Detroit took off on time, without incident.

Scott abandoned his Gene Petrone alias using new credentials and a new identity on this next leg of his journey. His boarding pass reads Steve Still, from Grosse Pointe, Michigan. From the back of the plane, he surveyed the few passengers on-board. Once the plane leveled off, he nodded off to sleep feeling relatively secure. He arrived in Detroit rested and walked inside the terminal watching carefully for any tails. He went in and outside the terminal trying to catch anyone trying to follow him. Once he was certain he was in the clear, he entered the lobby of the Marriott Hotel adjacent the Detroit Metro Main Terminal.

He checked into the hotel. He was given keys to Room 1230. It was 11:15 in the morning. He never went to his room. Instead, he left the lobby of the airport hotel and jumped in a waiting Lincoln Town Car, one of a fleet of gypsy cars outside the lobby of the Marriott at the Detroit Metro Airport.

Twenty-five minutes later, a Canadian immigration official was asking questions, as he sat in the back seat of the Lincoln as the car was stopped at an immigration booth on the Canadian side of the Detroit-Windsor Tunnel.

"Citizenship?" grunted the immigration official from his booth at the end of the tunnel. "Canadian, sir. From Toronto, heading home."

"In Detroit long?"

"No sir, short business trip to the States."

"Eh, can I see your passport?"

Scott hands him his passport through the window. Passports became a requirement, even at border crossings to Canada, immediately after 9/11. The immigration official inspects it, scans it and looks back again at Scott. Finally, he stamps it and returns it to Scott. "Welcome home, Mr. Engleman," he says. "Thank you. Good to be home," Scott replied, as the driver heads into Windsor.

He now is using yet anther false identity. A new passport, under the name of Bryce Engleman, gives him cover now as a Canadian from Toronto. He had to go through Detroit to use his latest passport, as the last foreign travel stamped on it was Detroit, just a few days earlier. All forged so well that it would fool even the FBI's stringent tests for authenticity. The driver reached his destination another 15 minutes later at Windsor International Airport.

Inside the terminal, Scott went to the Air Canada ticket counter and purchased a round trip ticket to Vancouver. He had no plans to return to Windsor but it would help disguise his true plans, if traced. The flight had one stop in Toronto, with a one-hour layover. He needed to change planes in Toronto. He paid for the ticket with a credit card with Bryce Engleman's name on it. It was scheduled for departure in less than an hour at 1:00 pm. He headed to the security line, which was short. He felt confident that his carry-on bag would not be hand searched, after it was scanned. It already cleared baggage scans in North Carolina. In his travel bag, in a separate compartment, he had packed his revolver with his body underarmor and rolled it into a special compartment. Max Leonhardt had designed the carry-on bag, with this special lined compartment made of space age lunar rock components and other titanium fibers that can disguise munitions, guns, knives and explosives. No scanner available at any airport or checkpoint around the world would be able to detect any trace of any weaponry in this travel bag in the special compartment. The only risk was if his travel bag was physically opened and searched by airport security.

Windsor International is a small airport on the southern border of Detroit, Michigan and shares one of the busiest airspaces in North America with neighboring Detroit's Metro International, a major hub for the behemoth auto industry in America. Airports became ghost towns after 9/11, however, as few people dared to fly. Federal Transportation Security Agents carefully scrutinized anyone that did fly.

Scott passed through the security line without a hitch, despite the scrutiny, and waited for his flight to board. He felt relieved that he was not being tailed or searched for by border agents. Before long, he boarded his flight, an Embraer ERJ-190, a small jet and took his aisle seat, towards the back of the plane, the last aisle seat available when he checked in. Scott surveyed each passenger as he walked down the aisle. He was confident that he had shaken any tail when he left the Detroit Marriott. Still, he remained vigilant to danger ahead.

The layover in Toronto allowed him to eat a quick meal, down some painkillers, and further ease his shoulder pain with a J. P. Wiser's 18 year-old blended Rye Canadian whiskey. Once he boarded the Air Canada flight to Vancouver, he took his seat in the rear of the Boeing 747 and took some small pleasure when he realized he had the three seats together to himself for the long flight. When his plane lifted off, he propped his head with a pillow, finally drifting off in a sound sleep.

He arrived in Vancouver sometime after 9:00 in the evening. He took a cab from the airport to the Pan Pacific Hotel. He checked in under the name of Robert Emmett, a US citizen and businessman from the state of Virginia. His passport showed a most recent border entry into Canada from Calgary days earlier. Scott, now as Bob Emmett, checked into a suite facing the waterfront in downtown Vancouver.

As soon as he entered his room, he unpacked and put his loaded gun on the side table of his bed. The bedside clock illuminated 10:39 pm. He stripped and took a long, hot shower before getting into bed. He was still exhausted, even after sleeping nearly five hours on the long flight from Toronto. He picked up the phone and ordered breakfast from room service for 6:30 in the morning. He also requested a copy of the NY Times be delivered with his breakfast. After the call, he lay on the bed drifting off feeling reasonably safe. He knew he wasn't tailed getting here. Before he nodded off, he wondered what tomorrow would bring?

Room service arrived the following morning at exactly 6:30 with a bountiful tray of scrambled eggs, bacon, coffee, orange juice, assorted fruits, rye toast and a copy of the morning's NY Times. Scott was restless. Despite powerful drugs he took for the pain from his injuries, he still awoke almost every hour on the hour. After starting to eat, he reached for the Times. He couldn't help but notice the ad in the paper on the bottom of page one. It was a picture of a little girl named Alex behind her lemonade stand. He got up and went over to his bag. He unzipped one of its many compartments and pulled out one of the several mobile phones inside. He went back to finishing his breakfast before he made a call on the mobile phone.

No one picked up his call. He let it ring three times before hanging up. He hit the redial. Again no one picked up the call. This time he let it ring only twice. He hung up again. It was code for Leigh on the other end to know he was safe. If it is safe to return to the States, she will call him back on the mobile he just used. If he didn't hear from her, he would destroy the mobile phone immediately so it couldn't be traced.

His mobile phone rang in 10 seconds. "Yes," Scott answered. "Sorry, I must have a wrong number," Leigh replied.

That call played out just as rehearsed. If Leigh called him back on another one of his several mobile phones within an hour, he no longer needs to run. He could start over with a new identity as Jack Barrett, an engineer with McDonnell Douglass. No known enemies to fear.

While he waited, he picked up the house phone dialing the extension for airlines. He found a flight to Palm Beach International from Vancouver leaving at 11:45 in just over 4 hours from now. It had one stopover in Houston but he'd arrive in Palm Beach around 10:30 in the evening. He booked it under the name of Bill Simon, another new identity for Scott. No sense taking chances now, he thought. Simon's passport showed Scott as a businessman from Los Angeles.

Then he waited for Leigh's call.

Leigh called back from Washington D.C. She gave the all-clear signal to Scott with a plan to meet in Washington D.C. He changed the plan telling her to meet him at Palm Beach International instead. He had it well thought out. He gave her his flight information, but intentionally never mentioned which identity he was using to get there. She understood his continued need for secrecy, unwarranted as it might be now. It did not give her much time to make plans to meet in Palm Beach in the evening.

After a few calls, Leigh piloted her own private jet, a Hawker 1000, the smallest in her UNIT's fleet based at Landmark Aviation at Dulles Airport, and arrived in Palm Beach International in the evening, just prior to Scott's arrival. Her contact at the airport had a waiting Jaguar XKR

Cabriolet ready for her and she drove over to the main terminal to pick up Scott.

After Scott arrived, she drove north to a safe house the UNIT owned on Jupiter Island in Hobe Sound. It was a mansion on the beach, secluded from neighbors. The UNIT had acquired it and the Jaguar in a drug cartel bust several years ago. They use it as a safe house, when not in use for clandestine meetings. It was late when they arrived last night. They went straight to the beach with bottles of wine and built a fire.

They had much to celebrate.

CHAPTER 31: REUNION

Palm Beach & The Treasure Coast
October 3, 2001

Sunrise. Three days have passed since the assassination of Osama Bin Laden. No one knows Bin Laden is dead. A nation girds for war.

Overlooking the breathtaking view of the Atlantic, Scott and Leigh are talking quietly, almost whispering, in white robes on navy chaise lounges by the pool. They had just showered together and are now nursing slight hangovers from the evening before with cups of coffee. They sit admiring a timid rising sun being filtered by autumn's billowing white clouds in this tropical paradise. It is the first time that the two have been together since the meeting at the White House with the President, just days ago. The danger that existed then is finally over.

They went for a short stroll on the beach after their sunrise coffee. They were wrapped in each other now, physically and emotionally. The sounds of seagulls welcomed them to the beach while the strong, rhythmic lapping of surf to sand comforted their reentry into their new world together. A world comprised of secrets, terror, violence and danger. Not a great mixture for two warriors no longer in their prime, wrapped in a whirlwind of love once lost, now found again, at a time in their life when neither was seeking, or expecting it.

The passion of a night before created a visible aura around them now. It's as if the high rising flames from an open fire pit on the beach under the stars last night never extinguished. It had started slowly with a kiss, a lingering kiss that ignited a passion neither was willing to admit, yet couldn't deny. Until it exploded, permitting them to yield to the ecstasy of two hearts becoming one. Stars shined light on their intertwined bodies throughout an intense evening of human rapture, as they learned how to love again.

After this morning's walk on the beach, Leigh and Scott rode into town for breakfast. Scott put the top down in their convertible and drove through Jupiter Island south to a restaurant on the inlet called Bonaparte's. It's an intriguing open-air restaurant on the Intercoastal waterway with woven Tiki huts and Banyan trees towering overhead and hand-chiseled coquina stone pathways underfoot. They left their car with the valet. Several Bloody Mary's later, interspersed with sampling almost everything on the eclectic breakfast menu, including sweet French breakfast crepes like the Bonaparte, the Josephine and the Moulin Rouge, both Scott and Leigh began to realize that their time together was growing shorter by the minute. When the bill came, Scott picked it up.

"Allow me. Or should I say, allow Jack." As he placed his black American Express card in the check folder. "Thank you Jack. We both should start getting familiar with the new you."

"As a black card holder now, I may start getting discerning who I hang out with…"

"Don't get snobby on me, cowboy."

So Leigh…who gets these bills anyway?"

"Oh, don't worry, you will have to pay your own bills, even as I christen you Jack Barrett officially today. But I do have to ask you a couple of questions about money which we didn't finish last night."

"Please Ms. McClure, must we talk financials at breakfast?" he said sarcastically.

"Ha. You already know Uncle Sam is rewarding you to the tune of $25 million dollars, tax-free. A checking and savings account has been set up in your new name with the first million. We'll deposit the other $24 million dollars in any way you want. I am going to provide you some names of accountants and brokers in Palos Verdes, California your new home. Any questions?"

"Hmmm, LA – you're hiding me on the West Coast?"

"Thought you could use a change of scenery…Now, I remember you had Khalib Seergy's Wall Street firm wiring cash into about 20 different Swiss Bank accounts for close to $200 million dollars. Might I ask what's going on with that?"

"I think you are bordering on a personal question there, should I just take the fifth on that one?"

"You may, cowboy, but you think you went too far on that one?"

"Hell no. You should rest well knowing I also have a slush fund for our next assignment. Any more questions?"

She just smiled at the cowboy across from her. "I guess we should have given you a different identity than Jack Barrett. Robin Hood would be more appropriate."

"Funny girl, you…but I also have a question for you. Whatever did you do with that scared little man, Khalib Seergy, from Wall Street?" asked Scott. Leigh smiled, "Let's just say he is a prisoner of his own design, for now."

Scott laughed. Then he added a handsome tip to the credit card slip that the waitress had just brought back under his new identity. Jack told Leigh that he was only picking up the check to make sure the credit card was activated and then he mumbled something coyly about hearing how it was so expensive to live in LA. How was he ever going to afford it? She yanked his arm playfully and they headed out. They traveled south to Palm Beach with the top down. They were going shopping. He needed clothes.

They spent their last evening together enjoying a bottle of Chateau Rayas as they dined on Hogsnapper and Chilean Sea Bass at a waterfront table across from the Lighthouse at Jetty's restaurant. Scott is taking on his newest identity, as Jack Barrett, America's newest secret agent in stride. He knew all too well, though, that his life post 9/11 is now as a lone wolf, an invisible man. The romance he has with Leigh will always be a long distance one. They both know it.

Back in the mansion on the beach later that evening, they lay side by side, spent, covered only by the sweat of passionate lovemaking between two lost souls. They did not speak. Jack didn't want this moment to end. Leigh is thinking the same. He knew, as she did too, that their future is complicated by their past and directed now by their service to country. Their life is to be intertwined from now on, but their work will always supersede this new and complicated relationship.

He has no clue what his next assignment will be. He only knows that there will be one and with war ahead, probably sooner than later. Leigh already knew his next assignment, but she would hold it back until he recovered from some of the wounds of this last deadly mission. America is at war. They are the secret soldiers sworn to defend their country. What else can they do?

He looked over at her, gently touched and kissed her cheek. She rolled back into him. There was little time left here, he knew. He is headed to Sweden tomorrow without her.

CHAPTER 32: CHANNEL CROSSING

Gothenburg, Sweden
October 4, 2001

In a remote archipelago near the second largest city in Sweden, sits a lone Scandinavian beach house property on one of the most beautiful wildlife preserves in the country. It is the summer home of one of Scott's best friends. They met more than a decade ago when Scott's firm started doing business with his company, Volvo, a Swedish automotive company. Together, they began working on the launch of a new car in 1990 that would save the car company. As time went on, their roles grew, their businesses matured, their world became smaller as they traveled it wider. Distance no matter, across oceans and continents, the friendship grew only stronger. Axel Andersson could be as trusted as no other friend Scott ever had.

Leigh had never met Axel. Yet, she found talking to him over the phone on such a dangerous and peculiar request relatively easy, just as Scott promised it would be. He was what Scott called a "stand-up guy" meaning simply, you could count on him. To do the right things, right. When Leigh had to find a temporary safe house for Dr. Osman and his wife, until she could get the U.S. witness protection system to approve her request, both she and Scott knew they had to find a remote hideaway. Scott knew that Axel Andersson could be trusted, that his interim location was secluded and safe, and that he would not be putting his friend in danger.

Scott was right. Axel not only took the fugitives in because it was a favor for an old friend, he told Leigh that it was a privilege to honor

Scott's memory in this way. He knew his friend Scott had perished in the World Trade Center on 9/11 and knew no different now. He was quick to promise Leigh that he would be there for anything that Scott would have wanted him to do in the future, as well. Swedes by nature can be the kindest humans on the planet, but they are still human, subject to the same frailties that beset the entire human race. But once in a while, someone arises like an Axel Andersson to grace the universe and everyone benefits, not just his friends.

Scott arrived in Gothenburg just hours ago before daybreak. He stands on the bow of a speedboat in the North Sea thinking about his reunion with Axel and his wife, Monika. His hair is blowing wildly in the wind, as he stood staring out at a Swedish archipelago just a little more than a mile from view now. It will be a shock for them to see him. They are probably still pondering his death and reeling from the aftermath of 9/11, even this far from New York City. They still are hiding two fugitives from an American Special Forces Op in their custody, Dr. Osman and his wife. He stood planning on how to break the news of his resurrection, as carefully as he could. He certainly did not want to put them in any additional danger.

Scott loved the North Sea. How a Scandinavian moon casts sensational shadows, like dreams, over its whitecaps and endless archipelagos. How the moon here is so prodigious that it appears at night to rest on rock islands on the horizon from its own weight. As he stood facing this night in a headwind, he felt he could touch this mammoth moon. A whirlwind gently massaged the vessel, as if to let Scott know the future was a journey unknown. The wind rushed by yet it was the waves, not the moon, that gave voice to this sea tonight. Upon hearing that voice, Scott remembered that Beowulf had crossed this channel before him having slayed a dragon in a foreign land, only to face another in the future, closer to home.

His mind was racing. Uncertainty never bothered Scott. Fear never changed his course. Although he never denied how fear was a potent motivator in his line of work. Doing ordinary things uncommonly well is one thing. Doing extraordinary things when you feel incapable of doing them is quite another. Fear has that awesome power to channel great strength, as much as it has the contrasting power to weaken or paralyze you.

Tonight, on this sea, he was overcome by loneliness despite knowing that he was on the cusp of getting some of the people he loved most back into his life, if ever so temporarily. He didn't know what he wanted anymore. Perhaps he just was tired of playing Sisyphus, pushing the boulder up the hill only to watch it roll back again. Nature constantly tugged at him. The forces of nature around this boat engulfed his senses. A cloud whisked by the moon and when it passed, a halo appeared again around this oversized moon.

A moon shadow cast over him standing tall on this rare and beautiful boat in a mystic sea. It was no ordinary boat. It was a mahogany 1928 Classic Sedan Express Cruiser, designed by John Faul, in Switzerland and now owned by Axel, who kept it moored in Gothenburg. Axel was already at his summer home with his wife Monika, who had ferried over just a few days earlier when Nick Anthony and Bryan Taylor used this same cruiser to ferry and hide Dr. Osman and his wife further north in Axel's father's secluded fishing village on the west coast of Sweden. Axel thought it best to spend some time in his own summer place keeping a low profile for a few days while he was hiding Scott's guests at his father's summer fishing isle.

So much was happening with his senses at sea this night that Scott decided to swim the last mile to shore from the speedboat to relax. He also needed time to think. Swimming is his refuge. He felt at one now with the wind, the waves, and the water and wanted to race into his future as if each stroke would lunge him closer to finding the truth. If he didn't know who he was before his wife's death, how could he ever know now?

What is destiny for a ghost?

New York City
The same day

Scott's son, James, was just finishing lunch at Ivy's near his law school downtown, his favorite late lunch spot in Tribeca. It had been his dad's favorite Italian lunch spot too, primarily because he liked the owner, Steve. He said that Steve had a gift for the restaurant business. He was an expert observer, great listener, and combined his sense of humor and natural charm to make anyone that came into Ivy's feel like you were the most important person in the world.

James felt the same way too, but felt even closer to Steve since his father died on 9/11. Steve kept the restaurant open 24/7 with meals free of charge for rescue workers at the World Trade Center site, which was nearby. Today, Steve came up to James to tell him he had a phone call. He could take it at the bar.

Scott's daughter, Sara, was in a French class at NYU in Greenwich Village, when someone entered the class and interrupted her instructor. Her instructor turned to the class and asked Sara to join them outside. Sara's antennae went up, danger was nearby.

Outside the classroom, Sara was told she had an important phone call waiting for her in the administrative office down the hall. Inside this administrative office, she took a deep breath before taking the call. She listened and only said a few words before hanging up. After the call, she called her brother on his mobile phone.

"Did you just get a call from…" she trailed off as James interrupted her in midsentence.

"Yeah, I did too. Crazy thing is that there really is a limo waiting for me across the street. Just like she said." Sara mused, "TFW, don't you think? Should we go?" There was a slight pause before James said playfully: "I've never been inside Gracie Mansion. Let's go." Sara was hesitant, "You sure about this?" James insisted: "Get in the car, Sara. Dad would do it."

"But he's not here anymore."

"I know Sara. But what if this is for real?"

"OK, but if the car doesn't head straight to Gracie Mansion, I'm jumping out." James laughed, "I'll be right behind you. Bye."

"Bye." Sara said with a bit of reticence yet with an equal dose of curiosity. They had both received phone calls from someone named Leigh McClure. Neither of them knew her. She apologized for the short notice, but told each of them that a brief ceremony honoring their father's heroism on 9/11 was being held in Gracie Mansion on the Upper East Side within the hour. She invited them to attend the ceremony. She attributed the short notice to the President of the United States, George Bush, who requested the ceremony be held while he is in town today. Because of 9/11 aftermath security, it had to be short notice. She told them separately that a limo was waiting now to bring them immediately to the ceremony.

Across from Ivy's, a black limo for James stood out on the corner of Greenwich Street and No Moore and the parking lot adjacent to the Tribeca Film Center. Limos in this part of Tribeca were common sights, as movie stars would drift in and out of the Tribeca Film Center. This one, however, had his name on it.

Yet, these were uncommon times. Traffic was blocked from this section of Tribeca by the military. Ivy's was just blocks from the still burning buildings that smoldered day and night in this restricted area near the devastation in and around the fallen twin towers, known as the World Trade Center. All you could see on these cobblestone streets were the convoys of trucks of rescue workers and construction crews on their way to work at the former World Trade Center. They were no longer working to find survivors. In between these convoys, there were passing brigades of the National Guard in Humvees on the streets of lower Manhattan, below Canal Street. Then, there was the hourly endless parade of water trucks cleaning the streets of pulverized people who simply went to work on 9/11, on a glorious New York sunny day never to be found.

Sara's limousine sat alone, on the street, in front of the arch at Washington Square in the heart of Greenwich Village and New York University, a short walk from her French class. There was a gaping hole in the landscape above this historic park, where the twin towers once stood in the distance overlooking old men playing chess, nannies watching over children, and where the graduation of young NYU students from around the world occurs annually. The landscape is as vertical as it is horizontal so the absence of the once proud totally out of scale lost buildings commands as much attention as it did when it jutted out at the sky.

Every sense and sensibility is afoot in this city. Whether it is the architecture, the restaurants and bars, the museums, parks and zoos, the shops, the neighborhoods, the festivities and festivals of the street, Broadway, world class Universities, the sideshows of the sidewalks of New York or just the endless parade of people in a park like this - walking, sitting, dancing, kissing, holding hands to running, crying, solitary silences in the midst of a crowd, so many people reading on a park bench alone - you realize that all of the humanity huddled here revel in a life with the knowledge that you are a part of something larger than yourself. Because here in such a setting, you can see it, hear it, touch it, smell it, and mostly feel it. Every day in the city, no matter how hard anyone works, someone is working harder. For everyday in the city, you will experience life in ways that no one can shelter you from. It will make you laugh. Or cry. There is no middle ground in a city like New York. It is as exhilarating daily as it is frightening. You can only leave it when your heart no longer races to its beat. There is no safe haven in this city. Never was. 9/11 reminded us.

James and Sara arrived in separate limousines at Gracie Mansion early in the afternoon. Their cars arrived nearly in tandem. Sara was first and she saw James getting out behind her as they glanced at each other and then came together with their hands out in a gesture of cluelessness as to this strange last-minute event in honor of their father. They stood together in the driveway in front of Gracie Mansion feeling a bit lost. This was a magical place they had looked at admiringly so many times before, but only through the handsome black metal gates from their walks in Carl Schurz Park, that surrounded the official home of all the Mayors of NYC.

Now, they were on the inside, looking out.

Leigh met them at the front door, flanked by the Secret Service who patted them down prior to walking them down a corridor to the Mayor's ceremonial office in the then Mayor Rudy Giuliani's home. Inside the office was not the Mayor, who was at the United Nations, but the President of the United States. President Bush told them that their father was very much alive and well and that they would see him soon.

It hit James and Sara like a thunderbolt immediately. Leigh could feel the shock waves. Emotions ran high throughout their briefing, learning their father is still alive and well. The next twenty minutes with President Bush helped make this unbelievable news real. It was still too much to expect that they would comprehend that their relationship with their father would need to forever be changed. It already had.

The President had Leigh brief them on the elaborate cover-up and faking of his death to allow him to work undercover for the government. She fell short of telling them what he had accomplished already as a phantom agent. She told them that their father would remain a secret agent and impressed upon them that they could never let anyone know that he survived the events at the World Trade Center on 9/11. Not only for their father's safety, but now that they hold this secret, their own safety.

After the President left, Leigh briefed them on the plan to see their father. She told them they were about to leave to another country to see him by morning. Sara and James didn't respond. They didn't even ask where? They just hugged each other. Then they hugged Leigh.

Leigh rode with Sara and James to Butler Aviation field in Newark, New Jersey. Ollie Girl was excitedly waiting for Sara and James in the back seat, which set off another emotional reunion. Travel bags had been prepared for them with clothing for their trip to visit their father, in Sweden, a family reunion some 4,000 miles away. Leigh made sure they had had Ollie's favorite dog snacks onboard too. They would all arrive in the morning, after a fuel stopover in Germany. Leigh was not accompanying them.

The North Sea
Sweden

When Scott dove in, Nick turned the boat's direction north back to Axel's father's fishing village, to pick up Doctor Osman and his wife for a flight to the United States. The water was cold, but unusually warm for the North Sea, about 71 degrees Fahrenheit. Not too cold for Scott swimming in fast, beautiful, arched strokes that would power him to the shore by sunrise.

He reached the shoreline and a wide expanse of beach on the archipelago surrounded by rocks from prehistoric times. The sun was now shining. In his waterproof bag slung around his torso, he found his clothes still dry. He dressed. He sat by the sea. Massaged his sore shoulder. He waited.

He waited as long as night became day. Axel was heading in his direction, up at sunrise, jogging down the beach just as Scott knew he would be. Scott let him pass by without seeing him and then he started running until he caught up to him.

Two friends meet again.

Axel looked at the man jogging in step with him. He just kept staring. Finally, he stopped. He said that he came here every morning since 9/11, here on this beach, looking out at the sea to speak with his friend Scott. He asked Scott if he is real? Scott embraced him.

They spent the entire day and evening talking, eating, and drinking with Monika joining in, always with a smile, wise words and perhaps a dash of disbelief. She always believed that their friend Scott from America was larger than life. Yet, she never expected him to resurrect, as she told Scott in her winsome and whimsical style. Scott didn't have to stress how important it was that no other than the two of them and his two children are ever to know of his existence.

For their safety.

The North Sea
Later the same day

Nick Anthony had just picked up the Doctor and his wife on the dock next to a whaling skiff and lobster shanty, right on schedule. They headed south to Gothenburg, a several hour cruise from this quaint fishing village.

The Doctor and his wife huddled in a hug-like fashion as they turned back to the dock upon departure as if to say goodbye to a good friend. Nick watched them in fascination. Who were they saying goodbye to? There was literally no one on this secluded fishing isle.

On the swift cruise to Gothenburg, Nick is thinking about the Hawk. He picked him up at the docks at a port in Gothenburg just after midnight and took him in the direction of a remote archipelago on the North Sea. They acknowledged each other when they met at the dock, but didn't speak during the long cruise to their destination. About a mile from shore, the Hawk told Nick to slow, as the Hawk took out night vision binoculars and looked to the shoreline. After a few minutes, he told Nick to stop. Nick shut down the engines. He remembers their conversation of just hours ago.

"I need to get off here. As soon as I dive in, start up the engines and head to your next destination to pick up the Doctor and his wife. You never saw me. Is that clear?"

"Yes, sir," Nick replied. "Is there anything I can do for you, sir?"

"No, Nick," He personalized his goodbye and continued: "Thank you for all you have done for me and for your country. Safe journey, soldier." Nick didn't know what to think. He replied, "You too, sir." Then he watched as the Hawk went to the stern, grabbed his travel bag, stripped bare and put his clothes inside it, then wrapped the bag in a plastic sheath, tied it around his neck and dove into the water. Vanished.

Nick started the engines and nudged the power to full throttle. As he raced across the North Sea about an hour before daylight, he was happy to see that the Hawk had survived the mission in Tora Bora and wondered what his mission was here in Sweden?

Later that evening

At Gothenburg's International airport, Bryan Taylor taxied down the runway just before noon with Nick Anthony as his copilot and his two now familiar passengers on board, Dr. Osman and his wife, Ayda. Destination: New York City. Bryan told Nick to get some sleep. Nick would be piloting back on this round-trip flight with what Leigh had told them was the two most important people they would ever fly across the Atlantic.

The Grumman AC-37A had become a phantom in the skies criss-crossing the Atlantic since 9/11. Upon arrival at Newark International, Leigh and Fran were at the Butler Aviation terminal waiting. Fran met the Doctor and his wife by the side of the aircraft as they exited. She quickly escorted the Doctor and his wife to another jet, a Learjet parked next to the one they just deplaned and boarded it.

Fran sat with them onboard telling them they were now headed to a private executive airfield in Charleston, South Carolina. From there, they will be driven to their new home on Kiawah Island. She briefed them on their new life, and after answering their initial questions introduced them to two other passengers – U.S. Marshalls from the Federal Witness Protection Program.

Meanwhile, Leigh met with Bryan and Nick as they depart the AC-37A, as a maintenance crew immediately started cleaning it, restocking it and refueling it for a round trip to Gothenburg.

Inside a waiting area sat James and Sara, and Ollie Girl.

CHAPTER 33: HOMEFRONT

October 7, 2001
Four Days Later

Scott sat between his son and daughter on a large oversized mansion of a rock, on an archipelago in Sweden. Together, they looked to the stars and the moon as if his late wife, their mother, could hear their separate thoughts, each sitting in silence, and somehow make sense out of any of this, for any one of them.

At the same moment, the President of the United States sitting in the White House Treaty room was delivering a live televised message to the world: America is at War in Afghanistan. The first 1,000 soldiers had arrived on horseback in OPERATION ENDURING FREEDOM. They were directing the bombing campaign today.

"Since September 11, an entire generation of young Americans has gained new understanding of the value of freedom, and its cost in duty and in sacrifice. The battle is now joined on many fronts. We will not waver; we will not tire; we will not falter; and we will not fail. Peace and freedom will prevail..."

The war on terror had just become official when an Arab TV station broadcast a strongly worded threat to all Americans by Osama Bin Laden.

That message by Osama Bin Laden had been videotaped before September 30th.

ALMOST A DECADE LATER

CHAPTER 34: DOUBLING DOWN

North Waziristan, Pakistan
April 28, 2011

Sheikh Mohammad Fateh al Masri, a rising superstar in Al Qaeda and its senior military commander, was entering a small, nondescript, camouflaged compound. It was a militant hideout for Al Qaeda leaders in Pakistan. He was delivering a script to Osama Bin Laden to use in a video to be taped for broadcast on Al Jazeera. He did not know that he was meeting Osama's double.

Ayman al-Zawahiri had been using his Osama doubles sparingly since Osama Bin Laden's assassination in 2001. He kept one in the field with him at all times and the other still secured in the mansion in Pakistan. If he enlisted Osama's public persona, it was on videotape only and strictly for propaganda and recruiting purposes. On rare occasions, he would send videotape threats to America for Al Jazeera broadcasts but al-Zawahiri was too smart to play this card too often.

He knew the U.S. government, under Bush, knew that Osama Bin Laden had been killed by the Northern Alliance during the run up to war, so he was cautious not to overplay this dead hand. Still, he was unafraid to play it, when he could, because he knew that his secret was America's too.

Politics play powerful roles in war and peace. He suspected that this elephant-sized secret was probably never passed on to the Obama administration. That was a good thing for al-Zawahiri but it would cause other problems for him too, as he had to keep Osama Bin Laden's death a secret within his own Al Qaeda network. That meant he had to use the double only periodically and that still exposed a high degree of risk, if the truth ever surfaced. But Ayman al-Zawahiri had kept the secret now for nearly a decade and the charade held so his use of the double minimized the need to use the double publicly much, if at all.

He was also street smart. He knew never to be anywhere physically near Osama's double. He suspected that American Predator drones were tracking the decoys. He firmly believed that the American forces were hoping for the day that the two would appear together. It was one reason he dispatched Sheikh Mohammad Fateh al Masri to meet Osama's double today without him; the other was to keep the myth of Osama alive in his own ranks. Sheikh Mohammad Fateh al Masri was now the highest-ranking Al Qaeda leader behind al-Zawahiri. He was carrying on the meeting not knowing Bin Laden was a double.

Only two doubles were left after OPERATION HAWK'S NEST. McClure did everything she could to track any movement of the doubles in Ayman al-Zawahiri's possession on a daily basis in the years that followed. Al-Zawahiri was correct in his assumptions. This morning she received an alert, one she had long been waiting for.

Sheikh Mohammad Fateh al Masri was embracing the faux Osama Bin Laden when the hellfire missile hit the compound. The entire compound was vaporized in an instant. Not only were there no survivors, there was not a telltale trace of a human body under the rubble. Scott, in his Afghan disguise, had just left the area on horseback after calling in the coordinates.

No one in the U.S. Government knew anything about a faux Osama Bin Laden dying in that compound. They had approved the drone attack to kill al Masri. Mission accomplished. When al-Zawahiri received the news, it was just another setback for the Al Qaeda leader. He had nothing to gain by going public. He even denied that al Masri had been killed.

There was only one double left. He was still in hiding, in exile, in a mansion in Abbottabad, Pakistan. The current administration in the United States, and the CIA, were unaware of the existence of this decoy. The only person left from the prior administration that knew about the double, after the transition of power, was Leigh McClure, head of the Unit still assigned to the President of the United States. She never told. No one asked her. Today was her last day at work. She was retiring and handed over the reigns to her trusted deputy, Max Leonhardt. But she had one final loose end to fix.

The moment that Sheikh Mohammad Fateh al Masri was confirmed killed, Leigh activated final instructions from the longstanding Top Secret OPERATION HAWK'S NEST. It was in the planning for years. Max Leonhardt was now in charge. She handed him the TOP SECRET CLASSIFIED file on a new Special Operation code-named: "Operation Double Mirror".

CHAPTER 35: OPERATION DOUBLE MIRROR

Somewhere On The North Arabian Sea
May 2, 2011

Midnight. An eagle, wings spread and talons extended, carrying a banner in its beak hung in a wooden seal above the head of the table in a secure conference room aboard the flagship of the United States Navy Carrier Strike Group One. The room was empty, not for long.

The captain of the USS Carl Vinson wasted no time in assembling the sleeping officers to a secure conference room onboard rigged with the most advanced telecommunications and satellite devices in human history. The highly trained naval officers, many from Annapolis, wasted no time in getting to the hastily summoned meeting, as a meeting at midnight at sea with the Admiral was indeed no ordinary meeting. Something of major consequence was in play. The meeting ended at exactly 0100 hours.

At 0200 hours, the siren sound of the Bosun's Call could be heard distinctly on the deck of the USS Carl Vinson. 6,068 sailors and two commandos from SEAL Team 6 stood at attention in the pitch dark of an open sea except for the rush from runway lights on deck and from above from an unusually bright star filled night with the enhanced rare occurrence on this particular night of a Supermoon. The impact of such radiance on a darkened ship the size of a city on the high seas was surreal. The sea however remained dark, windless. It cast no shadows on the sea.

As the siren sound of the pipes died down, there was only the sound of silence. Not a whisper from the sanguine sea. Not a single sailor moved, except for three sailors. Sailors assigned to a rare burial at sea.

The crew watched at attention as a body wrapped in a simple white sheet was slipped off the stern of the aircraft carrier. In a single, swift and strange event, in a simple Islamist burial practice aboard one of the US Navy's most sophisticated nuclear war machines, the dead body of Osama Bin Laden in a weighted bag slithered to the bottom of the Ocean.

Another Bosun's call swept the scene to end the macabre ceremony. Mission accomplished.

As the body slid into hell, the roar of jet engines ignited simultaneously at the bow of the super carrier filling the night as six F-18's came to life, getting ready to take off on the main deck. But even the pre-planned roar of these ferocious fighters could not drown out the joy of the voices of 6,068 celebrating sailors with two of the SEAL Team's 6 warriors who bravely took down Osama Bin Laden that night. The F-18's took off, one at a time in night training exercises. The ceremony was officially over.

It was the first time the U.S. Navy was enlisted to bury a head of a terrorist organization. No one on the crew of the USS Carl Vinson would ever speak to what happened this night. They took an oath.

CHAPTER 36: SECOND ACTS

On a cliff-side home facing the Pacific
May 2, 2011

Scott settled in as Jack Barrett in Palos Verdes, California when he returned from Sweden in late October 2001. Leigh found him refuge in an exclusive, private gated community in Rolling Hills Estates on the Palos Verdes peninsula, just south of LA. It was a perfect cover for a phantom. No neighbors to deal with in a secluded, discreet house with a pool on a cliff facing the Pacific. It offered solace for Scott and Ollie Girl, especially their long walks in the early dawn along McArthur Trail, high above Portuguese Bend, staring out at the Pacific. Most importantly, it offered a safe harbor for treasured visits from his children.

Leigh further provided his cover with an office inside Northrop Grumman Space Tech complex in Redondo Beach, just north of the Palos Verdes peninsula. The CEO of Northrop Grumman was a former CIA field agent, a Texan who had long ties with Leigh. He didn't know who Jack Barrett was or why Leigh needed him to have an office in his Redondo Beach Space Tech group, but he didn't hesitate when Leigh asked him. Jack's cover was complete.

He would never show up at that office though. His real office didn't have walls. His new missions began almost from the time he unpacked his bag almost a decade ago.

Tonight Jack was home swimming laps when he heard the telephone ring. He put his arms up against the edge of the pool, picked up his secure mobile phone and answered it. "I'm in the pool, Leigh. Can this wait?" Leigh answered: "You need to get out and turn on the TV now." He sensed her urgency. He jumped out of the pool, grabbed a towel, and headed to his living room through sliding doors from the pool. He turned on his TV.

There was a breaking news segment. The President of the United States of America was walking to a podium in the East Room of the White House. Within minutes, President Barak Obama addressed the nation:

"Good Evening, Tonight, I can report to the American people and to the world that the United States has conducted an operation that killed Osama Bin Laden, the leader of Al Qaeda…" During his address, he told of the targeted operation to bring Bin Laden to justice at his compound in Abbottabad, Pakistan. After a firefight inside the mansion, Bin Laden was killed. Jack turned off the TV after the address was finished. He picked up his mobile phone.

"Leigh, you still there?"

"Yes, Jack."

"Do you believe they really don't know?"

"What does it matter? It's finished and trust me, that's good for all of us." They sat on the phone in silence. 3,000 miles separated them but they could feel each other's heartbeats. Both sometimes wondered if keeping the actual death of Osama Bin Laden a secret really had altered history? Was the nation kept safer because his death was kept secret or more dangerous? Would we have invaded Iraq? Was an Arab Spring inevitable? Would anyone ever know that this Osama Bin Laden killed today was just a decoy? Did it alter American politics or world history? Leigh spoke up again: "Jack, this news is what we have been waiting for a long time. I'm on my way. My flight arrives in LAX tonight. Time to celebrate."

"It is. Send me your itinerary. Can't wait to pick you up."

Leigh hung up excited to be able to see Jack again, yet she also had a new assignment for him. He was being sent to Wuhan, China, posing as a scientist from Stanford, to get inside a new suspected bioweapons laboratory.

In some ways, this news would make Leigh and Jack Barrett's lives less complicated, yet terrorism and possible wars they spent trying to thwart became more complex, as technology innovations vastly disrupted the new world order as they grew older. Still, they were not haunted by the unanswered questions of their past because they already knew part of the answer. Because the stories untold of the clandestine missions that followed Operation Hawk's Nest after 9/11, until today, reveal a partial answer. One thing is for certain: There never was another attack on the scale of 9/11 on the homeland of the United States of America.

Or were attacks just thwarted and kept secret? Those files currently remain highly classified: TOP SECRET.

Jack had just hung up with Leigh when his telephone rang again. From the corner of his eye, he thought he saw two men crouch and hide near his pool equipment shack outside. They were dressed in black military fatigues. He didn't answer the call.

THE END

ABOUT THE AUTHOR

JOHN FITZGERALD is from New York City and formerly president of his own production company at the Tribeca Film Center in lower Manhattan, ten blocks from the former World Trade Center. He has written and worked with presidents of companies and countries, celebrities in film, music and sports and with literally thousands of citizen heroes from around the country. He has written scripts and speeches for most of his adult life and now devotes his time to his own material. "Of all the people I have worked with during my career, the most satisfying has been with selfless Americans who make a difference in their community." His writing is inspired by their actions.

John Fitzgerald now lives and writes by the sea in Hobe Sound, Florida.